PRAISE FOR F. NELSON SMITH

JACK TUESDAY

"The rapid pacing, a cast of vividly-portrayed characters and numerous elements of surprise make this story difficult to set aside."

— BlueInk Review, Starred

"With satisfying nods to postwar intrigue, Jack Tuesday is a thrilling police procedural novel in which a dedicated detective is subjected to dark suspicions."

— Clarion, Foreword Reviews

PERPETUAL CHECK

"Perpetual Check is a page-turner with a resolution readers won't see coming. It will please anyone who appreciates interesting characters and mysteries that deliver the unexpected."

— BlueInk Review, Starred

"Clever and surprising, Perpetual Check is a thrilling novel set during the intersection between the decline of the Soviet Union and the dawn of the computer age."

— Clarion, Foreword Reviews

NO STRAIGHT THING

"Ultimately heartwarming despite its macabre circumstances, No Straight Thing is an engrossing historical mystery."

— Clarion, Foreword Reviews

"With its vivid atmosphere and unforgettable characters, No Straight Thing is a treat for fans of suspenseful historical fiction."

— BlueInk Reviews, Starred

JACK TUESDAY

GAMBIT

Published in North America
Red Deer, A.B.
Canada

Paperback ISBN 978-1-989071-43-4
Hardcover ISBN 978-1-989071-44-1
Ebook ISBN 978-1-989071-45-8

JACK TUESDAY: GAMBIT

"If you're going through hell, keep going."

—Winston Churchill

1

Edmonton, Alberta 1972

The hair on Jack's neck prickled as he unhooked Pharo's leash and let the dog dart ahead along the path to the three-storey walk-up. He glanced up, his eyes stopping briefly at his former apartment on the second floor and then up to the balcony above it. Max leaned casually against the frame of the open sliding glass door, studying him. Jack waved, but his son turned away and vanished inside with no acknowledgement. Jack's jaw clenched, and he ran his hand through his hair, tugging on the ends as if it would pull the answers to raising a teenager free. He expected a certain amount of time to get used to each other, but the fifteen-year-old had defected from an East German swimming meet in Seattle to find his father. Why didn't Max show more enthusiasm now that he was here? Jack had naively expected immediate affection, but from the moment he'd collected Max from the RCMP in Vancouver, all he got was wariness and open coldness.

Pharo chortled and impatiently poked his nose at the heavy glass door, tongue dangling out of his mouth in the August heat. Jack mock-bowed the dog through the door, then raced him up the stairs. On the second floor, Pharo scampered down the hallway.

"Nope, nope." Jack sighed and leaned over the banister of the stairway. "That's not our place anymore. Up another flight. Remember?"

Pharo sat, head stubbornly set straight ahead.

"You can sit there, but I have to work." Jack continued up the stairs. Halfway, he heard the dog's nails on the tiles behind him. Jack stepped to the side, and Pharo deliberately slowed, padding past him up the rest of the stairs and acquiring a decided limp on the last three.

"Your con isn't working." Jack tilted his head, noting how the dog's *injured* leg switched sides mid-stride.

The move from the one-bedroom apartment on the second floor to a three-bedroom on the third floor happened with Max's arrival. Overnight, he went from bachelor to a family man in need of more space. Glen, the building's caretaker, suggested the apartment on the top floor.

"It's a three-bedroom. Hard to find three bedrooms," he stated. "And it's got a private laundry area in the basement." He wiggled his heavy eyebrows as an enticement.

"I thought it was reserved for the owner of the building," Jack said, searching his memory for the owner's name and coming up blank. Come to think of it, he couldn't recall ever having seen him either. "Who is the owner, anyway?" He'd always given Glen a cheque with a numbered company as a payee. A sudden suspicion that it might be a criminal hit him, and he dismissed it just as fast.

"Well, ask," Jack had agreed, not hopeful. Within a few days, he had it, and with a rent less than he expected to pay.

"I mentioned you're a good tenant and didn't cause problems," Glen said gruffly as if that settled the matter.

Now, it was home, but not as far as Pharo was concerned. Jack linked it to the Basenji's prolonged two-month kennel stay while hospitalized after Brodie's death.

He stood before the apartment door, steeling himself to greet Max, and plastered a cheerful grin on his face. No matter how patient he'd been in giving Max time to adjust, he couldn't shake the same thoughts. Despite searching for him being his sole reason to escape, Max's actions gave off a sense of regret.

He joined Max in the kitchen. Pharo rushed to his water bowl and drank noisily, then pushed his wet nose into Max's hand, getting a pat in return. Max wiped his damp hand on his pants, and half smiled at Jack, grey eyes cautious and shoulders hunched.

As if he doesn't trust me.

"Coffee smells great," Jack said, thinking his voice was a trifle too hearty. He shifted awkwardly on his feet, glancing at his son, unsure of what to say or how to bridge the gap between them. Especially to an almost fifteen-year-old. Who knew it could be so hard?

"Such good coffee. So plentiful every day." Max took a slow, contented sip, his grey eyes brightening as a satisfied smile tugged at the corners of his mouth. The expression disappeared as he lowered the cup from his mouth. "Bacon and eggs are also out."

Jack gave him the thumbs up. "Good. There's a full day today, and I'll be in court this morning."

Max pushed back a messy strand of dark hair from his forehead. It brought back a sudden memory of his mother, Ursula, who had the same colour hair and the same action when she had a concern.

"Why do you have to go to the court? Are you in trouble?" His brow furrowed, and his gaze flickered.

"Hey, it's okay," Jack assured him. "It isn't me they want. The accused is a biker gang member I arrested. His trial is today. Assault and drug dealing charges. I have to give my evidence of his guilt."

Max turned down the corners of his mouth. "In GDR, it is only for the prisoner to show up and hear his sentence," Max said, his tone expressing doubt that Jack's evidence would make a difference.

Jack paused and took a breath. He laid the strips of bacon into the frying pan until they began a satisfied sizzle. He eyed the bacon and kept his voice normal. "Well, this guy's defence lawyer will have something to say about that. He'll cross-examine me to ensure my case is airtight and my evidence is secure. Even if the man is guilty, he could go free if his lawyer finds a loophole."

"What is this loophole?"

"When the defence finds a law or regulation that leads to the judge dismissing the charge."

"Everyone can see this?" Max seemed to find the idea intriguing.

"Yes, of course."

"I want to see."

"I can arrange that, but another time, when I am not testifying. Anyway, don't you and Tommy have plans for a summer day? Go swimming, maybe? It's going to be hot." Since defecting from a competitive swim meet in Seattle, Max had shown little interest in continuing his competitive career since his arrival. He ignored Jack's attempts to investigate local competitive clubs.

"Going up to ninety degrees. Around thirty degrees centigrade," Jack added. "Doesn't that tempt you?"

His son's shoulders tensed, rising around his ears. His stony look at Jack and twisted lips expressed the typical teenage *what-does-it-take-for-you-to-understand?* expression. "You are so sure that political asylum is enough?" he muttered, not for the first time.

"Max," Jack kept his voice neutral. "You're well protected. I'll admit that if someone wanted you bad enough, the pool would be the first place to look, but you aren't famous, and your contribution to East Germany isn't considerable. So why would they go to extreme measures to take you back?"

"You know little about the Stasi." Max rolled his eyes, effectively dismissing Jack's attempts at logic and poured himself more coffee.

Jack took the hint. Best he found a lawyer, he reminded himself. One who knew how to keep Max safe and get him settled into Canada legally, with Jack as the sole guardian. He shouldn't put it off much longer.

"Which reminds me," he added, continuing his thoughts aloud while he pushed the bacon around in the pan, "school starts in just over a week. We need to make an appointment to find where you fit best. The principal will evaluate your grade and get you settled. Maybe in the same grade and school as Tommy?" He raised his eyebrows at Max. "Okay?"

Tommy, the teen Jack had met through Mira Zamborski, an elderly Polish woman, lived in the apartment building across the street.

Max had said Tommy's father was Roark Sullivan, but there was no mention of a mother. Jack didn't ask, fearing Max would look at it as interference or questioning his friendship. Jack's throat tightened, and he became aware that many new sensibilities were necessary to get to know his new son. Every nuance seemed to influence their budding relationship. Give it time, he told himself. We solve nothing in a day. Experience from questioning teenage delinquents told him they used mistrust of elders as a shield. Thoughtfully, Jack eyed Max, setting out dishes. He'd have to give him space to adapt in his own way.. After all, he had been adept at avoiding his Stasi handlers in Seattle and making his way to Vancouver, where he defected at the border crossing. It required initiative and a lot of bravery. And planning, which bothered Jack somewhat. Maybe someday he could ask his son about that. The RCMP in Vancouver had only given him a sketchy detail.

Once again, Jack had to shake off the feeling he was fumbling through fatherhood.

AT noon, the judge dismissed Jack from the stand. He hurried out of the second-floor courtroom and positioned himself so that he had a view of both exits on each side. Waiting for his target.

He heard the judge declare a muffled adjournment until after lunch, and a moment later, the doors opened. One of the first out was a man with brown hair pulled back in a ponytail, dressed in jeans and a white tee covered with a denim vest. He eyed Jack moving toward him, raised his eyebrows, and stepped to one side, letting Jack come to him. Jack grabbed him by the elbow and pulled him farther from the traffic.

"I spotted you from the witness box." He narrowed his gaze and locked on Anderson. His voice carried a sharp edge. "Care to tell me what interest Luke has in a drug case? Or is the Jackson gang into drug peddling now?"

Anderson stood, his thick arms folded and showing off bulging biceps, stretching his tee across his chest. He leaned back against the wall, his expression unreadable as he offered, "Nothing to do with Luke," and left it at that.

"Then what?" Jack persisted, wondering if Luke wanted to bring his business back to Edmonton. Worse, trying to involve Jack like last time? Stomach clenching at the thought, he leaned in close, eyes piercing into Anderson's calm brown ones.

Anderson sighed patiently. "I was in the area and saw you arrive. Maybe Luke wants me to assess how you perform." He half smirked at Jack. "Or maybe he asked me to watch for a particular person attending the courtroom. You know the drill. Information is gold."

Jack tried to make sense of the remark, concern growing. Was Anderson trying to tell him something? The biker's blithe stare told him nothing. "Is that a piece of information I should hang my hat on?"

Anger flared briefly in the other man's eyes, and Jack pursed his lips with a new thought. Had Anderson rejected his undercover role and joined the Jackson Gang for real, with Jack's brother Luke as his boss? Jack had promised to keep his secret with the proviso that Anderson would give fair warning if Luke's operation affected Jack. Jack had long ago rejected his family and taken up an existence apart from any connection to his brother or his life.

Anderson shifted his feet, reading his mind. The muscles in his arms flexed. Jack's lips formed a sneer, more for show than anything, sending his own message that he could destroy Anderson at any moment. Anderson's gaze hardened—the promise of consequences clear without a word. Anderson tilted his head to one side, then the other. Jack saw his eyes take in the surrounding area to assess if anyone was interested in their meeting. "You and I may have an understanding, Detective," Anderson murmured, "but if I consider I am in danger, our agreement can change on a dime."

"Well, then. Are you here as Luke's fixer? Setting up another meeting to move in on the Rebels? Again? After we ran him out of town last spring with his tail between his legs?"

Anderson's lip curled up at one end. For him, it was smiling. "Luke does whatever is in his family's best interests," he said like he knew something Jack didn't, sending another tingle down his spine. "His motto is there is more than one way to skin a cat."

"His family? What family?" Jack narrowed his eyes. "It had better not include me. The next time, he won't have time to run away. And you can tell him that's a promise."

Anderson only looked at his watch and stepped around Jack. "I have some things to do before I head back to Winnipeg." With that, he walked down the staircase in no hurry.

Why was Anderson here? His mind went over the biker's trial this morning. His investigation had not come up with any connection to Luke. Who else had been in the courtroom? Jack mulled it over. Had Anderson given him a clue when he mentioned it was to watch Jack himself? But why? Jack worried about the question all the way to the courthouse exit.

"Officer Tuesday?" The familiar, lilting voice with the Jamaican accent made him grin with delight. He turned away from the door, putting Anderson out of his thoughts.

"Jassy? What are you doing here? Not in any trouble, I hope." She had been Dr. Pavic's receptionist. Jack remembered the doctor who had been treating his amnesia before being murdered. They exchanged glances, the memory of that day still fresh—holding Jassy back as she trembled, trying to stop her from seeing Dr. Pavic's bloodied body slumped in the chair. He briefly squeezed her arm now. "It's so nice to see you again. It's been too long," he said, surprised by how much he meant it. He hadn't forgotten her kindness during his own troubles.

"I'm employed in a law firm now," she said. Jack's eyebrows rose a notch.

"I'm in charge of the library," she said, answering his unspoken question. "And I search for cases and precedents."

He threw his head to the side. "I thought you'd be after another medical job."

"I'm sorry," she said and sighed, brushing past his small talk. "Meeting you is my prescience." She gazed around, inspecting the area, then took his arm and pulled him aside from the doorway. "I planned to get in touch with you, and now here you are."

Puzzled, Jack chewed the inside of his cheek, but he said nothing, waiting. The colour around her cheeks got a little darker and flushed. "It's just, well . . ." She drew closer. "Can I pick your mind? I mean, I thought you might be the person who can advise me on . . ." She waved a hand. "Can we just sit down, and I can explain?"

"Sure. Here? Or over lunch? On me."

Her fingers drummed against her bag, and she kept darting quick looks toward the exit. "I must get back to the office. Mr. Kepler was waiting for a document he needed for court. It only arrived after he left, so I brought it. "

"I'm a client of the same law office. My lawyer is Winslow." Jack told her. "Actually, I need to make an appointment to—"

"Please, Detective," she interrupted, then smiled in apology, exposing her white teeth with the cute gap between the two front ones. She gestured towards a bench beside them. "There isn't much time."

Jack sighed and fell into step behind her, weaving through the steady stream of people pushing toward the security desk and jostling for space at the elevators. The courthouse bustled with life, its sleek, modern design looming overhead. From the outside, the six-story building resembled an inverted pyramid, each floor jutting outward. Inside, the bright, polished halls seemed to funnel the crowd toward their destinations while Jack and his companion slipped through the chaos, moving against the tide. She sat, leaving a scent of her perfume in passing. He had a sense of spring flowers, light and just barely there.

She took a deep breath. "It's your opinion I'm after. Like this." She paused and swallowed. "What if someone notices an abnormal activity in a record or too many activities traced back to one person?' She clicked her tongue and frowned. "I'm not being very clear, am I? But the problem is that the one who discovers the anomaly doesn't know what to do. I mean, should the person whose name appears on the record be told?"

Jack locked eyes with her, his gaze softening as he noticed hers dart away and her lips pressed into a tight line. "Would they view knowledge of that anomaly as a crime?" Jack saw her shoulders stiffen at the thought.

"It might." Her posture eased, a hint of relief flickering at his genuine concern.

"Has . . . this person," Jack asked carefully, "followed up with the questions? Asked other people if the observations are as serious as they seem?"

"Not really. I tried," she replied. "Trusting someone with the knowledge is the issue." Jassy's nervous fingers plucked at an invisible piece of lint on her dress. "Even asking other people who may have answers is taking a chance. They may construe it as spying into files that have no business being looked at. Besides, the head of the firm could be innocent or involved. How is one to know?" She shut up, and when Jack said nothing, added in a rush, "But if whoever noticed the records does nothing, it could cause a charge of abetting the unusual activity." She silently stared at Jack, eyes wide. "I thought of you and knew it would be safe to ask your advice." Her eyes pleaded with him to agree.

"Does the knowledge pose a danger to that person?" Jack asked carefully, avoiding a suggestion that it be so.

She swallowed and nodded. The colour drained from her cheeks, betraying the churn of fear and doubt etched across her round face.

"Jassy?"

She sprang to her feet, eyes wide in guilty surprise, and Jack rose with her. He turned an easy smile at the lanky figure of Howard Winslow, who furrowed his brow and adjusted his glasses, squinting at the scene of Jack and Jassy, heads together in intense focus.

"Jassy and I are old friends," Jack said quickly, his grin broadening as if enjoying the lawyer's surprise. "I haven't seen her since . . . well, for a while. It's been too long." Jack's glance travelled between the two of them. "Am I keeping her from work?"

"Sure, we keep our staff close to the grindstone," Eyes still curious, Howard shook Jack's hand. "Need I ask what brings a cop to the courthouse?" Jack snorted a laugh at Howard's joke, hoping to soften the atmosphere.

"Detective Tuesday says he wants an appointment to see you," Jassy slipped in easily, as though that was the reason for their conversation.

"I have a new son," Jack agreed, "and I need him to be legal."

"I read about it in the paper," Winslow said, relaxing now as he shifted to face Jack directly. "A snippet that said little. Some months ago now, wasn't it? Interesting."

"I asked the paper to keep it small, and there was no follow-up," Jack said. "He's still afraid someone may come after him, but the paper had to run a story. The fewer people know where he lives, the better. He's only fifteen and starting at a new school."

"And doesn't want to be an object of sensation," Howard finished. He pushed his glasses up on the bridge of his nose again with his forefinger. Jack smiled. Howard always used the gesture when he was about to issue a solution. "Come in tomorrow morning first thing if you can make it. I'd love to meet him. Bring him and all the papers you have that prove he's yours. You know the drill." Winslow glanced at his watch, then at Jassy. "I'm due in court soon. It looks like half our firm is here. Bernie is already here for one this morning, and now me this afternoon." He nodded at Jack. "There he is now," he added, his tall form seeing easily over Jack's shoulder.

Jack looked and saw a thickset, pudgy figure pushing through the door. He assumed it was Bernard Kepler. He looked back for

Jassy, but she had left during his conversation with Howard Winslow. Surprised, Jack had seen no last look, no touch of farewell. Her disappearance gave him the illusion of vanishing to avoid notice. Too bad Winslow had interrupted. Despite Jassy's poor evasive technique about a third person, she was obviously the one who'd noticed the anomalies. Whatever they were, they had frightened her enough to include any or all of the principles of Gordon, Kepler, and Winslow et al. Jack headed back toward headquarters, wondering how to arrange another conversation with her.

Jassy was one of the few people who had not treated him as a pariah when they suspended him from the force. He would not leave her hanging in the wind, her concerns unanswered. Her faith in him left him with a pulse of chivalric energy. Tomorrow, he'd find her after he met Winslow and ask her out on a date. He stepped out of the courthouse with a smile tugging at his lips. It'd been too long since he had been on a date. Remembering their pleasant back-and-forth encounters while he waited in the doctor's office, his pace quickened. Maybe even more than one date. Whistling, he got in the car to find a place for lunch before he went back to headquarters.

The call came into the squad room just before he was about to leave at the end of his shift. A hit and run at the corner of 103 Ave and 124 Street. The victim was deceased. A young female, I.D. of Jasmine Harrison.

Jack wondered why he never inquired about her last name. For him, she was always just Jassy with the bright smile.

2

"*I* want the case," he told his Detective Sergeant, Paul Wager, meeting the man's gaze with unwavering resolve. There is more to this than a hit-and-run."

Wager looked up from the papers before him, his expression vague. "You going off on one of your weird hunches again? Tilting at windmills like Donny—what's his name?" He snorted and rolled Jack's report on the morning's court appearance into a baton. He held it up, brandishing it as if to club Jack with it.

"Listen, Wager, she cornered me this morning at the courthouse and wanted to talk to me. She hinted that the firm might not be entirely honest. I'm . . ."

"Forget it, Jack." Wager cut him off, slapping the report against the desk for emphasis. "I've sent Chen to the scene to talk to the officer in charge. Go home—your shift's over. Let them work without your dreamed-up theories muddling the facts. Chen will spot anything out of the ordinary." The newest detective constable, Ethan Chen, joined the squad and replaced Mark Ackland. Ackland had been suspected of leaking information to the gangs, allegedly under the instructions of former Detective Sergeant Steven Hawke. Ackland was now serving in the boonies as a precaution.

Jack sighed, conceding temporary defeat. "Is it okay if I'm late tomorrow? I made an early appointment with Howard Winslow. I need to sort out Max's school and finalize his legal status in Canada—and mine as his father."

Wager eyed Jack over the top of his reading glasses. Something he'd gained, Jack noticed, along with his new position as Detective Sergeant. "How's that going? Not so great by the look of you.." His tone was oddly detached, as if he were observing rather than sympathizing. "Being a father not living up to your expectations?"

"I can't seem to get close to Max. Half the time, I think he resents me. I'm walking on eggshells half the time, and the other half saying stupid things, deciding for him. I think of his journey to reach here and wonder if he thinks I'm an idiot."

"That's three halves," Wager said, lips twitching under his moustache.

"You're no help."

Wager took his glasses off and set them aside while gesturing to the chair opposite him in one deliberate movement. Jack sank into it and massaged the back of his head with his fingertips, trying to ease the tension.

"Have you tried asking him what the problem is?" Wager's voice softened. You might think you have good people sense, but it's usually easier to just ask. At least it might start a conversation about what he feels. The kid probably has a million questions about you. Maybe he's wondering if you really want him. All his worldly knowledge comes from his life in East Germany."

"I'm thinking drugs, steroids," Jack blurted out.

Wager's eyes widened. "That's a leap, even for you. Any sign?"

"He's lanky. Although he has the ideal swimmer's build, his muscles seem large for his age. And he has a quick temper. Moods." Jack looked at Wager, helpless to explain more. "Drugs could be a reason."

"That's a bit flimsy, Jack. Or are you hoping it's drugs rather than your company?" Wager teased, but his expression tilted into a frown. "You've seen swimmers' physical builds. Constant training develops the arm and shoulder muscles—I'm envious." Wager grinned, then creased his forehead. "But then again, I've also read the rumours that East Germans are cheating. . . . Disgusting if it's true. Sacrificing kids for medals?" Wager shook his head and shuffled the reports on his desk, choosing one. Their meeting was over. "Do what you have to do. Get him to a doctor for tests."

Jack drove home, musing about Wager's suggestions and his upcoming appointment with Howard Winslow. As he crawled along the High Level Bridge in the evening rush, he pondered the ordinariness of life rushing on while minor tragedies disrupted other lives. Did Jassy have a family or a boyfriend in Edmonton? His ignorance about her personal life left a sour note. Stalled traffic pushed gasoline fumes through the open windows. A cool breeze coming off the river, its current moving sluggishly, mirroring the crawl of traffic, provided some relief. It must be near ninety degrees now. Jack got out of his car and took off his suit jacket. The traffic inched forward, and an impatient honk behind him told him to get moving.

Later, Max took Pharo out for a run while Jack chopped eggs, lettuce, cold meat, and whatever else he found to make a chef's salad. *Pharo could tell me what's going on in Max's head,* he thought irrationally. The dog would check Max's bedroom each night to ensure he was in bed before settling himself. And when Max was with Pharo, his demeanour shifted to something more typical of a teenager, a sight that poured hope into Jack's vision of a happy family. Yet, Pharo remained Jack's dog, a small reassurance that he was still the Alpha male in the house, even if he sometimes doubted his ability to handle a teenage son. He sliced a loaf of crusty bread to accompany the salad and prepared a pitcher of iced water with lemon slices.

Over dinner, Jack told Max about their early appointment the next day. "You'll need to come too. He'll have questions I can't answer, and besides, he has to see that you are a live, breathing person, and I am not trying to pull a fast one."

Max furrowed his black brows. "If something is fast, why pull it?"

"Making a false statement so I could adopt an orphan or . . . never mind. *'Pull a fast one'* means to deceive him."

Max gave a nod of agreement while his eyes scrutinized Jack's face for any hints of dishonesty. When they reached Jack's eyes, Max's own dropped to his plate. *What's that all about?* Jack inwardly grimaced and vowed they'd have the conversation that Wager suggested tonight.

But after dinner, Max slipped out the door with a casual mention of Tommy's new Fleetwood Mac LP. His description gave Jack the impression it would not be his genre of music. He kept his opinion to himself, glad that Max would listen to it across the street and fetched a bottle of Pilsner, taking it and a copy of *Maclean's* magazine to the balcony. Pharo padded along after him, peered through the metal slats of the balcony, and, after finding nothing worth barking at, curled at Jack's feet to commence grooming.

Jack stretched his legs, catching the last rays of the sun, and opened the magazine, read the letters to the editor, then leafed through the magazine, skimming the articles. *"Substandard Arms Industry"* caught his eye, and he stopped to read. The piece accused Canada's arms manufacturers of producing inferior equipment due to corruption. Jack's experience immediately balked against the accusation. During his Army career, his equipment had never been substandard. Quite the contrary. The article also criticized Canada's peacekeeping efforts, suggesting they were a façade for warmongering since our forces stood by and let violence occur during the conflict. All of Canada was under the influence of the United States. Jack gave the magazine a healthy shake. Shocked and angry, he checked the reporter's author, J. Ware, described as a political observer. *Never heard of him,* Jack thought. *Was he a military expert?* He may as well have come right out and said it was American Imperialism. Amongst the flim-flam, he searched for proof of the accusations but found only what sounded like truth. *Didn't reporters have some kind of ethics code?* Disgusted, Jack hoped he'd see letters to the editor in next month's edition refuting the claim. He tossed the magazine aside and finished his Pilsner.

JUST before eight o'clock the following day, Jack and Max arrived at a recently renovated building on 104th Street for their appointment. Gordon, Winslow and Kepler occupied the whole second floor of the four-story building. Jack carried a portfolio stuffed with Max's documents: the RCMP report, asylum statement, birth certificate, and a letter from Ursula confirming Jack as Max's father. Upstairs, the door with the firm's name was locked. The hours posted on the door told him opening hours began an hour later. He peered through the glass and saw Howard Winslow, hand up in greeting, coming to let them in.

Winslow led them into his office. He acknowledged Jack's introduction of Max with a handshake and critical inspection, then waved them to chairs in front of his desk. "He looks like you," he said to Jack.

Surprised, Jack's eyes swivelled from Howard to Max and back again. "I thought more like Ursula."

"Trust me, Jack." Winslow chuckled. "Any fool can see the resemblance."

Jack's face lit up with a proud grin as he looked at Max. Max stared straight ahead, his face sober. Jack resisted the urge to slap him up the back of the head. Why are all teenagers like zombies?

Howard was busy scanning the papers Jack had given him, his face pale and pouches under his eyes with dark circles. "I'm sorry about Jassy," Jack said. "I knew her pretty well from when she was Dr. Pavic's receptionist. More than that, she was competent and took complete control of winding down his practice after . . ." He hesitated.

Howard was staring at him, his expression pensive. "It's a terrible business. Poor girl. She just got off the bus from work. Some fool motorist swerving around the bus and not paying attention. I telephoned the police this morning, and that's what they told me."

Repeating it as an outside report was an odd way of putting it, Jack thought. He studied Howard's eyes. "I sense a reservation. Any doubt it was accidental?"

Howard flushed and shifted his attention back to the papers. He abruptly turned to Max. "You don't mind if I ask a few questions?"

"The papers we brought are not enough?" Max looked startled and uncomfortable. Jack hastened to assure him. "We expected a few questions. Right, Max? It's just to clarify details from the letters and records."

Howard gave Max a reassuring smile of his own. "For instance, your mother's letter mentions that she never hid your father's name from you. Do you agree with that statement?"

Max's shoulders relaxed. "She told me I must never talk about my father and just pretend we enjoyed living in GDR. She shared all her memories with me. Now, I know it was to prove who I was to the police at the border. How they met. He was an Army sergeant. She had decided she'd stay in West Germany despite Russia's determination to have all the East Germans returned to the West Zone. They forced her back." He turned to Jack and suddenly stated, his tone condemning. "I thought you'd be in the Canadian Army."

Taken aback at Max's impression he might still be in the Army, Jack took it at face value. Max had only heard about the past. "I had plans to bring her here before she disappeared. Shortly after, The Army transferred us back to Canada. A lifetime Army career didn't impress me; it was time to leave. I'd served my time." He didn't add that his entire existence and future seemed destroyed. As he explained, he realized they hadn't discussed Max's expectations or his impression of Jack during his time in East Germany and who Max had expected to meet when he searched for a father. Sighing, he tucked the subject away in his mind to raise again at his earliest opportunity. There were so many conversations that needed to happen between him and Max.

Dammit, there should be a manual somewhere.

Howard broke in, "Can you describe her work and your life there?".

"I told all that to the police who arrested me at the Border."

"Not an arrest, Max. They detain all those who make an appeal to enter Canada. To make sure they are genuine refugees." Howard held up the RCMP and Border Agent's report. "I know it is in here, and I'll read it carefully. But perhaps you can give me a brief version anyway."

"To see if it agrees," Max challenged. His mouth turned down. Howard didn't reply, just stared at him, his expression patient but not harsh.

"My mother worked in their nuclear program. In the end, they made her sick." Max's lips quivered. "She was a wonderful *mutter*. She could have treatment in Switzerland, but they wouldn't let her go." He took a shuddering breath.

Jack reached out and put his hand on his shoulder.

Max shrugged it off, sudden anger turning his face red. "She told me they wanted her there to assess and suggest new improvements to keep up with NATO weapons."

Howard's eyes widened, and he pushed his glasses firmly to the bridge of his nose. "NATO? How did they know what NATO had?"

Spies, of course, Jack thought, and Howard's expression told him he had arrived at the same conclusion.

Max pressed his lips together. "She warned me to keep her secrets. They put wiretaps in our house and in our rooms. We had to speak in code or outside the house. It was difficult. We had to be very careful. No slipups."

My god, thought Jack. A young boy trying to cope with talking about nuclear weapons? What was Ursula thinking? He opened his mouth and then shut it.

"She's gone now, though, isn't she?" Howard whispered. "What you say in this office is completely confidential. It's called attorney client privilege. Nobody can force me to reveal what we say between client and lawyer."

"They took her to meetings to discuss NATO's activities and how to arrange defence. So she heard their plans and knew they would execute her if anyone discovered information about those gatherings."

Max's face hardened, his mouth set in a line. "It was deliberate—to keep her chained up. She only pretended. I told them in Vancouver she was on guard day and night to keep them convinced she was in the fight to beat NATO and show that Russia was best." His bottom lip quivered. "It was hard. Took all her strength."

Howard continued after a long silence, where Jack hardly dared to breathe. "Noted." He made a few marks on his legal pad and said, "Tell us how she arranged for you to defect. She was courageous, and you have every reason to be proud of her."

"GDR was eager to excel in sports. Show the world how great communism is. We tried different sports." Max's expression cleared, and he seemed his age. "I hated them all, but she persisted. Finally, we agreed on swimming. I showed some gift. I know now that she planned to use athletics to get me out of Germany." His gaze shifted to Jack. "She made me promise to show you the list she made of all my records of competitions and scores. It's in my notebook that she made me take with me. To remember, she said." Max's lips trembled. He blinked hard and put his hand up to his eyes.

Winslow cleared his throat. "Very good, Max. That's all I need to know to proceed with your Canadian citizenship. Welcome to your new home, young man. Your forever home," he added, sounding like he was welcoming a stray animal. Howard rose and shook Max's hand.

To Jack, he said, "I'll let you know if I need more." He bent over his calendar. "An appointment in two days—" he glanced over his shoulder at Jack. "The same time as this morning?" Jack nodded.

"About Jassy," Jack prodded as they all headed for the door, Max ahead, seeming eager to leave. "I need to know more about the circumstances, Howard. She was special to me."

Howard's face tightened, and he put his hand on Jack's arm. "Jack, don't dig into matters that don't concern you. This is a firm issue. Anything else is too soon."

Too soon? "Meaning what?" Jack's heart skipped a beat. A familiar chill ran down his spine, reminiscent of the moments before an ambush in Korea.

Howard avoided his gaze. "Forget it, Jack. It's a discussion for me, Tim, and Bernie."

They reached the main reception area, where Max stood waiting. The room buzzed with muted conversation among staff and lawyers. As they entered, everyone's attention shifted to Howard and Jack.

"We're having a memorial for Jassy," Howard said before Jack could ask. "We can't just carry on like she'd never been here, can we?"

"Of course. I appreciate you made an exception to meet this morning," was all he could say. It was time to leave. Winslow's tight expression stayed with him until the sidewalk. Why did he need to talk to Gordon and Kepler about Jassy? What anomaly had Jassy found? Did Howard know about it, and was it severe enough that all partners, including Timothy Gordon, the senior partner, needed to consult about it?

He glanced over at the gathered group one final time. They had shifted closer to each other as though seeking comfort—except for one—an anxious girl behind the reception desk, clutching herself and staring at the floor. Her fear was palpable, unnoticed by the rest.

3

OUTSIDE, Jack squinted at his watch and made a face. He'd be late again.

"I will take the bus." Max scanned the street in both directions, looking for the stop.

"I don't know what number bus takes you to the south side. You may need a transfer," Jack said, cursing himself for being short on knowledge and suggestions. He chewed his lip, torn between offering a ride or taking him to work and arranging one.

"When I defected, I didn't leave my brain behind." Max's voice was full of scorn. "I will ask the bus driver for directions."

Jack put his hands up, palm out. "Of course. I'm sorry." He seemed to be forever apologizing to Max. "I'm not thinking straight. My mind is on the girl who died . . . Jassy. I knew her from a case before. We spoke the same day she died."

Max flushed, and his grey eyes widened. "Now it is me who must apologize. I will spend the afternoon with Tommy. He will show me our school."

"I'll see you at supper then." Jack watched him go down the street, a growing sense of distance between them lingering in the air.

"Simpson needs to see your face," Wager said as soon as Jack arrived in the squad room.

The truth was common knowledge among insiders—that Durand, the previous Deputy Chief of the Major Crimes division, was a corrupt cop who Tito had taken out. The official story for the outside claimed he died in the line of duty. Deputy Chief Lorne Simpson from Manitoba had taken his place, as opposite in appearance and method as could be. With salt-and-pepper hair, ruddy cheeks, and a pinkish complexion, Simpson favoured a decentralized command style, unlike Durand, who had craved control over everything.

"Fill me in on what he wants?" Jack asked Wager as they walked down the third floor towards the D.C.'s inner sanctum.

"You'll find out," Wager replied curtly. "Be respectful. No smart remarks. Hold back your usual wordplay. If you make me look bad, he'll automatically nix any future requests I might make on your behalf." At the door to Simpson's office, he stopped and eyed Jack. "Get my drift?"

"Yes, sergeant," Jack said crisply. "And I'll try really hard."

"Like that." A muscle twitched in Wager's cheek, making his mustache flare. "That—don't do that."

D.C. Simpson's office gave the image of a ship's bridge—minus the helm. Photographs of sailboats, some featuring Simpson with sunglasses, windblown hair, and a broad smile, played with each other along the walls. A model of a Bluenose, its canvas unfurled, seemed ready to sail right off the shelf. Why didn't the occupant join the navy and move to Nova Scotia? Lake Winnipeg could have been Simpson's summer playground with his sailboat in tow. Where could he moor his boat in Edmonton? Perhaps Pigeon Lake, south of Edmonton, would suit him.

Simpson didn't invite them to sit, and Jack noted Wager sidestep to a position just outside the deputy chief's direct line of sight, where he could still watch Jack. He frowned at Jack, narrowing his eyes and sending out warning signals.

"Officer Tuesday," began Simpson, tapping the point of his pencil on the desk. "About the hit-and-run death."

Jack's lips parted for a moment, but he pressed them together again, forcing a nod. What could this be about?

"It was an accident. Yes?"

Jack's eyes brightened with newfound energy. "Well, if I may just offer an observation," He said, ignoring Wager's scowl. "My lawyer is a partner in the same office where she worked. You see . . ."

"No, Officer Tuesday. Not *me* see. *You* see. You have no authorization." The office chair groaned as Simpson leaned back. His fingers drummed the desk in an erratic rhythm. "Tell me, Officer Tuesday, why is your personnel file an inch thicker than any other detective's?"

"I wasn't aware it was, sir." He stood in the at-ease stance, hands behind his back, and rocked back on his heels. His scalp prickled, and he felt sweat break out beneath his hairline. Now what?

"Because you like to sail too close to the wind? Just charge ahead without the benefit of trimming your sails?" Simpson's eyes gleamed at his nautical analogy. "I read your file, Officer Tuesday, and I see how you operate. This girl's hit-and-run, for instance. You went to her place of work to pry and gave the impression her death was now under police investigation."

"No, sir! I kept my appointment with Howard Winslow. A personal matter. Detective Sergeant Wager will verify that." He didn't deny bringing up Jassy's death.

Out of the corner of his eye, he saw Wager wrap his bottom teeth over his moustache and glare at him.

Simpson clasped his hands together, then, seeking confirmation of his suspicions, directed his gaze at Wager, whose pained expression had been replaced by one showing agreement with Jack's statement.

"I'm glad to hear it. Detective Sergeant Wager tells me that since your return to duty after last spring's fiasco, your actions have been professional and a credit to the force."

"Thank you, chief. Sir."

"In his morning's report to me, he also relayed your suspicions. But when I heard you were at the very place where she worked, I suspected you might be sailing into rough waters without a compass." His brow furrowed. "Again. I don't want another debacle that throws this division into stormy seas, Officer." Despite the stern set of his jaw, the corners of his mouth twitched upward, betraying a reluctant smile. "Not on my watch."

"Of course, sir. Just a faint wind on calm seas, sir."

Moustache bristling, Wager screwed his eyes shut.

D.C. Simpson's blue eyes developed an uneasy stare. "That's the ticket," he said. But the flicker of discomfort in his eyes solidified into a sharp, uncompromising look. "Depending on what your priority is, you must always adjust your sails to the proper course, detective." With that, Simpson abruptly waved them out.

"What was that all about? Why tell him I thought Jassy's hit and run was deliberate?" Jack and Wager marched back to the squad room.

"I only mentioned it as a possibility," Wager said. "How was I to know he'd been reading your file and got all antsy about the reports in there? It jiggled his liver, and he called me in, inclined to think we had a rogue cop on our team." He eyed Jack as they turned the corner. "He isn't far from wrong. You've toned down a bit, but yesterday, you had the look."

"What look?"

"The one that says to hell with everyone else." As they walked, Wager turned his head to Jack. "I thought you had seen the light and decided no more solo investigations. Or keeping things secret. Now you have that look again—the one that says you know what you know, and you're plotting a way to investigate it." Seeing confirmation in Jack's expression, he zoomed in close to Jack. "Forget it, whatever it is."

As they entered the room, Jack saw Hank Vassar straighten up from leaning over Bill Dyer's shoulder, his expression a cross between vexation and relief. Wager sighed, and Jack pretended to not notice, knowing that Vassar had been editing Dyer's usual careless reports.

William Dyer was the other Detective Constable, the last new arrival. His stocky build was already leaning on the side of chubby, and he kept his hair long with sideburns, just barely meeting regulation standards. Wager had paired Dyer with Vassar, and judging from the expression on Vassar's face now, it didn't sit well.

"Hand it over," Wager barked at Dyer, stretching out his hand for the report. With his other hand, he handed out a new report sheet to Jack.

"Another hit and grab. Probably connected with the same string of jobs last month. Take Chen with you. In fact, consider Chen your dearest and best partner."

Chen appeared at his elbow, nodding at Jack. A head shorter than Jack, wiry, late twenties, Jack guessed. And fit, Jack noted, reflex making him suck in his own stomach.

Jack turned back to Wager, who was pushing the report sheet at him. "Don't teach Chen any of your shortcuts," he told Jack. "One of you in this place is enough."

Jack's shoulders slumped, his voice just above a whisper. "Yes. Sergeant."

"Dyer, get over here," Wager's exasperated voice followed them out the door. "How'd you ever get this far writing sloppy reports like this?"

Chen rolled his eyes and tittered. "The next thing you hear will be Vassar asking for a new partner."

Chen maneuvered the car along Jasper Avenue toward their target jewellery store. The traffic moved smoothly along the wide main avenue, constructed long ago so that six carriages could easily travel along beside each other without snarling traffic.

Jack studied Chen's profile as he drove—posture uptight, grip on the steering wheel firm, yet relaxed. His gaze was steady, shifting purposefully from the road to the mirrors. Jack noted the meticulous way the younger man navigated even the most minor obstacles with quick deliberation. Young to be a detective, he thought, but Chen had the determined look of someone focused on actively pushing his career forward. He was going to be a policeman's policeman, Jack decided. Capable, knowledgeable, and hopefully reliable. He wondered if Chen's reliability could match that of his late partner,

Brodie, whose absence still felt like a void.

"Finished staring?" Chen asked as he continued west on Jasper Avenue.

"Just wondering if you like Chinese food," Jack improvised, forcing a grin.

"Why?"

"You could point us to the best place to eat."

"Sure I could. The half-white side of me is totally into Chinese food."

"Come on," Jack clicked his tongue against his teeth in a tsk. "Is that a knock? Don't put your thoughts into my head, Chen. Truthfully, I thought you and I might make a great team—your diligence and my brainpower." He flashed a grin.

Chen's mouth hung open, and he shot a glance at Jack, his expression half angry. "After you break me in, you mean?" He snorted and turned back to watch the traffic.

"Well, you are smart like Brodie, with the same drive to climb the ranks. I miss him, you know. Of course. Like any one of our own lost in service. More so because he was my partner since our rookie days together." He paused, then admitted. "My jokes comparing you to him are my way of covering up the memories, Chen. You'll learn that, but I'll mention it now." He watched as Chen considered it and then nodded his understanding. Jack smiled and changed the subject. "Why did you become a cop?"

At a red light, Chen relaxed, turning his head to meet Jack's gaze. "I always wanted to be one. My parents, especially my mom, didn't. She wanted me to take my MBA and go into business, finance— become a millionaire. She still blames my father for not stopping me." He laughed, the sound light and genuine. "I'm good at math, and I suppose finance suits me more, but being a cop drew me." The light changed to green. "I'm glad I did." he glanced at Jack and added, "I know the temptations and can resist them." Reminding Jack that he knew about what had gone on in the unit.

Hope he remembers that when he actually faces the temptation, Jack wanted to tell him but asked, "You attended the hit and run over by Oliver. A Jamaican girl, name of Harrison. Did you see anything that might make her death deliberate?"

Chen glanced over and grinned. "Wager warned me about you."

"Really." Jack kept his tone flat, his face expressionless.

"Yeah." Chen looked at him, his eyes curious. "A lot of guys say you're a nitpicker, always looking for ulterior motives. Going off on your own."

Jack's lip twitched. "Only when I had to. I've changed. Thinking outside the box isn't your thing?"

Chen brought one shoulder up to his ear in a shrug. "Dunno. You seem to be more right than wrong and get the arrests. The Chinese part of me might agree that signs are something to be noticed." He shot Jack a sidelong glance. "Whatever works?" But his twisted lips said he didn't believe it.

"I believe partners should bounce ideas off each other."

"I remember him, your partner," Chen said, sobered. "We lost a good cop." He glanced over at Jack. "But I intend to stay my own man, Tuesday. I can't be him, be your Sancho."

"To my Don Quixote?" Jack laughed. "You've been listening to gossip, Chen. It wasn't like that." His tone turned serious as he fixed Chen with a steady look. "I don't expect you to take his place. You've been talking to the wrong people. Ask Wager. He hassles me, but he knows I have this thing. Or talent? Curse? Forming a complete picture from details."

Chen's skepticism was evident in his furrowed brow. "For example?"

Jack pointedly inspected Chen, his gaze sweeping over him. "Your right thigh is larger than your left. You run every day to keep fit, but you probably play a game, like handball?" Chen's eyes widened. "You dodge toward the ball more with your right leg; repeated landings have increased your thigh muscle. You play with the left hand more than the right, even though you're right-handed. Your left palm gets sore and is getting calloused. Too proud for a glove? You probably golf with left-handed clubs too."

Chen's knuckles turned white as they gripped the steering wheel. "That hit and run," he said in a rush. "Nothing unusual stands out." He chewed his bottom lip, looking doubtful, probably worried he may have missed something. "Not anything that hit me, anyway," he amended, just in case. "One thing, though. She didn't get out at the usual bus stop, but before."

"And you know that, how?"

"The bus driver knows all his regulars and where they get on and off. The same crowd using the same bus to and from work. Like his work family, he says."

Jack leaned forward, interested. "Go on."

"He says she seemed upset, got off the bus and looked around like she was lost. He last saw her heading towards the street from the back of the bus. That's when she got hit. He didn't see it, but the people in the back of the bus hollered for him to stop when he pulled away."

"And I suppose nobody got the car's description?"

"A newer Chevy two-door. Blue. One person driving. One witness claimed two people were driving. Maybe Alberta plates. Who knows? The only thing they all agreed on was the driver didn't stop. There's an APB telexed to all offices for the car and all auto body shops in case one comes in for repair. Bound to be damaged." Chen swallowed. "It wasn't pretty. Poor girl."

Another pang of sorrow cramped Jack's stomach. He considered going to the scene himself and questioning nearby shops. But it would get back to Wager and might stop him from progressing on any new information. Until then, it was wiser to wait until he knew more.

Conversation ceased, and they arrived at their destination and got down to business. But all day, Jack's thoughts kept returning to Jassy.

After supper that night, he took Pharo to Kinsmen Park for an extended play session. The trees rustled with a cool breeze, providing some relief from the sweltering evening. To his surprise, Max agreed to come along. Jack chuckled as he watched Max throw the Frisbee, expecting Pharo to bring it back. But in the dog's usual fashion, Pharo clamped it in his mouth and dashed around the park, inviting Max to chase him.

"Basenjis won't play fetch," Jack laughed when an exhausted chaser finally dropped beside him. Max flapped the ends of his open shirt against his body to cool down. Dust clung to his jeans, which he brushed off with a rueful smile. Jack smirked to himself. Max had insisted he have two pairs of denim jeans, remarking that his friends in East Germany would be wild with envy. They were available there, but East Germany's manufactured jeans weren't the right material.

"Look at him," Jack said, nodding towards Pharo, who crouched in the grass, daring Max to chase him again. His wide, doggy grin was unmistakable.

Max flopped full out on his back, laughter spilling out freely. "It's good to let him think he's the master and I'm the dog." He laughed again and placed his arms behind his head. "He's a dog like I've never seen. Why does he make all those bad, sick noises when we are in the car?"

"He hates being in the car," Jack admitted, "and I have to pretend I'm going to drive off without him before he will get inside. Then he retches, hoping I'm going to stop and let him out. He's never really barfed inside the car, so I just let him whine and retch all he wants. Don't let him fool you. He's a real con." Jack sobered and gave Max a severe look. "Also, don't think he is just a play dog. He's got me out of more trouble than I can count. He's got a sense of people that I never dismiss."

Max stared at him, then at Pharo. "I won't. And I will always protect him. You can believe me. You are lucky to have him."

Jack felt like hugging him, but knowing what a teenager would think of a hug in the open air, he resisted. Was this the time to probe into his life and ask the questions that Wager had posed? No, he decided. This was a rare moment of ease, and why spoil it? Don't rush things, he told himself. He didn't want to be constantly in his face like his own father had been in his. Jack's mouth pulled down, remembering his father's unconcealed loathing.

"What is it?" Max asked. "Did I say something that was not proper?"

"No, son. Not at all. But it's late. Time to go home." He rose and put out a hand to help Max to his feet. "Only thinking how lucky I am to have you here. Safe."

Max stepped suddenly away, his thoughts frozen again behind a dark, withdrawn face. The friendly moment evaporated like mist.

Jack wanted to jerk him back roughly. Make him talk. Like he was a perp. He was tired of walking on eggshells. If Max wasn't happy living with Jack, why didn't he admit he would rather live elsewhere? Silly question, his mind answered. What else was the kid supposed to do? Numbness crept into his mind.

What am I thinking? He's here. He's safe. That's all that mattered. Whistling for Pharo, he let Max start away, toward the path up to the road. He wished Brodie were here. He'd know. His dead partner would know. *I miss you, Brodie. You, Maureen, even your sassy son, Ben. The outings we had. You were like family, and you'd know how to handle Max.* "Dammit, Brodie," he muttered under his breath, "Why'd you have to die?"

Jack shook off the unreasonable thought and focused on Howard Winslow. The legalities needed to be settled with no complications. One step at a time. First, the legal matters. The minute Max was officially his, he'd find out what was going on inside his head. Even if they both had to find outside counselling to achieve it. He shuddered at the thought. Taking things to the outside was not his bent. What if the fact came out that his own father had been the A-list crime boss in Winnipeg, and his brother continued when his father died? What would Max do with that information?

If Howard didn't produce something substantive at his next

appointment, he'd pester him to give it higher priority.

From there, his thoughts jumped to Jassy. All details pointed to an accident, so why couldn't he accept it? He couldn't yet link it to her revelation, but the circumstances gnawed at him. Something strange was happening in that office. And why had she gotten off the bus early? Had she seen something from the bus window that frightened her? He couldn't ignore two strange happenings that didn't quite fit with her death.

Pharo shot past him, racing to the top of the path by the High Level Bridge, yodelling at Max, already at the top waiting for him. They walked without speaking down the few blocks for home.

He'd not actively pursue an investigation under his promise to D.C. Simpson and Wager. Still, he'd keep it in the back of his mind and remain open to the possibility her death might not be an unfortunate accident. Hit-and-run deaths were not regular occurrences in Edmonton. And something felt decidedly wrong about this one.

4

THE next two days blurred into a routine of call-outs, reports, and interviews with suspects. True to his word, Jack avoided discussing Jassy's death, although reminders and worries about Winslow's progress in Max's certification lingered in his thoughts. At least Max's school arrangements were being handled—that was one thing off his plate.

Sprawled in an uncomfortable chair outside the principal's office while Max was being interviewed, Jack had nothing to look at but the hallway spreading in each direction. The scents of the place hit him: a blend of chalk dust, disinfectant, and the unmistakable odour of sweaty sneakers. No matter the school, the smell never changed. It brought back memories of his father's insistence on sending him and Luke to private school—this place was a far cry from that. The office door creaked open, and Jack snapped upright. The principal, Mr. Johnson, appeared with a smile. "He's right up to his age and grade level. Maybe more in Physics and Biology, but less in History, Civics, and English. Understandable. But on the plus side, a language. Russian and German." Mr Johnson raised his eyebrows at Jack, but made no further comment.

Jack flashed a look at Max, who only rolled his eyes. His lack of knowledge in Civics could be traced back to his compulsory attendance of Marxist fundamentals and participation in communist youth movement activities in the GDR. When Jack first commented on it, Max waved him off and vowed that while some absorbed it like religion, with the help of his mother, he wasn't one of them.

"We'll slot him in at Grade Nine." He shook hands with them both and left them. Max gave a thumbs up. "Tommy and I."

One down, thought Jack, relieved. He eyed Max and wondered if he should suggest a doctor's appointment. Maybe slip in a request for a drug test. But the idea of a positive result lingering on a medical record, complicating things later, made him pause. Maybe he should talk it over with Wager. The flood of questions pressed in—this new territory of guardianship, uncharted and unsettling. After Brodie's death, Jack's lack of family seemed his biggest regret, and here he was, thrown into the thick of being a single parent. Jack mentally shook himself. As they said in the Army, don't wish and don't go looking for trouble. Good advice.

Right now, his biggest material concern was money. A raise would help. New expenses continually ate into his savings. The latest hit was the ten-speed Raleigh he'd bought to match Tommy's bike. Once all the legal business was finished, maybe he could convince Max to get a part-time job. Then again, maybe not. Give him more time to settle in with his new school and environment. Shelve the idea for now.

Jack went to bed that night, pleased that his life was getting sorted and looking forward to his morning appointment with Winslow.

But when he arrived the next day, the receptionist barely looked in his direction, "Winslow isn't available."

"What's the earliest appointment, then?" Jack knew his voice was accusing as he struggled to hide his disappointment.

"A moment, please. I'll ask." Her eyes didn't quite meet his, and she twisted toward her phone. "Mr. Tuesday is here for his appointment with Mr. Winslow," she kept her back to Jack. There was a pause, the tension in her shoulders visible as she listened. "No, I can't do that," she whispered fiercely. "How about Mr. Kepler?" She listened again, then hung up and turned to Jack, a professional smile pasted on her lips. "We aren't sure when Mr. Winslow will be available, but if you'd like to take a seat, Mr. Kepler will see you."

He sighed and dropped into a chair in the reception area, Kepler or nothing, it seemed. Jack fidgeted for fifteen minutes outside Kepler's office. Finally, Kepler emerged from his office with a client, head bent and nodding respectfully. Kepler's manner was almost deferential as he used both hands to clasp and shake the other's hand. The client didn't appear to return the favour. A good head and shoulders taller than Kepler, he looked down at him, expression stony and his hand pulling away from the lawyer's after only a brief responsive shake, even wiping it against his suit jacket as if his palm was soiled. As he turned away toward the exit, cold grey eyes met Jack's, then sharpened, filing away his details. Jack's eyes didn't waver from the severe Slavic face. *Russian*, Jack decided, instinct flaring, *and he knows I'm a cop.* The man dismissed Jack, and he turned on his way. "Goodbye, Mr. Hudek," the receptionist called across her front counter, getting no reply, not even a nod. She made a face at his back as he swept past and out the door.

Bernie Kepler straightened as if he were now allowed, greeted Jack, and led the way to his office. "I'm sorry Howard isn't here today." He gestured to the chair. "Please have a seat."

Jack sized him up as he sat. Kepler was of medium height with a stocky build and dark hair cropped short. His blue suit, crisp white shirt, and thin silk blue tie—just a shade darker than his suit—gave him the air of expensive precision, if not exactly in vogue.

Shooting Jack an affable smile, Kepler opened a file, reading and shuffling the papers inside. Jack honed in on Ursula's letter. There didn't seem to be any forms or recent documents added to the file since Jack last saw it.

The lawyer frowned, then put his forefinger on the intercom. "Sheila. Can you just look on Winslow's desk, and also in his mail slot to see if there are any documents for," he looked at the file, "Bosch, Tuesday, et al."

"I checked this morning, Mr. Kepler," Jack heard her clear reply. "Nothing, I'm afraid. Unless something's arrived since. I'll check."

While they waited, Kepler straightened the papers, lining them up on his desk., "A son defecting from East Germany. Quite the feat for one so young." He carefully replaced the papers in the folder, then adjusted a paperweight on his desk.

"I'm glad he succeeded. It was an enormous risk and could have ended tragically." Jack kept his tone even, but the man's antsy behaviour wasn't lost on him. Kepler nodded, and they talked about Max's experience while Jack studied him. Kepler couldn't keep his hands still. One moment, it was the pens; next, the clock, a photo, a dictaphone—everything in constant motion. Straightening objects and replacing them in the exact spot. Uncomfortable, Jack thought. Why? Was it him? Because he was the police?

"Is Howard Winslow in court today, then?"

"What? Oh no. He's taking a personal day." Kepler's face sobered, and his eyes narrowed as if asking for a personal day was not kosher. "We're so busy," he mumbled, more to himself. But an anxiety flickered behind his eyes. Tiny beads of sweat glistened on his forehead. It wasn't even warm in the office.

Something wasn't right.

A soft knock at the door interrupted Jack's musing. Sheila stepped in, and Jack's eyes widened—it was the girl he'd thought was the receptionist the morning after Jassy died.

"There is nothing, Mr. Kepler," she reported.

Kepler's face turned red as he stared at her. Like she had lost the mail, thought Jack. She blinked and shot him a defensive stare. "I searched."

Kepler waved his hand at her as if she were a pesky fly and turned to Jack. Jack saw her hands clench in anger, but she quickly relaxed and lowered her gaze. "I'll tell the clerk to flag the documents as urgent," she said, quietly closing the door behind her.

Kepler turned back to the file, flipping through the notes with a frown. "Howard made a note here about a telephone call to Immigration requesting forms to complete your application. But beyond that, no further information. At least not that he noted down." Kepler laid both his hands on the desk, his eyes giving the message there was nothing more to be done.

Jack leaned forward. "So what happens now? Can we phone Mr. Winslow and ask him? He must be reachable."

Kepler contemplated Jack across the desk while his fingers tapped out a rhythm on the file folder. He took a deep breath, then pushed the file away just as the door to his office burst open, and a tall man with an officious bearing came in.

"Kepler," he said, then stopped short when he saw Jack.

Kepler stood. "Tim," he blurted and waved him inside. "Detective Tuesday and I are just finishing up. Our senior partner, Mr. Timothy Gordon," he introduced Jack. Gordon raised his eyebrows at Kepler.

"Winslow's client," Kepler added quickly, "a personal matter."

Jack exchanged greetings with Gordon and then shifted his focus back to Kepler. Why the need to justify Jack's presence? There was an open file on his desk. It should have been obvious that he was with a client. Kepler smiled at him. "I'm sorry, but we need the instructions from Immigration before we can proceed. I'll have Julie, Howard's secretary, notify you when it comes and set up another appointment. Perhaps Howard will be back by then."

Jack took the hint. "Please, as soon as it comes. I want to be finished with this."

"I agree," Kepler confirmed, while Timothy Gordon silently imitated the gesture by folding his hands.

As soon as Jack got back to headquarters, he consulted the phone directory for Howard's number. A woman's voice answered the ring. "Howard?" Was it Jack's imagination, or did she sound anxious?

He introduced himself as a client, only needing an update on a legality. "I had an appointment with him today, but I couldn't keep it," he lied. "Perhaps he can give me an answer over the phone?"

"I'm afraid not, Mr. . . . er . . . Howard is away at present."

"Can I get in touch with him elsewhere? The matter is rather urgent."

"No," her reply was blunt. "Look, I must hang up. I am waiting. . . . I'm expecting a call."

The line clicked, leaving Jack staring at the receiver with a frown. If Howard were taking a personal day, it wasn't at home. And his wife, or whoever answered the phone, sounded as if she didn't know where he was either.

His gut twisting with that familiar tension, Jack left his desk and sought out Wager.

"Give me this case," Jack demanded and threw himself into the chair across from Wager, making the sergeant's mustache twitch. "I had an appointment with Howard Winslow this morning. He wasn't there, and they gave me some crazy excuse that he was just taking a day off. But he had a lot on his calendar, which is why my appointment was early. I know Howard Winslow. He isn't the type to just take off with no word. I just phoned his house. Even his wife doesn't know where he is. Every sense I have is telling me something is wrong."

Wager gave Jack a long, unreadable look. The same expression he used when sizing up a suspect, silently weighing the evidence. "That's all you got?"

"This business with the hit and run. Jassy. And now Howard. I admit there isn't a lot of detail that stands out." Jack's confidence waned, listening to how it sounded when said aloud. He leaned forward, hoping to pique Wager's interest with body language alone. "It's all the small things that don't fit: her fear when she talked to me, the way she left the bus before her stop. Which she had never done before. The bus driver said she didn't do it with a purpose in mind. She just stood there at the door like she didn't know what to do next. And the car. Why didn't it stop?"

Wager sat back, biting his moustache. "We located the car," he said finally. "Don't look so hopeful. Stolen. Wiped clean and abandoned. Probably kids going for a joy ride and afraid to stop."

"No kids, Wager. Chen said witnesses saw one driver. Look. Do I have to beg? Clear it with Simpson, and let me work on this."

"Oh, here we go," Wager threw his pencil on the desk. "Or you will anyway?" Wager's tone was bland, but there was no mistake about the warning in his sharpened gaze. "We going to have a disagreement about this, detective?"

Jack relaxed. "No, sergeant. We are not. But if we don't go after this now, I have a hunch it'll come back and blindside us. And then, it won't be so easy to handle—take up even more resources. If that's what you're worried about."

The phone rang at Jack's desk. From his desk beside Jack's, Chen put up his hand to say he'd take it and went to answer.

Wager allowed himself a slight grin. "Alright, Jack. Give it all you got for one day, and then we will see where we are. For the love of Mike, just keep it clean, will you? No secrets. Reports every day so I can keep Simpson happy. I'll even give you Chen for backup. So make it snappy."

Jack exhaled, relief washing over him. He would have pursued it on his own, and Wager knew it. Easier to do it with the boss's blessing, though—kept things above board.

Chen interrupted. "The guy on the phone. Glen? Your landlord or caretaker? He wants you to call him back right away."

Jack's heart skipped a beat. Max. Was something wrong? He hurried to his desk and dialled, fingers tense on the receiver.

"There's a girl moving into your apartment. She said you're her uncle."

Lost for words, Jack's mouth went slack-jawed.

"I didn't know you had a niece," Glen reprimanded. "She never gave me a chance to grill her." Glen grilled all new tenants. Anything to do with the building he couldn't control put him out of sorts.

"I don't have a niece," Jack managed to protest, finding his voice.

"Anderson said she was."

Jack's heart dropped. A cold spot settled in his midsection. "Anderson?" Someone's idea of a joke?

"Remember that big guy who lived upstairs last spring? Anderson?

Looked like a biker? You want me to take care of it? I can't have this place become a kid-friendly building, you know," Glen's voice accused. "Bringing their friends and tramping up and down the stairs."

"I'll be right there." Jack cut the call and bolted for the stairs instead of waiting for the elevator. Was this something that Anderson cooked up? Or Luke? The reason why he was smirking at the courthouse?

Arriving home, he flew up the stairs two at a time. Outside his apartment, the aroma of cooking forced his stomach to growl despite the tension building in his gut. Jack shoved his key in the door and pushed it open, and the smell of something wonderful got stronger. There was luggage stacked beyond the door, a trunk, suitcases, and many boxes holding whatnot. Jack growled. Barely stifled anger threatened to erupt. It looked like ten people thought they were moving in.

The first faces he saw were Max and Tommy, all washed and polished, standing at the entrance to the kitchen, each leaning up against the doorjamb on either side. Both had fatuous grins on their doting faces, Tommy's hair plastered down with water, his overlong bangs glued behind one ear. Max had his chest stuck out to show off his pecs. Each boy held a cold drink of something that looked orange and bubbly. In front of them, where Jack couldn't see, he heard chopping and the banging of pans. Pharaoh, his loyal dog, sat between Max and Tommy, thoroughly entranced by whatever was happening in the kitchen. Not even a glance at Jack—his usual enthusiastic welcome nowhere to be found. Jack's eyes caught sight of the dining table—set for five. Jack's pulse quickened, and he frowned. Suddenly he had gained extra chairs?

A rustle of paper and Jack turned to see Anderson, Luke's bulky bodyguard and fixer, sitting on the couch, ankle settled lazily on his opposite knee. He scowled at something in a newspaper. "Who believes this crap?" he muttered and shook the paper again as if to get rid of a bug. He shifted his eyes to Jack and nodded a greeting. He still wore the same vest and tee, showing off his tattooed arms, with blond hair tied back in a ponytail.

Feeling like an outcast in his own house, Jack bristled.

"Oh, hi, Uncle Danny! I'm Olivia," came a high, muffled voice behind him. Anger seething to the boiling point, Jack turned slowly and saw the back of a dark head peering into the oven, the figure attached to it wrapped in a neat pair of bell-bottom jeans. At hearing 'Uncle Danny,' Max and Tommy turned to look at him, curious. "Who's Danny?" he heard Tommy whisper.

The form stood up from the oven; she was tall, with dark hair down past her shoulders. A flowered jersey, long sleeves rolled to the elbows, fitted tight to a slim body, and tucked into the low-cut jeans. She removed the quilted oven mitts and threw them aside. "Dinner will be ready in twenty minutes. I'm your niece. Carol Summers is my mom, and Luke is my dad."

Jack's spine stiffened at hearing the word Luke. Rage took his breath. Enough already. The invasion is over. Even if that dark hair had baby blue eyes to coax him. He opened his mouth to tell her so. When she turned toward him, smiling at him, her eyes weren't blue at all. Not both of them, anyway. One was blue. The other one was green. And she was drop-dead beautiful.

Jack sucked in his breath at the sight, rapidly hardened his heart, and ignored her. He bared his teeth at Anderson. "Get her out of here," he hissed, keeping his voice down so the boys couldn't hear. "She's not moving in. That's an N-O-T. Got it? Get her out. Right now."

Anderson's eyes glinted at him in amusement. "It's difficult to get Olivia out of things she doesn't want to get out of."

"There's always a first time. There is no room for her here. And you've no permission to butt in."

"Your brother owns this building," Anderson's tone was soft. "And the lease on your apartment."

Jack's stomach dropped. The information only increased Jack's ire.

No wonder Glen had no problem getting him the owner's suite.

"You really were spying on me in the courtroom?"

Anderson shrugged, unbothered. "Luke wanted to see what kind of parent you were."

"You kept tabs on Max and me?" Concentrating on Max had made him careless. Jack's ability to sense when he was being watched had disappeared. The realization only fueled his anger. Jack clenched his jaw, barely holding back from aggressively responding to Luke's insult.

Anderson flushed, confirming Jack's question, unable to hide his embarrassment.

"She's leaving." Jack kept his voice low and flat, leaving no doubt about his meaning. "I'm not sheltering Luke's spy for the mob. With my son."

Anderson hissed through his teeth and threw the newspaper to the couch beside him. "You want spies?" He jabbed a finger at the discarded newspaper. "How about chasing the source of lies spread in the newspapers instead of accusing an eighteen-year-old?"

"Not my priority." Jack waved the newspaper spies away. "Right now, the one in my home has my attention," he said, nearly spitting out the words.

"She's already enrolled at NAIT in the Culinary Arts program." Anderson's voice was steady, clearly playing the long game. "You'll get rent every month. One hundred, I'm told. Cooking's her thing, and she's got a generous allowance if you're worried about the grocery bill." Anderson looked around the sparsely furnished room. "By now, you'll have a good idea of the money it takes to raise a teenage boy. Don't tell me you couldn't use the extra."

It was the longest speech Jack had ever heard out of Anderson. Though he was following Luke's orders, it seemed Olivia's presence mattered to him on a personal level. For a moment, Jack could only stare at him, hardly listening to the meaning of his words. He opened his mouth to protest.

"Besides," Anderson forestalled his argument. "Olivia wants distance between her and her family. She's more like you than him." He pointed his finger at Jack, stressing the last words. "That's why she chose NAIT here and not in Winnipeg. She's using her mother's name and not Luke's. She'll take his money but wants nothing to do with her father and what he does."

"Good for her," Jack sneered. "Well, she can ignore him somewhere else. Not here. Not with us. She can take that mountain of luggage with her." He brightened. "Besides, there's no extra furniture."

"Already taken care of," Anderson countered, and with the audacity to smile. "All new in the empty bedroom."

Jack's blood boiled. Of course the rent had been lower than expected for a three-bedroom apartment. Instead of congratulating himself for being a good tenant, he should've been more suspicious. He opened and closed his fists, resisting the urge to throw a punch just for the action. Anderson's eyes narrowed, sensing the threat.

Jack took a deep breath to regain his composure. "You can take it right back out," he ordered softly, his resolve fixed.

"Ready!" Olivia called from the kitchen. "Start on the salad. Let's eat, everyone." The aroma of tomato sauce, pasta, and toasted garlic bread wafted into the living room. Pharo yodelled.

"Right after dinner," amended Jack, giving in for the moment. Anderson's lips twitched.

5

DESPITE the tempting aroma of the dish, he served himself a small portion. Max's gaze met Jack's from across the table, his eyes narrowing in confusion at Jack's set expression. After one mouthful, Jack had to admit the pasta was delicious. He took a small bite of garlic bread, which melted in a mixture of delight with the sauces. Chewing slowly to make it last until he could sneak another spoonful onto his plate, he stayed silent, concentrating on reading her without her being aware. Searching for something he could use as a weapon to get rid of her. She'd glanced once at him, then ignored him. Did he imagine a glint of anxiety in her eyes? He hoped so. It isn't a done deal, young lady, his own eyes told her.

"I heard how you ran away and came to Canada." Her complete attention to Max turned him beet red. She poked her fork at his arm. "That took guts. I can't imagine I would have done it."

Probably would have flapped her eyes and been escorted to the border, thought Jack, and shoved another forkful into his mouth.

Still flushed, Max shrugged. "I just saw an opening and took it. Not so hard. All I had to do was run fast."

"Especially when you're scared right out of your pants," Tommy sniggered, not to be left out.

"Of course," Olivia said. "I'd be scared too. Probably too scared to run." Max puffed out his chest, grinning. Tommy poked him in the side.

Olivia passed second helpings to Max and Tommy. Anderson, she mostly ignored. As if he were a servant, Jack thought. Amused, he glanced out of the corner of his eye and saw Anderson grinning at her, then he winked. Back to Olivia, he saw her happy flush and her expression, half pleading and bright with longing.

Jack eyed his plate, frowning.

"The food doesn't please you?" Olivia asked Jack.

"The best pasta I've had. You'll have to give me the sauce recipe," Jack's lips went stiff, and he couldn't bring himself to smile at her. She shot him a look of uncertainty, blinked, and then turned to Anderson again. Without lifting his head, Jack shifted in his chair and watched both of them.

She tried not to look at him but failed. Him, watching her talk, his soft expression telling her he noticed, then hardening into indifference. *Good God, she's in love with him.* Jack almost groaned aloud, and his already sour mood took a sharp nosedive. That clinched it. She had to go.

What if Olivia decided she wanted him and acted on it? He'd be in terrible danger. Months ago, Jack had discerned who Anderson really was when Luke decided Edmonton was the new city through which he'd launder his Gang's illegal money. Jack pushed the food around on his plate, appetite gone. Was Anderson mad? Undercover work already took a huge personal toll on mental agility without the added risk of a fling with the spoiled daughter of a crime boss. Jack glanced at Max and Tommy, grinning at each other, and felt his anger rising at this new threat his family could face. Anderson was staring at him, eyes speculating. Jack lifted his wine glass and took a generous sip, forcing calmness. Could his day get any worse?

After dinner, Anderson set off for Winnipeg. "Give her a chance," he said quietly to Jack. "Everybody deserves a chance."

Jack sighed, trapped for now. "Only on probation then. One slip-up, and she's out. No second chances,"

Anderson studied Jack's face and nodded. "You'll let her be? No prodding?"

"I am not in the business of abuse," Jack said shortly.

"Let it play out," Anderson said. "She needs this. The boss said her stay here was only allowed on the condition that you monitored her. She'll phone me if there's trouble. I'll come back to take care of it."

"Like a good fixer," Jack retorted, not hiding his bitterness.

Before Anderson left, Olivia hugged him, only reluctantly bringing her arms down. It wasn't an act, Jack decided. He heard Anderson's soft reply, soothing. "You'll be alright." She stayed close, her head nestling under his chin while he patted her. Then he gently pushed her away and left. She remained looking at the closed door for a long minute. It only confirmed Jack's worst fears. Lost in a renewed fit of depression, he watched Olivia directing Max and Tommy to cart off her trunk down the hall. Jack sat on the couch on the verge of weeping.

JACK woke early, with his mind ringing the alarm bells. He opened the blinds and peered into the sun low in the east but already lighting up a deep blue sky.

Swearing under his breath, Jack dragged himself to the shower, shaved, and then phoned Chen, telling him to meet at nine o'clock. After taking Pharo out for his morning walk, he left the apartment, grateful everyone remained sleeping so he didn't need to interact. The mass of luggage in the living room had disappeared. Where would it all fit in the third bedroom? Not in the small closet.

On the way down the stairs, regret gnawed at him. Why did he fold so quickly? She had wrinkled her pretty nose at him and beamed a glowing smile. She'd bewitched Max and Tommy with ease. Olivia's self-satisfied air wouldn't last long, Jack thought, gripping the steering wheel in frustration. "One wrong move and she'll get a surprise."

On 104th Street, the older buildings had been restored, transforming the area into a sought-after location with boutique businesses and offices close to the city's core. Jack parked in front of the door of the law firm of Gordon, Winslow, and Kepler. He checked his watch. At nine o'clock sharp, Chen was there waiting for him as instructed.

The morning sun blazed in a cloudless blue sky, promising heat. Jack slipped his tie knot down just far enough to still look put together.

"You talk to the receptionist," Jack told Chen. "Find out what you can about Jassy and if any of them saw anything odd the last week. You know what to ask. I'll see if Winslow is back."

He flashed his credentials at the receptionist. Her eyes widened in alarm until he introduced Chen, who nodded and flashed a reckless grin. Jack saw her worry instantly melt. She patted her hair and smiled.

"I need to see Mr. Winslow, please. Is he back?"

"No," the girl said, tearing her eyes away from Chen, "He's away on holiday."

Holidays? Jack inspected her smiling face. She wasn't lying—at least, she didn't think she was.

"Mr. Kepler, then?"

The girl hesitated but, after a moment, turned to her in-house phone. A few minutes later, Kepler's secretary appeared in the reception area.

"I only have about ten minutes to spare," Bernie Kepler told Jack after Sheila had shown him into the office. "So please make it brief."

"I need to know where Howard Winslow is," Jack said, his tone crisp. "He isn't at home. I've already asked his wife."

"She doesn't know where Howard is?" Kepler questioned, not answering Jack directly. "She told you that?"

Jack lowered his brows and stared at him. It was a strange remark. As if it was inconceivable that Howard's wife would say she didn't know where he was. Jack sighed. "Alright, Mr. Kepler. Enough dodging. You may as well tell me. Whatever it is, it involves Howard Winslow and has to come out sometime. Does it have anything to do with Jassy Harrison?"

"What? No." Kepler sat back in his chair and rubbed his temples as if it were a new connection he hadn't thought of. "Oh God, I hope not." He stopped rubbing his head and faced Jack full on. "No, no.

Of course not. But, before I say anything more, Mr. Gordon must also be present. We'll go to his office."

Once the three of them were settled in Gordon's spacious office—Jack on the couch, Kepler and Gordon in easy chairs—Kepler broke the silence. "We can't hide it any longer, Tim," Kepler said.

"Whatever you wish, Bernie," Gordon responded with an unsettling calm as though discussing dinner plans. "Perhaps the detective can suggest our next action."

Kepler took a deep breath, then exhaled through pursed lips. "We do not know where Howard is," he admitted. "Nobody else knows either. After this long, we have to assume he's missing."

Jack looked at each man, then took his notebook and pen from his pocket. He made a show of opening to a clean page and wrote Howard's name at the top. "A few details, please. How old is he?"

"Forty-two, I believe." Kepler looked at Gordon and got a nod in agreement.

"When did anyone last see him?"

"He left here about five thirty, the night before last. Said he was going to rehearsal and never arrived."

"Rehearsal?"

"He belongs to an amateur theatre group. It's down by the University somewhere. It's his hobby." Kepler's sardonic expression said he thought it was beyond their professional image. Timothy Gordon sat back and let Kepler do all the talking. "That's why he likes the courtroom. An actor in the real world, he always said."

"Who reported him missing?"

Kepler hesitated. "No report. Not official, anyway. His wife phoned yesterday morning and said he hadn't been home all night. She wondered if he'd had to pull an all-nighter over some case and forgot to phone her. I asked her not to report it."

"But now it's getting on for forty-eight hours?" Jack prodded.

Timothy Gordon interrupted. "No use letting the papers advertise our attorney is missing. What if they assumed he was on a bender or something, and our clients would think we . . . well, that he might be a drunkard or worse."

Jack thought back to his own dealings with Howard. "Why would that be the first assumption?" he asked.

Gordon shrugged. *He's probably used to people making wild assumptions,* Jack thought. "Well? Was Howard Winslow a drunkard? Or take off on wild sprees?"

"No! Of course not." Gordon snapped up, visibly piqued. Kepler's protest echoed the sentiment.

"Hospitals?"

"No. That's the first thing Catherine did. His wife," Kepler answered Jack's unspoken question.

"What about an angry client? Every case must not have a happy ending." Including his—the way things were shaping up. Jack forced his irritation down. They were clearly worried, but Jack's instinct told him they were holding back information. If so, it had to be connected to the office. Jassy's words, 'an anomaly,' came to mind. He narrowed his eyes at both of them.

"There are no cases that would involve him being molested or kidnapped. We always warn clients of the pros and cons of our litigation. I think we can dismiss that scenario."

"I need Winslow's address. His wife's name is Catherine?"

"Is this now an active police investigation?" Timothy Gordon asked and had the grace to look uncomfortable at Jack's expression. "I mean, is it possible to keep it from the press? At least for the time being. He may just show up again."

Jack's expression didn't change, though he noted the nerves creeping into Gordon's tone. Kepler handed him Winslow's address on a piece of paper, and Jack pocketed it. In return, Jack gave him his card with the usual instructions to phone him if anything changed.

As Jack walked out of the office and back toward the reception area where Chen waited, he couldn't shake the feeling that the men had just glossed over something important.

6

"*I'M* looking for Julie Holmes." Jack's tone diverted the receptionist's attention from her flirtation with Chen. She frowned at him, her expression unreceptive, and he softened his tone. "Howard Winslow's secretary? And I need somewhere private to speak. A few questions only."

She led him to a small interview room. "I'll find Mrs. Holmes," she stated, leaving him there to contemplate the four chairs and small round table, suitable only for a round of coffee or taking notes.

Half an hour later, Jack tucked his notebook away, none the wiser for the conversation. Winslow's secretary was older, experienced, and efficient. She answered each of Jack's questions with a directness that left little room for doubt. Her only sign of disturbance was her habit of crossing her arms over her body, hands cupping her elbows as if for protection. She gave brief answers; Winslow's cases were run-of-the-mill kind, with no particular problem with a client. Yes, he had an even temperament. Her mouth tightened, and Jack wondered if she was considering Kepler's treatment of his secretary, Sheila. Winslow got along with everyone in the office, a perfect gentleman with the staff and clients.

"Has any talk amongst the staff hinted at anything unusual?"

"Like what?" She frowned at him.

"Anything that might stand out and interrupt the normal routine of the Firm?"

"Certainly not." Her tone was definite, reproving him. But her eyes shifted.

"Yes?" Jack prodded.

"This office does not encourage gossip. And if there was anything unusual, I'm sure someone would have said something by now." She squinted a little as if realizing that Jack's question had been directed at that very thing.

"Not even about Jassy?"

Her eyes grew round. "Jassy has nothing to do with Mr. Winslow. Are you suggesting . . . ?"

Jack's face remained stern. "I don't suggest things, Mrs. Holmes. But the staff must have talked amongst themselves when she died."

"Well, yes, I suppose we all did." Her eyes deepened in sadness. "It is a different reason to talk about someone, though, isn't it?"

Jack got nothing else from her and gave up.

"Thank you." Jack handed her his card. "My phone number. If you think of anything, please phone me any time of the day or night. Any minor detail. It might be important, and you don't realize it."

As she turned to leave, he added, "By the way, do you know the name of his theatre group?"

"The Thespian Circle."

JACK met Chen in the reception area and recounted everything that had happened. "I'm hoping you learned something significant, even a stray remark. Now we know that he's missing."

Chen shook his head and shoved his hands into his pockets with a frown. "He's on holiday as far as they know. I slipped in a question about Jassy," he continued while they waited for the elevator. "She told me that Jassy seemed really frightened a couple of days before her death, but never said what frightened her. My instinct says it's her imagination after the fact. She couldn't give me any particular details about it, only an opinion that Jassy was wary of Kepler."

Chen rolled his eyes. "Not much to go on. I told her if she had anything concrete, let me know."

"Good work, Chen. That's more information than I got. I'd say all the support staff is wary of Kepler. He's rude to his own secretary, so I imagine he regarded them all the same way." Jack shook his head, recalling the lawyer's treatment of Sheila.

Outside, they stood in the still morning crisp air and pondered their next step. "Track down Winslow's theatre group," Jack told Chen. "It's called the Thespian Circle at the university somewhere. Find where it rehearses. There must be somebody on duty there or a phone number. And run down all members. Maybe Winslow had a private chat with one of them."

Chen nodded. "And you?"

"I'm going to go interview Winslow's wife. I'll meet you back at HQ later to compare notes."

The drive to Winslow's residence took him through the peaceful, tree-lined streets of St. Albert, a separate municipality in Edmonton's northwest that had resisted Edmonton's frequent attempts at incorporation. He parked on a quiet, crescent street shaded by Mountain Ash trees. The house itself—Craftsman-style, clapboard painted grey, darker grey window boxes under double-hung windows with fake shutters—looked warm and inviting.

Jack got out of the car, straightened his tie and put on his jacket, then started up the front walk as the front door opened. Two women came out on the porch step, hugged and separated. One stepped off the porch and started toward Jack. Nice legs, Jack thought, admiring the slim figure. The other woman stopped in front of her door and stared at him. She crossed her arms and took a firm stance, ready to dismiss a door-to-door salesman.

"Detective Tuesday?" the woman coming down the walk stopped. "It is you, isn't it?"

Jack hesitated, then recognized Edina Chambers. They'd met through her brother, Harry McNaughton, the reporter, murdered in the same case where Brodie had died. Edina had held the last clues, clearing Jack from the prosecution for Brodie's murder.

Jack smiled. "Yes, it's me again. Like a bad penny." He gazed past her at the woman he assumed was Winslow's wife, Catherine. Apparently, she changed her mind about waiting, for she turned and went back inside the house, firmly closing the door as a message.

"It's about Howard, isn't it?" Edina asked. Soft brown eyes inspected him, speculating.

"Do you know them well?" Jack parried.

"For years. Howard's my lawyer. But I knew Cathy first. We're old school friends and still volunteer together. I came to coax her out of the house. She's been sitting here, worrying herself sick." She sobered and shot Jack a worrying look. Her gaze lingered on him for a beat too long, a quick inhale signalling the unasked question before she smoothed it over with a tight nod. "I'm giving a birthday party a week Saturday," she announced instead, then grinned. "Mine." She rolled her eyes. "I'm turning forty." Pointing at her neat strawberry blond head, she added, "All downhill from here on. Bifocals, hearing aids, and counting grey hairs."

Laughing at her expression, Jack liked her all over again. "My next one, I'm afraid. I'll probably go bald from unsolved cases before I worry what colour it is."

Their eyes met as they shared another laugh. Looking at her, the world shifted for a brief second. Instinctively, Jack stretched out his hand, but whatever happened, it righted itself. She was already saying something.

". . . come to the party," Edina blurted out, then blushed. "I mean . . ."

"I'd like that," Jack agreed and meant it. "Still at the same address?"

Nodding, she handed him a small envelope. "Your official invitation." They stared at each other for a moment, Jack grinning foolishly. Edina nodded at him. "Until then."

He watched her walk away, and it was as if the earth moved with her. *Too bad she's married.*

Jack snapped out of it, embarrassed by the length of time he stared at her back end.

CATHERINE Winslow's dark hair hung just short of her shoulders—straight and heavy. It swayed with every sharp movement she made, framing her pale blue eyes—light yet striking against her dark lashes. The effect of dark against light made her seem exotic. Jack glanced around the living room, searching for photos, and found a few on a piano in the corner. Most of them featured the same teenage boy, including a high school graduation picture with both parents proudly flanking each side.

She noticed his interest, her expression softening just a bit. "Our son, Alan. He's at university. First year. He'll go into law after his B.A., of course." Or else, thought Jack, watching as she crossed her legs at the ankle, her back upright on the couch, Jack recognizing private schools and money. "My father has recently retired. A judge." Her pale eyes locked on his. "You may have even been in one of his courts."

Jack sat across from her and only nodded. She looked disappointed when he didn't ask for the judge's name.

He started in before she could tell him the name, as he knew she would. "May I ask a few questions about Howard, Mrs. Winslow?" *Forty-eight hours now. It's odd she isn't more anxious to know if he's found.* "Can you just walk me through the day he went missing?"

She wrinkled her nose. "He went to the office at the usual time. Told me he'd go straight from the office to rehearsal." She stared at Jack for a moment. "I suppose everyone should have some sort of hobby that takes one's mind off work. Howard's was an amateur theatre group. Mine is volunteering, social committees." She looked pleased with herself. Jack smiled at her, encouraging. Sometimes, he was glad he wasn't married. "You heard nothing at all from him that day?"

Her forehead creased a smidgeon. "No. But then, I didn't expect to. I never thought about it at all until one of the group phoned me to ask why Howard hadn't shown up to rehearsal. It didn't bother me. I just assumed a client had made him late."

"And what time was that phone call?"

"About seven o'clock."

"Can you give me the name of the person who phoned? A member of the theatre group?"

"I'm afraid I didn't write the name. The person told me, of course, but I didn't recognize it and assumed it was a member of the amateur actor's group. I have a phone number here if you wish to check."

"That would be welcome." Jack made a note.

Catherine clasped her fingers on her lap, her knuckles nearly white. "It wasn't until about ten o'clock that I had doubts. I wondered if he'd been in an accident, then told myself that if he'd had an accident and was hurt, I'd have been notified."

"Has anything happened like this before?" Jack asked. She only gazed at him, a puzzled look on her face. "I mean, has Howard ever stayed out all night before? Or disappeared without notice?"

She shot him a withering glance. "Taken a wild night off, you mean? Of course not. Howard does nothing on a whim. His mind doesn't work like that. They selected him for air intelligence when he was in the Air Force. If he'd been scatterbrained, they would have passed him over."

Jack sat up. "He had a career before law?"

She twisted the rings on her finger and inspected the enormous diamond there. "In the mid to late 40s, Air Intelligence posted him to Germany. He spent a few years there, I believe. Something to do with Russian propaganda. Tracing where it came from and stopping it from spreading." She gave a dismissive shrug, her eyes drifting to her nails. "Roughly along those lines. I didn't know him then," Mrs. Winslow finished as if Howard's life wasn't important before they met.

Jack let it go. "Why didn't you report him missing at once?"

"I phoned the office, and Timothy and Bernard insisted I give it another day. The publicity, you know. They said it wouldn't be good for the firm, and they assured me he would show up." She acknowledged Jack's unspoken rebuttal, adding, "I agreed but didn't approve. Now I wish I'd ignored them. It's been much too long." Her lips trembled, the weight of Howard's absence sinking in as if, for the first time, she truly grasped the gravity of the situation.

"Can you think of anything else which may help us? Old friends? Favourite eating places? Clubs?" Jack inquired, not hopeful.

"No, I'm sorry. It's all so maddening. When Bernard came this morning, I thought he was bringing bad news. That maybe . . ." Her chin quivered, and she pressed her lips together.

"Mr. Kepler came here?" Jack's interest sharpened. "Something brought him here personally?"

She waved her hand, brushing his visit away. "He just asked me if Howard had brought home a case file. He couldn't find it and needed it."

A case file? Didn't he trust Sheila to locate it? "And did he?" She stared at him as if forgetting what she said. "Have one? A file?" It was like pulling teeth.

"I was quite annoyed," she said while shaking her head. "Bernard should have known Howard wouldn't bring home any files. It was a silly question. And one of Bernard's files to boot. It would be highly unethical, something Howard would never do."

"Did he put a name to this case file?"

She stared at him as if he had brought a new twist into the situation. "No, and it was pointless to ask. He demanded to search Howard's study in case it was there. Of course, I had to agree. Otherwise, it would seem as if I were lying. Really." Catherine Winslow's eyes closed as if visualizing Kepler rifling through Howard's desk.

Kepler is missing a file? And he suspected Winslow of taking it? Was it connected? Jack made a note to interview Sheila and find out.

"He didn't even seem concerned that Howard was missing." Her tone was slightly surprised as if the thought had just occurred to her.

"I'm sorry, Mrs. Winslow. We will do our best and with as little press as possible. But making his disappearance public may be crucial.

Someone may have seen him. People just don't disappear without leaving any trace."

He thanked her and rose to leave. From her seat, she inspected him from foot to hair, then said, "When you arrived, you stopped to talk with Edina. Can I trust you weren't discussing Howard?"

Jack's face remained a mask of calm. Months of practice through torture and imprisonment as a POW in North Korea had made him adept at concealing his emotions. Since joining the police force, he allowed his expression to show interest only, finding that it encouraged a suspect to give more information. Glad now that he could keep his anger from openly showing, he said softly, "We never discuss our cases with the public, Mrs. Winslow," which encouraged her to blush, but she didn't turn her eyes away. Obviously, she wanted him to satisfy her own curiosity. Knowing he should walk away, the temptation to learn something for himself made him say, "I met her when her brother Harry died. She told me you had been school friends?"

Catherine Winslow relaxed then, sure that her personal cares were safe. "Yes, we have remained friends. Howard handled her divorce too." She started, her blue eyes widened as if realizing she had overstepped in revealing personal data.

Jack took his leave, silently cursing Gordon, Kepler, and Catherine Winslow. Someone like Howard Winslow didn't disappear without reason. If anyone in the public knew about it, new thoughts would replace memories after a day.

As he walked to the car, new thoughts replaced those of his interview with Catherine Winslow. Edina Chambers.

Divorced, huh?

7

BEFORE returning to headquarters to sort out his report and compare notes with Chen's, he decided to go back to the law office. Sliding into the hot car, Jack left the door open to catch any breeze and started the air conditioning.

His thoughts turned to Edina Chambers. She wasn't married after all and had invited him to a party. He glanced at the invitation: casual, outdoor barbecue after one o'clock. A rare invitation, and he welcomed it. It had been a long time since anything like this came along. No Luke, no Olivia, no chaos to face at home. Nothing waiting for him but his tangled feelings, which needed sorting.

When he arrived at the law office, Jack hunted out Kepler's secretary, Sheila Murray. "Time for short chat?" he asked her.

"I'll have to clear it with Mr. Kepler. . ."

Jack smirked and motioned with his uplifted palm to the phone as if saying 'please do.'

She grinned back with bright eyes, put her index finger on the intercom, and at Kepler's curt acknowledgement, told him Jack would like a word. Waiting for his reply, she gave Jack a wink and put her free hand over her mouth to hide her pleasure.

"I'll come out," Jack heard Kepler's reply. She grinned again, then sobered and bent her head to her notes.

"I need to borrow Sheila for a quick interview," Jack told him. Before Kepler could reply, Jack nodded. "Thank you," he said, assuming permission was a given.

Sheila didn't hesitate, immediately getting up to follow him.

"Make it quick then," Kepler growled. "Winslow's absence has set us back on our workload." He scowled at Sheila as if she wasn't holding up her end.

Jack waved his notebook at Kepler as acknowledgement and kept going. In the same interview room he'd used that morning, he pointed Sheila to a seat and sat on the other side of the small table. He started with the same questions he had given Julie, Winslow's secretary. The answers were the same, too, including no sign of anything unusual or disturbing about him, his clients, or the cases he handled.

"What about the missing file?" Jack asked finally.

Sheila lifted her head. "What file?" She leaned back and threw her arms out to the side. "Okay, now I'm going to be accused of losing a file? Well, it's news to me. I didn't even know one was missing."

"A witness told me that Mr. Kepler went to Winslow's house and asked his wife if he had taken home a file belonging to his client."

Sheila's eyes went round in disbelief. "Mr. Winslow took a case file? That's against our policy." She frowned, considering. "Not impossible, I guess. But Mr. Kepler's client? Which client?"

"I hoped you could tell me that."

"Sorry." Sheila snorted. "Mr. Kepler assumes I'm ignorant, so why am I surprised?" She tightened her lips and shot him a look full of bitterness. "Maybe he would have preferred Jassy as his secretary instead of me. She was the only one he had time for."

Jack busied himself with turning a page in his notebook. Emulating Wager's technique, he attempted indifference. "Yeah? How's that then?"

She screwed up her lips. "Maybe I'm being catty," she admitted. "But when he heard of her death, he almost fainted. I always thought it was a myth that people's faces could suddenly turn white, but his sure did. Mr. Gordon had to help him to a chair. He was shaking so much. We all saw it." She shrugged. "Maybe he was putting it on, but it was over the top if he was. It seemed to me he had more time for Jassy than he should." She winced and added, "I don't think anything was going on there. Don't get me wrong."

Kepler in a fainting spell? Jack tried to picture the lawyer as a shaken mess and couldn't come up with an image.

"No, me neither," he said, eyes on Sheila but not really seeing her. They sat in silence for a while, then Jack handed her the usual card and thanked her for her time. He wouldn't learn anything more. "My home phone number and at work. If you think of anything else."

Jack saw her back at her desk and went into the reception area. Julie Holmes was behind the reception desk, talking to the receptionist. When she saw Jack, she hurried around the other side toward him as though she had been waiting to see him. "Is there anything else we can do for you, Detective?" she asked, her tone bright. She came closer and, in an undertone, said, "I remember something."

"Well, as long as you're asking, I wonder if you can show me where your library room is located and fill me in on its function." Her expression shifted with a crease of her forehead, and he hurried on before she could object, "It isn't important, but only in the sense that I have a picture of how a law office operates. A complete picture, if you will."

Her eyes brightened as she caught on. "Of course, Detective. Come this way." She turned briskly, forcing him to keep pace as they walked down the hall.

"I remembered something unusual about Mr. Winslow," she breathed as they walked along. "He asked for a case file that I didn't recognize. I got the file for him and saw it was in Mr. Kepler's file storage area." She interrupted herself to explain. "We hired two more law students waiting to do their bar examinations, and we lack space. So we had to compromise and our law library shares space with active client files. We revised our admin procedures to ensure confidentiality."

Jack frowned, trying to picture the setup. "And how does that work?"

"We code the files. Each partner has his own scheme."

Not willing to discuss their administration and confidentiality rules in depth, Jack accepted Julie's description at face value. It did jog his memory about Jassy's revelation of seeing an anomaly. Could she access one of those codes? If she worked in the library, she could.

"And Jassy came into contact with these files?"

Julie hesitated at a door with glass insets. Jack saw rows of books and tables where two young men, who might be students or law clerks, bent their heads over papers.

"You don't really want to go in there, do you?" she asked.

"Is it usual for a lawyer to ask for a file belonging to another?"

"Not at all." She shook her head. "If two files are connected, it would be easier for the partner to just confer with whoever owns the other file."

"Got a name for me? The file Winslow wanted?"

She hesitated, looked over her shoulder, then back at him before she answered. "This is really putting me in a spot, but since Mr. Winslow is missing, and it might be relevant, I'll tell you." She narrowed her eyes at him. "But you didn't hear it from me."

"Hear what?" Jack replied, raising his eyebrows.

"Alois Hudek." Her lips puckered as if the name soured on her tongue. "An unpleasant client. He says he is Czechoslovakian in trade, exports, and imports. Mr. Kepler handles the legal aspect. Under the purchase and sale contracts, we hold the funds in our trust accounts until both purchasers and seller complete their obligations. Then we release the funds to Mr. Hudek." She paused.

"And do you find the transactions quite ordinary?" Jack pressed, sensing she was holding back.

"I wouldn't know. You'd have to ask Sheila that question. What puzzles me is I can't reason why Mr. Winslow needed the file in the first place." She looked at her watch. "That's my information. You're the one who wanted to know if I saw anything unusual."

Jack laughed. "I did, didn't I? Thank you, Julie. And the same again. If you think of anything else . . ."

Jack went back to headquarters in a better mood. He'd compare notes with Chen and sort his notes out into logical sequences and subjects for both of them to examine, tossing questions back and forth. Mentally recalling his notes, he decided he knew the source of the anomalies Jassy had found. For proof, he had only to know the contents of this *Mr. Hudek's* case file.

But if Kepler couldn't find it, where was it?

8

A small red sports car had swiped his parking spot in the apartment building's lot. Jack recognized the model, a Sunbeam Alpine, maybe 1968? One of the last manufactured, he guessed. He memorized the shiny, new plate's licence number. Annoyed, he parked in a visitor's spot, thinking the flashy car belonged to some over-privileged university kid arrogantly taking residence in whatever spot they pleased. He'd report it to Glen and let him track down the owner.

The man himself, toolkit strap slung over his shoulder, came down the stairs as Jack started up. Before Jack could open his mouth, he said, "I put together a chest of drawers she got from Ikea. Poor little thing, she was all thumbs." He saluted Jack with a cookie, waving it in the vague direction of upstairs. "Max was trying to help her but wasn't reading the directions right. Guess the English had him baffled." He took a big bite, mumbling through the crumbs, "Got paid in cookies."

Jack forgot the parking spot and tried not to grind his teeth again. They'd soon be stubs. "And here I thought you would tell me off for bringing another kid into the building." He couldn't help his sarcasm. "You never know how many more of her friends will show up, disturbing the peaceful atmosphere. Littering."

The idea didn't disturb Glen. "Not worried. She told me she had no friends—intends to concentrate on her studies, and has full respect for my rules within the building. I read her right the first time. You got a jewel there, Jack." His mouth shot cookie crumbs all over the steps, a big no-no of his number one rule. "Sometimes

I don't understand you. Must be a police thing." He passed Jack, mumbled something about ungrateful people who don't know how lucky they are, and then turned around.

"Oh yeah, by the way. I gave your parking spot to her. Sweet little ride. Brings class to the place," he added like Jack's Volvo 164E was a broken down hot-rod. "That spot is closer to the building and safer. She was carrying a load of groceries all the way across the parking lot." Glen's mouth formed a sympathetic 'O,' as if she were a cripple. "You now have parking spot number seventeen." Glen munched the last of the cookie and continued to his lair.

Jack continued up the stairs toward the poor little-all-thumbs thing, swearing softly and promising himself he'd find a way out of this mess. His judicious side reminded him he'd promised Anderson he'd wait. Wait? Wait for what? Jack's mouth turned down at the corners in disgust. "No way, José, not going to happen," he said aloud as he entered his apartment. Maybe if he packed up her luggage while she was out and parked it in the hallway, she'd get the message and decide it wasn't worth staying. His nose tasted something cooking. Not pasta this time.

Pharo bounded around his legs, chortling softly. Jack bent and ruffled his ears. "I missed you too." He bent down and ran both palms along the tan and white coat.

"I tried to feed him, but he wouldn't take it." Her voice sounded tentative, almost apologetic.

Jack straightened and faced Olivia, surprised at his feeling of remorse. His open disapproval, even hostility up against her resolve. Determination and fear showed in the set of her chin and stiff shoulders. Determination to stay and fear that if he threw her out, Luke would order her back to Winnipeg? How old was she? Eighteen now, he guessed. Jack looked into her strange almond-shaped eyes. Her one green-tinged eye was the same colour as his, inherited from his dead mother. It enhanced her looks and gave her a mystery. Her skin was smooth, a summer tan giving a golden sheen over her delicate cheekbones. She was beautiful and would become more so as she matured. Anderson must have a hard time resisting. If he did.

"I trained Pharo to not take food from anyone but me," he said. "It's to make sure nobody feeds him what isn't good for him."

"Like what?"

"Onions, chocolate, or grapes are the main ones. Or poisoned food . . ."

She looked startled for a moment. Huh, never thought of that, did you? The thought cheered him.

"I'm glad it's the training. I thought maybe he didn't approve of me, either." She looked down at Pharo, then shot him another tentative smile. "I know you suspect I am here at Dad's orders. But I'm not."

Jack waited. If she says, I promise, then I'll know she's lying.

"Tomorrow, I'm going to complete my registration at school. I've waited my whole life for this day. It's all I ever wanted to do. I'll do my share here, and more. Be Max's big sister? Help him adjust." At his raised eyebrows, she said, "He told me how he came to be here."

Red flags fluttering, Jack butted in. "You had a family chat? Traded histories? Including me?" Great, he thought.

"No, I didn't," she said, her voice flat. "I avoided any talk about our relationship. I don't care what went on between you and my dad, and I don't care what either of you do—does." Her head shot up. "Take it or leave it. Dad said I couldn't stay in Edmonton if you weren't here to watch me." Her lips twisted. "He doesn't trust anybody, including me. But that's his problem, isn't it? If he makes me go home, it will waste three years until I'm twenty-one. Then, I'll go. For good." White around her lips, she faced him. "So, it's your decision."

Pharo took a tentative step toward Jack from the living room beside the couch. Jack put his hand out, telling him to stay, knowing the dog had tested the emotion in the air. He obediently moved away, alert to Jack's signal for any action. Jack, however, never took his gaze off Olivia, studying her.

"We'll do it your way," he agreed and meant it. "But you're right, whatever it is between Luke and me is nobody's business. I'd extract your promise to keep it that way." Her shoulders slumped in relief, and she nodded. "And my name is not Danny. It's Jack Tuesday. I have no relatives, so if you call me Uncle, remember it's only a complementary title."

She gave a quick nod. "Right. Anything else?"

"You're the daughter of a childhood friend. Better keep his name Luke. We both grew up together in a Catholic orphanage called St. Joseph's." Her eyes formed round circles, but Jack continued, keeping his gaze steady. "Just in case anyone asks. Don't volunteer it—the place burnt down anyway."

A small, awkward giggle escaped her. "Well, Uncle Jack, it's nice to meet you." She held out her hand, and Jack responded before he thought. The hand was soft, but the handshake was hard. He found himself momentarily caught off guard, recognizing the steel beneath the surface. Even at eighteen, she was cool, determined, and aware of her strengths.

Despite trying to remain neutral, he couldn't control a nudge of approval.

"But we'll stay out of each other's way as much as possible."

"Won't that make it hard to keep an eye on me?" Her eyes shimmered with unshed tears.

Jack cocked his head at her, acknowledging the jibe. Against his promise, he still hoped. *If she believes I'm not watching, she'll forget to be careful. She's a teenager, after all. They all cut loose. When I catch her, Luke will make her leave.*

"If I hear one whiff of my police business and any connection to Luke, you're gone," he said aloud.

"You won't," she said. Jack waited, half expecting a breathless promise, which would show it meant nothing. But she only looked at him, curious, hesitant, as if she expected more.

"What?"

"You're not wondering what else Max talked about?"

What had he missed? "You said he told you how he got here." His attention sharpened on her.

She looked at her watch and held up her hand, palm out. "Time for a check." She opened the oven door, and Jack's mouth watered, already tasting the meat roasting inside. Olivia shut the door and turned down the oven temperature before turning back to him.

"You were in the Army." She raised her eyebrows for confirmation.

Puzzled as to the relevance, Jack nodded. "When I was with his mother in Germany,"

"Max said it shocked him when he found out you were a cop."

Jack's eyebrows rose. "So?"

Olivia looked at him like he was dense. "Police? East Germany? Stasi?"

Jack almost laughed until he saw she was serious. "Surely to God, he knows I'm not like the East German Stasi!" But in Winslow's office, Max's tone was accusing when he said he thought Jack was still in the Army. "Doesn't he?" he questioned, suddenly unsure.

"The East Germans tell lies and feed propaganda to their people non-stop. Everybody knows that. How else can they get everyone to believe communism is great?"

Jack stared at her, jaw slack. She was what? Eighteen?

"I read a lot, and I also went to school," she said, reading his doubting expression. Then she smiled, a pixie smile as if she'd just had a happy memory. "And Anderson mentions it a lot. To keep me from turning socialist, he said."

Anderson. Of course. He'd have inside intel. Jack inwardly smiled at her admission, then had a pang of warning that he couldn't transmit to Anderson. Conversations like that led to admissions about preferences and other things. She was no dummy. Had she guessed? Had suspicions? Regardless of her feelings about Luke's crime business, Jack was sure family loyalty would take over if anything threatened him. How many years has Anderson been undercover? Unknown, but was it too long?

But that was Anderson's problem. He knew the dangers. Turning his attention back to Olivia, he said, "Max is smarter than that. And his mother told him the truth about the Communist agenda."

Olivia shrugged. "Okay, but he can read too. Our papers and TV don't always show the police in a friendly light. I told him not to believe it when he hears them called pigs."

Shocked, Jack had no answer. Was he so blind that he didn't realize that Max might compare the propaganda he'd internalized and see some truth in it when our own papers run down the police? Who fed these stories to the papers in the first place? He'd just assumed it was students on a rebellion power trip.

Olivia turned back to the kitchen. "It's a hot kitchen tonight, but the roast is big enough that we'll have cold cuts the next few days. Tomorrow, I will be busy getting my classes and books straightened out." She turned around and faced Jack, saying pointedly, "Just so you'll know where I am."

"You only have to leave a note. In case someone wants to know. Or you get kidnapped by slavers. Otherwise . . ." Jack almost added a spiteful hint that only Anderson might care but didn't.

"Good to know," she grinned. "Tonight, we'll have it with gravy, mashed and Yorkshire. Grandad's favourite." She shot Jack a smirk as his eyebrows rose. "Granddad Sommer. For dessert, pineapple squares."

Jack kept his curiosity to himself rather than ask how her granddad felt about her move to Edmonton. Asking questions brought familiarity.

Telling himself he didn't want information about her family, he yanked off his tie and undid the top button of his shirt. The room was warm.

"You've got time for a shower before dinner. And Max is at Tommy's. They'll both be here soon."

Feeling like he'd just been told what to do as well as think, Jack curled his lip. *Almost like being married,* he thought, rebellious, then caught himself. His resentment simmered, fueled by the realization that he might have been in the dark about things for months, and now a teenager was schooling him.

As if on cue, the door opened, and both boys clumped in, noisy and full of energy. Four eyes checked the kitchen, making sure Olivia hadn't left town while they were out. Tommy had gained a fresh shirt, jersey in a loud pattern of checks or something. And a haircut. His usual see-through bangs and scraggly hair ends that looked mouse-chewed were now shaped to just below his ears. A bit early for the first day of school cut. Jack wanted to laugh.

"Ohh, nice haircut, Tommy," Jack heard as he headed to the shower. Under a finishing cool spray, he thought of Max's short hair. He'd said he was going to let it grow from his almost shaved head, but it never seemed to thicken out. He ran his hand over his own head, wondering about steroids again. The idea conjured up a vision of himself strangling the person who gave steroids to an unsuspecting boy, and once again, he vowed to have Max tested. Something he was sure Max would resist, as he resisted everything Jack did. But why? When Jack picked him up, the immigration officer said Max was excited and happy to know his father had been located. So, what happened? Getting no answers to his questions, Jack got out of the shower.

Maybe it was a holdover of Olivia's cheerful conversation at the table and cementing her spell over them, but Max's attitude was relaxed while they walked with Pharo to Kinsmen Park after dinner. Or was it his new knowledge that forced him to see Max differently? Either way, Jack pushed the worries out of his mind and decided to enjoy the rare, peaceful moments. "Let's play Pharo's game with a twist," Jack winked, tucking the Frisbee under his arm. Max grinned and ran to the other end of the field. He matched his stride with the speed of the Frisbee, as only an athlete could, and easily snatched it out of the air just as Pharo caught up. The dog leaped up, expecting Max to throw it to him, but Max threw it back to Jack with such speed and accuracy that Jack swore he heard the Frisbee sing. It stung the palm of his hand enough that Jack had to massage it. He looked at Max, standing casually, waiting for him to return the throw. The accuracy of Max's aim was unusual for a flexible Frisbee. Jack had only to put out his hand to catch it. Still amazed, it took a moment before Jack tucked it under his arm like a football and ran across the field. Chortling, Pharo anticipated the rules of the game and ran back to Max, waiting for Jack to throw it his way.

"Not so fast, smarty," Jack mumbled, running back the other way. Pharo ran after him. Jack threw it to Max. Laughing, Max started running, and Pharo chased. All over the field, with Max dodging and weaving, playing the dog's usual game. Jack sat on the sidelines, winded. Smiling, he watched them, thanking all the gods for sending Max to him. The right moment would come to discover the reasons behind his son's behaviour. His mind turned back to Winslow and the interviews. Did he learn anything? He could never be sure until he reviewed them in depth. Sometimes, clues remained unnoticed until paired with other clues.

Pharo knocked the Frisbee out of Max's hands and ran off with it. "Score one," Jack hooted from the sidelines and clapped.

On the walk home, Jack put his hand on Max's shoulder. For once, Max didn't shrug it off. "You know now that we have shown Pharo a new game, he'll expect it every time we go to the park. Maybe we should have thought it over."

"I have never seen a dog like Pharo. He's smart, but he's funny too. In Germany, Stasi have dogs. Nobody would want to play with them." Max's mouth turned down. Jack felt his shoulder muscles twitch. "But Pharo is funny and knows what play is."

"Pharo knows people," Jack said. "I trust him with my life." He seized the moment. "Where did you learn to throw a frisbee like that?"

Max inspected Jack's face before answering, looking for hidden criticisms. Finding none, he said, "I don't understand."

"Frisbees rarely go in a straight line like that but curve around. Your throws find their aim and never waver. Fast, too, and accurate. I just admire it, that's all." He looked at his hands, pretending the answer was not significant. "And you use different techniques, I noticed. Some underhand, some overhand, some low, or high. The way you throw, it's like an art."

Max blushed, clearly pleased. "Mutter and I started because it took us outside. She always looked for us to do things together and exercise. We practiced different throws to compete with each other. She was very good." Max shrugged. "It was a common game for many people."

"I remember that she always had something different for us to do together, so I guess I'm not surprised." *Just happy to enjoy ourselves,* Jack though, suddenly wistful. Each day was spent as if it would never last. *Did she always know they would end?* He laughed to lighten the serious turn of conversation. "Never mind, Max. Pharo loves a challenge. He'll figure it out and beat you one day."

"Smart, for sure. I will wait to see what new tactic he invents to fool us." The teen's smile widened with each word.

"I love summer," Jack said, a swell of gladness in his chest. "And this chance to spend time together."

"Yes." Max kept his eyes averted, patting Pharo.

I wish he'd call me father, or better still, Dad?

"This NAIT that Olivia is enrolling at—what is it?" Max asked after a long silence.

"Northern Alberta Institute of Technology. A technical school as opposed to a university. People who wish to learn trades as a profession. It's an excellent school."

"Yes. She will teach them new things, perhaps."

Jack burst into a spontaneous laugh, and Max joined in, then added, "But she is beautiful, and I like her." He grinned up at Jack. "Too bad I am a relative."

"In time, you will find someone you like better," Jack said, sobering.

"At home, they were going to send me to a technical institute. They told me I had to become their electrician." Max made a face and kicked a stone along the sidewalk.

"You couldn't choose your career?"

"No." Max turned up the corner of their walkway to the front door.

"You can be whatever you want in Canada," Jack said to his back but got no reply.

Later that night, after everyone was in bed, Jack stayed up, pouring over the notes Chen had given him and then more he'd made after their verbal conversation. He'd spent all afternoon tracking down the members of Thespian Circle. Jack read what he'd discovered. Winslow's not showing up was unusual. He was always reliable, the first one there. As their chief organizer, he kept morale high. They were doing a Noel Coward play and now had to find an understudy for the meantime. They were a serious theatre group, meeting twice a week and once on the weekend.

Chen had rolled his eyes at the telling. "I got the same story from each one. How dedicated they were. You'd think they were going to tour with a Toronto opening."

"What about Winslow?"

"All much the same. They last met two days before Jassy's death. Everybody agreed Winslow was his ordinary self."

"So nothing?" Suspicious, Jack stared at Chen leafing through his notes, not looking like someone who'd spent an entire afternoon in the heat and getting nothing for his efforts.

"I asked myself what questions you would ask and thought about routines. If they met or had any conversations other than the rehearsal days." Chen smiled.

"Well?

"One thing out of the ordinary. Might be something. Or nothing."

"I'm going to strangle you in a minute," Jack hissed.

"The day that Jassy died, Winslow phoned the props lady," Chen looked at his notes, "I've got her name here." Jack cleared his throat; Chen shut his notebook and continued, "She who is in charge of props and costumes. All that stuff, and has a key to the building. Winslow told her he'd left a briefcase the day before and needed it. Could he use her key to pick it up? She agreed." Chen took a breath and looked at his notes while Jack's eyes threw sparks of electricity at him.

"She never would have mentioned it, but she said Winslow must have meant the costume room because it was all in a mess. She took it personally. It's her domain. Then she got all soft and forgave him. Probably because she remembered Winslow was missing. Even shed a tear and said it must have been important, and he may have been frantic—thinking he'd lost it."

Jack mulled it over. "Great job, Chen."

Chen grinned, pleased. "Thanks. I'm learning from you." He sobered. "Do you think we should go back to the law offices tomorrow? I have that uncomfortable feeling that we're missing something connected to Winslow's disappearance."

"The same thing crossed my mind." Jack's lips curved into a subtle, affirming smile as he acknowledged the point. "Maybe this time, we should trade places. I'll talk to the receptionist while you have a go at the rest of them. In the morning, we'll set up what we concentrate on."

"Right," Chen chipped in with an animated point wag of his finger. "There is more to learn there; we just have to ask the right questions to find out what."

"Right," Jack said, "and one of them is Howard, who takes a day to suddenly miss his briefcase."

"You'd think he would miss it before he even got home or as soon as he got home."

"Winslow was in court the day that Jassy died, so maybe he didn't have a chance to go after it."

Chen cocked a dubious eyebrow at him.

"And even more important," Jack added. "Does the briefcase have the missing Hudek's file inside?"

Now, slouching back into the couch, Jack rubbed his eyes and packed away his notes. Hopefully, tomorrow, something would jump out at either him or Chen. He smiled at the thought of Chen. It was looking as though they would make a good team. Better than months ago, when he only had himself and ghosts to argue with. There seemed no right or wrong way to look at this mystery. His mind was a blank. Chen might think they've missed only the links, but his gut told me that small happenings like a missing file, followed by a disappearance, were only the beginning, and things were going to get worse.

9

A heavy weight settled on Jack's feet. He raised his head off the pillow to find Pharo curled up over them. A surge of concern prickled at him; Pharo only crept onto Jack's bed if he was sick. The dog opened his eyes, stretched a leg out, yawned, and went to sleep.

Jack carefully slid out from under the dog and barefoot padded into the kitchen for Pharo's bed. He put the round bed in the corner of the bedroom and snapped his fingers. Pharo stretched his neck, glowered at Jack, then reluctantly rose and traded the bed for his own. His paws stomped on the cushion, mashing it to his satisfaction, and he slumped into it, giving Jack a last reproachful look.

"Don't like all the people milling around in the kitchen?" Jack whispered, fondling Pharo's ears. A bushy tail did a tentative swish before Pharo uncurled his head and pushed his nose against Jack's leg.

Jack went back to bed, but sleep was gone. He stared at the ceiling, planning his day. He'd go back to the law office first thing. With his new information about Hudek, he could probe. And Timothy Gordon—what did Jack really know about him? Did the firm of Gordon, Winslow, and Kepler want for money? Jack drifted in and out of a restless doze until the alarm jolted him fully awake.

Chen was waiting for him, lounging against his own car, when Jack pulled into the headquarters parking lot. Jack parked beside him, exited the car, and eyed Chen. "Been waiting long?" he joked.

Chen fell into step beside Jack as they headed toward the building. "Just a word before you go inside," he said. "I heard the D.C. talking to Wager when I left last night, and he isn't happy about us making a case over Winslow."

"He gave us until the weekend," Jack stopped at Chen's expression. "Didn't he?"

"Wishful thinking. Simpson said one day's investigation had revealed nothing interesting." Chen grinned, "His words were, the water against the Winslow ship is less dense than what surrounds it." Chen snorted, then laughed out loud. "His way of saying it's a lame duck."

Inside, Wager confirmed the decision. "He's right in one respect, Jack. We can't spare the manpower. If you want to pursue it in your own time, be my guest." Wager chewed his moustache. "That being said, here's what we'll do. There are two cases on your desk; you and Chen can double up or go single on them. Odds are you'll get both done in half a day." He took a breath, and his eyes gave out a message. "Be careful and go by the book; otherwise . . ." he left the rest hanging. Jack took it as more of an order than an observation.

On the way out of the building again, Jack and Chen stopped at the main reception desk in front of Rollie Burton, who was staring down at a piece of paper.

"You got a minute, Rollie?"

Sergeant Rollie Burton was the Komodo dragon of the reception area. Close to retirement, he often bragged he'd been a cop since God was a little boy. Common gossip said that Rollie and the Chief of Police, Alec Mackie, were joined at the hip. Jack had taken advantage of the rumour before. Without Rollie's help, he would never have been able to prove he hadn't killed Brodie.

"What's the word, Rollie," Jack said in way of greeting. He introduced Chen, who sketched a salute. Rollie nodded to Chen, sized him up in two seconds, and turned back to Jack. "Word says you have seen the light and joined the rest of us. Or is it short-lived, and you're in deep again? When I retire, I'll swap that phony gold watch for hearing you've bowed to authority for good."

Chen put his hand over his mouth and turned away.

"Ha-ha," Jack showed his teeth. "You see before you the new me. Don't listen to claptrap. I'm here for your brain. Ever run across a lawyer called Timothy Gordon? Or Bernard Kepler? Howard Winslow?"

Rollie looked at Jack sideways. "The guy that's missing?"

Jack nodded, not surprised that Rollie knew. He had every case filed away in his head, present and past. "Yeah, I know Gordon, but only because he was a youngster when I was on the beat. He was a good defence lawyer, too. But fair and never tried to pull anything fancy. Right up front all the way." He kneaded his chin with his thumb. "I don't know the Kepler guy. Or Winslow either. Their names have never crossed my files, as far as I remember. So, guess they're clean." He eyed the constables working in his admin section, then at Jack. "If they are under Gordon's oversight, they should be alright. Is that it?"

Not sure whether he was disappointed or not, Jack nodded. Could Gordon have changed through the years? It was possible. "Thanks, Rollie. I owe you one."

"And be sure I'll collect," Rollie promised and ducked under the gate to go behind the counter.

As they drove out of the parking lot, Jack turned to Chen. "Let's get this done as fast as we can. Then, are you willing to work with me on this?" He watched Chen's shifting expressions—doubt, reluctance, excitement, and finally, resolution.

"Sure. Wager hinted at it." He looked at Jack for reassurance. "Or did I get the wrong impression?"

"Wager sometimes allows me to follow my gut instinct," Jack informed Chen, recalling a time when Wager had criticized him for acting independently, which was frowned upon by everyone. "As long as we don't abuse it and get Simpson on his back, he'll let us dig deeper." He hoped he was right and examined Chen out of the corner of his eye. Whatever fallout came from this, he'd keep Chen out of it.

"The missing file seems to be front and centre. I want to find out just how many people knew about this file. I'll try to talk with

Timothy Gordon. Has he really got his finger on what's going on in that office? I want to get a feel for his persona. And Jassy—she may have said more than they are letting on. After a death, sometimes people bestow sainthood on them." Sheila had also said Bernie Kepler's reaction to Jassy's death had been extreme. As a lawyer, Kepler surely couldn't have a morbid aversion to news of death?

"Do you want me to come along?" Chen's gaze held, a subtle lift of his brow asking for the green light.

Jack nodded. "Your job is to assess the clients. We can't get a direct line on the backgrounds of the three partners, so let's start by looking at who their clients are. It will give a picture of the overall tone of the firm. Especially see what you can find out about this guy, Hudek. He's supposed to be Czech. And a puzzle."

Chen moved his feet back and forth as if the task might involve unwanted leg work. "There's nothing in our records. I've already checked."

Jack adjusted his grip on the steering wheel as he devised a plan. "While I'm wandering around talking to people, you can wait. Pretend you're bored, and talk to any of the staff and play to their knowledge. They always see a lot more than they let on." He leered at Chen. "The receptionist already likes you, so put on the charm. You can start by flattering her job, working in a prestigious law firm. Must be exciting. You know the score. As long as it doesn't look like obvious probing." Jack frowned at the prospect. Touchy, that. Might prompt complaints to Simpson.

Chen pursed his mouth, upper lip curling. "I thought you wanted me to talk to the secretaries."

"If you get the chance, butt right in and do your best. Two views will give us a clearer picture."

"You gonna be long?" Chen sighed. "I won't have to fake being bored—I will be."

"Ever want to be a spy when you were a kid?"

Chen turned his face from the traffic to Jack. "Sure. Am I supposed to be learning from you?"

Jack laughed, thinking Chen's personality was a lot like Brodie's. As long as he didn't start spouting Robert Service, the poet Brodie idolized.

While Chen headed to the entrance, Jack took a moment to gaze up at the discreet sign on the second story announcing the law offices of Gordon, Winslow, and Kepler. A cloud scudded across the sun, bringing a sudden coolness, and his forearms began to tingle. Was it the loss of heat or a reminder that the questions he asked next had to be the right ones? He wouldn't get another chance, as Wager warned.

Catching up to Chen, he muttered, "Let's see who's moiling for gold in this place,"

Forehead creased, Chen shot Jack a puzzled look and followed.

A middle-aged lady who inspected him up and down to see if he was suitable to grace Gordon's office reluctantly showed Jack into the inner sanctum. Jack took the opportunity to slip in a question. "Has Howard Winslow been in touch?"

"No." The word dropped like a brick, implying he was out of line. "If that's the reason you want to see Mr. Gordon, I'm afraid he has no time." She took a pitbull stance in front of him.

Jack raised a hand in quick reassurance. "Personal matter only."

Inside, Gordon took off his glasses and laid them on the document he was reading. "Good morning, uh . . . Detective Tuesday." He gestured to a chair. "I have some information for you regarding your son. The documents look fine and should prove no problem." The lawyer let his hands clasp together over the papers and smiled. Like he'd done a thousand times, thought Jack. He noticed the sharp cut of the grey suit that draped Gordon's shoulders in a way which proclaimed it a bespoke measurement. A handkerchief just peeked over the jacket pocket, matching the blue silk tie. Yet, beneath the polished exterior, Jack could see it—the tired sag under Gordon's eyes, deep shadows hinting at sleepless nights.

Jack nodded, masking his scrutiny. "I appreciate it. When can I expect the final papers to come?"

"There is a requirement for a medical certificate stating the boy is in good health," Gordon said and shrugged. "Only a legal refinement, I suppose. But you will have to comply and pay for the doctor's visit." He gave an apologetic smile. "Until Max is a Canadian citizen, he won't be registered for health care."

Jack leaned forward, concerned. "Didn't the RCMP cover that when they processed him?"

Gordon put his glasses back on and shuffled through the papers. "Doesn't seem so." He eyed Jack over his glasses. "Is there a problem?"

"Not for the medical charge." In truth, Jack hadn't thought of registering him for health care. Another parent slip up. "It's just . . . Max has an aversion to doctors. He might put up a fight."

Gordon said nothing. He just examined Jack, his eyes suddenly probing, aware. Jack saw another Gordon—one where experience had taught him to observe and miss nothing. Jack suddenly felt he was on the witness stand in a courtroom.

"The report says Max defected from a swimming competition in Seattle and made it to the U.S./Canada border. That takes courage and planning." Gordon looked from the report to Jack. "Has he talked about how he managed it?"

"His mother did the planning years before," Jack replied indirectly. He pointed at Gordon's desktop. "All examined by the authorities and confirmed."

Gordon put his palm out. "I'm not questioning it, Detective Tuesday." He gave Jack a reassuring smile designed to put him at ease. "I have seen reports that too many East German athletes are breaking records at a suspicious rate. Some experts suspect drug use. Your expression says you've seen them too."

"Unconfirmed reports. The Germans spend a huge amount on their athletes, so it's bound to show excellent results and be resented by other countries."

"I'm sure." Gordon took off his glasses and gave Jack a piercing stare. "Get the doctor's certificate, detective. It probably will work out just fine."

Jack gave in. "In the next few days, you'll have it." Gordon looked at his watch, then Jack, hinting the interview was over. Jack didn't move.

"Would you mind answering some questions about Mr. Winslow?"

With a crease between his eyes, Gordon glanced at his watch again.

"Brief questions," Jack hurried on, "As long as I am here. I'm sure you are busy taking up the slack that his disappearance caused. It's about one of your clients. I would ask Mr. Kepler, but I believe he is away at court." Jack crossed his fingers, hoping it was true.

"I'm sure you know I will not discuss any of our clients," Gordon's tone was severe. His word final.

Jack scratched the back of his neck, trying for clumsiness. "It won't be anything that isn't already in public knowledge. I merely want to know where I might contact him. His name is Mr. Hudek?"

The mention of the name hit a nerve—Gordon's eyes flickered, widening for just a heartbeat before he cast them downward, his expression quickly hidden behind his lowered lids. Jack had to admire him, the man whose long experience in law had not deserted him when he needed it.

"I'm aware he is our client, of course, but I only know the man by sight. His business is export and import, I heard." Gordon shrugged off his short reply. "One of our many smaller accounts, I think. You'd have to ask Mr. Kepler for his business address or even the name of the company. Though, I imagine a quick look in the telephone directory could help, no?" Gordon lifted his eyes, puzzled. The unsaid message inferred a policeman should have no trouble finding such basic information.

"Has Mr. Hudek and his business been operating in Canada for some time?"

Gordon's eyebrows furrowed. "May I ask what the interest is? Nothing to do with our firm, I trust."

Jack shrugged. "Oh no, another matter altogether," he said, not sure himself if it was important. "I wondered about the lot of immigrants who left Czechoslovakia in 1968 during their Prague Spring. If he were one of them, his import business seemed to prosper rather quickly. Remarkable how keen their business sense is."

"Are you saying that's a bad thing?" Gordon's voice carried the hints of genuine confusion, but Jack noticed his eyes focused on Jack's manner.

"No, the opposite," Jack hurried on, aware that Gordon was an accomplished barrister who read people like books. "As you know, trade with Russian satellite countries—not exactly known for fast action—normally included a lot of back-and-forth to iron out procedures." He leaned forward as if in confidence. "We have had some inquiries regarding customs. It's not our bailiwick, but people sometimes think policing covers all kinds of intelligence. It sparked my curiosity." Jack smiled apologetically and lifted his shoulders, accenting the vagaries of being a cop.

"Yes. Unfortunately, I don't have that knowledge either." His answer was vague, and he looked as though the idea intrigued him. He barely acknowledged Jack's goodbye and his promise to deliver Max's medical report.

On the way past her desk, Jack read the nameplate labelling the pitbull as Helen Roberts. She didn't look at him, probably rating him as one of Gordon's minor clients.

Jack left, satisfied that Gordon knew much more about Hudek than he admitted. Rightly refusing to reveal any information about his client was logical, but that small moment of surprise at the mention of Hudek's name said everything. His attempt to downplay Hudek's significance was equally revealing. Kepler had treated Hudek as if he were royalty, and the staff thought he was important. If indeed he was, his fees collected by the firm couldn't be minor, as Gordon claimed. Jack went to find Kepler's secretary, Sheila, again. He met her at the door of her office.

My coffee break," she explained. "Your partner is a hit with the girls down there. Wasting time. They'd better watch someone doesn't see them." She pointed her finger at the ceiling. Jack assumed toward the pitbull residing there. "Mr. Kepler is away. In court for one of Mr. Winslow's cases. He's trying to get a stay. Judges hate it when the named lawyer doesn't show up." She grinned. "Makes them crabby. Kepler has to convince the judge he can cope."

"Any news about Mr. Winslow?"

"Nothing." She pursed her lips. "I'm getting worried. I hope he isn't in trouble or lying in an alley somewhere. His poor wife. Imagine not knowing where your husband is."

Jack nodded and made a sympathetic noise while considering Catherine Winslow's imagination. Sheila sat behind her desk. She opened a drawer and took two pieces of paper out. She placed a carbon between the sheets and inserted them into her typewriter. Peering sideways at them, she decided they were crooked, reinserted them, and muttered, "We are supposed to get those new typewriters soon, word processing things or something. I wish they'd hurry up."

"Jassy," Jack said.

Sheila looked at him over the typewriter. "What about her?"

"She looked after the library and the case files, bringing them back and forth. Right?"

She gave a slight, uncertain nod, her eyes narrowing.

"Just getting it straight," Jack made himself busy playing with the bobbles on her desk. "Did you talk to her much?"

"All the time. Coffee break, or during work, of course." She looked puzzled, then picked up her headphones and plugged them into the Dictaphone. About to put them on her head, she glanced at Jack, still waiting, a question in her eyes.

He came right out and asked. "Did Jassy ever tell you she noticed anything odd about the files? Odd, as in something wrong? Even illegal?"

Sheila's grip around the headphones tightened. "Jassy had a vivid imagination."

"Jassy had an excellent education. She had a designation in business administration and finance." Jack leaned over Sheila's desk and whispered. "If she noticed something amiss in the files and mentioned it, I don't think it would be imagination."

Sheila said nothing. She just stared, first at him, then at her typewriter.

"One of your files is missing, Sheila. The Hudek file. I learned that Mr. Winslow asked to see it. Have they found it?"

"How should I know?" At his knowing look, she added, "I haven't looked." She glared at Jack. "Probably not."

"Is Mr. Hudek an important client? Brings in substantial fees?"

Sheila's eyes narrowed. "That's our business. We don't talk about our clients."

"I know that," Jack said, his voice crisp. "But he's one of your biggest, I'll wager."

Sheila said nothing but didn't deny it either, just smiled at him knowingly. Then her eyes widened. "Do you think the file is connected to Mr. Winslow's disappearance?"

"And Jassy's death?" Jack's tone was brutal.

Sheila stared at him in horror. "No! Now, you're getting into fantasy land, imagining things. What are you implying?"

"Was there anything going on between Jassy and Mr. Kepler?"

"Whaaaat?" Sheila drawled, eyes rounded in disbelief. A giggle bubbled up. "Are you crazy? Jassy and him?" Her laughter took on a hysterical note. "If you saw Mr. Kepler's wife, Miss Lottie, you'd never in the world think he'd stray. He worships her and wouldn't hesitate to leap off a tall building if she asked." She gave him a look that said she wondered about his sanity. "Oh, that's too hilarious. Wait until I tell the others." She looked at him like he was a comedian. Heat rushed into Jack's face, and she giggled again.

"Good to know," he said aimlessly, then forced a grin on her. "Shock always brings out the truth."

"Sure," she said, putting her headphones on before turning to her typewriter.

A final snort followed him out the door as he went to find Chen.

10

CHEN met him in the hall. "Just coming to get you. As ordered, I phoned in a check with Sarge. He wants us back at headquarters, pronto."

They hustled out to the car, and as Chen slid behind the wheel, he exhaled heavily. "God, what a bunch of gossips. I'm exhausted just after an hour. Imagine listening to it all day."

"Don't look at me for a medal." Jack gave him a sideways glare. "What did you get?"

Chen pulled out to the main road, flicking his eyes between the traffic and Jack. "Hudek is a big wheel. Lots of consultations, lots of business transactions. Money in and money out. Staff are expected to bow and scrape when he appears, but nobody likes him much. He's demanding and acts like he's King Tut, as they call him. But they admit his billable hours add up to plenty. That's about it for him."

"So we have a picture of someone on the move with business expanding like gangbusters. All in four years at most, maybe less, depending on when he arrived. And yet, Timothy Gordon insists that he is a minor client." Jack puckered his lips. "Why, I wonder?"

Chen shrugged. "Maybe he's afraid the competition will steal him as a client if they knew."

"No. There are rules in their world against poaching clients." Jack put it aside. "What else?"

"Jassy was well-liked and good at her job. But the last week, she was disturbed, upset. Winslow's girl, what's her name? Julie admitted that Jassy had talked to her about Hudek. Just ordinary remarks, then suddenly asked Julie if she found him creepy and suspicious."

"And did she?" Jack straightened, all ears now. "Find him creepy?"

Chen raised his eyebrows. "Julie thought Hudek was off, all right, but she admitted lying to Jassy. Out of loyalty to the firm, she scolded Jassy for insinuating Kepler's clients might not be upstanding. But then Jassy dropped a bomb—said she thought Hudek was pulling one over on Kelper. And worse, that the transactions in his file looked . . . shady. Maybe even illegal."

"She said that? Illegal?"

"Julie shut her up right then. Told Jassy that the partners don't allow illegal activities, and they would know the difference better than Jassy would." Chen smiled. "Julie was still angry when she told me. She ripped into Jassy and said the job didn't include looking into case files."

Jack scowled, the pieces not quite fitting. The Jassy in his mind wasn't a snoop. "And how did Jassy defend herself?"

"Jassy got a little hot herself and told Julie she had dropped an armload of files and had to sort the documents into their correct folders. So, of course, she had to read a bit to know which file." Chen screwed his lips together as if he doubted her reason. "Seems like a convenient excuse."

Jack considered the idea, then dismissed it. "Jassy was used to handling confidential files," he told Chen. "She was a secretary in a shrink's office and wouldn't deliberately read a file. And I'd argue that a shrink's case files would hold more secrets than you'd find in a law file." Taken all together, it didn't add up, he thought, recalling Jassy's anxieties at the courthouse. "She always came across to me as practical and competent, not paranoid with a vivid imagination. When we talked, she was petrified. But who was it, and how did that person find out what she saw?"

"The way they yak at each other in that office," Chen sniggered. "They remind me of my grandmother's tea parties. So, who knows? My bet is someone deliberately squealed." At the corner of Jasper and

99th, Chen stopped in the left turn lane for a red light. Tapping his fingers impatiently on the steering wheel, he said, "I asked Julie if she had told Winslow about her conversation with Jassy. She didn't deny it nor admit it, but I think she must have if he read the file."

"Kepler would have known," Jack said. "Jassy also approached Sheila, Kepler's secretary, who decided that Jassy imagined it. It wouldn't stay a secret long. All it takes is one person to pass it on, and then anyone could have overheard."

Both were silent as Chen turned the corner and continued down the block to the parking lot. "I wonder if one of them was Hudek," Jack mused as they got out of the car. On the way to the building, he said, "Nice work today. You might've been drowning in gossip, but you came out with plenty of info we didn't have before."

Chen's grin widened as he opened the building door and waved Jack inside. "Can I expect you'll treat me to lunch tomorrow?"

"Don't hold your breath," Jack went past him.

"A coffee will do," Chen amended from behind him.

Wager looked up from his desk, a scowl on his face. "About time you two showed up. Did you forget where you worked?" He pointed his pen at Jack. "Simpson wants you. He isn't pleased. What have you done now?" He stood up and pointed to Chen and then Chen's desk. The order was explicit. Chen obeyed, rummaged at his desk for paper and pen, ducked his head, and began writing.

"I swear, Jack, if you think you're dragging Chen into your antics and shining a negative light on our unit, you'd better think again. Consider this your notice. Now get down to Simpson's office." He flicked his hand toward the door in dismissal.

Simpson roared at Jack, his florid cheeks turning redder. "I got a complaint from Timothy Gordon, who informed me it was highly improper to ask questions of a lawyer about one of his clients. Have you heard of client privilege, Detective Constable Tuesday? Or is that a foreign concept to you?"

"No, Sir," Jack said, snapping his head upright, genuinely

surprised. "I went to Gordon for personal reasons—he's handling my son's permanent residency paperwork. Just a legal matter, sir. Nothing more."

Simpson's sharp blue eyes bore into him, unwavering. Jack thought he saw a twitch in the corner of his mouth. "And I suppose a question concerning Mr. Winslow's disappearance just conveniently slipped in during conversation?"

Jack's insides relaxed at titch. The D.C. seemed familiar with asking impertinent questions and may have used it himself in the past.

"No, Sir. I confess I asked him if he could share the address of one of his clients. But I didn't ask about their legal relationship. The client's name was Hudek, and I am sure that his association with Gordon and partners has something to do with Winslow's disappearance. You see—"

"No, Detective Constable. Stop right there." Simpson stood up, emphasizing his order. "As you are aware, there is nothing illegal about Winslow's disappearance, and you are to stop your questions immediately. Wasting time and manpower while other cases need addressing is not what the serious crimes unit is about. Do you understand?"

"Yes, sir." About to make a smart turn, he paused. "If I find anything that changes the case, might I . . ."

Simpson glared at him. "You know the drill, Detective Tuesday. It would have to be unshakeable. Concrete. And through regular channels, not vigilante style. Get your act together and practice teamwork, Detective. I don't like cluttered personnel files."

Wager's eyebrow waited, raised in question when Jack returned.

"I'm supposed to produce evidence, but only by way of a Ouija board."

Wager pinched the bridge of his nose, his fingers massaging his forehead like he was fighting off a headache. His scowl deepened, but he didn't speak immediately; he just stared at Jack. Finally, he threw his hands up in the air in surrender, muttering, "Why do I even bother?"

"Chen and I had some success today," Jack hinted, hoping Wager's curiosity would overcome his reluctance.

"Okay, what have you got?" Wager waved Jack to the chair across his desk and listened. His expression became all business, intact, fixed, and unreadable, but Jack knew his mind was recording every word and nuance.

When Jack was finished, Wager leaned back and crossed his fingers over his stomach. "Well, in my opinion, the D.C. is right. There isn't even a suggestion of anything illegal going on. It may only be business secrets being shared and short-cutting other competitors. Cutting your competitors' throats isn't against the law. But . . ."

"Why would Jassy be afraid of that?" Jack interrupted. "And why would Winslow be interested in Kepler's client? Unless . . ."

"Unless it's money," Wager forestalled him. "From what you said, the law firm's sole purpose with Hudek is acting as a conduit for loads of money transferred in and out. If there's an illegal game here, it's undeclared cash, maybe even tax evasion." He paused, bottom teeth gnawing at the edge of his moustache. "The real question is, how's the money being moved? And from where?" Wager's posture stiffened. He rubbed a hand across the back of his neck. "Jack, we're treading on thin ice here. If we're talking international money transfers, we're way out of our jurisdiction."

"Or," Jack added, getting excited at the idea. "What if it's not just about the transfers? What if the money's being funnelled into something else?"

Wager's eyes narrowed, then took on a resigned expression. "Back to money laundering again? That's a stretch, even for you."

"Look, Wager. This guy is from Czechoslovakia. After the country's attempt at freedom, the USSR has clamped down tighter than before." Another thought lit up his face. "Maybe this guy isn't legit, and that could be what Jassy found out. We don't know a thing about him, and we can't find out—we don't have the resources." Jack shot a pleading look at Wager, who folded his arms.

Jack winced under his inspection. The sergeant had a way of seeing a person's thoughts, which made him a first-rate interviewer. After a long deliberation, he nodded. "Okay. Suppose I might have a contact who can help with that. But," Wager stared hard at him, warning. "Only just supposing. Nothing more. I'll see if I can get information about this guy. Satisfied?"

Jack nodded and grinned. "Yes. Thank you."

"Stay out of trouble until we get some feedback. Dammit, Jack, why do you always get involved with Commies?" Wager's mouth turned down.

"Because, Paul, we're in a cold war. Our government is so soft on Moscow, China, and Cuba that we're crawling with foreign agents . . ." Jack trailed off, leaving the rest unsaid.

Wager's eyes stayed locked on Jack, his fingers idly fingering his moustache. The silence stretched, thick and heavy, except for the annoying click of Chen's ballpoint pen as he thumbed the tip while checking his report. Aware of Wager's tendency to let silence stretch to the breaking point, Jack kept his mouth shut.

"Tomorrow's Friday, and Labor Day weekend is coming up," Wager said. "A chance for you to get quality time with your son. For the sake of God and my ulcer, hold off prying and keep out of trouble. Take the weekend off, but you're on call." Wager turned back to his desk, but Jack saw him take an exasperated gulp of air.

Before heading home after his shift, he phoned Dr. Griffin and made an appointment for Max, explaining exactly what he required to the nurse. With another task ticked off his list, Jack started mapping out the weekend with Max—some history lessons at Fort Saskatchewan, and on Sunday, maybe taking the airbus to Calgary and visiting Heritage Park.

But his plans unravelled the moment he stepped into the apartment. Olivia and Max were setting the table. Jack noted there were three places—Tommy must eat at home for a change.

Max spotted him first and rushed over, beating Pharo to the door. "Mr. Sullivan is taking Tommy fishing this weekend. I can go too if you say it's alright. We leave early on Saturday. We will sleep in a tent and camp outside."

Giving himself time to think, Jack bent to greet Pharo. The excitement in Max's face sent a jolt of disappointment through him.

"Where is this place he is going to camp and fish?" he asked.

"It's called Pigeon Lake." Max laughed. "A funny name for a lake."

Jack grinned back at him and decided not to voice his own plans. "Yes, I know it." Maybe a couple of hours' drive southeast. "Of course you can go. If that's what you want," he added, half wistful.

"Yes, thank you. I will tell Tommy right now." He rushed to the phone.

"You're also going to be rid of me for most of the weekend," Olivia said, her voice low but carrying a note of excitement. At Jack's stare and unspoken question, she altered her statement. "Well, not the nights. Only the days. Monday is the first full day at school, and this weekend is orientation. They urged students to attend to acquaint themselves with the campus and the clubs they can join. All that stuff."

So, he would have the weekend to himself. Not that Olivia's absence would bother him, of course. It would be like the old days. "Just you and me, pal," he looked down at Pharo, whose bushy tail gave a tentative wave as if he wasn't sure whether Jack was pleased.

Max hung up the phone, practically bouncing, "I will go see if I have the things to stay in a camp, and we can buy more tomorrow if I need something."

"Hold it!" Jack held up his hand. "I made an appointment for you to see Dr. Griffin on Tuesday after school. Immigration needs a medical report before they complete the papers." Max stared at him, not acknowledging he heard. "It's okay, Max. It won't take long. He'll just listen to your heart and make sure you look healthy."

Olivia laughed, and Max looked at her. "Piece of cake, Max. You'll be in and out in five minutes."

Max shrugged. "Okay." He pointed to his bedroom, a question in his eyes.

"Go on. Check it out," Jack said, grinning. Face alight again, Max did.

Retreating to his own room, Jack changed into more comfortable clothes while his mind wandered. He leafed through the telephone directory and copied a number to the pad. Checking around to see if he was alone, he dialled a number.

"Edina? It's Jack Tuesday here." He listened, then added, "No, I definitely have accepted next Saturday, but are you free this Saturday?" He hurried on, not waiting for a reply. "What I had in mind was a pre-birthday gift. A dinner date. A chance for uninterrupted conversation before you have to mingle with crowds of people. You will? Great. I'll make the reservations. I'll pick you up Saturday at seven." As he hung up, a rare twinge of excitement stirred in his chest, a small grin spreading across his face. He turned—then froze.

Three pairs of eyes lined up, staring at him.

Olivia's were laughing, like his invitation was the clumsy, insecure schoolboy kind. Jack stared back at her, not hiding his scorn, daring her to say what she was thinking. Max's eyes were round, and his eyebrows raised up to the middle of his forehead. What, Jack thought, like maybe I'm too old to date? Pharo came over and stood beside him. He looked at the two across from him, showing them his loyalty. Jack grinned and patted him.

"Dinner's served," Olivia said, turning away from the table. She giggled softly. "He's normal after all," he thought he heard her say.

Jack flushed, tightened his hands into fists and visualized pitching all her clothes down the garbage chute. "A few bits and pieces at a time would work," he whispered to Pharo, wondering why he never thought of it before.

Later that evening, Jack phoned Roark Sullivan to confirm Max's plans for the weekend. He had met Roark a couple of times, briefly, and had a solid impression of the man—a big Irishman with muscled arms, clear blue eyes, and an open, honest face. Roark struck Jack as a hard worker, someone who put his job and family above all else. Still, Jack wondered where Tommy's mother was, though he never asked. The way Tommy had doted on Mira Zamborski when she lived on the top floor made sense now. A mother or grandmother substitute. Jack remembered how diligently the boy had run errands for her.

"Are you sure you don't mind?" he asked Roark. "Max is excited and looking forward to it. Probably his first experience that isn't sponsored by group doctrine, if you get what I mean. Is there anything that I can contribute? I don't have fishing gear, and suppose you have enough for both of them." He listened while Roark reassured him with the usual commitments. He suggested they get a beer sometime before hanging up. After, Jack wrote the doctor's appointment and address on the calendar in the kitchen while Olivia watched.

"Max's appointment on Tuesday is at four thirty." He pointed to where he'd written the address underneath. "Near the University Hospital. If I get caught up at work, can you make sure he makes it?"

"I can do that, but are you sure you can trust me?" Olivia said, her tone dry.

"Don't get smart," Jack shot back. "I just want you to remind him, that's all."

"I'll do better than that and drive him. He won't hesitate to get a ride in my Sunbeam. And I don't have any classes after three o'clock on Tuesdays." Turning away, she looked back over her shoulder at him. "You know, it would be better for you to relax a little. Sometimes, I think I'll come home and find my suitcases all packed."

The way she read his mind stopped him cold, and he fought to keep his face neutral. "Nope, we agreed on a probationary period, and I'll stick to it." Still, her jab had found its target, and he felt his face flush. "On the plus side, thanks for seeing to the appointment. And the veal scaloppini tonight? I've never tasted better. For what it's worth, you will be a success at NAIT."

Her lips twitching at his grudging compliment, Olivia sniffed and turned toward her room.

Jack thought about Max's weekend, asking himself if it was safe, then scolding himself for being a worrywart. He wouldn't be alone and vulnerable. Besides, vulnerable and Max didn't rhyme. Capable and Max did. But just then, Jack had a fleeting memory of something he'd heard, seen, and witnessed. In Simpson's office? No, it was gone. Nothing.

He headed to his bedroom, worrying at his memory. Pharo was stomping his bed into submission before finally curling into it, his eyes on Jack. Jack got ready for bed and rolled into it, mashing his pillow a la Pharo before being satisfied.

He turned his mind from the illusive memory to Saturday and his date with Edina.

Whatever he had buried in the back of his mind would eventually surface.

11

FRIDAY came and went, unusually quiet. Jack supposed petty crimes were put on the back burner as people squeezed the last days out of August when minds got busy with a new school year and the ending phase of summer.

Jack eyed Wager whenever the phone rang, hoping it might be his answer to queries about Hudek. That is if Wager had called as promised. Mid-afternoon, they had a call-out. One of the snatch-and-grab victims phoned in to say he saw one of the perpetrators who robbed his store. This time, he had the foresight to use his camera for a positive I.D. He had the photo ready for pick-up. Jack and Chen welcomed the break from writing reports and took the call.

On the way back to Headquarters along Jasper Avenue, Jack idly watched people on the sidewalk. Nearing the corner of the Chateau Lacombe, he straightened. "Slow down."

Startled, Chen braked. "What?" he said, glancing over.

By now, they had passed the corner, and Jack turned and looked back. "It's Hudek. I'm sure it's him. Find a place to turn around."

"Which way was he going?"

"South. I want to see if that's where he's headed."

"If he's headed there and walking, we got a bit of time. Hold on," Chen said and stepped on the gas. He took the first turn south, then west on Macdonald Drive, doubling back toward 101st Street. Jack swivelled his head up and down the street, searching.

"There," Chen said, spotting him first. Hudek was just reaching the corner. Not losing a moment, Chen eased the car into a line of cars heading into the entrance to the hotel. He found a temporary drop-off spot and parked, leaving the motor running. Hudek came into the walkway, and as he passed, Jack turned his back, leaning over the seat as if to pick up something from the back seat.

"Okay," Chen said. "He didn't even look."

"Don't be too sure," Jack replied. "People like him watch without turning their heads. He probably knows every action around him."

Sure enough, Hudek paused at the entrance to the hotel and looked first in one direction, then toward their car again. Jack held his breath, keeping himself out of sight; Chen looked straight ahead, drumming his fingers on the wheel as if waiting for a passenger.

"What's he doing?" Jack asked.

"Oh, oh, He's coming back this way. Right at us."

"Get out, quick. Go open the trunk."

Without hesitation, Chen obeyed. Jack felt the trunk opening, then slam shut again. Chen climbed back in, his movements smooth but tense.

"He got waylaid by someone. Let's get out of here." He put the car in reverse and turned the nose to the exit.

From the other side, Jack took a fast look at Hudek. He was facing a man who gripped his elbow. A stocky, muscled man with a butch haircut. Jack summed him up: suit jacket, jeans, and a wide-legged aggressive stance. As Chen turned away from the exit and joined the evening rush, Jack saw Hudek turn and continue to where they had been parked.

"Too close," Chen remarked. "Why the dodge? We had every excuse for being there. Work related."

"I didn't want to risk a complaint to Gordon, who'd call Simpson, and we'd be in for another dressing down. From Wager too."

Chen grunted, his grip on the steering wheel relaxing. "Get a load of the brute he was talking to. Looks like the tough bodyguard type. Why would Hudek need a bodyguard? Do you think he's staying at the hotel?"

"I do. No car. Which means he either was out for a walk or had a short distance to return to the hotel."

"By himself, which would upset a bodyguard." They both sat for a moment, thinking about it.

"Hudek might live somewhere and is coming to the hotel for another reason,"

Jack shook his head. "There are no living arrangements close enough, and it's late afternoon. He's coming back to where he lives."

"Okay, so now what does that mean for us?"

"Not much," Jack said, grinning. "But we know where to look if we need it. A lead."

Frowning, Chen stared at him, eyes full of suspicion and unspoken curiosity. He opened his mouth, then closed it and went back to watching the traffic.

Thinking of the weekend ahead, Jack stopped in at Canadian Tire on the way home and bought a sleeping bag. Max pounced toward him as soon as he got inside the door, eyes lighting up when he saw the sleeping bag. Packing it under his arm, he pulled Jack toward his bedroom. "Can you check all my equipment? I've laid it out on the bed."

Feeling a nudge of happiness, he followed Max, pleased that the boy wanted his opinion. Inside Max's neatly packed bag were PJs, an extra t-shirt, pants, socks, and a warm jacket with an attached hood in case of rain. Bug repellent, sun lotion, soap, toothpaste, washcloth, and towel. At the bottom, Jack's hand closed around a hunting knife in its leather holder. He held it up, eyebrows raised in a question.

"I bought it when I ran," Max explained. "In case I was in a corner. I will take it." His tone left no alternative.

"You know how to use it safely?" Jack asked.

Max nodded. "Mutter made sure."

Jack's heart tightened. It saddened him that Ursula had thought it necessary to teach him how to defend himself like that. "Perhaps you can leave it here this time," Jack advised gently. "If anyone sees you with it, they may get the wrong idea. Especially Mr. Sullivan." Max looked unsure, but he nodded.

"What about swimming trunks?" Jack changed the subject with a smile. "A lake without taking your swimming trunks?"

Max chewed his lips. "Someone might see me."

So there it was. "You still believe someone from East Germany is looking for you?" Jack. Of course. Again, he knew the swimming pools might be the first place they would search.

Jack nodded, placing a hand on Max's shoulder. "I understand why you're cautious. But why not pack them, just in case? Better than to regret you didn't. You've been granted asylum. You're safe now."

But then, Jack's thoughts darkened. If an agent from the GDR wanted Max back, would asylum be enough? He frowned but quickly masked it. "Pigeon Lake is large. Odds are that nobody will know you're there."

Max nodded and got them out of the bottom dresser drawer. Jack added the new sleeping bag to the pile. "You're all set," he concluded and gave a thumbs up.

Early the next morning, Jack helped find room inside the station wagon for all the luggage and supplies.

"Sure you have enough?" he joked.

Roark grinned. "Thank goodness we aren't hauling the boat. My buddy owns the campground and has a sweet fourteen-foot Mirrocraft he lets me use. All I have to do is give him fish."

Jack waved, seeing only the fully packed trunk as the car went down the street. Left alone in the morning sun, he stood in the middle of the road, unsure whether he relished the sudden quiet, the vacant feeling of emptiness that comes from saying goodbye. Pharo licked his hand as though he felt it too. "Got the whole day, you and me," Jack said to him. To think, a year ago, he'd wished he had a family; now he had one in spades and admitted it was tiring sometimes.

Except for Olivia upstairs, Jack wouldn't change a thing about his life now, especially for where he was almost a year ago, suspended and accused of Brodie's murder. But if he was honest, the week with Olivia living with them hadn't been the disaster he'd imagined. True to her promise, she'd kept out of the way, and the food was good. Maybe too good. He might gain weight. Complete trust in her, however, would be foolish. There was still the chance that events in their lives were of interest to Luke. He couldn't let his guard down. But today, Olivia would go off for whatever she planned, and he and Pharo could relax. And there was always tonight and Edina. Jack whistled as he climbed the stairs.

With breakfast done, the kitchen clean, and Olivia finally out of the house for the day, Jack refilled his coffee mug, settled into the living room chair, and skimmed the newspaper's contents. The Watergate scandal continued to unfold, with Nixon issuing yet another denial. Jack barely glanced at it. The hockey series against the Soviets wasn't looking too promising for a Canadian victory. The word Czechoslovakia caught his eye in an item at the bottom of the page. Jack zeroed in on it. Military officers who had taken part in the Prague Spring were now farming experts. A lot of emphasis highlighting their expertise being a significant contribution to national progress. There was more of the same, but Jack quit reading and frowned. Who in their right mind would believe that rubbish? After August 1968, Russia had likely arrested every Czech military officer. Amazing they hadn't been shot. Jack snorted and then sobered. Maybe they had been. How would anyone know? Why were the papers printing these lies in the first place? He rattled the paper as if to dislodge the item, then turned to the crossword.

THE maître-D of the LaRonde room on the top floor of Chateau Lacombe greeted Jack and Edina with a warm smile and showed them to a table by the windows.

Edina's eyes sparkled as she took in the magnificent view. She waved her hand toward the vista. "I didn't expect this. I took a guess that you'd choose the CN Tower." She wore a sleeveless linen dress, the blue colour matching her eyes. Jack appreciated his own view, watching her settle into her chair.

"How astute. I did think about the CN Tower," Jack said truthfully. Until he'd seen Hudek outside the hotel. " But I decided this was the best spot to celebrate your birthday." He ignored a small guilty twinge while he surveyed the diners in the room, wondering if Hudek would show, then caught himself. The date with Edina came first, above all else. "The view at this time of the day is extraordinary."

"It's lovely." She gave a contented sigh, sat down her bag on the window ledge beside her chair, and gazed over the river valley expanse below.

"A double payback," Jack said, handing her the menu and opening his. "If it hadn't been for you giving me Harry's notes, I'd still be in suspension limbo." He made a face. "Probably worse, actually. As for your birthday present." He grinned. "Saves me combing the stores for something showy but worthless."

She laughed. "Now I'm glad I didn't tell you I won't tolerate birthday gifts next Saturday. The first one to offer me a gift gets tied to the nearest tree until all the good food is gone."

"You're more dangerous than you look." The corners of Jack's mouth turned up. "But I should warn you about something."

Eyes curious, she looked at him over the top of the menu. "What?"

Jack pointed to the window ledge. "The place isn't called LaRonde for nothing. It turns a full circle every eighty-eight minutes. Your belongings go with it." Jack neatly caught her purse beside his chair and handed it over.

"I forgot that." Blushing, she tucked it behind her back. "Just goes to show how long it's been."

A waiter—a white shirt, bow tie, and black pants—showed up beside the table, introduced himself, and looked inquiringly at Jack.

"Chateaubriand for two. Medium?" Jack got Edina's approval. "And a Merlot. Australian."

He turned back to Edina, who gave him an appraising, slightly curious look. "You do this often?" she asked. "Knowing the wines and food pairing, I mean?" She floundered and blushed again, looking uncomfortable now. "I'm sorry. You just seemed so . . ."

Jack rescued her. "I was in the Army. Stationed in Germany for a while in the fifties." Revealing he'd been educated in private schools would only raise questions he didn't want to answer.

"The Army?" Her eyebrows grew together across her nose. "You must have been terribly young."

"Just eighteen when I joined." Jack filled in the blanks. Usually, he hated to talk about his time in the Army and his tour in Germany, but Edina's rapt attention and questions about Germany at that time kept him talking. The wine glasses were refilled. Jack wanted to know more about her. So far, his knowledge was limited to her brother Harry. As a top-notch crime reporter, he uncovered the true identity of Brodie's killer. Then he'd been murdered, but not before leaving revealing tapes with Edina for Jack to read.

She confirmed she was divorced. "Married too young. There wasn't much for a girl to do just out of school. Teacher or a nurse. Neither appealed to me. Neil is living in Strasbourg, France and works in some position European Parliament. We've stayed friends, and he remembers I helped his career. With what he settled on me and Harry's estate, I don't want for much."

"The two young men who were at Harry's funeral. Sons?"

Edina laughed. "My sister's children. They loved Harry, and the feeling was mutual. No, Neil and I put off having children until his career was secure." She put her knife and fork down and frowned. "I suppose it was fate. Not having children from a broken marriage. Still . . ." She sighed.

"I'm sorry," Jack said. He picked up his wine glass. "Here's to life."

"Of course," she agreed, saluting him with her own and taking a sip. "Tell me about Max. Becoming a father isn't all roses, I should think."

Just then, the waiter appeared with a dish, which he laid down with a smooth twist of his wrist. "The chef's compliments," he stated. "Pitted dates in strips of bacon, then roasted until crisp." Jack looked at him and grinned. The waiter smiled back. "It's just to whet the appetite."

"Looks delicious," Edina said, reaching for one and placing it on her small plate. She took a bite. "Um. Caramelized."

Jack helped himself. "Their way of telling us we may wait a bit for the main course. But I don't mind. Where were we?"

"You were going to tell me how lovely fatherhood is."

So, Jack told her about Max and his lack of appreciation for Olivia's sudden appearance. He pressed his lips together and answered the obvious question. "She's the daughter of a crime boss."

"Good heavens." She lowered her eyes, shielding her curiosity.

"It's all tied up with the mess Harry was in and the money laundering and illegal gambling that went on."

She looked at him then, and when he opened his mouth, she said quickly. "Am I invading your privacy now?"

He tilted his head and smiled at her. "Olivia is trying to live without her father's influence. She's even taken her mother's name to distance herself from him. Somehow, she thinks I might be the answer." He chose another chef's amuse-bouche. "I don't like it, but I'm going along with it for now."

Edina laid her hand on Jack's arm, and a warm tremor rippled up it. "Stop, Jack. That's enough. Harry said you were a good man. For that alone, I'll volunteer if you need any help."

Jack nodded, surprised at the relief flooding through him that she hadn't rejected him. She trusted him without explanation. He stared at her, realizing he'd have been devastated if she had, and wondered at this new knowledge. A light filled his insides. Their dinner arrived, and conversation improved as they ate, chuckling over anecdotes and Jack's army experience. Both expressed some amazement when they found their opinions agreed on almost everything.

"What?" she asked at last, smiling at him as though he had asked her if she could read his mind. He had, but of himself as well. I'm not going to let you go, he decided. Ever. He grinned and took her hand. "Cheese? Dessert?"

"I can't. It isn't mannerly to say one is full, but I am. How about just coffee?"

Table cleared and coffee in front of them, they watched the new scenery spread out in the west, the sun setting over the valley, contrasting with trees whose leaves started to turn golden. Edina's eyes wandered around the room, surveying the people and the windows on the other side, blinking against the setting sun reflecting off the windows of the buildings. Jack saw her eyes dilate, and her jaw fell. She gasped and abruptly turned toward Jack, raising her hand to shield one side of her face.

Edina?" Jack looked at her, then turned his head in the same direction.

"Stop. Don't turn around." Edina whispered and put her hand on his arm. Jack obeyed.

Edina let out a soft laugh and leaned toward her hand on his arm as if she were whispering a compliment. "My God, Howard Winslow. He's wearing a bellhop's uniform." She forced out another soft laugh.

Shocked, Jack stared at her, then recovered and leaned toward her as if sharing the joke. "It can't be." He picked up his napkin, patted his mouth, then his forehead, showing he was warm, and sneaked a quick glance across the room at a tall slim man leaning against the coffee bar while the waiter loaded a tray with four cups of coffee. A bellhop waiting to deliver an order to a guest. The man turned to look around the room, and Jack averted his head, but not before he noted blond hair, a moustache, and glasses fixed on a large beefy nose.

"No, I don't think so. The same body build, though," he said, agreeing with part of her statement.

Edina shook her head. "I've been in his office and house too many times. I'd know him anywhere." She gave a sideways glance. "Look again while he's facing the other way."

This time, Jack took a longer, harder look, mentally cataloging the man's features. Just then, the bellhop used his forefinger to push his glasses against his nose, and Jack frowned. The bellhop turned toward them, but Jack was already focused on Edina, feigning an intimate conversation.

"He saw me," Edina said. "Us. Jack, it's him, for sure. He turned his back too fast. Now he's practically running away. He did that thing with his glasses again. Pushing them up on his nose as if they're too big." Edina slapped her napkin on the table and rose. "I can't believe it. Let's go."

Jack stayed where he was, thinking of Hudek in the same hotel, trying to put two and two together.

"Aren't we going after him?"

"I'd rather talk about it first."

Edina slowly sat down again, frowning. "What's to think? He's got some explaining to do."

"Well, yes, but not so fast. What's he doing here, of all places, as a bellhop? Why disappear in the first place only to end up here? He's got to be in trouble. If we expose him, we won't learn anything and may cause actual harm."

Edina relaxed, and her face softened. "Of course. I should have remembered that you've been asking questions." She sighed. "You have information that I don't. So, what's the plan, Detective?"

"First, you can't tell his wife or anyone else that you've seen him, or it'll be all over the papers." Jack looked around for the waiter and his bill. "I'll try and find out what he's calling himself. Until I know more, it isn't safe to approach him." He broke his musing, facing her. "But the next step is for me to take you home and report this to my sergeant."

Edina shook her head. "No, Jack. You can't leave me in a flux."

Jack only looked at her, eyes narrowed.

"I saw him first. I get first dibs."

Jack's mouth dropped. "This isn't like who saw the dollar on the sidewalk first." At the stubborn face staring at him, he said. "Okay. Let's discuss this like two grownups."

"That's better," she said and leaned forward. "I can help."

Exasperated, Jack's fingers massaged his forehead. "And how's that?"

"Suppose I go downstairs to the concierge's desk and pretend I need to leave a tip for a certain bellhop but can't remember his name. I can describe him, though."

"And what if he is in the front lobby, and they call him over?"

Edina shook her head. "He saw us, and the way he hurried out of here means he will make himself scarce. If he is near the front desk, I'll just get back on the elevator." She considered Jack's doubtful expression, scrunching up his mouth with distaste. "How else are you going to find out who he is? You? The concierge will know you are a cop right away and go dumb."

Jack sighed, telling himself he was mad. He rubbed his chin. "Against my instincts, but give it a try." As she rose, he put his hand out. "Can I trust you to be careful? This isn't a game, Edina. It can turn bad right away."

"Jack, I am an intelligent woman. I think before I act. I'll make sure there are people around the concierge's desk, so he won't pay too much attention to me. I'll just pay a visit to the washroom first." She picked up her purse and stepped away before he could protest again. He'd never encountered a woman like this since Ursula and was slow on the uptake. Going after her now would only cause comment amongst the diners. She passed the waiter on the way, and Jack watched her stop and say something. It must have been a compliment, judging by the smile on the man's face as he handed Jack the tab.

12

IN front of the elevators outside La Ronde, Jack shuffled his weight from one foot to the other with his hands shoved into his pockets. Each time, the people getting into the elevator held the door open for him with questioning looks. Jack would point at his watch and wave them away. At the point of getting in the next one to look for Edina, she appeared as the door slid open with an air of calm control, though her hair was noticeably fluffed as if caught in the wind. She held the elevator open, gestured for him to get in, and put her fingers to her lips in a silent gesture that promised answers, but not yet. On the way down, she combed her fingers through her hair, smoothing it. *Why had it been mussed in the first place?* His head spun.

They headed outside into the cool night air, still without exchanging a word between them. Edina broke the tension with a soft laugh as soon as they settled into the car. "His name is Howie. Howie Westlock," she said. "Not very imaginative. Same initials."

"Actually, a smart move," Jack said drily. "Did anybody see you asking questions? Anyone near enough to be interested?"

"Not a bit." Flushed with success, Edina laughed and brushed him off. "Like I said, I waited until he was busy, then fluffed myself up a little before I went down," she ran her fingers one last time through her hair and added with a smirk, "so I'd look on the fussy, forgetful side—the type who forgets where they put things. He hardly paid attention."

Jack squirmed, asking himself if it had been a good idea to let her have her way. If he was being honest, he felt left on the sidelines and was shocked at his prickliness.

"Anything else?" Jack hunched his shoulders, fighting against the edge in his voice.

"No, but I handed over ten dollars for poor Howie for being so nice—so conscientious."

Jack winced. A mistake. The concierge would remember.

"We forget the people who work behind the scenes," Edina said in a high voice.

"Howard is sure to ask about you. Did you leave your name?"

Edina's pursed lips huffed air at Jack's statement. "The concierge was too busy eyeing the ten-dollar bill."

"Howie is sure to want your description. He might recognize you from upstairs. Blue dress and all." *Damn*, Jack thought, I should have insisted on her going home.

"I left a piece of toilet paper carelessly tucked into my dress in the ladies' room. He mostly stared at it and not my face. I was just an old fusspot."

Jack turned onto 118th Avenue and continued west toward the St. Albert Road. He kept his eye on traffic, not daring to look at her with a straight face.

"The concierge agreed, but Howie lives right in the hotel, in an area they keep for staff rooms. Usually, it was just because they worked late, but poor Howie was new to town and hadn't found a place to live yet. He agreed to always be on call, so the arrangement to live in suited them both." Edina laughed and poked Jack in the ribs. "How'd I do?"

"Great," Jack said, damning himself yet welcoming the result. Already planning his next move, he looked over at Edina. *Go for it*, he told himself and took a deep breath. "It's a bit soon to say it, but do you mind very much if I stick around in the future?"

Jack studied her face for some clue as to how she felt. She stopped laughing, and her eyes went wide, looking at him as if she'd not heard right.

"Well, I won't reject it outright," she finally said softly. Jack waited for the postscript. "You don't waste time, do you? And yes, it's a bit soon to expect decisions, though." She chuckled then, her eyes sparkling and faced the front. "But if we want to see how it works out, you'd better keep your eye on the road. We can't keep driving around the traffic circle all night. The right lane exit for St. Albert is coming up."

"Yes, ma'am," Jack said, exhaling with a grin, soaking in the good energy swirling around the car. There was something wonderfully genuine about her — no pretenses, just vitality and spirit. He could already tell she'd never let him settle into anything dull.

JACK took his time driving back to the hotel so that he'd arrive after eleven o'clock. Leaving his jacket in the car, he rolled his sleeves to the elbow and sauntered the block and half to the hotel entrance, where the doorman looked him over.

"I'm not a guest," Jack smiled at him. "My friend Howie, Howie Westlock, works here. Invited me for a drink after work." Jack peered at the doorman. "I've been to see him a few times, and I've never seen you before. New, are you?"

"I've been a doorman ever since it opened in 1966." He looked Jack up and down, sizing him up. "Weren't you here just a while ago? With a lady?"

Jack shook his head and opened his eyes wide. "Thanks for the compliment. Maybe someday, but not so far." He poked the doorman in the side with his elbow. "You're pretty sharp, sizing up the guests. Guess you see a lot of different types."

"The stories I could tell." The doorman rolled his eyes and gave Jack a friendly grin. He looked like he welcomed some company from the monotony. "Want me to track down Howie for you?"

"Well, I don't want you to take the time," he said, mentally crossing his fingers. "I can just sneak up. He's on the top floor, isn't he?" He paused at the doorman's quizzical expression. "Or did I get mixed up with the Mac down the Street?"

"No, and there aren't any staff quarters. Not here, anyway. I think Howie made some arrangements with the management. On the first floor, at the very back, over the maintenance room." The doorman's attention passed to a car entering the driveway, and Jack took the opportunity to scurry to the hotel entrance.

He found the room after several false leads. Past the café and kitchen and through a staff-only door. Another hallway with store rooms, the noise of a laundry room, another with tables and lockers. It was taking too much time. Someone would eventually spot him and start asking questions. He twisted the knob on another door. Locked. Not seeing a private sign, he pressed his ear against the door and listened for a moment before giving it a good knock.

"Nice digs you have here, Howie," Jack said as he pushed his way in. He turned and faced Howard. "Close the door, and let's talk."

Howard closed the door and leaned against it, facing Jack. Black circles under his eyes, he stared at Jack, who wondered if he'd slept ever since his disappearance. He still wore his blond wig, and Jack noted the change in his face. A bigger nose, cheeks fatter, but still the same horn-rimmed glasses. Howard put up a forefinger and pushed at the bridge. Jack grinned and tilted his head, examining.

"Good job at disguise, though. Stuff your back gums with foam to fill out your cheeks, pad the nose. Wig. They missed the props you stole from your theatre group, by the way."

Howard pushed himself away from the door and sat on the edge of his cot. He gestured to the lone chair in the room. "I saw you and Edina Chambers upstairs but hoped my uniform would cover me. People look at the uniform and never the face. Most people . . . except you."

Jack sank into the chair, leaning forward with his elbows resting on his knees, choosing to hold back the fact that it wasn't him who made the connection. He leaned forward, forearms over his thighs. "Why, Howard? What's going on?"

His hand shaking, Howard rubbed his forehead. "First things first. Anyone else know you saw me?" His narrowed eyes bore into Jack's.

Jack shook his head, not liking what he saw in the lawyer's face. Fear, indecision. Anger.

"It's important, Jack. How did you get in here?" He waved his hand at the room, meaning the whole hotel.

"I told the doorman I was a friend, and we'd agreed to meet after your shift."

Howard pursed his lips, tilted his head at the ceiling, and let out his breath. "Great. Just great."

"Relax Howard. It's okay." Jack spread his arms wide. "Look at me. I know enough to keep quiet about recognizing you, and I impressed Edina to do the same. She'll keep it to herself, Howard."

Howard's pinched face still held doubt.

"I know how to slip past security," Jack added. "I'm not an amateur at this. And I met nobody inside the hotel." He met Howard's eyes and ducked his head a few times to urge the man to speak.

Howard let out a long, weary breath, his shoulders sagging as if the weight of his secrets had finally caught up to him. He rubbed his eyes with trembling fingers. "God, it's been so long since I've had to do this. It never used to be this draining or nerve-wracking." His voice cracked, and he shook his head. "You know I used to do Intel work in Germany after the war?"

Jack nodded, but Howard wasn't even looking at him. He was studying the floor.

"Rooting out propaganda from the Russians. They were trying to undermine our recovery work in West Germany." Howard's top lip curled. "Their Agitation and Propaganda Section. Set up to guide the masses into Marxism. The disinformation that went on was powerful, and the Commies weren't only in the East German sector." He looked up at Jack then. "I don't have to tell you what went on. You faced it yourself in the fifties before the wall went up."

Jack leaned back and nodded. Ursula. She only returned because of threats to her family, who were still residing in the Eastern Sector.

Howard's voice grew quieter, but there was an urgency there now, the kind that came from carrying the burden of terrible knowledge. "It's happening again, Jack. But this time, it's here. Bigger, more dangerous. The lies, the misinformation—it's targeted. Carefully crafted to take advantage of people's fears, their discontent."

Jack thought of the item he'd read that morning and Anderson's hint about reading the papers if he wanted to find spies. Jack wrinkled his forehead. How often did he analyze newspaper articles of events he knew little about and accept the views if they coincided with his own? If he wasn't familiar with the actual subject, did he take information at face value? Or check that the authors were bona fide and had facts to back up their accusations? Who took the time unless it affected them directly or knew the information was false?

"Still," he said, "How can they lie about a world event? Global reporters would have different versions. Surely the right people would know the difference?"

Howard let out a bitter laugh devoid of any real humour. "You'd think so, wouldn't you? But no. The world outside the USSR is the enemy, remember? The goal isn't to convince everyone but to confuse enough people. Create doubt. And a lot of little doubts, over time, become consensus." He paused, his expression darkening. "That's how they chip away at relationships—like ours with the States. Spread just enough lies to make Canada look weak, like we're under US control. They want to ruin our economic ties, make us look vulnerable."

Howard's eyes drooped as if suddenly too tired to continue. "Already, anyone who objects is accused of witch-hunting and war-mongering."

"Well, it isn't as though many people read the papers," Jack said. "Who's got time these days anyway?

"Disinformation is widespread, Jack." Howard sat straight and looked side to side before continuing, "It spreads through papers, pamphlets, anything people read. Now imagine—just imagine—if someone found a way to slip propaganda into every household, into your morning coffee, into the gossip at work. It starts small, harmless even. But by the end? It's a full-blown conspiracy theory."

Jack had nothing to say in retort. Instead, he shifted the conversation. "When you say it's here, do you mean here, as in Edmonton?"

Howard hesitated.

"Howard," Jack pressed, his voice soft yet firm. "It's no crime to write an article, even with lies. It's despicable but not illegal."

Howard's face tightened. The small of Jack's back tingled. "It's got something to do with Kepler's client, right? What do you know about Mr. Hudek?"

The shift was subtle but sudden. Howard's gaze locked on Jack's, not the look of a man ready to break, but one resolute in his purpose. "What if I told you Hudek is dangerous?" His words were calm but carried the weight of something darker. "That this goes deeper than I ever imagined. And I only have part of the evidence. What would you do with that information, Jack?"

Jack's throat tightened, his mind racing, but Howard wasn't finished, a wry smile creeping on his face. "I have attorney-client privilege on my side. I am not obliged to reveal anything. You know that. But I've heard of your reputation—remember you sent me McNaughton's tapes that cleared you of murder. So, I've gotta ask— do you still keep secrets from your superiors?"

Jack stared back at him, his voice now cold. "Is Hudek receiving money that's not kosher? And how's that money used? If it's flowing through a law firm, that's laundering. That's criminal."

"What if they come after you, Jack?" Howard said, his voice quieter now, more persistent. "You've already seen it happen. Your son—talk to him. You know he's been subjected to this kind of indoctrination. This could even touch him."

The words hit Jack like a punch to the gut. His son?

Howard's eyes bore into his, but then he smiled gently. "His file's at our office. He talks about the Stasi and indoctrination. Remember?

What if someone is afraid Max will go public? Refute all the lies?" He spread his palms as if laying everything bare. "I'm not saying it hasn't already been said before, but he is a defector. The Soviets don't like defectors saying bad things about them."

Just like that, the elusive piece of memory came to the forefront. During the interview with Howard at the office, Max said his mother kept a list of his swimming records and meets to show Jack. But Jack knew Ursula never made lists. "She said they were always used against you," he said aloud.

"What?" said Howard, his eyebrows meeting with a crease.

"Nothing. I hope." But anxiety tightened his chest, pulling him toward a darker possibility. What if those records weren't what Max thought they were? His pulse quickened, but he forced himself to calm down. Max was safe at the lake for the moment.

"Timothy Gordon has taken Max's case," Jack said instead. "Will anyone else in the office have a reason to look at it?" Jack asked carefully. He didn't mention Kepler's name lest Howard realize Jack knew of the connection between the missing Hudek file and him.

"No. It's safe with Tim." An impatient wave of the hand dismissed Jack's concern. Howard glanced at the clock on the bedside table while massaging the back of his neck. "Your call, Jack. Stay or leave? But if you leave, I've got to go too, and all of this," his hands swept the room in a grand, desperate gesture, "will have been for nothing. They'll kill me."

"Like Jassy?" Jack asked.

Howard's face darkened, his reply a low murmur. "Like Jassy,"

Jack sighed, the weight of everything he'd learned tonight settling on his shoulders. "Howard, if they killed Jassy, you know I can't keep quiet. Besides, if your suspicions are right, it's beyond the Edmonton police. It's in the RCMP's realm. For sure, it will surface, and I'll be in real trouble." He moved in on Howard. "You can't continue with this alone. Give it up, Howard."

Stubborn, Howard shook his head. "I'm close, Jack. Just a few more days. They're starting to trust me—I'm hearing things, conversations that'll lead to methods, names. Without it, we'll have nothing." His eyes were wild with determination, a man teetering on the edge of something dangerous. "If you get anything, anything at all that changes this, tell me. I'll get out."

Jack stared at him momentarily, a fire blazing behind the man's eyes. It reminded him of himself and told Jack this was a losing battle. "Until Monday, Howard. No more." Jack said, the words heavy on his tongue.

An image of Wager floated into his mind, leaving him feeling rotten.

13

HOWARD took a deep breath of relief. "Jassy thought she'd spotted irregularities in a file. I found out third-hand from Julie, who heard it from Sheila. I already knew when I saw you both talking in the Court House." Howard's lips thinned into a grim line.

He shook his head, regret settling over him like a dark cloud. "And brushed it off. To my shame. I even read Jassy the Riot Act, which stated that it infringed the rules to read client files. If only I'd . . ." He clasped his hands over his head, fingers digging into his scalp. "Well, never mind. Still, it nagged at me. Because of Hudek, I suppose. He's a chaser."

Jack's brow furrowed. "A chaser? What's that?"

"A head for business. Always scheming, always working an angle. Ruthless in pursuing his aims, too. A chaser. Like a used car salesman—tailoring his pitch to the mark, playing on his prospect's likes and dislikes. Ask them to call him by his first name. It was all an act."

Jack raised his eyebrow and said, "Sounds like a con man to me."

"No, this guy doesn't only promise. He actually produces the goods."

"And what is he selling exactly?"

Howard shifted in his seat, looking exhausted. Rubbing the back of his neck to stay alert. "He says he is an importer-exporter. Import goods from Czechoslovakia. But mostly exports goods needed there."

"If I recall correctly, Bohemian crystal is the sole worthwhile item from there."

Howard allowed a smile, small and tight. "Nope. Czechoslovakia is abundant in producer goods, meaning consumer goods are short. Ordinary things like sewing needles and ballpoint pens. Products we take for granted. According to Hudek, he imports machinery and parts and exports scarce consumer goods."

"And Gordon, Winslow and Kepler only process the paperwork?" Howard nodded, but his teeth chewed the corner of his lip. Jack narrowed his eyes, reading doubt. "Something not quite right there?"

Howard leaned back and closed his eyes for a long minute. Jack wondered if he had fallen asleep and had a twinge of pity. Should he leave him and talk tomorrow? He braced himself and was about to nudge Howard.

"The short version, a lot of money transferred in at frequent intervals," Howard said. "Not much transferred out. I listed them all, and the transactions don't relate to the amount of business he says he does. Unless . . ." Another pause, and he looked at Jack as if he expected a hint.

"Unless the business is a cover, and the money is being funnelled for something else entirely." Howard's stare didn't waver, offering nothing, but his eyes invited more comment. Jack obliged. "He lives in this hotel, doesn't he? And that's why you're here. To suss him out."

Howard smiled. "Right. And it's a slow process. I've only just managed to become his favourite errand boy and gofer. I got into his room once and found written material. Lies, some truths, but twisted facts which aim to misinform." Howard got up and stretched, looking weary, then paced back and forth in front of Jack. "I agree that writing lies isn't illegal, but I also found a list of names taped to the bottom of a drawer." Howard shook his head. "Very careless. I would have found a better place."

"Probably thinks we're not bright enough. What names?"

Howard paused mid-stride and waved the question away. "A few I recognized—mostly Edmonton businessmen. But that's not the point. I'm convinced it's a full-blown cell with a designed purpose, and Hudek's the leader." Howard peered through his glasses over his phony nose with eyes hard as flint. "That's what the money's really for."

Jack's gut tightened, recalling his days in Germany. "A cell? That means he's answering to someone. Who's his handler? Gotta be someone giving him orders."

"That's the question, isn't it?" Howard's voice got more even, more relaxed, Jack thought, as if having someone to bounce his ideas off shared his worry. "Historically, it's someone connected with the diplomatic corps. Who, if exposed, has immunity. No embassy in Edmonton, so looking at someone out of the city?"

Jack mulled it over in his mind, then shook it off as irrelevant now. "Shouldn't we be more worried about what and who Hudek is handling? How many people does he have under his control?"

"I don't know." Howard frowned. "But if there is a cell, those people do whatever harm they can conjure up. Illegal things. Right now, it's only a suspicion . . ." He trailed off, casting a glance toward the door. "People visit him. It looks like business visits, but I'm not convinced. I need to hear what they're saying. Get inside those meetings."

Jack's heart took a dip. "Good heavens, Howard. If it's true, it's way beyond our scope. The RCMP? Don't you think it's time you told Gordon and Kepler?" He stood and decided to test the waters. "Unless you think Kepler is in on it?"

Howard reeled, put his palm against his forehead and sat on the bed again. "No. Kepler is as straight as they come. He would never condone this setup. They'd have to put a gun to his head first." Howard's expression turned thoughtful. "And I can't inform the RCMP yet or anyone. They will send people into the office to snoop around. Impossible to keep quiet. Word would get out, and we'd be ruined. Think of Gordon and all the staff affected." Howard shook his head. "Impossible. And what if my suspicions all prove untrue?"

Jack conceded the last point but felt the need to push the first. "But Kepler. Blackmail?"

Howard chuckled. "He's got nothing in his life that would be open to blackmail. Kepler's brusque, even autocratic, but he's a good man."

"But his reaction to Jassy's death—I've heard it was extreme. Gordon had to step in and help him. That's not the reaction of a normal boss. Howard. Kepler dotes on his wife. Would he be open to blackmail if someone threatened his wife?"

"Yes, he would, for her." Howard rubbed his chin, thoughtful, then shook his head. "But it's moot. Kepler has nothing to gain as far as motive. He's already a solid partner in the firm and never indicated he isn't satisfied. There is no chance of his partnership being threatened."

Howard gave a pointed stare at the clock. "Let's call it a night."

"I can't just sit on my hands, Howard. I know a couple of civilians— not cops—who could tail Kepler. Might reveal an important connection. They will keep their mouths shut."

Howard looked indecisive. "I don't know. Right now, I am too tired to think, and that's unsafe. Get lost, Jack. Be careful going out."

Jack stood. "How will you let me know?"

"I'll phone you. At home."

"And what if I need to contact you?"

Howard paused, mulling it over. "Got any informers?"

"Some," Jack admitted. "Why?"

"What do they do when they need to talk to you?"

"They give me a place and time," Jack explained. "I subtract one from the time and meet them. I do the same if I want to see them."

"Okay. Let's do that."

"Hold on. How?" Jack lifted his hands in frustration.

Howard gave him a tired smile. "The same way you found me. If you need me, wrap a note in a two-dollar bill and slip it at the concierge's desk with my name on it. Then, I'll phone you."

Alarmed, Jack asked, "How did you know I left the bill?" He crossed his fingers, praying he wouldn't hear Edina's name.

"I recognized your style. It had to be you."

All the way home, a gnawing feeling unsettled his gut. Full of remorse, he wished he hadn't promised Howard more time. Now, he would have to stand by, chewing his fingernails, hoping events didn't turn sour. At worst, a death he may have stopped. Since the last fiasco with the old Deputy Chief, Wager had trusted Jack's word he'd do no investigations himself without informing proper channels. Breaking that rule could merit a suspension or worse. He couldn't chance confiding in Wager now. He'd sooner face a rearing cobra.

And then there was the part about Max. Howard's reference to his son whined in his head like a mosquito buzzing by the ear. Jack couldn't shake the feeling that Max was somehow tied up in all this. He told himself he was chasing shadows. Worrying about his promise to Howard was enough.

By the time Jack arrived home, it was after midnight. At the top of his floor, he noticed the apartment door just closing. Instantly alert, he waited momentarily, listening for Pharo's warning. Then, standing to one side, he pushed at the door against the resistance on the other side. Relaxing when he felt no threat, he gave a firmer shove and stepped inside. Olivia stood just beyond the door, her expression shifting from fear to guilt to defiance. The moonlight streaming through the windows lit up her delicate features and luminous skin. Whatever genes she had inherited from both families had combined to make her beautiful, Jack thought. No wonder Luke worried.

"Been out on the town?" he inquired, slipping past her to where Pharo waited to lick his hand.

"My new classmates," she said. "We went out for dinner to get acquainted. And no, we weren't drinking," she answered his unspoken question. "Anyway, what do you care?" She put her key in her handbag and then looked at her watch. "Bit late to take your date home, isn't it?"

"As you said, you are your own boss," Jack said, ignoring her effort to switch the subject. "Luke, being Luke, has probably taught you to keep yourself safe. But as long as you are in my house, I expect you to show Max you aren't an irresponsible teenager with a license to do whatever you want." Suddenly exhausted, Jack slumped and hooked the leash on Pharo for his nightly trip outdoors. "Next time, be good enough to leave a note that you will be late. In case Anderson phones, and I have to tell him I don't know where you are. Goodnight, Olivia."

Returning from his quick outing, while Jack readied for bed, Pharo gave him a sour look for not taking him on a longer walk and did his usual stamping dance, beating his bed into compliance before he curled up in it. Despite his exhaustion, Jack stared at the ceiling, searching for answers to actions he should take in the coming days.

THE next day, Sunday, around midmorning, Chen knocked on the door, timing his appearance just as Jack, having showered and dressed, poured his first coffee. He fetched another mug and poured one for Chen without being asked. Pharo met him at the door and sniffed around him while Chen patiently waited. Pharo finally gave him the okay and nosed his hand. Chen obliged and rubbed Pharo's ears.

"A heads up that you may be called in. We had a murder last night." Chen took a sip of coffee and gave an exaggerated, grateful sigh after a sip. "Gee, that's good." He followed Jack into the living room.

"Who?" Jack rattled off at Chen, suddenly nervous. Surely not?

Chen shot him a surprised stare over the cup held up to his mouth. "Why? You expecting something?"

"What? No. Wager promised me the long weekend, and I thought I might be called in. I don't mind. Max is away fishing for the weekend."

Chen raised his eyebrows. "Not mind? Are you mad?" he asked mildly, sharpening his gaze. "It isn't that lost file again, is it?" Chen plunked himself on a chair and said, "Please don't make me go back to that law office. I can't stand sitting around with a bunch of girls and pretending I'm in heaven. I'm supposed to be learning from you." He shook his head. "Just so we're clear, I'm not. If that's what I'm supposed to be learning, I'm changing careers." He then sucked in his breath, and his eyes rounded in amazement as he peered over

Jack's shoulder. Some of Chen's coffee slopped out of the mug as he rose to his feet.

Sighing heavily, Jack turned. Olivia had appeared, dressed in shorts and tee, flat slippers and tanned legs, heading to heaven knows where. One hand pulled at her hair while the other slipped a band around the ponytail. She smiled at Chen. "Hello."

Jack waited for Chen's mouth to close and his face to return to its normal colour.

"Uh, hi. Um, I'm Ethan Chen. Jack's partner." He put out his coffee mug to shake, then pulled it back. "Just Chen will do," he added. Jack saw his great effort to look casual.

"I'm Olivia, Jack's pseudo niece," she shot Jack a sugary smile, then pointed to the kitchen and said to Chen. "Have you had breakfast? I'm just about to make it. You're welcome to join us."

"Yeah. Thanks. That would be great," Chen said, a little too eagerly. Olivia disappeared behind the counter in the kitchen. Chen gazed back at Jack as if he'd just witnessed a miracle.

"Your mouth is open," Jack said.

Bewitched, Chen's lips sketched a silly grin. He sat carefully as though any slight bump might knock him from a dream.

"She's got different colour eyes," he informed Jack in a delighted whisper. "It's called heterochromia something."

"I know," Jack whispered back. The poor thing, he almost added.

"It's beautiful. She's beautiful."

"Drink your coffee and tell me about the murder." Jack tried to be casual. "Who's on it?"

Chen gulped and came back to earth. "Oh. Wager put Vassar and Dyer on the scene. The owner of a pawnshop. Looks like he got the wrong end of an attempted robbery. That's all I know. You might be called in if anything else comes up, and I'm on late shift." He chanced a glance at the kitchen. "You're her uncle?" He looked hopeful.

"Only in name. A daughter of a friend from way back."

"Oh," was all Chen could muster up. Still whispering despite the preparation clatters coming from behind the kitchen wall. His eyes widened, hopeful. "Is she staying for long?"

"She's enrolled at NAIT."

"Ah. What's her subject?"

"Cooking." Jack stifled a laugh.

Chen nodded wisely, grateful. "That's good." Adoration on his face, he watched Olivia set three places at the table, then breathed in the food odours wafting into the room. Pharo wandered over and lay down near the kitchen. Jack was thankful Basenjis rarely drooled, or he'd drown.

Soon after, they sat at the table with orange juice, omelettes with side dishes of green onions, grated cheese, tomatoes, toast, marmalade or jam, bacon, sausage, croissants, and fresh coffee. Jack didn't join the conversation, only watched Chen and Olivia attempt to wow each other, although so far, Chen seemed to be the only one wowed. Olivia was a natural. She didn't use coy gestures or inflection in her actions or voice. Jack begrudgingly admired that she didn't flaunt her charm or use it as some tool of manipulation. Being herself gave her more influence than she probably even realized. Jack sighed. What was he going to do? He couldn't weaken. She had to be out of his responsibility, leaving no connection to Luke. Luke, who never did anything without a detailed plan, was up to something. And Olivia was the first tease even if she wasn't aware of it. And there was now Edina in his life. He'd have to confide in her, which might darken her view of him and end a promising relationship before it got properly started.

The phone rang at the end of their meal, and Olivia jumped up to answer before Jack could put down his napkin. After a breathless hello, she handed the receiver over to Jack, openly disappointed.

"You're in deep again, Tuesday," Wager growled. "What have you been up to now? Get in here. I've heard from my contact."

Mystified, Jack hung up. Surely, it couldn't be about Winslow. Nobody had seen Jack leave the hotel. *Unless* . . . Jack's heart skipped.

She wouldn't. She promised. The phone rang again. Olivia jumped up, face shining in hope.

"Jack?" said Edina. Jack shook his head at Olivia. "Tea and scones will be ready by early afternoon, after two o'clock. I'll expect you after that." Her voice sounded anxious but questioning. "As we agreed." A slight emphasis on the word. He got the message. That her agreement meant she wasn't about to be left out of his visit to Winslow. Jack's suspicion lifted, and he chastised himself for his first suspicion.

"I've been called in for a case," he said carefully. "A bit of trouble, and we're running shorthanded, as usual. I'll let you know. Sometime today. I enjoyed last night, by the way. It's nice of you to say the same." He glanced at Chen and Olivia at the table, both openly eavesdropping.

"Oh. Got people listening, do you?" Edina confirmed, amusement ringing in her voice. "I'll keep the kettle boiling." Jack interpreted the comment to mean she was eager to hear.

They said goodbye, and Jack quickly finished what was left of his meal. Chen insisted he help with the cleaning up, saying it was his job at home. Right, thought Jack, and saw Olivia's smile when Chen started collecting dishes from the table.

"Maybe it's time I got out of my parents' basement and found my own place," Chen said later to Jack as he was leaving. "Are there any vacancies in this building? By any chance?"

"No." Jack closed the door in his face.

14

WAGER pointed Jack to a chair across his desk. Jack dutifully sat and waited under his sergeant's long accusing stare. "What gives?" Jack finally broached, hoping his visit to Howard wasn't the main topic.

"My contact phoned back this morning and used the same words," Wager leaned forward, both elbows on his desk. "He said he requested available files on Hudek and got a reaction he didn't expect. He was told to wait, and instead of the file, he got collared by a couple of Intel people and ordered to accompany them for questioning." Wager rolled his eyes. "So I got an earful when he called back. I had to tell him who wanted to know and why."

The sergeant chewed at his moustache. "You'd better have told me everything you know, or so help me, Tuesday, I'll throw you to the wolves. I've a good mind to do it, anyway." He paused, his face unreadable as always, then muttered, "If only I could think of a reason."

Jack opened his eyes wide, letting his eyebrows reach his forehead. Inside, he sweated. Now what? This is worse than Howard let on, or else he was playing Jack for a fool. "Everything we talked about is all I know, Wager. I can't believe the law firm is involved in anything associated with RCMP Intel. It's a simple case of a missing person. And a missing file with Hudek's name on it. It's supposed to be a routine background investigation. And now, suddenly, it isn't?" Jack spread his hands. "How were we to know that?"

Wager sighed. "We weren't. And that's what I told my contact. But he advised us to let it go. He has no idea why, but he said if we were smart, we'd forget it. And just concentrate on the guy we're looking for. And what about Simpson? Imagine his reaction."

"What if we find out there is a connection?"

"Cross that bridge if and when we get to it." Wager's eyes sharpened on Jack. "Do you know anything else, Jack? Truly? You'd better not be hiding anything I should know."

Looking across the desk at Wager, Jack's chest tightened, and for a moment, he considered confessing. The memory of Winslow's fear at the prospect of Hudek finding out who he was, along with Jassy's face, intruded, and he clamped his lips together. Still, Winslow had to stop. Now.

"You know as much as I do," he said, hating himself and Winslow even more. Wager said nothing; he just inspected his face, looking for lies.

"Chen said you'd had a murder," Jack changed the subject. "Do you want me to come in tomorrow? I can do an early shift. Max comes home from camping just before dinner. I'd like to be home then."

Wager blinked. "That would be good." He looked at his watch. "You got any plans for the rest of today? I know it's your day off, but I can use you if you have nothing else to do."

"I've an appointment in St. Albert this afternoon. But I'll come in tomorrow," Jack replied, lifting himself from the chair. He phoned Edina from his own desk, warned her he was on his way and then left, his thoughts casting a dark shadow over the bright afternoon.

Once inside, he could tell from Edina's narrowed eyes that she noticed his mood at once. She didn't probe or ask—just filled the silence with casual chatter about their dinner last night and the food as she poured tea. She slid a plate toward him with a teasing smile. "Try these," she said. "Devon cream and strawberry jam on a fresh scone is pure bliss. Trust me." Jack relaxed as he listened to her speak, enjoying her company and the room, its comfortable furniture, papers and books scattered about, giving it a neat but homey atmosphere.

"I can see you aren't interested at all in what I found out about Howard," he said finally, teasing.

"I'm going to kill you in a minute," she retorted. "I hardly slept at all and had to bake and keep busy doing inconsequential things to keep myself sane."

Jack's smile faded as he shared a condensed version of what had unfolded—Howard's plea to keep his secret a little longer and the precarious agreement Jack had made. "It's not good, Edina. I'm already in trouble. I got called in today and accused of going off on my own. I didn't lie, but I didn't tell all I knew either. Not good."

"What? They found out that we saw Howard?" Alarm flickered in Edina's eyes.

"No. Just the person who Howard is spying on. I'm not even sure Howard isn't keeping other secrets from me. He was adamant that he'd be in deep trouble if we didn't keep my promise. I believe him. And there isn't any way I can get him to stop or question him further. It's too dangerous. There may be people I don't know who are involved. I wouldn't even know if they saw me approach him." Jack's fist beat a tattoo against his thigh. "It puts me between a rock and a hard place. I've been a fool."

He reached over and took her hands in his. "And Edina, I'm concerned that someone will place you at the hotel last night, and you may be in danger. It's so important that if anyone gets that idea, plead total ignorance." He squeezed her hand so hard that she winced. "If anything happened to you because I let you in on it . . . I don't know how I could stand it."

Edina gently pulled his hands away from hers and flexed her fingers. "I am a grown woman, Jack, and I know when to keep my mouth shut. And I can do it without giving anyone a reason to suspect me. Don't doubt me, Jack."

What else could he do except agree? They gazed at each other, both with worried looks. Stubborn, Jack had the last word. "I agree, but with a proviso. Preparation is everything, isn't it? We'll plan and forestall questions which may arise. Just in case?"

"I bet you were a boy scout." Edina laughed.

Jack returned the smile, but his mind was still running through every potential threat, every angle they might be missing. Together, they had grilled each other until each knew how the other would react. Watching her, he regretted more and more that he had not trusted his instincts and stopped her dash to the concierge. Now he'd found her, he could only imagine she was in danger like Jassy. He couldn't bear the thought, but it persisted well after he left for home.

Jack parked in his reassigned parking space and told himself he needed to cool off from overthinking. He'd take Pharo to Kinsmen Park. There was always a cool breeze from the river and lots of shade. Poor Pharo. In the last week, Jack had neglected him, and that was no way to treat his best friend.

There was a note plastered to the fridge in big block letters. A poke at Jack's suggestion to Olivia, no doubt. A placard more than a note. It said she was out, his dinner in the fridge. All he had to do was warm it up unless he preferred cold. Jack ripped it off and binned it. He opened the refrigerator and saw slices of beef beside slivers of cold celery and carrots, with pickles and mustard in a side dish. Crusty rolls covered with a linen napkin were on the countertop. Jack considered a cold beer but closed the fridge door and dangled the leash before Pharo, who yodelled his agreement.

It was indeed cooler in the park, where Jack took Pharo to the riverside. Pharo did his typical mad dash in circles until he found used chewing gum. He'd pick it up, chew awhile and then eject it, continuing until he found another. Jack watched for a short time until he shouted his usual "Drop it! Disgusting. You're supposed to be trained," wondering at the dog's ability to find gum while on the run. Pharo seemed to grin at him but obeyed and came over to Jack to be petted. "You're a menace, you know that? One of these days, it's going to backfire, and you'll swallow a gob." Pharo wagged his bushy tail in agreement, sat down beside Jack, and started licking himself clean.

"Your dog is a cat?"

Jack had seen the man coming down the path toward them—hands behind his back, stopping now and then to look up at the High Level Bridge and his surroundings. Getting away from the heat as Jack and Pharo were.

"No. He just cleans himself like a cat," Jack said, studying the man. Tie loose around his neck, shirt sleeves rolled up to his elbows. Linen pants, part of a summer suit, but missing the jacket. Perhaps left in the car. He had an accent. Not Canadian.

"Hot today." He took a handkerchief out of his pocket and wiped his forehead. The man inspected Jack with the same intensity— his intelligent eyes flashed amusement.

"You're cooling off the same way I am" the man continued, a chuckle escaping his lips. "But I can see you're already wondering what I am doing here." He paused for effect, surveying the space around them. "I was coming to see you at your home, but saw you on the street and thought—why not here? It's as good a place as any and much more comfortable."

Pharo stopped cleaning and closed in on Jack, pressing himself against his leg and facing the man. Jack put a cautionary hand on his head.

"Have we met before?" Tension crawled up Jack's spine. A German accent.

The man looked surprised. "Of course not. Why should you? My name is Alec. I followed you because I have some . . . sensitive questions."

"You have an odd way of introducing yourself, Alec." Jack hooked on Pharo's leash and made to walk away.

"Wait," The man put out his hand. "Please. I agree. My wife says I always start in the middle when I ask a question." He pointed to a nearby bench. "Can we sit, and I'll start at the beginning? I just need advice. It's important."

Jack looked the man over again, and curiosity tugged at him. "Why me?"

"Please." Alec motioned again to the bench, and Jack reluctantly followed, Pharo still glued to his side.

"It's delicate." He began as they walked, his voice low. "I hope you don't think me intrusive, but I think you can advise me. I read you have a son who recently defected from East Germany."

Jack halted. "Stop right there, Mister. I will not discuss this. Are you a reporter?"

The man's hands flew up in surrender. "Goodness, no! Please, hear me out before you walk away." Alec sat down on the bench and took a deep breath. Jack stood in front of him. Pharo rumbled softly in his throat and pressed against his leg. "There is a niece, mine, who lives in East Berlin. She is my dead sister's daughter. You understand I love her like my own. It's been three years since I saw her last. Her latest letter—she's begging for help. She wants out, even just to West Berlin. She is only nineteen. She doesn't know what to do. I want to get her out. You can help."

"No, I cannot," Jack said firmly. "If you think I arranged my son's escape, I did not. I wouldn't know where to start."

"But still, your son did manage it. I'm hoping that he knows people who can help her. Who she can get in touch with."

Jack laughed, a short, sharp bark that startled even Pharo. "Are you serious? He only saw a chance to run and took it. No help." This man was starting to come across as a nutcase. Or was he just an idiot? Even if I knew anything, why would I tell him? He could be anyone.

Logic told Jack to walk away. If this man was who he claimed, or even if he wasn't—why would Jack involve himself in something this risky? But as Alec sat there, fumbling through his words, his ineptitude gave a strange ring of truth. There was something so raw, so unpolished about his plea that Jack felt a sliver of doubt creep in.

"I know what you're thinking," Alec broke into his thoughts. "My wife says I am silly. But also desperate." He touched his forehead as though trying to ease a headache. He looked sincere, and Jack's pity increased. What if Max were in the same situation as his niece? Behind the wall, Ursula dead, alone, with only the distant hope that Jack was somewhere out there.

"I'm sorry," he said and meant it. Because what could he do? He knew nothing and would never question Max for the information this man wanted. Max would take it as mistrust that Jack doubted his story. The door would shut between them forever. "I can't help you. I wish I could. As I said, it wasn't planned, just luck and grasping at an opportunity."

Alec wiped his face with a handkerchief again and slumped on the bench. "I suppose I can expect no more," he said, then his forehead creased, and he looked up, with hope. "But . . . could you tell me if your son still has friends there? Or relatives? Anyone he might be in contact with? Maybe he has names, addresses, something . . . even an old address book?"

Stunned at his persistence, Jack could only stare in disbelief at the credulity. For a moment suspicion pinged at the back of his head. He stepped back. "This girl must mean a lot to you to risk asking me that."

"She means everything!" Alec's voice shook, naked agony written all over his face, and when he locked eyes with Jack, it made him feel instantly guilty for doubting the man. "I know what you think of me. I think the same. I am a fool for approaching a policeman with questions like this. A policeman who suspects underlying motives for my questions." His eyes implored Jack. "Maybe you think I have ulterior motives, and I get it. But I'm not here for that. I'm here because I have no one else. It could be illegal to bring names and addresses from East Germany—I don't know. But why would it be?" He ran a hand through his hair, shoulders sagging. "When I read about your son, I thought . . . here's someone who must've had help. Someone who had to plan all this. I had to try."

Jack sighed, dismayed that his fears about being taken advantage of were now sitting right in front of him. Alec, with his clumsy desperation, was precisely the kind of person Jack had been afraid of encountering after that newspaper article. Yet, there he was, with his pleas and his pain, so transparent.

Jack sat down. Pharo didn't like it and pulled on his leash. He wanted to leave. "Look, Alec, think about it. She's the best person to find someone to trust. It would be impossible to work an escape from this end."

Alec sighed and nodded. "I suppose. Still, can't you ask him? Your son?"

"No, I will not. He's only a kid and has been through enough. Besides, he had nothing but a swimsuit when he ran." That should do it.

Jack rose. Pharo danced around his feet, and pulled on the leash, eager to get going. The mosquitoes were coming out for their supper. He gave the man, still slumped forward, a last appraising glance. Was he for real? If he were acting, it was a superb performance. But Pharo didn't like him, and that was good enough for Jack.

By the time he got home, he'd banished the strange encounter at the park from his mind. He ate the cold cuts for supper, thankful he didn't have to attempt to prepare it himself. He snickered at how quickly he'd grown accustomed to someone preparing meals for him. And a variety, all delicious. *Well,* he consoled himself, *we are useful guinea pigs for her to try out what she learns at NAIT.* He opened a bottle of Pilsner and walked toward the living room, but as he passed Max's bedroom door, he stopped short, just staring.

Might as well do it now when he wouldn't be interrupted.

Feeling slightly like an invader in his son's bedroom, he convinced himself it was necessary. He started searching, making sure to not leave any signs of disturbance. In the dresser's bottom drawer, he saw a Doritos chip bag folded into a bundle the size of a paperback book. Without touching it, Jack sized it up. Max had bought a bag of Doritos in Spokane, he surmised and kept the semi-waterproof package to secure something else. It looked safe to handle. No traps. Jack carefully slid the rubber band from it and withdrew a notebook. He turned it over, inspecting both sides, looking for a pin, traces of powder, a small piece of paper, strand of hair; all traps to warn of intruders. When he saw nothing, he opened the notebook, still careful in case something loose fell out. Breathing easier, he leafed through it, looking at pages randomly. It was the record that Ursula had kept of Max's swimming meets. The place, the competitors, Max's scores. A belt around Jack's chest tightened, and he blinked, eyelids stinging, thinking of Ursula carefully keeping a record of their son's achievements for Jack to see.

Why hadn't Max shown it to him then? He sighed, realizing he knew why. A lack of trust. Somehow, it wasn't there. Even Olivia had noticed it. Jack ran his fingers over a page, reading the words Ursula had penned; the cities, names unfamiliar to him. He noted one name. Harris. Odd name for a German, he thought.

Jack chuckled. There may have been more than one soldier leaving behind a child. He put everything back together, stopping at the door to ensure the room was as he'd found it. The kid was neat. Everything in its place, another sign of indoctrination, he thought. Somewhat down in spirit, he closed the door and went to the fridge for another beer. Later, in bed, he wondered if Max missed his competitors, likely encountering the same ones at every competition, studying their styles and weaknesses, and striving to outdo each other. Amidst the thoughts spinning around his head was the fleeting idea that Max regretted his escape. Just as fast, he dismissed it. Max's life and future prospects were just beginning. He'd be home from his fishing trip tomorrow and start school the next day. Things would settle.

With a tired smile, Jack finally let sleep take him.

Jack reported in for duty the following day. Thank goodness Wager didn't mention Howard Winslow, and no news came in about it either. Not that Jack expected any. Chen looked glum, and Jack snickered to himself. He wondered if Chen would mention moving into the apartment block again. But perhaps an overnight think took him out of his enchantment with Olivia and got him back into real life.

The day was hectic, keeping Jack on his toes—mostly with paperwork. He finished up his reports with one eye on the clock. On the way home just after four, weekenders and the end of holiday people clogged up the roads. At least they had enjoyed a fun-filled long weekend, the last of the summer. But the day had that lingering scent of sun-crisp leaves recovering from a morning frost. Last-minute school shoppers with short tempers didn't help the traffic, and crossing the river to home seemed to take forever.

Fifteen minutes after he did, Roark Sullivan's station wagon drew up to the curb, and Jack ran outside to help unload. Roark looked hot and frazzled. Tommy and Max not so much. They looked happy until Max saw Jack, and his smile faded. Jack's enthusiastic "Welcome home" did nothing to bring it back. Max grumpily got his backpack and sleeping bag out and made to take it inside without a word.

"Hang on there, Max," Jack called after him, stepping closer and lowering his voice. "Thank Mr. Sullivan for his trouble."

Red-faced, Max returned back to Roark. "I apologize, Mr. Sullivan. Thank you for a great weekend. I had such a good time and learned a lot about fishing. I hope next time you go, you won't forget me."

Roark patted Max's shoulder. "I enjoyed your company, Max. There'll be plenty more times. You can count on it."

Max shot Jack a venomous look, picked up his gear, and headed to the apartment. Jack watched as his son dumped his backpack on the step, fumbled his keys and let himself into the building. A mix of hurt and a simmering rage twisted in Jack's gut. His fists clenched at his sides, his jaw tightening. Roark, thankfully, was instructing Tommy and failed to notice the tense exchange.

"Take what you can carry, and I'll pull around into the parking lot, and we can unpack the rest. I'll be along shortly. Just a word with Jack." Tommy threw Jack a quick look, then obediently loaded himself up and started across the street to their apartment block.

"I brought back a couple of walleye for you. Not too big, so they're tasty. They're on ice, so if you pop them in the fridge, they'll be good for supper."

"Thanks. I have just the person who knows what to do," said Jack. "Guess you don't have time for a beer?"

"Another time. And my name is Rory." He indicated his clothes. "Can't wait for a shower." He pressed his lips together and looked uncertain.

Jack felt a tingle along his arms. "Everything okay?"

"Did you send anyone to keep an eye on Max at the lake?" Rory looked embarrassed.

Not hiding his alarm, Jack sputtered. "Certainly not. You see something fishy?" He grinned at the quip, then sobered.

"Sunday morning. Tommy and Max went swimming. They had a race. Nobody was around much, just a few early morning dippers." Roy's face opened in wonder. "You should have seen that kid go. Can he swim? I thought it was a machine out there. No wonder his shoulders and arms are so developed."

"He was a competitive swimmer," Jack said, with pride along with envy he hadn't witnessed it for himself. "But he's reluctant to swim here. He's afraid someone for East Germany will arrive and snatch him back."

"Poor kid," Rory agreed, but his face grew thoughtful. "After he got out of the water, someone who'd watched him came up to us. I thought he was just another person on the beach, but Max took one look at him and seemed frightened. The guy looked okay to me. He admired Max's technique and kept complimenting him, then trudged off."

Jack mused on it. "I think it will take time for Max to become used to swimming without fear. He's just adjusting. What makes him think I sent him? I'm worried about that."

"Because it wasn't the last time we saw him. We had an open fire going in the campground and a few campers sitting around bragging about their catch if you know what I mean." Roy laughed and held out his hands, measuring imaginary fish lengths. "The guy suddenly appeared and sat beside Max. He started asking him where he learned to swim like that . . . plus other things."

"What other things?" Jack's suspicion sharpened. "Describe him to me."

Rory rubbed his chin, considering. "Medium height. Not young, maybe late thirties, early forties. Dressed okay, not a bum."

"Did he give a name?"

"Al, or something like that."

Sweet Jesus, thought Jack. Fury shook him, and he clenched his fists. Rory saw his face, and his own lips thinned.

"You know him?"

"No. But someone like him approached me last night wanting information on . . . well, it doesn't matter. How did Max react?"

"He got up and moved. I thought maybe he just didn't like the guy, and I can appreciate he might be wary of strangers. But Max really didn't like him. I was ready to get up and tell him to move on. If it hadn't been for the people there . . ." The already large muscles of his biceps fluttered. "I decided to just let our indifference send a message, and he'd leave. But then . . ." he stopped, unsure, eyeing Jack.

Jack said nothing, just watching him, letting the silence ask its own question.

"I saw Max tuck a knife under his sleeping bag that night. A pretty big knife." Rory faced Jack squarely, his eyes angry. "I didn't say anything, but Tommy noticed. I don't like it, Jack. If there is any danger that Max might include Tommy in, I will squash this friendship right now."

So Max had taken the knife against Jack's wishes. "Rory," Jack gripped the other man's elbow. "Remember that Max grew up under the Stasi, always afraid they'd come to arrest him. People couldn't trust anybody, their friends, their neighbours, nobody. It will take a while to get over that. He's only a kid and bought that knife when he defected, just in case they caught up to him. He's never used it." Jack suddenly had clarity. *He thinks policemen are all the same.* "I am a cop, Rory. No wonder he thought I might have sent one to watch over him." He put his hand on Rory's arm. "Thanks for telling me. And I can't thank you enough for looking after Max, but please don't stop Tommy from being friends with him. It will just prove to him he can't trust anyone. Right now, I have to make this right." He turned to go.

"The fish?" Roarke reminded him. He took a bag of fish surrounded by ice from the cooler and handed it to Jack. His eyes drifted past Jack's shoulders. "Is that her?"

Jack sighed and turned. Olivia was rounding the corner from the parking lot, saw them and stopped.

"That's Olivia."

Rory laughed. "Tommy talks about her as if she'd drifted to earth on a lotus blossom. From here, she looks harmless enough."

"Finally," Jack said and laughed. "A man with common sense. Thanks for the Walleye, Rory. We'll talk soon." He left the man to his tasks and caught up with Olivia. He held up the package. "Dinner."

Jack followed Olivia up the stairs. After dinner, he decided. No more playing the part of Max's understanding father. He was the authority in this family, he told himself, and it was time he got some answers.

15

"IF you didn't send him, then someone did," Max's chin set in stubborn lines. "They never change, these Stasi agents. Always right beside us when we left the country. They followed us even when we competed in East Germany." He turned his back on Jack and started pulling things out of his backpack. "I know the method. He was after me."

Pharo, who had followed Jack into the bedroom, sensed the tension in the atmosphere and pushed his nose into Jack's hand to reassure him. Jack absentmindedly scratched his ears.

"Max." Jack got in between his son and the open backpack on the bed. "We're not done here."

Max recoiled. "Just like the Stasi. Never done. You can't trust anyone on the team, even when they are friendly. Stasi blackmails people to report on other people, even friends. I always pretended because they would not let me compete in other countries if I refused. They wanted reports on everything. Pictures of inside, places where we stayed, what Western competitors talked about, if they approached our swimmers. I always said I saw nothing."

He faced Jack, his sunburnt cheeks flushed further with anger. "Mutter told me you were a Canadian soldier, but now you are police. Your kind who come knocking at the door or wait in plain sight, so you are always aware they suspect you. Even here, I must be on guard." Max's voice quivered. He sat on the edge of the bed and lowered his eyes to hide the tears threatening to spill from them. Pharo moved closer, put his face on Max's knee, and gave a soft *'baroo'* noise in sympathy.

"I'm not your enemy, Max." Jack sighed and kept his tone gentle. "Sure, I am a cop, but unlike the Stasi or KGB, we don't harass ordinary citizens or watch them go about their ordinary lives. Were any of them unkind when the RCMP and Border Services picked you up?"

Max shook his head. "No. It was the first time I felt safe since I ran from Seattle."

"Yet you assume I don't want to keep you safe." Jack pushed away the backpack and sat beside Max. It smelt of lake and damp swimsuit. Encouraged that Max didn't shift away from him, he just sat and let his last words linger in the air. Finally, he said quietly, "You're my son, Max, and I love you. Just as I loved your mother with all my being. It broke my heart when she left me in Germany. That phone call telling me you were in Canada erased all that pain, and the bad years disappeared. I can't tell you what joy I felt."

Max looked up at him, searching Jack's face for lies. Jack's heart nearly stopped when he saw the longing in his son's eyes. He could only look back at him and nod his head. The tension in the room eased, and Jack finally took a breath. "Besides," he pointed at Pharo. "Dogs are good at reading people. Do you think a smart dog like Pharo wouldn't know a Stasi agent right off?"

Max's laugh quavered. "He'd know right away and bare his teeth."

"Right." The implication was plain, and Jack let it rest. "This man at the lake. Tell me about him. I think he was the same man who approached me in the park yesterday. He must have come right from the lake." He listened while Max repeated what Rory had told him.

"Mr. Sullivan saw he bothered me. I knew he and Tommy would prevent him from taking me if that was his aim." Max's mouth turned down. "I wondered why they would send an agent here to question me. It is a lot of trouble, even for them. So I thought he might have come to kill me and then brag that death awaited anyone trying to leave Germany." Scared eyes in a tight face turned to Jack.

"Did this man ask about anything you brought with you?" Jack leaned forward and massaged Max's shoulder to ease his son's worry.

Max wrinkled his forehead. "I didn't give him a chance to ask anything." He sat up straighter, then. "The man you saw yesterday. Was it him?"

"Yes, I'm certain." Jack told him how he approached him.

Max nodded. "Same name, only he said Alan. But his voice was begging, like he needed a friend, someone to talk to."

"That's him, alright." Jack wondered if the man's story was sincere, recalling his tone of desperation. "He told me his orphan niece, still in East Germany, was desperate to defect, and he thought you could give him names of people who helped you. He thought the same people might help her."

"Who could believe such a story?" Max's mouth curled in disbelief. "No one would give out names so easy. He wanted names so the Stasi could arrest them. Such a fool," He snorted, "to think you would believe him."

Jack chuckled, averting his gaze. "Thanks for the vote of confidence."

"What does that mean?" Max showed alarm.

"Only that I'm relieved you have faith in my judgement." Jack shifted the topic. "I sent him off with a flea in his ear. Convinced him you defected with nothing but your swimsuit."

"You gave him fleas?" asked Max, bewildered.

Jack chuckled again. "He had to be content with the small amount of information he got." He paused for a moment while Max patted Pharo and digested the meaning of the flea in his ear. "But it got me thinking of what you said you brought. A record of your swimming career and competitions so you could show me," Jack continued. "Why have I never seen it?"

Max stopped playing with Pharo's head and sat up. He said nothing, appearing to be thinking. "I don't know," he confessed. "I wanted to, but I put it away. Maybe I thought it might be painful for you to think of her." Grey eyes pleading for understanding, he stared up at Jack. "I want to be honest with you, but I hope you understand it is hard for me to see something she wrote. I miss her so much. She was more than a mutter; she was my only friend. We could speak freely. We said things, like a code, that only we understood. She taught me everything." Nearly choking on his last words, Max stopped.

"Of course I understand," Jack said quickly, sorry now that he had mentioned the list. He put his hand on Max's shoulder. "Never mind, son. Anytime you're ready. We have a lifetime ahead of us." He squeezed his shoulder, emphasizing his words.

Disappointed and uneasy, he would have liked Max to show him now. He'd had the same uneasy feeling while reading random pages in the notebook. Was he missing something, or was it only Ursula's handwriting stirring up forgotten memories and sadness?

"Mr. Sullivan tells me you swim like a machine in action. He was absolutely astounded by your ability. I wish I had been there to see it."

"He did?" Max sucked in his lips, blushing. "I had a good time showing Tommy what I can do. Next time we go fishing, maybe you will come with us. Then I show you."

About to leave the room, Jack turned. "Max, Mr. Sullivan saw the knife you tucked under your sleeping bag," he said, reluctant to break the cheerful note. "I told him you were probably afraid that you might have to defend yourself, but maybe you might tell him how it came into your possession and why you took it camping."

Max's eyes widened, and he stiffened before dropping his eyes to fidget with the hem of his shirt. "I'm sorry. You told me to not take it, and I did anyway."

"He worried why you didn't trust he would have protected you. Also that Tommy might get hurt, son. You must understand that boys your age in Canada don't need a hunting knife. As a matter of fact, a knife in your possession will concern any policeman in Canada. You definitely cannot carry it to school, or you will attract big trouble, and not just from me." Max stared at the floor, the corners of his mouth twitching as he absorbed the information. Jack noted the slight nod of his head, a silent acknowledgment, but Jack suspected he only listened out of politeness. "Better turn in early tonight. School starts tomorrow, and then Olivia will take you to the doctor. His medical report is the last step to make you and me legal. Then, we'll celebrate big time." Jack gave a thumbs up and left, hoping he gave Max plenty to reflect on.

He emerged just as Olivia headed into hers. Jack stopped and glared at her. Had she been outside Max's door the whole time? She turned and stood her ground.

"I can read your face and the accusation," she said. "Yes, I heard your talk about the knife, but that was all. I finished cleaning up the last of the dinner and getting rid of fish guts. So, it was purely by accident. I walked by just now." She waited for Jack to reply.

"Hearing what we say isn't the point. Though I wonder how much of it gets back to your father."

She drew herself up. Her mouth opened, then shut. She tossed her head and turned away without reply.

Jack's words stopped her. "Or Anderson, then? Who will then tell Luke?"

She stopped, her face toward the door, then slowly turned, fists clenched at her sides, as if controlling herself from lunging at him. The tension radiating from her was palpable, like a coiled spring ready to snap. Jack braced himself for the storm. "Am I the only one to remember we had a pact? What goes on in this apartment stays here. If you haven't already noticed, between classes, cooking, and homework, I don't have a lot of spare time to meddle in your affairs."

He didn't hesitate and shot right back. "You don't have to cook every day. I can make meals, too." He studied her face, uncertainty creeping as he met her gaze. "I thought you enjoyed cooking," he added lamely.

"Don't try that on me," she snapped, her voice sharp as a blade. "You're as bad as my father. Cooking is my life." Her eyes narrowed at him. "So now you threaten to shut me out of the kitchen, too? I was referring to my time limits, and you know it."

Ashamed of his loss of control, Jack flushed at her barb. "Okay. I deserve that, and I apologize." He took a deep breath, then another, and exhaled in a long puff. The time was now to say it. "I realize NAIT will take up most of your time, Olivia. As it should do. After all, it's why you are here." He moistened his lips. "But now you're all set up, Luke may agree that you find your own place. You might even move in and share costs with a fellow student. I could speak to Anderson. Together, we'll find a place."

Olivia stared at him, eyes wide, the colour leaving her face. "It's too late," she whispered. "There are no vacancies. Any reasonable place is gone now that university is in, and you know it. If Dad finds out you want me to leave, he won't argue; he'll just yank me out." She opened her mouth, closed it, and shut her eyes. "You can't hate me that much," she mumbled.

The door behind him opened. Max peered out, saw Olivia's panic and said, "What is wrong?" His voice trembled.

Jack closed his eyes, lifted his head to the ceiling and sighed. "No, Olivia, it isn't dislike. It's indifference," he said and saw her wince. "What I hate is coming to my home and finding the situation already arranged without my input. As if I am one of Luke's gofers. We dance around each other, trying to be civil. The entire atmosphere is crazy. Luke purposely engineered this situation, and he's using you to show me he has the last word. He is controlling my life through you. It's intolerable." Jack leaned against the hall wall, frustrated. "Moving out is the only solution. I'm sorry."

"He's forcing you to stay here?" Max was obviously confused, his head turning between Jack and Olivia until Jack's eyes told him to back off.

"Why should my dad care about controlling you?" Olivia's expression was bewildered. "He said you left years ago. You were my age, and he never saw you again." She shook her head. "No. You're wrong."

Surprised, Jack considered. "Anderson never told you that Luke and I met here. Last Spring?"

Her eyebrows shot up, expression clearly surprised.

Jack gave her the short version. "He thought he'd move some of his operations into Edmonton, and I made sure he failed. He had to leave in a hurry."

Olivia laughed. "You're kidding." But unsure, she examined his expression and saw he was serious. Her face lit up, and her eyes twinkled. "Too precious."

"Anderson didn't tell you?" Jack pushed. Maybe she really was innocent.

Her laughter turned into derision. "No. Believe me, I'd be lucky to get an answer if I asked Anderson what the weather report says." Her tone was bitter. Her eyelids blinked away tears. "I thought he . . ." She pressed the heels of her palms against her eyes for a fast second, then away. "Never mind. But whatever your situation is with my father, it's half what mine is." She came towards him and leaned against the opposite wall as though they had discovered a mutual bond. She folded her arms and crossed her feet, ready for a cozy chat. "At least you got away scot-free. I'm in a prison where even the warden is against me. Only the other inmate likes me." She smiled at Max, who shot her a smile back.

Jack sighed and clasped his hands behind his head, fighting a temptation to sympathize.

He gritted his teeth. Damn Luke. There must be ways to get rid of him for good. Maybe even turn the tables on him. Jack felt some excitement at the idea. Let the spying work from that side. Find his intentions and turn them against him. Two can play at this game.

Across from him, Olivia mirrored his posture, she may not have been plotting, but she pouted, her lower lip jutting out as her brow furrowed in frustration. They stared at each other in a long silence, hoping the other had a solution. Max watched both of them. Pharo came into the hall. He planted his feet at the corner of the living room and gazed at them crowded into the narrow passage, exchanging distrust with each other. He did a tentative tap dance, asking for his nightly trip outside. Silence reigned.

Jack felt a snicker rising in his throat. He pressed his lips together, desperate to smother it, but the effort backfired, resulting in a sneeze that morphed into a choking snort. Olivia dropped her hands and looked at him, startled, then worried. Jack put his palm against his mouth, but she saw his eyes sparkle, and her concern turned to amusement. She gave a tentative laugh. Behind Max, Pharo yodelled, and Max yelped in a surprised jerk. Jack pointed his finger at Max and laughed out loud. Then Max laughed. Soon, they all were laughing at their ridiculous stalemate.

After a few minutes, Jack waved his hands to regain some semblance of authority. "A big day tomorrow. Max, make sure you put your dirty camp clothes in the laundry basket. Sort what you need for school tomorrow. Olivia, get to bed. You need your beauty sleep. And I'm tired."

Despite the Mexican standoff, Jack lay in bed, looking at the ceiling for solutions. He went over his talk with Rory. He knew he needed to address Rory's concerns about the incident at the lake before speculation festered into something bigger. If Max lost his friendship with Tommy, how would it affect the fragile trust he had with his new life? And why was Max withholding the notebook from him? The excuse was overly sentimental and didn't gel. Ursula had told Max she'd made up the notebook especially for Jack to see his son's life as he was growing up. So, if that was the sole purpose of the notebook, why hold it back? He frowned. What he'd noticed in the notebook pages still pinged at the fringes of his mind.

16

JACK arrived the next day and found Chen leaning against the entrance, arms crossed, a smirk lurking at the corners of his mouth. Jack didn't need to ask—Chen, ever the forecaster of bad news. How did he always get advanced information?

"You're in for it again." Chen stepped aside and held the door open for him. "Straighten your tie and comb your hair. Simpson is asking for you." He shot Jack an evil grin. "Along with two plain clothes in there."

Before Jack could respond, Chen left him and sprinted up the stairs. He took a breath and followed more sedately. He couldn't help but peer out the stairway door on the third floor to see if anyone was in the main foyer leading to Simpson's office. Seeing nobody, he darted through and down the corridor and through the squad room door.

Wager motioned for him to come over, his other hand fidgeting with his mustache, a sign that he was about to blow up at anyone nearby. Usually, it was a suspect in for an interview, but today, it appeared Jack was the target. Assuming a look of innocence, Jack raised his eyebrows at him.

"Simpson wants us in his office, pronto," he only said, voice controlled but strained. His eyes told a different story, holding tension and blame. "His secretary says the D.C. looks like someone whose sails have suddenly lost wind at the last lap of the race."

Jack couldn't help a stifled snicker.

"When he was in the lead," Wager added, turning Jack's snicker off.

"Whatever it is, it's nothing to do with me, Paul," Jack insisted, trying to sound convincing. Had Simpson found out about Winslow? Better to tell Wager first off. "Can I talk to you first? You need to hear this."

"Nothing to do with you? It's always to do with you," Wager grumbled, ignoring Jack's request. He grabbed his suit jacket from the back of his chair, straightened his tie, and motioned for Jack to follow.

They waited outside Simpson's office until the door opened, and they were called in. Simpson's face was rosier than usual. He had his uniform jacket on, all correct and buttoned. He indicated the two men seated on the couch in front of the small table. No introductions.

Jack's eyes flickered to the older man—bristly, short brush cut, and clean-shaven face—then to the younger man beside him with a neatly trimmed mustache and slightly longer, mousy brown hair. Both men appraised him in turn, expressions stony. RC Intel, Jack concluded. He hazarded a glance at Wager, wondering if he saw the same, but his face was neutral. Simpson pointed to the two empty chairs on the side facing the two men. He sat behind the desk, waiting, eyes portraying nothing. This isn't the first go around for him, Jack thought, and found a new respect for the D.C.

"Detective Constable Tuesday," said the older man. The younger kept his eyes on Jack. Wager, he ignored, and Jack knew that this man would remember every word he said.

"This man Hudek. How did he come to your attention? Start from the beginning, and please tell me everything you know about him."

"May I ask why?" Jack ventured, "So that I can stress any points that interest you?"

"Just answer the Staff Sergeant, Tuesday," Simpson ordered, tone brisk.

Jack started with his conversation with Jassy and told the whole story in sequence, sticking to relevant points, Howard's disappearance, and their investigation so far. Instinct told him to leave out Howard's reappearance as a bellhop at the Chateau Lacombe and their conversation. He reminded himself Howard's safety depended on keeping silent. Best to add information later than try to retrieve it.

When he finished, both men stared at him, examining his expression, their eyes hard. Jack hoped his weren't transparent. In the long silence, he blanked his mind using an old army trick. Concentrate on a brick wall, seeing only bricks and nothing else.

"Thank you, Officer," the older man said finally, "for relating the facts without additional enhancement. Now, what about your conclusions? Any opinions, anything that occurred to you during your investigation?" Four pairs of eyes swivelled to Jack. Wager's and Simpson's telegraphed a mutual warning not to wander into the land of fantasy. Wager shifted in his chair and stilled. Jack got his message.

No tilting at windmills.

Jack forged ahead. "Hudek is not what he seems to be," Jack started, feeling Wager's electricity jolt. "His business. He's been here maybe four years but has a thriving, lucrative setup. It's common knowledge in the law office where he finalizes his transactions."

Jack saw the younger man nod. "You deduced that how?"

"From our initial questioning, before we decided to halt our investigations. I could only conclude that by the number of his transactions, his business was thriving." Jack didn't look at Simpson but felt the man's uneasy shift in his chair. The older man only said, "Continue."

"It grew too quickly, considering he likely had no contacts before he arrived. The missing file bothered me. I knew Jassy. She is a solid personality and not one for flights of imagination. Her death still bothers me." Jack shrugged. "But just a hunch, I admit. Everyone agrees that Hudek's lawyer, Bernie Kepler, is morally solid and ethical but is afraid of his client. Maybe because he is important to the firm because he brings in substantial fees. Kepler may be too eager to please." Simpson cleared his throat, and Jack added quickly. "There is no foundation for that opinion, you understand."

The younger intel man's mouth lifted at one corner. Jack continued, "But it isn't conjecture that Howard Winslow examined Hudek's file. And now Winslow has disappeared. Another totally uncommon action. Winslow's wife says that he has a history of Army intelligence, and I wondered if when he looked at Hudek's file and personal actions, he deduced that Hudek might be an enemy agent."

Simpson's voice intervened, his tone sharp enough to splinter concrete. "Stop right there, Officer Tuesday. You have slipped into flights of fancy," He turned to the Staff Sergeant. "Not one shred of evidence, let alone a suggestion, in any of the reports. As I told you. I cannot, in all good conscience and police procedure, allow Detective Tuesday to continue along this line." He glared at Jack, telling him he'd let their side down. "He cannot assume the lawyer's disappearance has anything to do with his law firm or the people who work there."

"Well?" The older man's voice was calm but commanding as his eyes pinned Jack. The younger man leaned forward slightly, his gaze keen with interest.

"As I said, a lot of money has been moving around since Hudek started his export-import business. My question is, where is that money going? What firms received export permits for all that money, and are they making profits? The appropriate taxable profits? To account for that amount, a lot of goods have to be imported from Czechoslovakia. Besides glass and industrial parts, what else is there? Does Canada import a lot of industrial parts?" Jack shrugged. "Maybe we do. If a communist satellite can produce reliable parts, that is."

"Jesus," whispered Wager quietly under his breath.

"Detective Constable Tuesday." Simpson's face, already flushed, darkened to a furious red. "As far as the Edmonton Police Service is concerned, these are unsupported suppositions. Even if there is any inkling of truth in what you claim, and there is not, we don't investigate foreign interference." His voice rose with each word. "We are not in the business of chasing spies. Are we clear?"

"Sir. Yes sir. I know that. They asked, and I answered."

Simpson's jaws grew rigid with tension, and the air inside the office grew thick. Jack could feel Wager's eyes drill into him with the unspoken plea to 'shut up.'

"Deputy Chief," interrupted the Staff Sergeant. Jack wondered about their names. They hadn't offered any. Names would be fake anyway, he decided. They never give their real ones. "Officer Tuesday is right. I asked for his opinion. We are here for information only." His eyes zeroed in on Jack. "However, as far as this Police Unit and you are concerned," he nodded at Jack. "All investigations must be halted. Everything. Furthermore, our talk here is in confidence and any reference to it, or us, will remain in this room." He paused, looked at his partner for a moment, and added, "We already have an ongoing action on this man, Hudek, and interference will not be tolerated." He eyed each of them in turn. "Do you understand?"

Simpson breathed a sigh of relief and threw up his hands, palms wide. "That is the best news I've heard all day." His gaze slid over to Wager, his earlier anger dissolving into tired resolve. "You have your orders, Detective Sergeant. Goodness knows we have enough cases in hand without nosing around in matters that don't concern us."

"Yes, Chief," Wager said, and they both looked at Jack as if he was a parolee who failed to keep up his end of the parole conditions. Resenting the dressing down in the presence of others, Jack pressed his lips together. Out of the corner of his eye, he saw the younger man shoot him a sympathetic grin and shrug. Jack cheered, sensing he was familiar with the same lecture.

Just great, thought Jack, his thoughts turning to Winslow and a new danger. *I have to warn him.* From what the staff sergeant said, they definitely had an agent in place. Winslow might jeopardize him, and vice versa. Cursing himself for ignoring his first instinct and getting into a pact with Howard, he wondered if he could get the Staff Sergeant alone and let him know.

Aware the others were watching him, Jack straightened. Pressing his lips together, he lifted his shoulders and let them drop as if relieved to let a burden go. "Happy to get back to normal, sir," he told Simpson. The staff sergeant looked satisfied while the younger man lifted one corner of his mouth in a half smile. As usual, Wager just stared at him, poker-faced.

Wager led the way back to the squad room, head lowered, not looking at Jack or discussing what had gone on.

"Sorry, Wager," Jack said, his voice low as they reached the squad room door. "Just goes to show what one brief phone call asking for information can balloon into an ugly mess."

Wager didn't reply, but at the door to the room, he turned to Jack. "If you've kept anything from me, Jack, I won't cover for you." His voice was cold, his tone final. "Whatever trust I've had left will be gone. Keep that in mind."

Without waiting for a reply, Wager walked through the door, leaving Jack standing in the hall, chastened. Jack's stomach twisted. He despised himself for deceiving Wager, knowing full well what would happen if he confessed about Winslow now after what had just gone down with Simpson. The fallout would be brutal. I've got to warn Winslow to back off completely, Jack thought, feeling the weight of the situation settle heavily on him. Winslow would have to resurface on his own and deal with whatever came. He made a mental note to warn Edina to be extra vigilant.

When Wager began assigning the morning cases in the squad room, Jack was grateful to be left out of it, happy to blend into the background for once. That night, as Jack left the building for his car in the parking lot, he found the younger RCMP Intel leaning on the fender, waiting for him.

"Got time for a coffee?" He straightened and glanced at his watch. "How about a hamburger? I haven't eaten since breakfast. And I could use the company." Without another word, he waited for Jack to unlock the doors and slid into the passenger seat.

Jack bent to peer at him through the driver's window. "Maybe you'd rather come to my place for dinner . . . Mr. . . . er, got a name?"

"Dave will do. No, I have a date at the airport. Only time to grab a coffee and burger. I thought you might know a good place for one." He raised his eyebrows. "Are you going to get in, or does the car move by magic?"

17

"THIS is actually a good burger. Fries too." Dave wiped crumbs from his moustache, the napkin catching a smear of ketchup as he reached for a clean one from the dispenser.

"You should try the toasted Danish," Jack said absently, his mind consumed with thoughts of Harry McNaughton—Edina's brother—and his murder in the alleyway farther down the strip from them. They sat in Faucets, a cozy diner on the city's south side at 104th Street. Jack gulped the rest of his coffee and searched for the waitress to come by with a refill.

"Toasted Danish? There are such things?"

"They make their own," Jack told him.

"You chose a good place, then," Dave mumbled over a bite of his hamburger.

"And you're already halfway to the airport," Jack agreed, hinting that maybe Dave's flight would have an early check-in, letting him get on with figuring out how to warn Howard. He studied the person across from him. He wasn't as young as Jack first assumed. The smooth skin didn't hide the faint lines around his mouth and eyes, signs of someone who'd seen more years than his boyish features suggested.

Dave dipped a fry into a glob of ketchup and bit the end off. "Quite the dressing down you took from your Deputy Chief. I'm sorry we were there to see it. Embarrassing all around." He inspected his cup, saw he needed coffee and waved his arm at the waitress. They waited while she refilled their cups and squelched away on sponge-soled shoes. Jack watched her zigzag around the tables for a moment before he looked back at Dave and shrugged. "Not the first time."

Dave chuckled. "I suppose not." He read Jack's expression and added, "Yes, we did a check on you. So we'd know what we were up against." He grinned again. "Don't worry, we forget as soon as it's cleared."

"Sure you do." Jack's tone dripped with sarcasm. "I am used to getting a dressing-down. In the Army, officers rant at other ranks a lot. Empty blustering, to show who is boss." Seeing Dave purse his lips, he grinned.

"And you thought that's what we are?" Dave asked, a quizzical expression in his eyes.

"Well, in my experience, your sort are a lot of arrogant snobs who regularly ignore the law and smile while you do."

Dave's eyebrows rose in an arch as Jack spoke. "Not a fan, then," was all he said, seemingly unconcerned.

"What's your rank, anyway? Sergeant? Constable? Inspector?" Jack saw a waver in Dave's eyes, leaving as soon as it flashed. "Ah, it is, isn't it? You outrank the Staff. I thought so."

"Why?" asked Dave. For the first time, Jack saw unfeigned interest. "Why did you think so?" he asked, but not confirming Jack's guess.

"You listened, digesting everything and everyone in that room. Your Staff didn't order you to take notes. You should tell him the way he sits, it defers to you. I saw him glance at you a couple times to see how you reacted."

"I'll tell him," Dave chuckled. His eyes swept over Jack's face again. "Now we've got all the preliminaries out of the way, you can tell me what you didn't say during the interview. And I have no doubts you are holding back information." He shot Jack a smile that wasn't a smile, just a thinning of lips over his teeth. "So tell me where your missing lawyer is. And what he is up to."

Dave's eyes hardened. He pushed aside his plate and leaned forward. "Either tell me now or face the consequences. This is not a game, Detective. It's life or death."

Jack flushed. "I'm aware of that. And yes, I discovered where Howard Winslow disappeared. But only yesterday. Well, late Saturday night. And no," Jack held up his palm to forestall the inevitable question, "neither of us were aware you might be involved. I read him the Riot Act and told him to stop whatever the hell he was doing. You know what lawyers are like. All persuasion and practiced lawyer talk. He swore he was that close to finding the evidence proving Hudek is an agent and only needed a bit more time to clinch it." Jack related the entire story, where Howard was and their conversation. "In any event, I intended to put a stop to it today, even without your order. You cornered me in the parking lot instead, and here I am instead of warning Howard that his time is up."

Jack pushed aside his cold coffee, closely watching Dave's face. "If I'd have told you, you would have just barged in on him, and he is in a precarious spot. In jeopardy, even."

Dave frowned at him like he were speaking a foreign language. "A poor excuse, Detective. We have the means of extracting people who are at risk. All without harm." Dave rubbed his forehead with his fingers. "You've added another headache for us. You and this foolish lawyer."

"He doesn't know you're already involved," Jack hastened to lessen the mess. "Give him a break. He's protecting his law firm solely because of its misuse of their trust account. Think of their trouble if the Law Society moved in. Howard thinks he can remedy it before it gets that far." Jack nodded at the disdain on the other man's face. "Howard was in Germany after the war with Air Force Intel, doing exactly that kind of investigation. He thinks he can handle it."

"Be that as it may," conceded Dave, "as soon it was clear it wasn't the case, that same experience and his profession didn't beg him to refer it to the proper authority." Lips set into a straight line, Dave closed his eyes. "God save us from meddling fools."

Jack flinched, wondering if the remark included him. He supposed he deserved it, going against all his instincts to give Howard what he asked.

When he glanced at Dave, he found the man watching him closely, almost as if reading his thoughts. "Does anyone else know what you've told me?" Dave's eyes narrowed, distrust creeping into his gaze, scrutinizing Jack's every movement.

"No, of course not," Jack lied. "I was going to tell my Detective Sergeant today, but the meeting intervened. Who else would I tell?"

"Normally, I'd turn you into your D.C. for your outrageous behaviour," Dave said. "And see you suspended." His eyes locked onto Jack, the intensity radiating off him. "Your D.C. told us your case record is flawless. He likes you but said you had to be whipped into shape two times a week, or you'd treat the police service as your private Army. The entire department puts up with you because your hunches are solid." Dave's lips curled into a smirk. "He says you'd give a saint an ulcer while you're doing it. Why, I wonder? Who are you really?"

Surprised to hear that Simpson didn't dislike him, Jack kept his expression neutral. "I'm not a wild card or a rogue if that's what you're wondering. I like my job and the people, and I try to do the best job that a cop is supposed to do." Jack shrugged, raised his eyebrows and hoped he looked perplexed. "Although my army career might set me apart. I was young then. Korea taught me to think fast, always have a mate's six and use some initiative." He sighed and crunched the napkin he was holding into a ball.

Dave gave him a speculative look. "Yes, your experience there would have shaped your outlook." Jack waited, but Dave said nothing more about Korea and his POW experience, although odds were he would have been aware of it if he'd investigated his history. Voicing a wonder about who he *really* was meant that his investigation stopped short at Jack's enlistment in the Army. Would he now ask about his life before the Army? Jack was ready with his stock answers.

"I'm due at the airport soon." Dave peeked at his watch. He grabbed the bill and reached into his pocket, bringing out some loose change for a tip. "It was a good hamburger, by the way."

Jack rose. "I'll send a taxi driver to the hotel with a note to Howard. I'll ask him to phone me at home. Urgent. That's the end of my involvement."

The man across from him paused and fixed him with a steady look. "Be careful. I could arrange to have him ousted, but your way is quicker. Just don't make it worse." Dave stood, eyes still locked with Jack "Let's pray it isn't too late." He walked up to the front and the cashier. Shaken, Jack followed. Should he ask Dave if their man was in with Hudek, then told himself not to push it.

Dave's implication that they could retrieve Howard confirmed his suspicion they had a man inside. But the danger was that Howard didn't know and that ignorance could put both men at risk. Jack winced, feeling partly responsible. Howard had been stubborn about staying, but Jack told himself it had been only a day since they'd talked. There was still time.

Jack headed to the airport, concentrating on busy evening traffic as an excuse to dwell in his thoughts instead of conversation. On the approach road leading up to the airport departure level, Dave finally spoke. "That son of yours. Settling in okay, is he?" Jack shot him a quick glance. Of course he'd know Max's background, seeing as his department was responsible for Max's vetting.

"He's made some friends but is still adjusting. We both are, but we're making headway. He started school today." Jack smiled, showing off his pride. "He had no trouble passing the tests."

Dave smiled and pointed. "Go there, at the CP sign," he said, "he's had no real trouble, then?"

Startled, Jack braked a little hard behind a parked tour bus unloading passengers, throwing them both forward against the seat belts. *Real trouble?* "Like what?" he asked, thinking of Alan—Alec or whoever he was. He looked over at Dave. "Something you're not telling me?"

Dave chuckled. "Don't get your knickers in a twist. It's just conversation. These questions are second nature to me. Sometimes I forget how they sound. Doesn't mean there is anything going on." Before Jack could reply, he opened the passenger door, reached over, and slipped a paper into Jack's breast pocket. "My phone number in case you remember anything else. Ask for Dave and leave your name. I'll call you within minutes."

Jack nodded, hoping to never see the man again. He pulled away behind the empty tour bus, the driver smiling as though relieved he'd seen the last of his passengers. Habit made Jack check his rearview mirror. He saw Dave standing by the curb, looking after him like he'd forgotten something. Like he knew more than he was telling.

"Of course he does," Jack said out loud. "It's his stock in trade." Jack sped up on the exit ramp leading to the road from the airport. He'd be late getting home. Thank goodness Olivia was taking Max to his doctor's appointment. He considered how he was going to deliver the envelope to Howard containing a two-dollar bill and an urgent plea to phone him at home. Maybe he'd better just find him and tell him straight that he'd been blown. Otherwise, Howard, being Howard, might just ignore it. After dinner, he'd take Pharo out as usual and drive to the hotel. He'd find a way to slip the concierge a note for Howard. Jack took a deep breath. It was past time to end the investigation into Gordon, Winslow, and Kepler. Obey instructions. Perhaps it was a lesson telling him to listen more. Poor Jassy.

He drove beyond his old parking spot occupied by the little Red Sunbeam Alpine and continued to the number seventeen at the end of the row. Lately, his days and life consisted of nothing but making concessions in one thing or another. He got out of the car, his mouth drooping into an upside-down 'u.'

At the front entrance, Glen was giving four boys the business. Jack hoped none of them were Max's friends. Glen wasn't fond of kids running through the building making a noise, as he repeatedly told Jack.

Close up, he saw they were older. He assumed they were headed for a seminar on the second floor with Professor Waterman, who tutored university students studying for their Master's degrees. Glen opened the door for him. "They are stalking Miss Olivia," he said, as though she were a Southern princess and he, her majordomo. "Poor little thing doesn't realize her attraction. The place would be crawling with boys if I didn't keep an eye out. As if I didn't have enough to do around here. Still, it's a good thing somebody's looking out for her." His glare told Jack he was deficient in that respect.

"Yes, today's been a good day all around," Jack said as he stomped to the stairs.

While inserting his key, he heard Pharo prancing behind the door. Jack bent and made a fuss of greeting him, grateful for the wiggling dog and eager affection. His mood lightened. In the past months, after getting Jack's full attention, Pharo had his domain invaded by Max and now Olivia. The Basenji dancing beside him, Jack continued into the kitchen area where the aroma started him salivating.

Olivia looked up from a pot she was stirring on the stove. "We're having Beef bourguignon. Not real, but sort of. From leftover beef." Her eyes sharpened. "You're a bit late. Bad day?" Her frown became suspicion, then alarm. "Or something else?"

"Smells good," he said, standing up a little straighter. "Relax. Nothing to do with you." Her shoulders eased, telling him he had guessed correctly and sending a pang of shame through him. Did he have her on pins and needles every day, wondering if he would evict her?

"Where's Max?"

"In his room. I drove him to the doctor. It didn't take long. He had a short physical, and then we went to the lab. They took some blood tests, and we came home." Still stirring the pot, she nodded to the table. "Needs setting."

Obediently, Jack got out the place settings, then went down the hall and knocked on Max's door. Hearing a grunt, which he took as an invitation, he entered.

"Hi. Just wondering how you got on your first day," he leaned against the dresser. Max was lying on the bed, reading a sheet of typed paper, others spread out around him.

Max shrugged. "I expected work right away, but we didn't do much," he indicated the paper he was holding, "Just got a list of books we have to buy and met the professors, I mean teachers."

"Doesn't sound exciting, but necessary for new students, I suppose," Jack said, feeling Max was giving him the short version all teens thought adults needed to hear. For reassurance. He smiled.

"We have to go to different rooms for different subjects. The new pupils had a guided tour of the labs; one for Chemistry and another for Physics." He grinned up at Jack. "Ours back home are better equipped."

Jack raised his eyebrows. "Really?"

"Nothing but the best equipment to train minds for service to the state." Max quipped, "But it will be a challenge to draw conclusions to questions when there is not the equipment to prove it."

"Oh. Okay." Jack had nothing to say about equipment. "Everything go alright at the doctor's?"

"Yes. I love 'Liv's sports car. It attracts jealous looks." Max grinned.

"The doctor ask you questions about your medical history that you didn't know?

Max looked confused. "Just if I had measles, chicken pox and that stuff. I answered everything what I knew." His brow wrinkled. "But I don't know why he asked questions about extra food or nutrition while training."

Jack's spidey sense sparked. He slouched over the dresser, seeming uninterested. "And did you get extras?"

"Of course," Max stated, as though it was a given that he'd been treated as an elite. "We all had vitamins and extra nutritional supplements to keep up our physical condition. Training is exhausting and frequent. We have to replenish what we have lost in physical exertion." He sounded like he was repeating a slogan.

"And how did Ursula take that?"

Max shrugged again and continued reading his list. "I never told her. It was only a few vitamins, and I don't have to tell her everything." Again, he sounded as though he were repeating jargon. Jack let it go, cursing inside.

Olivia's voice called them for dinner. Max leaped up. "Good, I am hungry."

"Me too," Jack said. He waited for Max to lead the way, but Max hesitated.

Jack's eyebrows rose in a question. "Something else?"

Max shifted his feet. "I did not want to tell you because you didn't like my actions when I saw him at the lake. But Tommy said if I don't tell you, you will be even more cranky when you find out."

Jack froze. His lips seemed stuck together. "Saw who?" he managed.

"The man at the lake. He followed me again today."

18

"LAST call, guys," Olivia shouted again. "It's on the table."

"We'll be right there," Jack replied, his voice echoing down the hall. He turned to Max. "Same guy? You're sure?"

Max shot him a dirty look. "I am not stupid."

"I know you aren't." Jack raised his hands in mock surrender, hiding his exasperation at his son's reaction. Why was he always on the defensive? "It's something I didn't want to hear, so confirmation is a natural response, Max. You know, like any normal parent." He prodded Max in the midsection and got a blank stare in return.

The unmistakable sound of a pot being set down a little too forcefully came from the kitchen. Olivia was running out of patience. "Thanks for telling me and not keeping that bit of information to yourself. It's always a bad idea in matters like these." *I should know,* his conscience chided him. Another dish rattled, and Jack prodded Max again, this time out the door. "Right now, let's eat. I have to go out later, and I'd like you to come with me. You can tell me the total story."

After Olivia's dinner, her beef concoction was served with a fresh crusty loaf, Jack washed the dishes, and Max dried them. Later, when Jack took down the leash, Pharo ran to the door and eagerly followed the two. When it seemed they were heading for the car, Pharo suddenly became interested in examining the bushes and every blade of grass. Max snickered and waited for him. "Ignore him and keep walking," Jack advised.

Both in the car, Jack rolled down the window and started the car.

It wasn't until he shifted into reverse and started backing away that Pharo rushed to the car. Max got out and opened up the back door. Pharo put his front paws inside and scrabbled his back legs helplessly, faking hardship to get inside. Max laughed, lifted the dog's backside and shoved, closing the door quickly before the dog changed his mind.

As they cruised down 109th, Pharo settled into the back, a steady stream of disgruntled yawns and quiet whining filling the car. At the corner of Saskatchewan Drive, Jack stopped for the red light.

"Did you tell Olivia you were being followed?" Jack asked over the retching noises from the back seat.

"No," Max said. He pointed his thumb toward the back seat and let out a spontaneous giggle.

"He expected to go to the park; he's complaining," Jack grinned. Then his tone shifted. "This man—Alan, Alec, or whoever—didn't try to approach you again?"

"No, he didn't, but he didn't hide from showing himself," Max muttered with a grimace like the memory left a bad taste in his mouth. The light turned green, and Jack eased the car forward and down the short ramp to the High Level Bridge. "Why do people think all teenagers are stupid? Do the boys my age in Canada never think of serious things?" When Jack didn't answer, he continued, "Tommy is not like that. He is serious."

Jack remembered Tommy's diligence in looking after Mira Zamborsky. "Yes, Tommy is different." He wondered if Rory's influence was the reason and felt a pang of jealousy. Would he ever hold that kind of weight in Max's life?

"That man, Al. I shall call him Al," Max kept talking, and Jack had the wits to stay silent. "When we came out of the doctor's, and after I went to give a blood sample, he was still there. Talking to another man. Trying to seem natural so I would believe he was there to meet someone and not following me." Max snorted. "Fat chance."

Fat chance? That was a new expression. Learned from Tommy, no doubt. Jack chuckled silently. "Did you get a good look at who he was meeting?" He chanced a glance at Max. "Good cops always notice the little details, you know."

Max looked interested and proud. "Yes, I am the same. Mutter told me that too. He was tall. About the same as you. About 182 centimeters? Dark hair, well dressed." Max concentrated. "He looked like an important man. You know, like a boss."

"The boss of Al?"

Max considered. "Maybe. They seemed to be having a serious conversation." He laughed. "They didn't see us go. I would like to see his surprise when he saw Olivia's car was gone from the parking."

Jack smiled but kept his focus on the road as he turned down Bellamy Hill Road toward the Chateau Lacombe Hotel. Where to park? He still had no plan to deliver a message to Howard. He decided on a quick in-and-out delivery, waiting until there was a line to the concierge. His eyes darted to the entrance—a steady stream of guests moving along the short entrance roadway, dropping passengers off and then moving on, the doorman preoccupied. Perfect. He could slip the envelope onto the desk unnoticed.

He pulled into a short-term parking spot and turned to Max. "Won't be a minute," he said and got out, feeling in his pocket for the prepared envelope. He moved swiftly toward the entrance, weaving through the crowd and slipped into the hotel behind a guest and bellhop struggling with a cart heaped with luggage. As soon as he crossed the threshold, he spotted Howard coming toward him, a fumbling guest just behind him. Jack held up his hand for attention. Howard's face shifted from surprise to alarm, eyes scanning the lobby for curious faces.

"Howie," Jack beamed, ignoring his panicked expression and shoving the envelope at him. "Glad I caught you. Just a small thank you note from the wife and me." He grabbed Howard's elbow in a crushing appreciative gesture, leaning in just enough to whisper, "Get out now. You're blown." Not waiting for a reaction, Jack spun away, heart thumping against his ribs. He was back in the car in seconds, closing the door and starting the engine in one motion. Max was slouched low in the passenger seat, long legs folded awkwardly, trying to make himself invisible. Minus his usual greeting, Pharo was also hunkered down low in the back seat.

"What?" Jack glanced over and raised an eyebrow

"Drive away quickly," Max whispered, "before he sees me."

In complete agreement to hurry away, Jack was already reversing and lined up behind another car leaving the hotel driveway. His eyes flickering to the rearview mirror. "He-who?"

"That man standing on the top step, talking to the servant in hotel uniform. He's the man who I saw with Al today."

Jack's hands tightened on the steering wheel. He chanced a quick glance as he passed the entrance. Howard came through the door, and the tall man beside the doorman turned and beckoned to him. It was Hudek. Looking servile, Howard obeyed his silent summons. My God, why hadn't he run? What was he doing? Sick, Jack's gaze silently willed Howard to look up and see him inside the car, but in a flash, Jack had driven by, and the opportunity disappeared.

"All clear," Jack announced moments later. Max straightened up and scowled. "Suddenly, I am not liking this. I have the same feeling I get in East Germany when I know something was wrong." He stared at Jack, looking miserable. "I thought it would be better once I got to Canada, and I could relax?"

Jack swallowed hard. A safe place? He wished he could believe that. He laid a hand on Max's forearm, giving it a reassuring squeeze, though his pulse raced. "We'll figure something out," Jack said, trying to inject certainty into his voice. "You don't have to be afraid. You're safe here."

Beads of sweat broke out on Jack's forehead. Fear raised the hair on his forearms. He should know better. He was risking Max's confidence just to make him feel secure.

"What are you thinking?" Max said. "Your face is arguing with itself." He tittered, trusting him, which made Jack feel worse.

"I'm thinking about your safety," Jack replied. "If you feel in your bones that you cannot trust this man, you have to go with your feelings."

"But you just said different." Suspicion narrowed Max's eyes.

"I know. Just make sure you are reading the man's actions right. It's easy to feed your imagination with false signals." He glanced over at Max. "Be careful, stay in crowds, never alone. Don't let fear overtake you. Trust your own strength. Okay?"

"Yes, I understand," Max said. He shot a grateful glance at Jack. "Thank you."

Wow. Jack thought. No resentment at advice or protestations of not being stupid. Just acceptance. Things were looking up.

"Let's take Pharo for a Frisbee game at the park on the way home," Jack said as they drove onto the High Level Bridge. At the word 'park,' Pharo sat up and yodelled a 'yup.'

Jack set his face in pleasant lines, but his mind was a whirlwind of dark thoughts. Was Alec part of Hudek's network? Maybe one of his Canadian importers? Given his meeting in the park, somehow Jack didn't think so. If he was sincere, why did Alec approach Jack for help? Why not Hudek, who by definition had many more contacts in the USSR than Max would? But if Alec was part of Hudek's group, that would mean he was pro USSR as well. Jack damned himself, his jaw clenching—for it meant that the man was a convincing actor and Jack had fallen for a con.

His thoughts shifted to Max, and Jack forced himself to focus. Max is safe, he repeated in his head, trying to believe it. He had to be. But the nagging fear refused to let go. *They think Max has something—something they want. What?* Jack had told anyone within earshot that Max had nothing but the clothes on his back and a swimsuit when he ran, yet they persisted. What about the notebook? But Jack's sneak peek had seen only a list of competitions. Publicly available to anyone. But the question made his heart race, tightening his chest with anxiety. Was Max really in danger?

Howard was the only one who heard Max say that Ursula had made a memory book for Jack. Howard wouldn't have recorded that in any legal files—it was just idle conversation, not something a lawyer would note down. Still, Jack couldn't shake the fear that Howard's involvement was a loose thread dangling over their heads.

He prayed Howard would leave immediately. Jack's warning had been clear enough. He sighed. Howard was a big boy willingly playing a dangerous game. *Concentrate on Max. Enjoy what's left of the evening.* Even as he thought it, a creeping unease tugged at him, refusing to let him relax.

19

JACK leaned toward Chen—his back to Wager—and dropped his voice low. "I need a favour, Chen."

Chen glanced at Wager, then at Jack. He raised an eyebrow but gave a tentative nod.

"Phone the concierge's desk at Chateau Lacombe and ask for Howie, the bellhop. Tell him you have a parcel for him and want to verify his address. Confirm it's the hotel."

"Your hands broke?"

"I phoned him once already," Jack fibbed. "He might recognize my voice."

"Who's Howie?"

Jack sighed. "An informant, if you must know." He shot him an impatient frown. "Do we have to have a written charter over this? Will you do it or not?"

Chen grunted, a weak, non-committal sound, and reached for the phone book. While Chen looked up the number, Jack went over to Wager's desk, partly to distract him from Chen. "Got a minute?" he asked.

"What's on your mind?" Wager kept on writing, not looking up.

"The raid we did last spring on McGruber's."

Lip screwing up at one end, Wager quit writing. He shot Jack a wary glance. "What about it?"

Jack bit his lip and scratched behind one ear as if the subject gave rise to a new thought. "Heard some chatter that the Jackson Gang may come back into town for another try at setting up operations."

Wager's eyes locked in on Jack, encouraging, as if Jack were a suspect and knew more than he was telling. Jack obliged. "No solid info. Just a rumour, but wanted to run it past you. Do you think I should follow it up? Get a head start on whether anything is true. I have a contact who might know more if you get my meaning. It's a long shot, but better to find out sooner than later, right?"

Wager drew in his breath and let it out with a harsh sigh, which meant he wasn't buying what Jack was selling. "You're not feeding me a bunch? Just so you can keep on digging at this Winslow thing?"

"No, Wager," Jack flatly denied it, even knowing it was partly true because he thought Apple may have heard rumours about Hudek. But his primary aim was Luke. Was he still in partnership with McGruber, money laundering, with plans to return to Edmonton?

"It's real. Like I said yesterday, I'm off anything to do with Winslow and Company. I only have to deliver Max's medical info to the law office and get his papers. When he is permanent, I won't go near them again." He spread out his palms. "I'm open to your orders, Sergeant." He grinned.

Wager swung his head back and forth and pinched his lips, saying he was unconvinced. "I guess an inquiry won't hurt. Just don't take all day." He bent over his paperwork again. "And phone in every hour to see if I need you for something else."

"Can I take an hour for lunch?" Jack asked with an innocent smile.

"Get smart with me, and I'll change my mind," Wager warned, his hands busy shifting papers into piles.

Jack returned to his desk and sent Chen a silent question. Chen shook his head and spread out his hands. Jack raised his eyebrows and dragged a finger across his throat—gone for good—and Chen nodded.

Looks as though Howard finally got the message. Relieved, Jack dialed Edina's number.

"It's me," he said when she answered.

"Hello, me," she replied.

"Got time for lunch today?" Jack said. "How about twelve at Boston Pizza in St. Albert? It will be a quick eat and run, I'm afraid." He left it hanging, hoping she'd pick up on the haste and conclude that he had news.

She did. "I'm submerged in final party arrangements, but a break will be lovely. I'll see you there."

He pulled into the parking lot later and spotted her smiling at him from the window. His mood lifted just seeing her. Stepping out of the car, he spread his arms wide and pressed a hand over his heart, exaggerating a dramatic sigh as he walked toward her. "Fool," she said as he came inside and hugged her. "I'm not seventeen and gullible, you know."

The hostess led them to a table, handed them menus, and took their order for coffee. In a moment, she was back. Edina ordered a BLT and a cup of chicken noodle soup. Jack seconded it.

"So, what's the news?" Edina's blue eyes watched him as he casually stirred cream into his coffee. He launched into the story, keeping his voice steady while her expression grew more serious with each passing detail. The story ended with his warning to Howard, leaving out only the part where Max had seen his follower talking to Hudek.

"I had Chen phone the hotel, and Howard quit his job as a bellhop."

"Thank goodness for that," Edina said. "He couldn't keep on the way he was, anyway. Howard always impressed me as being smarter than that."

"I'm off the case," Jack said, draping his arm over the arm of his chair. "After I get Max's final papers, my reason to visit the lawyers is gone. I suppose time will tell if Jassy's death had anything to do with whatever is going on in that place." Disturbed at the thought, he pressed a fist against his mouth.

The waitress appeared with their soup and sandwiches. "You aren't pleased with that idea." Edina sat back and patted her napkin over her lap.

He took the top piece of bread off his sandwich, inspecting the contents before setting it back down. "I'm disappointed, to be honest. I like to see the end of a case. Leaving it in the middle somehow smacks of incompetence. Like it'll just end up buried in a cold case file."

"There's that, I suppose. But it's their fault if it turns out bad for the law firm." Edina lay down her soup spoon. "Sad for Tim Gordon, though. He's suffered enough these past years."

Jack's ears perked up. "Why?"

"His son." Edina put down her sandwich. Her eyes clouded over. "Not a good ending. He was in Korea, and when he came home . . ." She stopped and eyed Jack. "I'm reluctant to go on. It seems like gossip. You didn't know?"

Jack shook his head. *Korea?* He racked his brain, trying to remember a similar name. Nothing came. But not unusual. Different outfits. And then it may have been when Jack was in a North Korean camp. He didn't want to think about it. "Now you've gone this far, my dear one, you can't leave me hanging."

She laughed. "No, I suppose not. His daughter and son. I believe the daughter lives somewhere in the States. His son came back from Korea in terrible shape. Nerves, I think, or what they used to call shell shock. They had him in the veteran's hospital in Calgary for treatment, and for a time, he seemed better. Then he got worse, and the Veteran Affairs people said they couldn't do anything more. Timothy took him down East, but apparently to no end. I heard he tried private psychologists, but I guess they didn't help either." Tears flooded her eyes. "The son shot himself."

"God," Jack said and put down his sandwich. His chest tightened, a swarm of bees buzzed in his head, and without warning, he was back there, in the mud and filth, the days without washing, sleepless nights listening to the Chinese vile taunts, mocking, just before a sneak attack. He swallowed hard to stop himself from yelling out a warning.

Edina just looked at him, wordless, then put her hand on his arm. "Alright?"

"His wife?" He managed to blurt out.

"Their marriage couldn't take the trauma," she whispered, tone reluctant. "They were both gutted and separated shortly after. Catherine Winslow told me his wife now lives in the States with their daughter, who is a teacher at a university. In Wyoming, I think."

Jack squeezed his eyes shut, blocking the images.

He felt her hand on his arm. "I'm sorry."

With effort, Jack drew himself up. "I'm okay." He choked. "It's just . . . I wasn't expecting to hear that he killed himself. It happened to some, I know. I'm glad you told me. I will see Gordon in a different light now. No wonder Howard went to such lengths to protect the firm from scandal. It makes his efforts and bellhop disguise understandable."

Edina nodded agreement. "Timothy Gordon threw himself into public service. To forget, I suppose. Whenever there's a charity function, he's in the thick of it. He's something in the Chamber of Commerce and the Rotary Club too."

"Cops grilled by him in court say he's sharp and doesn't miss a thing," Jack said, pushing his plate aside. "Let's talk about something else now. How are the party arrangements coming? Need any help?"

Edina relaxed, as he hoped she would. He couldn't help but study her face, noticing for the first time how truly pretty she was. It surprised him—when they first met, he'd assumed she was older, mistaking her nephews for her sons. But now, sitting across from her, warmth spread through his chest, a quiet comfort in her presence. There wasn't a thing about her he didn't like.

"I'm just about there," she said. "But you could come a little early and help with arranging chairs and furniture and carry dishes." Her lips curled up at the corners. "All part of that business of seeing if you want to keep me or if it was just the cocktails speaking."

"You'll see. I'll be up front, all washed and combed." He thought for a moment. "Do you mind if I bring Max along? I think it's time you met him. Or is this just a grown-up party? No kids allowed."

"Kids are fine. My nephews will be there. They aren't that much older." Her forehead puckered for a second. "Actually, there should be a couple more. I'll check and make sure they're coming. Why not? I'd love to meet your son. What about the girl . . . Olivia?"

"No." Jack was firm. "She is renting space from me, but I am not fussy about including her in my courtship."

"Okay, no courtship observers allowed." Edina laughed, then added, "But that means I'll have no party. The whole crowd will be curious as soon as you turn up."

"Except them, then." He glanced at his watch. "I'm sorry, I have to check in before my Sergeant sends out a squad car." Jack signalled for the bill. As they waited, Jack turned serious. "Edina, please don't let your guard down until we know for sure the Howard thing is settled. If you see anything at all suspicious, you know what to do."

Her playful demeanour faded, the sparkle in her blue eyes replaced by genuine concern. "Yes, I do."

Outside, Jack kissed Edina on the cheek, squeezed her hand, and said goodbye. "Saturday," he confirmed with a grin. "I can't wait. Don't forget me by then."

"I'll try my best," Edina teased, "but there's a handsome postman who comes around every day. If you forget Saturday, he might want to take your place."

"That'd be a shame." Jack smirked. "I shovel sidewalks in the winter."

"That does help." She smiled back at him—her eyes continuing the conversation without words, and Jack struggled to leave her.

He stopped at headquarters and reported to Wager. "I'm still trying to run my source down. If you have nothing for me, I can try another hangout."

"Dispatch says a tip came in about some arsehole dealing meth out of his house. The sergeant at the scene says he found something suspicious and needs someone to investigate. You and Chen are it."

"What did he find?"

"Didn't say. He wants us to look at it and see if it hits us the same way it did him." He handed Jack the address.

When Jack arrived, Chen was already there, waiting outside a fairly new house in the Westmount Community—an area where middle-class families were just starting to settle. Not a neighbourhood where one suspected their neighbour might deal drugs.

The sergeant opened the door and gestured them inside. "Owner's disappeared," he explained as Chen and Jack slipped by him into the front hallway. "Either had a tip-off or bolted long before the call to Dispatch. Might have even been the one who called it in himself."

The sergeant's last words and decidedly pale face sent a chill through Jack. There was a melancholy atmosphere amongst the group of constables, not really doing their normal business, but instead hanging around, whispering with each other. Chen and Jack eyed each other, both reading the thick atmosphere. "Let's see what you got," Jack ordered.

The sergeant said and led the way to a back bedroom, past an officer quietly standing guard. The sergeant stopped at the doorway while Chen and Jack entered the room. Jack saw nothing unusual until Chen gasped and paled. On the bed, on top of a pillow, was something that Jack took to be the ragged remains of a stuffed toy. Until he looked closer. A blond hairpiece—a pair of horn-rimmed glasses with cracked lenses sat atop what he initially mistook for a nose, but underneath was something more grotesque. Bloodied. Jack curled his tongue against the roof of his mouth, constricting his throat while he bent for a closer look and jerked upright, taking a step back and bumping into Chen, whose face had turned green.

"For all that's holy—" Jack shuddered and swallowed the bile rising in his throat.

"Is that a tongue?" Chen whispered and gagged.

Jack turned to the sergeant. "You touch anything in here?"

The man shot him a dirty look. Jack's eyes blinked with a silent apology. "Where's the phone?"

The sergeant pointed his thumb over his shoulder. Unsteady on his feet, Jack found the wall phone, gently wrapped his handkerchief around the receiver end and dialled Wager's number with a pencil.

"We've found Howard Winslow," he choked.

20

"*IT* was Howard's wig, his glasses, the damn putty nose . . ." Jack's voice trailed off as he wrestled with the absurdity of it.

"You knew all along where he was?" Wager's tone was dangerously mild, his eyes fierce. They bored into Jack's. "Damn it, Jack, there is no excuse for this one."

Jack felt his gut twist at the accusation, bile creeping up his throat. "No, Wager. I didn't know until Saturday night." He rubbed his cheeks, searching for the right words. "We were told it wasn't a police affair, remember? After the meeting, I headed for Howard to tell him it was over." His confession only tightened the lines of fury on Wager's face so that Jack could almost hear the gears grinding out a fitting punishment. He hurried on. "The other plainclothes RC that sat and let the Staff Sergeant do all the talking? He waylaid me outside after the meeting with Simpson. An Inspector, no less. When he said they had an inside man inside Hudek's organization, I had to tell him." Jack swallowed hard past the lump in his throat. "He practically ordered me to keep it all to myself, or it would blow their work wide open. It put me between a rock and a hard place. You know there's only one way they operate. Their way."

Jack's hands clenched. "He agreed I had to warn Howard, but nothing more. Which I did." He rubbed his temple with a forefinger, the weight of the last few days bearing down on him. "What Howard did after that was his call."

"If you had told us as soon as you saw him, maybe he'd be alive today." Wager glared at him, and the raw truth hit Jack like a blow to the chest. "No getting away from that. You're in big trouble now, Jack. Despite what the inspector said, Simpson has to be told."

"I feel responsible, Wager, even when I know I'm not." Anger directed only at himself burned under his skin and made him sweat. "I tried to tell you, but we were hustled into Simpson's office on Monday morning before I could. What if I had mentioned it in front of two plainclothes RCs when Simpson didn't know?" The answer was plain on Wager's face. "Hell would have been a refuge. I warned Howard on Saturday that he could expect no cover. The stubborn ass wouldn't budge. What else could anyone have done if I had told you? Anything?"

Wager pursed his lips while Jack talked. "Nothing," he said finally. "The same thing you did. We couldn't go storming into the Chateau with any force. What Howard was doing wasn't illegal." His expression hardened, summing up his opinion. "How can a person of his calibre be so stupid?"

"To him, it was about protecting the firm, primarily Timothy Gordon. He suspected the firm's trust account was being used for transactions that had no sellers or buyers. Against all Law Association rules, not to mention tax laws, and they'd be in big trouble if the Law Society audited them. Might even face disbarment. And if rivals caught wind of it . . . ?" Jack gave a humourless smile. "People do stupid things when under pressure."

"You should know," Wager said drily. He swivelled around in his office chair to face sideways. "You've got a habit of letting your sympathies dictate your choices." His hand raised, Wager stopped Jack's protest. "Right now, there's a murder to solve. Number one, it's a certainty Winslow's dead, but where's the rest of him?" He shuddered. "Disgusting. Whoever ordered it wanted to leave a message that said, 'Keep your nose out and don't talk.' We'll make sure the papers don't know about that part. The outside person who does will be the guilty party. Or knows who did it."

Jack nodded. "Hudek is the number one suspect. Since it's now a murder investigation, are we clear to go ahead with an investigation? The inspector left me a phone number. Should we let him know?" *Not that Dave would care that Howard was dead,* thought Jack. Because Howard left it too late or else ignored the knowledge that death meant nothing to these guys. Their credo came first. If it protected them, it was good. Anything else was bad.

"Well, we have to find his remains so he'll have a decent burial. What about his family?"

"I can do it," Jack said, dreading it but feeling sympathy for Catherine Winslow, hoping she had family to help her through what was to come.

"Take Chen with you," Wager ordered. "Tell her as much as you think best for now. You'll have to question her again. Maybe Winslow left notes or said something she forgot about. Give me that inspector's number, and I'll phone him, and maybe I can shake loose more information. Get authorization to pursue it. What a mess." Wager blew a noisy breath from between pursed lips and glared at Jack. "Damn and blast it, Jack. Why is it always you? Why am I always in Simpson's office talking about you?" Jack had no answer.

Before Jack and Chen left for St. Albert, he phoned Edina and told her.

"Oh, Jack. Poor Catherine. Call me from her house, and I'll be there in five minutes. She shouldn't be alone."

Chen drove in silence from the station. Jack shot him a look as they went through the underpass on 109th, a notorious dip in the road that turned into a miniature lake after rain. Today, it was dry, and Chen didn't slow down as he usually would, his eyes fixed ahead. "So," Chen finally ventured, "how are things?"

"You mean other than Simpson and our present case?" Jack replied innocently.

"Chen shrugged, staring out the windshield. "Other things. Life." He paused. "How's Olivia?"

"Okay, I guess. I hardly see her. What with her schedule and mine." Jack hid a grin.

"Ah, yeah, I suppose you don't talk much." Chen's mouth turned down, and he said nothing more. Jack let him chew on his thoughts until they reached the traffic circle at Westmount toward the St. Albert trail.

"What are you asking, Chen?" Jack took pity on him.

"She ever mentioned me?"

Jack resisted the impulse to say no. "Honestly, Chen, I have had no time to speak to her since you were there. I assumed she'd got a heavy school schedule, and you know what our hours are."

Chen's face cleared. "Can I come to dinner again sometime?"

"Sure, Chen. You're welcome anytime. Just let me warn her ahead of time." Jack sighed and mentally rolled his eyes at Chen's expression. "Only so she can add to the menu."

"Oh yeah. Naturally." Chen said, face clearing.

Catherine Winslow opened the door to them, her gaze flicking over Jack, then settling briefly on Chen before she stepped aside in silent invitation. Inside, she faced them, hands behind her against the closed door. "It isn't good news, is it?" Pale blue eyes darted from Jack, rested on Chen momentarily, dismissed him, and returned to Jack.

"Can we sit down, Mrs. Winslow?" Jack led the way to the living room.

A youth appeared, drawn by the voices. "Mom?"

"John," she said, reaching out a hand. He came to her and supported her arm. "What's wrong? Is it Dad?" His eyes found Jack and stayed there.

Jack took a deep breath, steadying himself before meeting their anxious stares. He chose to remain standing but waited until they settled, Catherine's fingers gripping her son's hand with a desperate firmness.

He could only do this in one way. "I'm sorry, Mrs. Winslow. We believe your husband is dead."

"What? Believe?" John said. "What does that mean, exactly?"

"You're his son?" Jack had to be sure. John nodded.

"We found evidence of a murder in a house in Westmount," Jack said.

"What evidence?"

"I can't go into detail, but it was something that belonged to him, and the scene showed clear signs that a crime had occurred."

"Blood?" John asked. A choked gasp from his mother stopped him from listing more details. "Not his body?" he said instead.

"I'll not describe the crime scene," Jack stated firmly. "But it was enough to prove your father did not survive. I'm so very sorry."

Catherine Winslow's dark lashes blinked rapidly over her eyes. "There can be no mistake? You're sure?" At Jack's nod, she put her hands to her face and moaned. Her son stared at Jack's face, looking for signs that he might be unsure. Like father, like son, Jack thought. Howard would have looked the same way, demanding certainty behind the sorrowful words.

Jack softened his tone. "Is there anyone we can call, Mrs. Winslow? Family? Friend?"

He got no answer. John pressed his lips together, holding his mother. A bleak expression in his eyes gradually appeared. Jack recognized the signs. After hoping it isn't true, he's now wondering how it affects him, the first thing a child of the deceased thinks. When he realizes that his life had changed in a mere moment. Pity rose in his throat. "Please believe we will not stop until we find answers and the person responsible."

John looked up at him. Face blank. "What happens now?" His words were tinged with frustration as if the order of everything had been blown to pieces. "How can we have a funeral or even a memorial? Or make up an obituary?" His voice rose. "What the hell do we do now?"

"John," whispered his mother. "Not now. Please."

He gripped her harder. "I'm sorry." His voice broke, and his lips became a thin line.

"I'd suggest waiting a few days before you put a notice in the paper," Jack said, a smattering of authority in his voice. "Answer all questions that you want to inform family members. By then, we will have more information." He didn't add, perhaps, a body.

John gave him a sour gaze and waved the suggestion away.

"We are doing everything we can," Jack said, knowing it wasn't comforting. "But I have some questions?" Catherine looked at him, eyes wide in shock. Jack continued on, directing his investigation at the son, who might be better posed to answer. "It might be important. Did your dad ever mention anything unusual or related to a case? Particularly if it is a name that wasn't familiar. Anything at all? Even if you think it is trivial."

John shook his head, then had a thought. "The evidence you found at this place in Westmount. How old was it? My father's been gone for almost a week. Was he killed then? If not, where was he?"

Jack was hoping the subject wouldn't arise. His eyes examined John. *He's sharp.* "A witness saw him at the Chateau Lacombe Hotel on the weekend. Posing as a bellhop."

Disbelief darkened John's face. "No way," he snorted. "What kind of police are you? That's the most ridiculous story I've heard." Jack didn't look at Chen, knowing his expression would mirror John's disbelief. Jack should have warned him.

"Our source confirms it," Jack assured him. "Your dad thought the firm was in danger, but he thought he could find evidence at the hotel." He left the rest unsaid—that Howard had downplayed the danger to his peril.

"That preposterous!" John shouted, face twisted in rage. "You're incompetent fools."

"Shut up, John," Catherine hissed. She gave a wan smile at his shocked expression. "It's true."

"Mother. No." John's expression dodged between puzzlement, dismal, hope, and despair. Jack understood. It was easier to feel angry and hopeful than to deal with an unrecoverable loss.

"Howard was the fool." Her voice was bitter. "It's too late now to deny it. He thought he was back in Germany in 1950 or whenever he was there."

Jack chose a chair, sat, and motioned Chen to do the same. Pouting somewhat, Chen sat and deliberately took out his notebook and pen, narrowing his eyes accusingly at Jack.

Jack ignored him. "Maybe you'd better tell us what you know," he said to Catherine Winslow.

"He phoned me. Saturday night. It was late. So strange." She frowned as if wondering if it had been a dream. "After midnight, I think."

After I'd spoken with him, thought Jack, heart heavy. *Had Howard already sensed he might not make it out?* Jack's stomach knotted as he realized that phone call might have been a farewell. He'd given Howard just a day to wrap things up, but had Howard ever intended to heed his warning? The sinking feeling made Jack almost wince.

"Mom." John's voice interrupted his thoughts. "You knew where he was? And didn't tell me? Why the hell not?" John half rose as if to leave the room. His mother put her hand out to stop him.

"John. Just listen." She turned back to Jack. "He told me he needed evidence, and I had to keep it quiet. That Gordon, Winslow, and Kepler's existence was at stake. Their reputation." Catherine's mouth turned down in horror. "Not only the firm's reputation but ours personally." Her hand squeezed her son's arm. "Your future." John pulled his arm away from her grip and leaned into the corner of the couch in a sulk. "He told me everything and phoned me so I wouldn't worry. He wanted assurance that I was with him. I told him yes, one hundred percent." Her glance at John was defensive. "He believed that Gordon had suffered enough without losing his reputation. As well as ours."

For her, reputation would do it, Jack mused. "Did he give you any names?" he asked, leaning forward, studying the slightest shift in her expression. "Or mention what evidence he had already found?"

"No, nothing else. At first, I tried to talk some sense into him. It all seemed so . . . distasteful." That much was true, Jack decided, watching her curled lip. "If he'd only discussed it with me before the fact, we may have planned it better. In the end, I had to agree because there was no way Howard would stop, and he told me it would be dangerous."

Holding a tissue to her eyes, she added, "Well, he found out, didn't he? Fool."

"Are you certain he didn't leave anything else with you?"

She only shook her head, still dabbing at her eyes.

She was lying. Even John stared at her, eyes wide, as if he were seeing her for the first time. Maybe he was.

Jack stood. He had reached the limit of what he could get from her today.

"You should really phone someone to be with you both."

She raised her eyes to him. The light blue framed with dark eyelashes showed naked sorrow. She's going to be blaming herself by tonight, wondering if she should not have agreed to keep his secret. Jack didn't envy her and felt sorrow. Life wouldn't be kind to her in the coming weeks.

"I'll phone Edina," she said, looking at John.

"I'll do it," he said, leaving the room without looking at his mother, his gaze bleak and fixed.

Head resounding with the same questions he had, Jack predicted.

"You cannot blame yourself, Mrs. Winslow," Jack said, not wanting to leave without offering some comfort. "You did everything you could with the information you had. We'll catch whoever did this. I promise."

As he and Chen walked out to the curb, the weight of what had just transpired pressed heavily on him. "I hate this part of being a cop," he said aloud as they walked toward the curb and the car. Chen grunted. "Worse if it is a kid," he said, his words clipped and hard. As if he had seen a stark reminder.

Jack nodded in agreement. Once you see something, it can't be unseen.

"I also hate going into an interview without all the information," Chen added. His eyes grew thoughtful, and Jack knew he was censuring himself for missing the significance when they'd discovered what remained of Howard's disguise. Jack let it go.

"Did you believe her when she said Howard didn't give her any names?"

"No. Howard is . . . was a lawyer. He'd make notes, even if they were cryptic. He couldn't hope to remember all the details. The whole reason he phoned her was to leave a clue if something happened to him. So where is it?" They drove away in silence, looking for a coffee shop after Chen suggested that they stop.

"Would she be foolish enough to look-see at what he left without telling anyone?" asked Chen.

They were in the parking lot of the Dairy Queen on St. Albert Road, sitting in the car with their hot coffee. Jack took a healthy gulp, found it too hot, and slurped most of it back into the cup.

"Agggh," Chen's mouth twisted in distaste. He delicately sipped at his own cup and offered no more comment.

"Oh, she'll want a look-see, alright," Jack answered, flicking his burnt tongue against the roof of his mouth. "But not to go after Hudek. She isn't the type to act on her own. I think she's only interested in what information Howard left. See if it gives her some power with the law firm."

"You mean sell the information to the firm? Like blackmail? If you don't give me extra, I'll send the papers to the police?" Chen left his mouth hanging open and blinked.

"Or the Law Society," Jack agreed. "Convincing herself she deserves whatever she can get because of Howard's sacrifice to save the firm."

Chen's brow creased in thought. "So what is our next move?"

"I have an idea," Jack smiled. "I know someone who might help her decide."

Chen rolled his eyes. "Forget I asked." He threw his hands in the air in surrender and expelled his breath in an exasperated growl. "But remember, I'm not your partner if you get into trouble with Wager and D.C. Simpson," he added firmly, his face set in stubborn lines. He gulped his hot coffee, then spurted it back.

JACK unlocked the door and heard the music as soon as it opened. *'Nice Work If You Can Get It.'* Soft and Low, Billie Holiday's words sung out, clear, and husky. The heat rose in Jack's chest, anger that *his* vinyl was playing on *his* Grundig stereo system. Olivia's snooping through his collections.

She was sitting in the chair, head thrown back, eyes closed. He saw the tears on her cheeks. Beside her, Pharo was giving himself a bath, licking his front legs. He raised his head, got up and silently padded to him, bushy tail wagging. Jack closed the door with his foot. She snapped up straight, wiped her cheeks and faced him.

"Please don't mind," she said, holding out the cover with Billie Holiday's face smiling out at him. Sensing Jack's disapproval, Pharo padded over to her and sat facing Jack as if to show him where his sympathies lie.

Jack bit back a snarl and tried to appear casual. "I'm surprised you like her." He came closer, inspecting her face, looking for clues to her grief. Her eyes were distinctly different colours today, rimmed by lashes still damp, not defined by mascara. She didn't need it. Her face was a perfect ration of features, he decided. From her mother? He tried to visualize Carol Sommer but couldn't conjure up an image.

"I do. My Mom was a big fan. Whenever I needed . . . something . . . she'd make tea, and we'd listen to Billie Holiday while she talked, and I'd listen, or she listened, and I talked." Olivia impatiently wiped away a tear.

Jack sat on the couch, leaned against the arm, and faced her. "You need one of her somethings today? School not going right?"

"No, NAIT's everything I hoped it would be." She inhaled. "It's not that," she said and stopped, frowning, and examined the back of the vinyl jacket.

Where was her mother? I never asked about her. Jack thought, kicking himself for missing a connection. "Does your Mom approve of you here? In Edmonton, at NAIT, and not the tech school in Winnipeg?"

Olivia looked up at him, her eyes snapping from surprise to something sharper.

"My mother and father are divorced. She lives in Vancouver with her new husband and family."

"I'm sorry," Jack said, wincing. "That's rough." He wondered if he should come right out and ask why she wasn't there, too, instead of with Luke.

"You're wondering why I didn't go to Vancouver," she forestalled him. Her lips twisted in a tight smile. "Can't you guess? My father didn't contest a divorce, but one proviso was that he had custody of me. She wouldn't agree, but I convinced her to take it." She stared straight at Jack. "There was no use both of us suffering. Besides, it wasn't as if he mistreated me. Dad gave me everything I wanted. Within reason."

Jack could think of nothing to say.

"We write to each other." She smiled a secret smile. "We have ways of corresponding. I haven't lost her completely, and when I'm twenty-one, it will be different." She sounded more stubborn than convinced.

"Anderson," Jack hissed.

"What about him?" Her eyes focused on him, and Jack saw sudden worry and even fright.

"He's your contact with your Mom."

Her face tensed, then softened as she searched his eyes for something—perhaps a promise. "You won't say anything?"

"Of course not." In truth, it shocked him she might think he would rat on her.

A shiver of relief passed over her as her shoulders dropped. She looked away. "I'm not sure of anything anymore," she murmured, more to herself than Jack. "Anderson's always been my anchor. He knew when I needed help, and I knew he'd keep me out of trouble with Dad but would never reveal my secrets." She blinked fresh tears.

Jack studied her for a long moment. He decided to just get it over with. "It will never happen, Olivia. Your dream is impossible."

Her eyes opened wide with shock, then filled with sheer terror, as if she saw her life ebbing away. "I don't know what you're talking about," she protested.

Jack shifted along the couch, nearer to her. The record stopped, and Billie's voice with it. Pitying Olivia, Jack wanted to take her hand. She was so young and vulnerable. But he had to tell her.

"Anderson. I know you love him, but it's impossible. Anderson can never leave, and if Luke finds out about the both of you, the world won't be big enough to contain his rage. Besides, your affection for Anderson may not be as strong as you think. He is years older than you."

"So what?" She rose, laid the vinyl cover on the turntable and turned to him, eyes blazing in anger. "You're so wrong! He loves me anyway. I'm sure about that."

"Olivia, listen to me. If you hate what Luke does, how long would your relationship with Anderson last? How soon would you hate him too?"

Her face crumpled, and she sank into the chair again. Pharo stood and put his head on her knee. She stroked his ears, all the while shaking her head, denying Jack's words. "No, he'll work it out."

At that moment, Jack hated Anderson for not nixing the situation from the start. Jack had guessed months ago that Anderson was an RCMP undercover agent, and Anderson had not denied it. They had an unspoken agreement. If Jack was in any danger from Luke, Anderson would let him know, and in return, Jack kept his silence.

And if Olivia knew that, her eyes could not hide it from Luke.

"I don't doubt your word, Olivia. I'm sure his feelings for you are sincere. There's the rub. You're a smart girl and know how risky it is. Luke would stop at nothing to axe your relationship, even if it means Anderson's death." Confronting her pasty face and eyes full of bleak pain, he halted his speech. "It will work itself out, Olivia. It just needs time. You'll see," he said instead. It sounded lame, even to him.

She only gave him a glassy stare as if she'd already shut out his words.

The door banged open, letting in Max and Tommy, full of noise and laughter. Olivia jumped up. "I'll get a meal started." She hurried into the kitchen.

Left feeling miserable, Jack stood and pinned a grin on his face. Both boys tramped past as if he were a post and went down the hall. Pharo raced behind and got there just before the bedroom door slammed shut.

"Traitor," Jack muttered and sat again. Elbows on his knees, he put his head in both hands, wondering how to make Olivia feel better. He exchanged Billie Holiday for Louis Armstrong and his trumpet, turning the volume down.

Could this day get any worse?

21

THE following morning, Jack rushed to Dr. Griffin's office to collect Max's results. A sullen sky, matching Jack's mood, spread a flat, gray imprint over everything. A distant rumble chased him through the door as if searching him out, especially reminding him of his forgotten raincoat at home. Dr. Griffin held up the envelope containing Max's medical report and waved Jack into his office. "Just a quick word."

Jack's heart skipped a beat. "Something wrong with Max?"

"Only a few anomalies you might clear up," the doctor motioned Jack to a chair.

"Max was a competitive swimmer?" he started, and Jack nodded. "He has developed muscles to show it, so I questioned him about his background." Dr. Griffin hesitated.

"I've read the rumours about East German doping," Jack contributed, forestalling the doctor's question. "In my work, I'm not ignorant of signs. I've noticed Max's mood swings. But my guess is he is adjusting to Canada and me and coping with the loss of his mother. He's also afraid someone will come after him and take him back to East Germany."

Dr. Griffin's lips curled downward. "So I gathered. It's a heavy load for a boy."

"But I asked him if he had been given drugs," Jack hastened to add. "He said no, only vitamins."

Dr. Griffin rolled a pen between his fingers. "He told me the same thing. I believe him. I asked him how long he had taken them, and he said a few months since he turned fifteen. But I ordered blood tests to determine if he was given testosterone or anabolic steroids."

"And was he?" Jack's heart took a dive and knotted in his stomach.

"I am not sure. The same goes for his urine tests. I would like to follow up and run tests for hormonal imbalances and normal liver function." At Jack's frozen expression, he added, "He's good to go, Jack. And my report says so." He pulled a piece of paper toward him and scribbled on it. "Vitamin D and calcium won't hurt. Some Vitamin E and NAC." He handed Jack the paper. "Real supplements. Information is all listed there. Have you noticed any muscle weakness?"

Jack thought of Max's Frisbee throws. "He seems strong to me. Normal."

Dr. Griffin rose. "Let's order another sweep of tests in three months. See what's different, if anything." As they shook hands, he added, "You can tell Max whatever you feel he needs to know, and I guess he does, but I foresee nothing drastic. We'll make sure."

Jack cursed all the way out to his car. Vitamins, my foot. It's child abuse. What's the matter with the International Sports associations? Can't they set rules and make test procedures mandatory? He put the report in his pocket and carried on to work.

"Any word on the search for Winslow?" he asked Wager during a later break.

"We've got everything and everyone we can rustle up to search for his remains," Wager told him. "Now, I'm thinking the river is the logical bet, although it is shallow and sluggish right now." Wager trailed off, looking grim. "Or any dumpster."

Jack frowned. "Is there a chance it was a fake tongue? Not human?"

"Not according to the M.E." Wager eyed Jack, amusement glinting in his eyes. "Simpson is one step away from accusing you of knowing where he is and keeping it to yourself."

"Thanks for nothing, Wager," Jack snapped and immediately regretted it. Wager's usual staid expression shifted a trifle.

"What's up with everyone today?" he growled in irritation. "Chen is walking around like he's lost his favourite teddy bear, and now here's you, sucking lemons. Good thing I've got Vassar and Dyer to carry the load. You two are useless."

"Home life," Jack said shortly, thinking of Olivia along with the doctor's report in his pocket. "Not much sleep last night." He told himself to get a grip. "I was thinking about that anonymous call. It's odd the caller pointed us to the house but left no hints where we might find Winslow's body."

"How's that, then??" Wager asked in his usual mild tone. But his fingers moved along the edge of his moustache as if priming it for a trim.

"That maybe Winslow's body was in the house when he called, and he assumed we'd find him. But the house search was clean?"

Wager shuffled papers on his desk. He scanned one sheet carefully, then looked at Jack. "No blood traces unless they were all wiped." He checked another report. "Doesn't matter how thorough, especially the room used to do their . . . cutting, it is impossible to wipe every trace away. Garbage bins held bloody towels and rags. Indicates an effort to make it all look normal. We checked the outside structures, garage, shed. Nothing."

"Why hide the body, though? It seems like adding an ornament too much."

Flopping the reports down on the corner of his desk, Wager leaned back, half spinning in his chair. "Sending a message. Plain and brutal—the penalty for sticking your nose where it doesn't belong." Wager's mouth twisted with disgust. "Hiding the body's just an extra touch, to show they don't mind the extra work—proving they can, and that life's cheap in their world. Bastards."

Jack agreed. "Was there a garage entry from the alley? With a dirt floor or concrete?"

"The reports only mention they searched all outside structures. And no soil disturbances in the yard."

"Any old flower beds? What about beside the garage? Any space between that and the fence next door?"

"I don't know." They eyed each other, silent, both thinking the same thing. Wager sighed. "Damn." He reached for the phone.

"I'll go out there and supervise," Jack said.

"Take Chen," ordered Wager. "If you find anything, he'll be a witness."

"You think I'll keep it to myself if I do?" Jack glared at Wager, openly ready to argue.

Wager shot him one of his impenetrable looks and turned his attention to the phone.

"Yes, he does," Chen confirmed, appearing beside him. "Let's go."

Outside, the early morning clouds had shifted away, leaving a blue sky, but the wind was still chilly, just in case people started to think Indian summer might last forever.

Chen strode to the driver's side, but Jack snatched the keys from his hand and pointed him to the passenger side. Chen took one glance at his expression and obeyed. In silence, Jack drove West toward Westmount.

After a few blocks along 118th Avenue, Chen scratched his head and half turned to Jack to speak.

"If you mention anything about keeping secrets, I'll throw you out of the car," Jack snapped without looking at him.

"No, it isn't . . ." Chen began.

"And no, you can't visit tonight. Olivia is busy." Jack stepped on the gas, considering turning on the siren so he could speed through all the traffic lights.

BY seven o'clock, the clouds had gathered again, but an even cooler breeze fanned over the yard, bringing with it an odour of freshly dug soil, weeds and decaying plants. On each side of the house, nosy neighbours and their looky-loo friends were peering over the fence, trying to see inside the canvas barricades set up to prevent precisely that. Most had become bored and gone inside, away from the wind, to their suppers.

"Perhaps we're wrong," Chen murmured, casting a doubtful glance toward the narrow space between the garage and the fence. They were sitting on the back step, watching the workers completely covered in disposable suits as they dug. Barely wide enough to walk but still a big enough burial site, it was the last place to check.

During periods of inactivity, they searched the house again, each taking a room and then swapping to check again with fresh eyes. They concurred that Howard passed away in a small basement bedroom. It smelled of soap and antiseptic, household bleach, probably. A clumsy effort to get rid of the blood. Had Howard tried to convince them of his innocence? Jack's mind churned with the possibilities: his disguise ripped away, his arguments—explanations, pleas, maybe even an elaborate lie, trying to justify his hidden identity as something benign, a harmless secret. In Chen's opinion, the fact they'd killed him meant they were afraid and had much to hide, much more than just a phony export and import racket. And as the thought of Inspector Dave's asset floated back into his mind, Jack's gut twisted, and he shuddered. Did that asset take part in Howard's torture and death? No, his mind answered and told him to get a grip. More likely, he'd be part of the group making up the business cabal and not one of Hudek's personal henchmen.

"They have swept clean whatever happened here, anyway," Jack said, looking around the room, "wrapped it all up with Howard and dumped him somewhere. No fire either, I'd bet—they couldn't risk leaving anything behind."

Chen only nodded, eyes scanning over the floor and walls one more time. Jack turned away. "Let's keep looking. Howard might have dropped a clue they missed."

They made their way out onto the step and sat. "It beats me why people buy houses, then let the yard go to weed." He waved a hand around the backyard, one big weed patch, some three feet high by this point of summer. "This place could have a nice garden full of fresh veggies to cook. Good earth there."

"Don't suppose drug dealers are interested in gardens," Jack said. "Good place to hide a body, though. Just take off the top layer, then replace it. Nothing would seem disturbed." He cricked his neck and examined the back of the house. "Not a bad-looking house, really. I wouldn't mind one like this. Add a patio for the summer and have meals outside." His eyes wandered over the door, thinking of Max, Pharo and him living in a house. "All it needs is a coat of paint and a new door, and Bob's your uncle." His eyes flicked to the door jamb and then back. Something white caught the breeze and flapped gently—a piece of paper stuck in the aluminum edging.

Jack got up and tugged it out. It was small with a messy scribble across it, barely legible like the doctor's writing on Max's prescription. *In the file,* he read. He peered closer at the writing. Howard's? Jack turned the paper over. Nothing but a small smear of blood. *What file? Where?* He pictured Howard faking a stumble at the step and putting his hand out to cram a piece of paper there, a frantic last-ditch effort, knowing the people he faced would not let him survive. An involuntary groan escaped, His fist closed around the scrap.

"What is it?" Chen asked.

"Not sure. Could be a message." He showed it to Chen.

"In the file? Do you suppose Howard was trying to send a last message about the missing file?" Chen held it up to the light in case something else was written on it.

Or maybe a stray piece of paper," Jack said, putting it in his pocket. "I'll see what Wager thinks."

Chen looked at his watch. "I could use a coffee."

An officer in grubby coveralls appeared and beckoned them. Jack led the way, leaping up before Chen.

"Not deep," the officer said. "Wrapped in a bedsheet. Preserving some evidence, I hope." He led the way. Jack had a quick peek and went inside to phone Wager, who showed up at the site within twenty minutes with the M.E. and crime scene investigators. Within a short time, they had contained the whole housing site.

"It's Winslow, all right," Jack said. "Mutilated and still in his bellhop uniform. They would have grabbed him the same night before he got out."

"I want you to leave," Wager instructed. "Now, Jack."

"Wager . . ."

"I don't want you anywhere near this site. Simpson needs to be aware that no physical evidence links you to Winslow's hide-and-seek actions."

"Wager, you know me. That isn't what I do. Nor what I ever did."

Wager held up his palm, shutting Jack up. "I know, Jack. But those two RC plainclothes will turn up as soon as they find out. Simpson will go ape over it, soothing their feelings." Wager put his hand on Jack's shoulder. "I can read you like a book. You're already too hot to be useful. You want another suspension? Go home. Tomorrow is another day. Everything will still be here, but you'll be cooler."

"Do you want me to inform his wife and son?"

"I'll handle it, Jack." Wager glanced around at the crowd gathered in the alley. "The press will be here sniffing around soon enough. Best we see them first before the reporters do. I'll tell Mrs. Winslow that you'll be around to see her soon. By tomorrow, maybe we'll have more information." Wager didn't seem as if he believed it himself. He waved Jack off and beckoned Chen over.

Jack took a few steps back. "Tomorrow morning, I have to deliver Max's medical documents to Gordon. His final papers," he added at Wager's set mouth. "Not anything else. I swear." He almost added that the fresh news of Winslow's murder might reveal new insights from the reactions of the staff there. A second thought told him it wasn't the time to test Wager's temper. Instead, he said, "I'm taking the car, Chen. Get a ride back with Wager."

Chen nodded, then whispered. "Say hello to Olivia, will you, Jack? Can you ask if she'd be willing to go on a date with me?"

"Oh, for god's sake, Chen. Give me a break. Do it yourself."

Chen bristled, hurt. "I did. Once. She said she was busy. It won't kill you to ask, will it? If I phone again, I can't be sure she won't hang up on me."

"I'll ask. Anything to shut you up." Jack rolled his eyes as he watched Chen walk away, fist-punching the air in triumph.

After dinner, Jack took Pharo to Kinsmen Park. Just he and the dog, like old times. Jack sat on a bench and watched Pharo do his running-in-circles routine, looking for cast-off chewing gum. Jack curled his lips in disgust, mumbling under his breath but not calling out. If he pretended not to care, Pharo might lose interest in the game. The piece of paper he'd taken from the door was still in his pocket. In his argument with Wager, he'd forgotten to mention it. Now, he looked it over again, wondering if it was significant. An image of Howard stuffing it in the door while being hustled into the house grew in his mind. Was it his handwriting? It's in the file was not something that anyone would just doodle.

A file meant record keeping, and that house didn't have the character of people keeping office records. Sure, it's a drug house, but since when did dealers keep records as evidence which will send them up the river for years? He had to mean the missing file from the firm.

Pharo at his side, Jack trudged home, trying to shake off the brutal image of Howard's body discarded like trash in a forgotten corner of the earth. He gritted his teeth, feeling his anger simmer, the raw edge of revenge pulsing just beneath his calm facade.

By the time he settled Pharo, who was meticulously pawing and nudging his bed into place, Jack felt his own exhaustion creeping up, thick and heavy. He flicked off the light and sank onto his mattress, pulling the sheet over his head like a shield. Lying in the darkness, he forced himself to focus on the stale warmth of his breath beneath the covers, willing it to drown out the day's horrors.

22

WHEN Jack arrived at Gordon, Winslow, and Kepler the following morning, he found a *'Closed Due to Bereavement'* sign on the door. He peered through the slats of Venetian blind and saw shadowy movements. He knocked and then knocked again. The receptionist, her eyes red and skin blotchy, opened the door. Before she could speak, Jack waved the envelope at her. "I'm just dropping this off for Mr. Gordon."

She reached out to take it without a word, but he held it back.

"Is it okay if I come in for a few minutes? To offer my condolences?"

Eyes filling up, she shook her head. "Please, Detective. Come back tomorrow. We are all just devastated here." She wiped her eyes and closed the door gently on him.

It opened again immediately, and Jack turned, hopeful, only to be faced with Hudek. He made no attempt to step around Jack but closed in on him front and center, making Jack backtrack or be run over. The encounter felt too perfectly timed.

"It's time we speak," Hudek said, confirming Jack's suspicions. How did he know Jack would be here? He had no time to mull over the question, for Hudek gripped Jack's elbow and pulled him along the corridor. Feeling like an errant schoolboy, Jack had no choice but to walk with him. Only curiosity and Hudek's iron grip kept him from resisting. They stopped near the elevator door, where Jack circled Hudek's wrist with his own grip and gave a hard twist. Hudek let go, one side of his mouth pulling away. His version of a smile, Jack assumed.

"You have been curious about me," Hudek said, his voice surprisingly high. Jack had imagined something darker, more authoritarian.

"What gives you that idea?" Jack replied, massaging his elbow.

Hudek's eyes narrowed as if he wasn't used to being put off. "You are trying to convince me they were only minor inquiries?" Brown eyes, black and beady like a bear's, bore into Jack. "If so, then why did you spend so much time asking them?" He jerked his head back toward the law office. "You want to know about my business, what I do, with whom, and where I come from." He lowered his head closer to Jack's face. "Don't pretend. Why are the police interested in my business and my person?" Hudek's English was flawless, but the slight, precise emphasis on certain words betrayed his foreign origin.

Jack held Hudek's gaze for a beat, studying his steely composure before answering. "A girl from that office was murdered." He watched to see if the word made any difference to Hudek. It didn't. "It's my business to ask questions," he said and cast out a bait. "Are you objecting, or do you have information for me?"

Hudek's expression remained impassive, though his lips seemed to press into a thinner line. Cold eyes moved over Jack's face as if memorizing his features. "No," he finally spoke. "I have nothing to do with this girl. And yet, you are involving my name and office with your questions."

"Not only you. Any other client as well," Jack lied.

"You should have followed protocol for one of my station—a businessman. And approached me first with your questions. Perhaps then, you would realize that you endanger great accomplishments in my dealings with Canada." He paused, his eyes still on Jack.

"Yes, your business affairs." Jack purposely shrugged, making light of Hudek's ego and sending his own message. And then prompted, "And those include . . . ?"

Hudek drew himself up, shoulders squaring with a practiced dignity. "Opportunities for Edmonton business people to profit from import and export products needed by both countries. Goods they would not otherwise have access to." Hudek pointed his forefinger at Jack, warming up into his spiel. Here comes the next selling point, thought Jack. All it lacked was an overhead projector and transparencies showing profit margins. "A most important trade opportunity for both sides. The men who have signed up will be offended that you put their businesses at risk."

Jack frowned, pursed his lips as if thinking deeply about the proposition, and stayed quiet.

"As for me," Hudek continued without missing a beat, "I will not treat interference lightly." His gaze travelled slowly over Jack, assessing him with an intensity that was all the more chilling for its mildness. "Think carefully, Detective. Actions are always followed by reactions. Always. And where and when you least expect them."

Not waiting for Jack's answer, he turned away and pushed the elevator down button, his back to Jack—a final, deliberate dismissal.

Jack walked toward the office door again, inwardly shaken. Did he mean Max? No, he probably meant Howard. A warning that he might face the same end. But still, should he warn Max? He was already keyed up from his experience at the lake, and now he was starting school; Jack wanted him to settle into something normal. Max had spent his life steering clear of trouble with suspicious people. Jack would now have to trust Max's instincts. What else could he do?

Only slightly easier in his mind, he gave a sharp rap on the firm's door again. This time, Bernie Kepler opened the door, ushering out a petite woman, who stopped, startled to see Jack in front of her. He noted her in a fitted suit, curled hair perfectly coiffed and stiff with spray. She smiled at him, baby blue eyes wide and lips perfectly outlined in bright red lipstick. Kepler came out, and she turned to him, looking helpless and tiny. She leaned into him, and he protectively put his arm around her. Kepler's wife, Jack assumed.

"I'm sorry, but the office is closed to clients today," he said. He peered at Jack, and recognition came into his eyes. "Detective, no questions today. Please."

"Agreed, Mr. Kepler. I had business with Mr. Gordon but wish to convey my sympathies." He handed over the doctor's sealed envelope, telling Kepler its contents. "Howard was a good friend, and I'll miss him." He continued. "We won't rest until we find whoever killed him."

Kepler swallowed as if he had a knot in his throat and nodded. "It will be hard to carry on without him," he said, his voice hoarse. He turned to his wife. "Lottie, I'll see you at home." His eyes on her were indulgent, and he actually raised her hand and kissed it. Jack hid a smile.

"Yes, Bernie, love. I'll just nip to the store first, though. A black outfit to suit our loss. I don't have anything. This," she pointed to herself, "won't do at all, will it?"

"Of course, my dear." Kepler gave her an indulgent smile. "You are thinking ahead."

She put her hand to her husband's cheek. "Dear Bernie, I am so sorry. I will do everything to help you through your grief."

"I know." Ignoring Jack, Kepler reverently kissed her gloved hand again. "My love. Be careful, Lottie."

Jack held the elevator door for her and studied the ceiling, aware of her perfume, something flowery, spring-like, and not overwhelming. She sighed, adjusted her purse to the other arm as if impatient at the journey, and swept ahead of him out the front entrance without so much as a glance. Jack followed behind her. Kepler plainly adored his wife, and she knew how to keep him that way. If Kepler knew what Hudek really was, would he have imagined the same thing happening to his wife which happened to Jassy and Howard? Was he being blackmailed? Jack was just getting into the car when he saw Julie, Howard's secretary, coming down the street. She saw him waiting and tried to ignore him. He stepped in front of her.

"I'm sorry about Howard, Julie," he said. Her eyes, under swollen lids, sullenly acknowledged him. She didn't smile. "What are the police doing about it? Why stand here when you could be out hunting down whoever killed him? First Jassy, now Mr. Winslow, it's . . ." She stopped, waving her hands, unable to go on and looked at him helplessly.

"I feel the same as you do, Julie. Howard wasn't only a victim; he was my friend too." He squinted at her, thinking of the scrap of paper. "I have to ask you, though." She shook her head and tried to shove past him. "No time is a good time, Julie. But time is the enemy. If we wait for days to go by to ask questions, it's too late. The killer will vanish out of sight."

She stopped and let out a long sigh of resignation. "What?"

"It's that damn file. The one that was missing. I have a feeling it's important."

"That file? That's a laugh. Why does everybody keep referring to that miserable file? A lot of rushing around and searching for nothing. I already told Mrs. Winslow. It wasn't missing at all. Someone found it. I found it lying on my desk yesterday morning. All this time, it was just misfiled."

Jack stared at her. "Why on your desk? I thought it was Kepler's file?"

She said, "I don't know," in an annoyed tone. She waved her arms in dismissal. "What does it matter now?"

In all Julie's rambling about the file not missing, Jack seized on one reference. "Mrs. Winslow was asking about it? Why would she ask about it?"

Julie heaved a deep sigh. "Who knows?" She moved her feet impatiently. "Mrs. Winslow phoned yesterday and said Mr. Kepler came to her house looking for it and wondered if it had turned up. Of all the crazy . . ." She rolled her eyes.

"Did you look inside it?" Jack asked and got a withering stare.

"Noooo," she said, slowly drawing the word out as if he were dim-witted. "It wasn't our case. I put it on Sheila's desk." Julie stepped away. "Now, if you'll excuse me, I want to join the rest of them so we can mourn together."

His hopes dashed at finding nothing to show for his morning's efforts, Jack drove to Headquarters, reviewing the little knowledge he'd gained. If Catherine Winslow had asked about the file on a flimsy pretext, it could only mean it was important. It confirmed Jack's hunch that Howard had given her a source of information. Somehow, the file had appeared, and if Howard took it, how did it get back to the office? Was someone in the law firm an accomplice? Kepler? Perhaps. If it had something that incriminated Kepler, why put it in the file at all? Why not hide it in his own office? Someplace inaccessible to others? No, the file had routine transactions, but that routine included a direct threat to the firm. Unfortunately, Jack wasn't hopeful of ever finding out what Howard saw.

What goes into a legal file, anyway? Transactions, meetings with the client, Kepler's notes, fees, and bank transactions. The initial meeting with Hudek and the reason he needed a lawyer in the first place, he supposed.

"HEART gave out," Wager said, reading from the autopsy report. "The bastards tortured him to death is what it really means. His hands." He threw the report down on his desk and rubbed the stubble on his chin. His sleep-deprived eyes looked at Jack.

"What about his hands?" Jack said, prepared to hear the worst.

Wager picked up the report again. "Burnt. They held his hands over the elements on the stove." Jack sucked in his breath, and Wager pressed his lips into a tight line. "By the looks of it, Winslow's heart gave out before they got the information they needed."

"Jesus." Jack sank into the chair facing Wager's desk. "What could he give them anyway? Winslow was acting on his own. Except . . ."

A chill settled over Jack. Winslow could reveal that Jack had found him and the name he was using while a bellhop. Found out by Edina.

"Except what?"

"The file." Jack blurted. He told Wager about his encounter

with Hudek when he delivered Max's medical report. "Hudek is responsible for Howard's murder. I'm sure of it. He is Kepler's client, but I'm almost convinced Kepler's involvement is limited to allowing the trust account's misuse, even if that makes him complicit.'"

Wager's usual unreadable countenance broke. His face flushed with anger. "Well, that started this whole mess in the first place. He's just as responsible for Winslow's death." His fist clenched the coroner's report as if it were Kepler's or Hudek's throat, then relaxed. "I bet he thought one transaction wouldn't hurt, then it became another and another until he couldn't back out."

"They will have to explain it to the Law Society now," Jack said. "The cause of Winslow's death will have to go public." Did Gordon know about the transactions? Did the firm's head always have knowledge of the partners' actions? Surely, there were monthly reports on trust account transactions. Didn't they have to be audited? "We have to make sure they can't cover this up, Wager."

"You mean if the RCs decide otherwise?" Wager suggested.

Jack nodded. "This is pure murder, and it's up to us, as police, to find the killer. At least for his family's closure."

"And if it involves bringing Hudek in for questioning, how do you suggest we start?"

"If that's what it takes," Jack persisted. He rose and leaned over to Wager, knuckles resting on the desktop. "You can't be suggesting we wait for permission from those two plainclothes?"

"I'll talk to Simpson." Wager sighed. "I'm right in there with you, Jack, but . . ."

Jack turned away in disgust. "But wait until Simpson talks to them? Why doesn't Simpson just remind them what we're here to do—what our mission is?"

"Because if we don't, Jack, we won't have the assets to keep the investigation going. You know that as well as anyone." Wager stood and faced Jack. "Give me some credit. Don't think all I want is Simpson's permission. I'll give my strongest case. That's all we got right now."

Jack shrugged. "Dare we hope," he muttered, his tone weighted with doubt, and sat at his own desk, knowing he had to be fair to Wager's job.

Jack picked up a piece of paper and shoved it into his typewriter. Wager would do the best he could, and Simpson wasn't a rules-based deputy chief. He wouldn't be a D.C. if he was a patsy to officialdom. The force encouraged thinkers, especially Chief Mackie, and Simpson would know that. The thought buoyed him a little. Maybe Wager was right.

Jack ignored the paper in his typewriter, took a fresh sheet, and made pencil notes. He set out the facts known about Hudek in one column, arranging them by timeline, with a second column for suspicions and a third for possible sources to confirm those suspicions. He glanced around the squad room, hoping it would empty to give him a chance to call Edina. Evidence that Winslow had been tortured bothered him. Under torture, would Howard mention both Jack and Edina's knowledge he was posing as a bellhop? No, he thought, as the police, Jack's name wouldn't matter and maybe even help. But Edina would be in immediate danger.

He tried to recall every detail of his conversations with Winslow. Howard hadn't linked Edina's name specifically, though he'd certainly seen her with Jack at LaRonde. And Hudek hadn't mentioned her either . . . nor had he mentioned Max. Jack's jaw tightened. Too late now for second-guessing; he'd just have to keep Edina out of this however he could.

Finally, the squad room emptied, and Chen left to get a coffee. Jack phoned Edina.

"Oh, Jack, I'm so glad to hear from you. I have been with Catherine. It's so awful. But at least now she can plan a funeral."

"Listen, Edina. I'm in a hurry here, so excuse my abruptness. Is everything else okay? I mean, no odd happenings? No strange people you are not used to seeing?"

"Jack, what's going on?" Edina's voice was casual and controlled. "We talked about this before. And no, everything is normal."

"Edina. Howard died of heart failure. Please keep this to yourself. But they worked him over first. I am concerned that he told them you found out his name." Jack cursed himself. Why was he telling her this? He held the receiver against his forehead, wanting to take back the whole conversation. Had he lost his sense of professionalism? Hearing a tinny voice, he put the receiver back to his ear.

". . . just fine, Jack," she was saying, "And shocked too. I know what it cost you to tell me and why. Please, Jack, believe me when I say I won't misuse your trust. Jack?"

"Just be careful, Edina. I blame myself." Chen and Wager entered the room together. "I have to go. I'll phone you tonight. It might be late."

"I'll be here."

He hung up and shook his head at Wager's questioning glance.

At noon, Wager sent Jack and Chen to a case of B and E in the city centre, which kept them busy well into the late afternoon.

By that time, Jack was growing weary of Chen's moody adherence to duty while ignoring any friendly back-and-forth conversation. Aware of the reason, Jack cooperated with him, asking and replying in the strictest business terms, which only made Chen's mood chillier. *He's waiting for me to tell him I asked Olivia if she will date him*, Jack thought, *and won't ask, only give me the cold shoulder until I admit one way or the other.*

Finally, as they were wrapping up, Jack put Chen out of his misery. "Would you like to come home with me for dinner?" he asked.

Chen's eyes lit up. "You asked her?"

"I didn't have time, Chen." He knew his tone was peevish, "Winslow's murder has taken up all my thoughts." About to add the case took precedence over Chen's love life, he blew out a breath of exasperation instead. Judging by the disappointment on Chen's face, the message didn't register.

"You can ask her yourself," Jack said, struggling not to tell Chen to stuff it somewhere. "You aren't Cyrano de Bergerac, and Olivia isn't Roxanne, and I'm not whatshisname who delivers your messages."

"Christian."

"What?"

"Roxanne thinks the letters are from Christian." He said as if the play were ongoing.

"Shut up," Jack snapped. "I don't care. I'll tell Olivia you are coming for dinner. She'll be thrilled," he added. No subtle sarcasm there, he thought.

"Really? Can we stop somewhere so I can buy flowers?"

"Get in the car, Chen," said Jack, thoroughly crabby now, preferring the earlier chilly atmosphere.

Surprisingly, either Olivia was a talented actress, which Jack didn't doubt for one minute, or she enjoyed Chen's company. Jack sat in the living room drinking his Pilsner while he listened to them talk from the kitchen in between the chopping sounds of whatever it was being chopped. Chen described his grandmother's Chinese recipes. At least Max was entertained. Laughing, he set the table, listening to Chen's descriptions of his family's tactics to avoid the kitchen because the grandmother enslaved anyone in reaching distance for chores. She was head chef and didn't do prep work; she wasn't keeping dogs and barking herself.

In the end, they sat down to a chilled beet gazpacho soup to start, topped with a mixture of avocado, cucumber, onions, beet and dill. An enormous shrimp cobb salad with bacon dressing and crusty baguette followed. Chen asked for Olivia's recipe for the bacon dressing, but Olivia just shook her head. Jack had two helpings. Dessert was crème brule and coffee.

"Ah, so similar to my grandmother's recipe of Chinese steamed milk egg pudding, but without the crunchy sugar top," Chen said. He rolled his eyes and told Olivia she had a glorious future in the restaurant business, getting a pleased smile and thank you in return.

Jack sat and covertly examined the two of them, an idea forming in his mind. Maybe he should encourage Chen's infatuation. One never knew. It might replace Anderson. Olivia caught his eye and curled her lip at him as if reading his thoughts and nixing the plot before it began.

"Come on, Max," Jack said. "Pharo is itching for a game of frisbee." He patted his midsection and thanked Olivia for the meal.

Chen immediately rose and started clearing the table. "I'll clean up. Olivia can supervise me but do nothing else."

Olivia gave Jack a smirk and smiled sweetly at Chen.

Chen was gone by the time they returned from the park, and Olivia had books and papers spread out on the table. "Thanks for putting up with my coworker and not minding that I brought him home for dinner. He's been pestering me ever since he first saw you."

"I don't mind," she said without raising her head from her book. "He's rather sweet." *Says the mature, grown-up eighteen-year-old,* thought Jack. Accustomed to the attention, of course. He had to admire the way it rolled off her like a shower, and she didn't bask in it.

"Someday soon, I'd like to bring Edina so you and Max can meet her." Her eyebrows raised in a question. "Edina Chambers?" Jack said.

"Of course." She grinned at him, her eyes speculating. "This is special, is it?"

"Yes," Jack answered thoughtfully.

She smiled then. "Oh, like that. Well sure. When?"

"When you have time." Jack scratched behind his ear. "Actually, she has a birthday on Saturday, the day after tomorrow, and is hosting a small party at her house. Would you like to come with me and Max?" He felt his face burn with heat at her astonished expression.

"You want my opinion of her?"

"No," he said firmly. "But I thought you might be at a loose end this weekend."

She flushed and looked a bit frazzled. "I'm not sure. I am hoping . . ." her expression changed to uncertainty, then at his piercing stare, guilt.

"You hope Anderson will call?"

"A visit, actually." She sat up straighter, defiant. "Or I can accept Ethan's invitation for a date. He'll take me sightseeing. Either way, I will be busy Saturday night."

Jack studied her for a long moment, undecided whether he should comment. Meddling won out; Chen was his partner, after all. "I suspect you know that Chen is aiming for a serious relationship." He pressed his lips together to stop himself from saying more.

"Ethan Chen knows well enough that I only see him as a friend." Her tone was mild, but her manner said he'd gone too far with his opinions.

"Well, if you change your mind, the invitation is open." Jack left her to her homework. He wanted to say that if Anderson hadn't called for a visit already, the odds weren't in her favour for this weekend. Anderson might be smarter than Jack gave him credit for. Absence in both word and person sent a direct message when someone wouldn't settle for denial. He remembered the first day when he had ordered Anderson to take her away, and his reply that, "Olivia doesn't go easily."

Later, Jack took Pharo outside for a last outing and kept on around the block to clear his thoughts. The night was clear. Overhead, a large yellow-orange harvest moon stood out as though someone had trained a beacon on it. Pharo stayed close, pushing up against Jack's leg, needing confirmation of his presence. Since last year's fiasco, when Jack spent weeks in the hospital, Pharo had a fixation about being taken to the kennel by a stranger. "Not going to happen again," Jack told him, tickling his ears.

Turning his thoughts back to Winslow's murder, he mapped out his next steps for the investigation. He was sure Wager would be on board. As for Inspector Dave, he'd have to step aside or keep up.

23

"**SO,** are we good to go on the Winslow case?" Jack asked Wager first thing in the morning.

Wager grimaced as if he'd caught a whiff of something foul. "The short answer is a big fat no," he growled. "National Security and all that. The RCs are demanding all the crime scene information, the coroner's report, along with our reports. Everything." His voice became falsetto, mocking. "Nothing remains in our files pertaining to anything, anywhere, nowhere, nohow." Wager waved his hands precariously near to upsetting an evidence box on his desk.

Jack swore, loud enough to raise eyebrows. Hank Vassar, who wasn't Jack's fan and typically kept his distance, grinned and waited for the reprisals. Wager forbade black humour and cursing, saying the squad room wasn't a bawdy house. Nobody excused except himself. Vassar moved closer to hear the rest of it, Dyer right behind him.

"Okay, that's enough," Wager commanded quietly. "We don't have the manpower for a full-fledged investigation, even if we borrowed from other crime units." Wager gathered papers on his desk and pointed to the box. "Chen. Get over here," he barked. "You make up the list while Tuesday and I sort out this mess before we send it. I don't give a rat's ass how fast they want it. They aren't getting one piece until they sign for it. In duplicate."

Jack pulled a crumpled scrap of paper from his pocket, the one he'd found and forgotten to log, and handed it to Wager with an explanation. Wager scowled and told Chen to add it to the inventory.

"It doesn't seem right." Jack began pacing to contain his frustration.

"They get the credit for all our work, plus copy our conclusions."

"Simpson isn't that easy," Wager said. "He got their promise to bring us in when they wind it up. We'll get credit and make ourselves look good."

"I'll believe it when I see it," Jack grumbled. He opened his mouth to argue further, convince Wager to go back to Simpson, then thought better of it. "Inadequate, that's what they think we are."

"Too bad, Tuesday," Vassar said, "those poor Mounties don't have people as sharp as you. Maybe you should offer your advice so they can get on with solving it."

Wager roared. "Can it!" His gaze swept over Chen, who was busy starting his list. "Vassar, you and Dyer take over the B and E case for now. Chen will fill you in." Chen made a face.

"We've got the biker drug case to prepare for," Vassar protested. "Court date in two days."

"Oh, pardon me," Wager drawled, menacing, "I thought you were showing the rest of us how you handle your caseload. I assumed you had time to spare."

Vassar clamped his lips together, backed up into Dyer, elbowed him away, and stamped to his desk.

Wager eyes lit on Dyer next. "Dyer, I'm still waiting for that report on the juvie case. Was there assault, or wasn't there? You've had it for a day already." Dyer ducked his head and followed Vassar to his work spot.

"You!" Wager barked at Chen and Jack. "Sit. Let's get this done."

BLUE skies and sunshine greeted Jack on Saturday morning as he slid open the balcony doors. The crispness of fall wafted in, mixed with the faint scent of burnt leaves. Outside, the boulevard was lined with a blend of yellow and green foliage, stirring in him a faint, unrealistic hope that summer might stretch on for another month.

In the kitchen, Olivia hummed as she made breakfast while stealing repeated glances at the clock. Jack wondered if there was a no-return hour when hopes of Anderson's call would dwindle. In spite of himself, his own thoughts waffled between hoping her wish would come true and praying it wouldn't.

"Edina's birthday is today," he said. "What kind of cake do you think I should buy?"

"Buy?" Olivia drawled in a pseudo-shocked tone. "You want to buy a cake?"

"Well, she might bake one, but nobody should have to bake their own birthday cake."

Olivia threw her hands in the air. "I'll make her a lemon chiffon cake. It won't take long."

Jack managed an innocent expression of delighted surprise, congratulating himself on planting that seed. "Thanks, Olivia. I'll tell her you made it special."

"Which I will, by the way." Olivia rolled her eyes, but Jack could see she was pleased that, for once, they weren't at each other's throats.

Max came out of his room, dressed in a shirt and jeans. His uniform. Jack eyed the small flowers on the jersey material. He knew the pattern was the latest fashion, but Jack's own tastes didn't conform. Maybe it was his army dress protocol, but the modern jersey prints always looked like pyjamas to him.

"Edina's birthday party is today," Jack told him as Max poured orange juice and drank without sitting down. Jack frowned. "It starts in mid-afternoon with a barbeque. We should be home by eight o'clock. Not too late."

Max sat the glass down on the table, forehead screwed up in worry lines. "We?"

"Yes, you and me. Edina said there would be people your age there, and I wanted you to meet her. This is the best occasion, when other people will be around to make it easier on you."

Max looked uncertain. He glanced over at Olivia, but she had suddenly found her coffee cup interesting. He looked back at Jack.

"Please?" Jack said, and after a slight hesitation, Max nodded. Jack smiled and silently thanked Ursula for bringing up a polite young man who was willing to please his parents. Though he could see that Max was not overly anxious to attend a party where he knew nobody, most of them adults. It said something that he was willing to sacrifice time for Jack's sake.

They left early enough so he could help Edina as promised. On the way, just across the High Level bridge, he parked beside a flower shop he knew on 109th. It didn't take long, and he put the wrapped flowers on the back seat with the cake in its Tupperware container.

As Jack waited for traffic to go by so he could pull away from the curb, Max said, "This afternoon at school, there will be tryouts for the football team. Not the football I know, but Canadian football. Tommy and I were going to try out."

The penny dropped, and Jack turned to Max. "The tryout is only one day? Just today?" Max nodded, looking unhappy, keeping his eyes on his hands and not on Jack.

Jack exhaled and sat back. "Oh. So if you come with me, you'll miss out." He turned to Max. "Did you want to be on the team?"

"I thought I might like to see how I do." He faced Jack. "I am sorry. If you don't want me to, I won't."

And miss out on what high school is, thought Jack. *Building friendships and all that team spirit? The stuff I missed out on?*

"I'll turn around and drive you back home," he said. "There'll be more birthday parties."

"No," Max burst out, suddenly happier. "I can go on my own. I'll just walk back across the bridge. Until you get home, I'll stay at Tommy's. We can rent a movie." He pulled down the handle on the door, ready to get out, as if he expected Jack to change his mind. "Thank you. Tell Mrs . . . Edina, I wish her a pleasant birthday, and soon we will meet."

He opened his mouth to tell Max to be careful, but his son was already halfway down the street. Jack watched him in the rearview mirror for a moment, sighed, and joined the northbound traffic.

By eight o'clock, the guests had gone, and Jack was helping Edina collect the disposables, napkins, ashtrays, and bottles scattered around the patio and inside the house.

"There. That's the lot, I think." Edina dropped the last bag and slammed down the garbage bin lid. Jack came up behind her and put his arms around her, kissing the back of her neck. She turned in his arms, and he kissed her long and lingering. "Mmm," she said, "tastes like more." He grinned and took her up on the invitation.

"Did you see all the knowing looks we got from your relatives?" he whispered into her neck.

"I did. Nosy parkers."

"I made sure they saw how devoted I was so that you're stuck with me. If you ditch me now, they'll think you're too fussy."

"And don't think I didn't notice, you scheming cop."

"Do you mind? The cop thing, I mean." He was half serious.

She leaned back in his arms to look at him. "No, of course I don't. I wouldn't have accepted your first invitation if I minded." Her lips curved in a smile. "As long as you realize, I'm the elder here, and you should always listen to your elders."

"Yeah, not even six months. I like older women, especially if they have the name Edina Chambers."

That settled it, he thought, feeling the warm sense of something right. It had been a good day, and as he headed home, he skipped up the stairs two at a time. Jack whistled tunelessly, relaxed and content with life.

Pharo met him at the door, tap-dancing around him, which meant he wanted to go out. Jack obediently fetched the leash.

Olivia poked her head out the door of her bedroom. "You're home early."

Hand on the door to go out again, he raised his eyebrows at her. "Didn't expect to see you home either. Wasn't Chen going to take you sightseeing or something?" Feeling slightly suspicious, he wondered if she was alone. Did Anderson arrive?

"I decided being alone would give me a start at an assignment," she said. "Did you have a good time?"

Jack grinned and nodded. "None better."

"And Max?"

"He begged off for a football team tryout at the school. He and Tommy."

Olivia came the rest of the way out of her room into the hall. "But . . ." she wrinkled her nose in puzzlement.

"But what? Is he still at Tommy's? He said they might rent a movie." Jack's voice slowed, his words trailing off at the expression in Olivia's eyes.

"But . . . he isn't . . . Tommy came to the door this afternoon and wondered if Max had decided to go with you after all. I told him you'd left together." Olivia came closer. "Am I telling on Max? Is he up to something that he didn't want you to know? That accounts for the phone calls. Somebody asking for you."

"What phone calls?" Jack said softly through stiff lips. *Lie? Max doesn't lie,* the voice in his head told him. But Olivia was still talking, and he couldn't hear her over the howling siren in his head. Panic seized his chest, sharp and tight, almost suffocating. The siren was still blaring. No, it wasn't a siren—the phone.

Carefully, he put down Pharo's leash and went to the phone. He thought nobody was on the other end, but then he could hear a soft, indrawn breath.

"Don't look for him. Don't report him, and he will be okay. When we get what we want, he will come home. If you disobey, we'll send him back to Germany."

24

"WHAT do you want?" Jack shouted into the deadline, his voice echoing through the silence.

He quickly dialled 911 with shaking fingers, then gave his name and shield number. "My son's been kidnapped. I need you to contact Detective Sergeant Paul Wager and tell him I am coming down to Headquarters. He needs to meet me there—now."

Behind him, Olivia stood wide-eyed, the pupils of her eyes large and dark. "Max has been kidnapped? Why? What . . . ?"

Jack brushed her aside. Pharo yodelled, startling them both. "I don't know. But lock the door and don't open it for anyone but me. Understand?"

Olivia nodded, wrapping her arms around herself as if suddenly cold. "What can I do? Anderson . . . my Dad. I can phone. They can help."

"No!" Jack snapped, sharper than intended. "Not one word to Anderson or Luke."

"But . . ." Her face twisted, near tears.

"I don't want Luke interfering. He'll make it worse." She stood there shaking her head in denial. "Olivia, stop," Jack ordered. "If Luke hears about this, his first thought will be to yank you out of a danger zone, and you'll be gone faster than greased lightning. Is that what you want?"

"No," she whispered. "But Anderson has connections."

"I haven't time for this," Jack said, his voice flat with anger. He took Pharo's leash and hooked it onto his collar. "I don't know when

I'll be back." He put his hand on Olivia's shoulder. "You have to promise me. Lock the door. Understand?"

"I promise," she whispered. "But why Max?"

Jack was already out the door with Pharo and didn't answer. He waited until he heard the deadbolt click in place, then left. Halfway down the stairs, he groaned. Edina. He'd have to warn her. If Max was taken by Hudek's people, then he could put pressure on anyone connected to Jack. In turn, Olivia and Edina could be used to pressure Max. Jack knew what they were after. It had to be the notebook Max had brought with him. The one Alec, or whatever his name was, asked about. Max had nothing else in his possession.

He climbed into the car, gripping the steering wheel so tightly his knuckles turned white as images flashed through his mind—Max being dragged back to East Germany, accused of betrayal, facing horrors Jack couldn't let himself imagine. Pharo whined in the back seat, a low, mournful sound that mirrored Jack's dread.

"ALL bets are off. I'm now in, no matter how deep it gets," Jack stood before Wagar, square and unyielding. "I won't wait until Simpson decides this is serious enough to phone the plainclothes and let them know." Pharo padded around the squad room, sniffing here and there and finally finding a familiar odour at Jack's desk. He went into the knee well and curled up, looking sorrowful.

"We've got notices out to everybody and a telex to every division across the city," Wager said, ignoring Jack's declaration.

"Telex? Those notices will just go up on the squad room's bulletin board. Anyone can see it. They'll hear it on the radios. Wager . . ."

"That's enough!" The sergeant put his palm up. "No bulletin boards, no calls. You know better than that. From what you said, Max must have been taken before, on, or just after crossing the High Level. We've got officers talking to every store owner along the way, asking if someone saw something." He paused and softened his tone. "Going public means whoever took him will know that you ignored their warnings. Do you want to take that chance?"

"No, Yes. I don't know. Maybe not." Jack groaned. "But the best chance of someone seeing him put into a car is someone on the street or in a car. Hudek knows that."

"Providing it was Hudek that took him."

"Who else? The candyman?"

Wager closed his eyes, telling Jack he'd ignore the sarcasm. "Let's assume it is him, then—and I believe you too, but if we faced Hudek with no evidence, we'll be worse off than we are now."

Jack opened his mouth and then closed it. He exhaled, puffing out his lips. "We have to find out where they'd take him. Call in every favour and informant and get their opinion. I'll go see Apple at McGruber's Pub." Apple was Hugo MacIntosh, Jack's army buddy. Apple had not come out of Korea intact, and Jack had kept tabs on him, helping when he could. In return, Apple gave Jack what information he garnered from street living.

Wager agreed but looked doubtful. "If Hudek is an agent, I doubt any of our sources will even have heard of him, or we'd have intel on him already."

"I won't know that until I try," Jack retorted, reading Wager's stoic face. He sensed Wager was intentionally dropping small objections, coaxing Jack into responding, maybe even trying to calm him.

"From what you've told me, Max isn't some typical teenage boy who will cry out for his mommy at the first sign of trouble. He's lived under the iron fist his whole life. I'm betting he knows how to survive when danger threatens." Wager shot him a smile under his thick moustache. "Underneath your panic, you know that as well as I do. Become the cop now, not the father. Think on that for a minute, Jack."

"I've been doing little else but think," Jack protested. "Max knows how to keep away from Stasi thugs and their ilk, but he's never been physically in their clutches. Questioned, maybe even tortured." Jack gulped, his breathing harsh, thinking of Howard Winslow. "He's just a kid, Paul. Will he be capable of resisting and holding together without lasting damage?"

Wager opened his mouth, then closed it. Wordless, they stared at each other for a long moment.

"Get on the blower and call this number, Wager. Please." And Jack laid Dave's card with his telephone number in front of Wager. "The inspector gave it to me. Ask for Dave and wait for his call back. No more hokum about national security from him." Jack no longer cared whether his voice showed his desperation. "It's gone way past that. I want your support, but if I have to go on my own, Wager, I will."

"I know that, Jack," Wager's voice was calm, matter of fact. "Okay, but no action without me. Got it? And I'll let Simpson know. He won't be happy, but then he's never happy about anything anyway." Wager chewed on his moustache, thinking. "It's been a while, and I'm itching for action too." He shot Jack a warning glance. "And you never heard me say that."

On the way home, Jack detoured toward 66th Avenue and 92nd Street to McGruber's Pub. At this time on Saturday night, the gamblers will have just arrived, hoping to win even knowing the odds were against them. Months ago, the place had been raided to uncover Luke's money laundering effort. Phineas McGruber had waved a document showing it was a private charity fundraising event. However, Luke's plan to grow his crime syndicate never prospered, and he left town. Jack had no doubt the illegal gambling was ongoing.

About to leave Pharo guarding the car, Jack instead hooked the leash to his collar and went to find Apple. At the back of the pub and up the rickety stairs to the second-floor landing.

Jack paused two doors down the landing, at the entrance to the pub's real wealth and where the customers addicted to illegal gambling gathered. Apple's welcoming smile at his knock faded when he saw Jack. He frowned at Pharo.

"Well, long time no see, Jack," he said, blocking his path. He looked over Jack's shoulder and scanned the landing for more police.

"What do you want? Or is it because you miss me?" Apple snorted, pleased with his joke. Jack noted that for once, Apple looked sober and couldn't help but smile back, hoping it meant that he'd tamed whatever devils had pursued him since Korea.

"I need your help," Jack said outright and saw surprise followed by suspicion flash across Apple's eyes. "Can I come in?"

Apple glanced back inside the room, hesitating. He stepped outside on the landing and closed the door behind him. "If you are asking me for another favour, Jack, forget it. We're quits, remember? I don't owe you anymore."

"You never did, Apple. Whatever is in the past belongs there. Not here." He stepped to one side and over to the railing. "I have a son, Apple."

"I know. He defected. People talk," Curiosity won over suspicion. "Waiting this long to tell me about it means you want something. Why me?"

"He's been kidnapped. Someone from East Germany. You know what those commies are like. They'll take him back unless I find him quickly." Jack gripped Apple's forearm.

Apple took a step back, eyes wide. "Oh God, I'm sorry, Jack. Bastards."

"Jeez, Apple," Jack choked, holding back tears. "He's a kid, just fifteen."

Apple brought himself up to his full height of five-ten. "What are you going to do?" Without waiting for Jack to reply, he added. "Are you here to ask if I know anything? Well, I don't, Jack. I would have let you know if I'd heard anything like that." He grimaced. "Even though you made trouble for Mr. Phineas, and he wasn't pleased."

The door behind them opened, and a croupier in a vest stuck his head out. "You're wanted," He jerked his head to indicate someone inside the room.

"Mr. Phineas, Jack. I gotta go. I'll keep my ears open, but that's a different kind of operation than what I'd hear about. Nobody will be talking about Commies kidnapping a kid." He turned to leave. "Sorry, Jack," he said, his mouth turned down, pitying.

"Let me talk to McGruber, Apple."

Apple's pity changed to displeasure and doubt. He inspected Jack's tight lips and pleading eyes and eventually sighed. "Wait here." Jack gripped the railing until his hands cramped, waiting. Moments later, the door opened, and Apple stood aside, inviting Jack inside. Jack, Pharo beside him, followed Apple past the poker and blackjack tables, hardly noticing the action. They entered a room down a short corridor.

"Detective Tuesday, or should I say Jackson?" greeted McGruber from his automated wheelchair. McGruber sported a natty outfit, formal tuxedo style, his usual evening garb. His face still had a neat goatee. His tiny body sat squarely in the wheelchair, stubby fingers resting on the arms near the automated controls. Intelligent eyes ran over Jack's features and then to Pharo, sitting quietly at Jack's side. "Mr. MacIntosh tells me your son has been kidnapped. Why do you think I can be of help? Surely you don't think I am familiar with agents of another government?"

"It's kind of you to hear me out," Jack said politely. "I'll be blunt because time is not my friend." He waved his hand at the room outside the door. "In your operation, you must be aware of many things, and right now, I need your observation skills." Jack briefly brought McGruber up to date on only what he needed to know. "You hear things, new businesses starting up, the sources of those funds, and their profitability," he ended. "Without naming names, if you wish, I would like to know who suddenly has become richer, receiving funds from exports, a source that wasn't there before. That sort of thing." He spread his hands out suggestively.

McGruber sat silent, eyes on Jack, taking it all in. Finally, he nodded. "Yes, that sort of thing. And why should I tell you, even if I have heard that sort of thing?"

"Because you're a Canadian. You are aware I am talking about agents operating in our country, spreading lies, recruiting allies to their cause."

"I know no such thing, Detective."

Jack frowned at him. "I just gave you details that are way beyond my authority to reveal, Mr. McGruber. Yes, it is my son, but he risked his life to escape, and for a fifteen-year-old, it required great courage. He deserves some help, not an excuse for pretending not to know. Don't you think?"

McGruber didn't react. His fingers fiddled with the buttons on the armrest as if memorizing their function. Pharo suddenly left Jack's side and padded to the wheelchair dragging his leash. McGruber's eyes rounded in alarm, his grip tightened on the armrests.

"Pharo." But the dog stopped in front of McGruber and placed a paw up on the footrest where the man's short legs protruded.

McGruber relaxed, snorted, and then ignored him. "Trained to beg, is he? You should take him on the street. Quite a performance. But it isn't necessary, Detective." He stopped and eyed Jack for a long moment. "There is a person," he said finally. "His stagnant import business appeared to suddenly improve. He bragged it was because he branched into kitchenware. It made me curious because I wondered if the market suddenly realized it is short of those items." McGruber smiled. "Glassware in the pub is always in need of replenishing, so I gave him a large order, asking for a discount, of course." He fingered his goatee, and Jack saw a small wrinkle form on his brow.

Jack read his mind. "He told you there might be a delay in filling the order. Because export documents from Czechoslovakia were difficult to obtain. The communists, no doubt."

McGruber's eyes sparkled as they met Jack's. A smile showed his small white teeth. "Yes. He was apologetic."

"And does this man have a warehouse, by any chance?" Jack held his breath, his chest constricting. Please, he prayed silently.

"Probably," McGruber nodded. "But I can't tell you where it is."

Jack let out his breath. "But you will make discreet inquiries?"

McGruber paused, searching Jack's face, then seemed to make up his mind. "I might."

Jack could only say, "Thank you," knowing sooner or later this favour would be called in. *Needs must*, he decided, not quite shaking off a dark cloud forming around him.

F. NELSON SMITH | 232

25

IT was only a little past ten, but a weariness of body and spirit sucked at Jack's energy as he and Pharo plodded up the stairs to the third floor. Had he made any progress? McGruber and Apple seemed the only leads with any promise, but involving himself with McGruber carried its own risk. Jack was in the dark about the man's true character and could only guess how much he would be committed to repaying favours. Commitments—once started would not stop. Small to begin with, then continuously ramped up. Testing the limits until one day, they would devour him. And if McGruber still had ties to Luke, this move could make things worse. Right now, though, he was too exhausted to think much beyond Max.

Jack slotted his key in the door but forgot it had been bolted from the inside. He rapped the door. "It's me," he called softly while Pharo huffed along the bottom edge.

She silently let him in, and once inside, he found she wasn't alone. Rory Sullivan rose from the couch. "I threatened to sit outside the door until she let me in," he said immediately.

"I used my head. I trust him," Olivia said, calm but resolute. "And I wanted protection if it became necessary."

Pharo padded to Rory, sniffed him over, and then to Olivia, who gave him a biscuit treat and rubbed him briskly along his side while Pharo wiggled in ecstasy.

"Tommy is turning himself inside out and made me come over. So, I'm here to help, and it looks like you need it." He examined Jack's face. "You look like hell."

"I made Pharo liver and carrots," Olivia said. "Is it too late?" Pharo beat her to the kitchen.

Jack nodded thanks and made a beeline to the phone, dialling Headquarters. "Any news?" he asked after identifying himself. "You're sure?" he asked after listening to the report. "Yes, I know that."

Smothering his frustration, Jack stifled a yawn and went to the kitchen, coming back with two Pilsners. He handed one to Rory.

"Tommy's a good kid," he said, nodding to Rory as a way of acknowledging his help without words. "He looked after Mrs. Zamborski like she was his own grandmother—made sure she never wanted for anything. Always suspected I had ulterior motives whenever I stopped by."

Rory nodded at Jack, showing his appreciation with a salute of his Pilsner before taking a gulp. He waited until Jack settled himself in the chair before he sat again on the couch. With arms crossed, Olivia stood by the balcony door, surveying them while listening to every word.

"Tommy's got this chivalry complex. He needs someone to care for." Rory agreed. "His mother . . . anyway, the kid's a walking charity." He leaned forward, his face grim. "What can I do, Jack? I assume the police are all out looking for him? One of their own is missing?"

Jack looked at Olivia, his eyes inquiring. She shook her head that she hadn't said anything.

"Anything the police are doing can't be made public," Jack warned and proceeded to give some essential details. "If I don't comply, they will stash Max on a plane headed for East Germany. I don't have to tell you what that would mean for him."

"They are East Germans? Commies? You aren't going to listen to that crap, are you? No, of course not," he leaned forward, looking at Jack. "Not that you can afford to tell them that. What do you need? My outfit, *Brewsters,* treat each other as family, and we look out for each other. We're pretty smart at finding things without anyone knowing our connection." Rory's glance swept over Jack. "People in the oil business are a bit like the place where you work. I just need to know what we're looking for."

Jack sighed, rolled the beer bottle between his palms, and opened his mouth to refuse Rory's offer. Then logic took over. He mentally thumped the side of his head. Tiredness was closing down his brain. "Brewster's is that wire rope facility in the new industrial section of Nisku, right?"

"Yeah, we've just moved to a new and bigger setup. The area has good access to the airport but is still being developed. But the advantage is that the owners know one another and know what they do. I know the guys in our outfit won't back off from a fight if that's what you're wondering." Rory's chin jutted out, and his biceps rippled as if to prove a point. "You can trust them to keep their mouths shut. The oil business is one secretive industry anyway, Jack. Too much competition. If we let out our customer's orders or plans to their competitors, our business would be finished."

"Would they know who owns which warehouse in the vicinity and who might rely on a close relationship with the airport and Customs?"

"These guys know more than they let on, so I would say yes off the cuff. I can find out. What are you after?"

"Not sure," Jack said slowly. "There was an iffy connection to a warehouse, but too cloudy to act on. Perhaps if your guys could snoop around? Find out if all the business ventures there trade openly. I'm looking for a business that is a front, not legit. It would be the sort of place that Max might be taken."

Rory raised his eyebrows, and his face cleared of doubt. "It's got something to do with that guy at the lake, hasn't it? I should have twigged that Max would know right off if someone wasn't on the up and up." Rory clenched his fists around his beer. "I'm sorry, Jack, I should have pasted the guy. Instead, I thought Max was . . ." He stopped and shook his head.

"I got taken in too." Jack waved the apology away. "They think Max has names. It seems important to them for some reason."

"Names? Whose? Why would a fifteen-year-old kid have names?"

"I don't know." Jack gave a brief account of his encounter with Alec in the park. "Max ran from Seattle with nothing but the clothes he wore."

Rory took another mouthful of beer and swallowed, his face thoughtful. "Maybe they were chasing some guy in Seattle and thought he may have slipped Max something to carry over the border?"

"I doubt Max would have broadcast his intention of defecting." Jack glanced at his watch, surprised his hands were steady when his heartbeat wasn't. "These people only ever believe their own version of facts anyway. He's been gone a good seven hours. I have to find him, Rory. Fast." His voice broke.

"Right." Rory stood, his lips tight. "I'll get on it, and again early tomorrow for those I can't reach tonight. My guys will be all over that area like fleas." He shook Jack's hand, gave him a reassuring pat on the shoulder, then nodded to Olivia and left.

Jack felt a glimmer of hope, albeit faint. Keeping the kidnappers thinking he was obeying their command that he didn't involve the police meant he now relied on McGruber and Rory.

Exhausted, he dragged himself into the shower before bed, yet once under the covers, sleep eluded him. He tossed and turned, wrestling with his pillow, the sheets, and most of all, the day's events—all the could-haves and should-haves weighing down on him. Finally, he sat on the edge of the bed, his head in his hands. Pharo woke, sat up and yawned, waiting for what was next. After a long moment, he padded over to Jack and put his nose on his knee. Jack petted him, then rose and went across the hall into Max's bedroom, Pharo keeping him company.

He fetched the package from the dresser's bottom drawer and took it into the dining area. Before he got down to business, he phoned Headquarters again but got the same reply as last time. After receiving assurances and a polite reprimand, he accepted the cops on the streets, and detectives were doing their jobs. To think otherwise meant he questioned his own organization as if it was something he'd be lax in himself. The thought calmed him.

Jack spread the contents of the package across the table. In his initial rush to open it, he'd overlooked an envelope inside. As he opened it, a small pile of photos slipped out—snapshots of Max growing up. Ursula was there too, the way he last pictured her, Max on her knee, a sober little boy facing the camera, unsmiling. Jack swallowed the lump in his throat, blinking away the tears blurring the two faces in the photos. Ursula, older, had large eyes with no expression but the same smile he'd imagined a thousand times over the years. Most of them were outside a building Jack took to be a pool; Max, in various poses, from a gangly kid to more recent. Some were of his training in the pool, and a few with a grinning Max holding a medal on a ribbon. Jack turned the photos over and saw Ursula's handwriting, stating the age and location. The last photo showed both of them, Ursula thin, her lips smiling, but the smile didn't reach her eyes. She must have been sick then. Jack clenched his fists. Would she have still been alive if she had not returned to the GDR? Did she die from nuclear exposure? Tears spilled down his cheeks. Scientists didn't often die from their work. His hand swiped at his cheeks. It was no use guessing.

The photos went neatly back into the envelope, and Jack picked up the notebook. Inside, he found each competition organized by class, location, and results—a careful record lovingly kept by a proud mother, Jack thought. He leafed through the pages, reading the locations and cities of the meets. All the earliest were in East Germany, and then Max had progressed enough to be entered into European competitions. Jack started to recognize the competitors' names, and Max's score in microseconds was sometimes better than one or two and sometimes behind. A small smile touched his lips as he imagined Max's thrill at beating an opponent who'd become his primary focus during those gruelling training sessions.

Curious, Jack focused on a few recurring names, tracking how Max had fared against them over time. He spotted the name Harris again. Odd, it was out of place. He told himself it wasn't odd for a new competitor to appear and continued searching. Frowning, he started leafing through the pages faster, searching. Finally, after another half hour, he began to doubt his senses, and names started running together in his head. He needed sleep. Reluctantly, he knew it was time to bundle the whole lot together and replace it. He tucked it in the same place and about to close the drawer, saw Max's knife at the back. The knife Jack told him to put away because it wasn't needed here. Maybe if he'd had it on his person, he'd not been kidnapped. Then again, he might have been dead for trying to defend himself and losing.

He replaced the knife and looked over the room before he left as if he might have missed a clue telling him Max's whereabouts. Pharo had curled up on Max's bed, his head on the pillow. The sight of the undisturbed bed and Pharo's mournful pose brought him to the brink of tears again. Hold it together, he silently told Max. I'll find you before another day is done.

He forced himself to bed, knowing he'd push his luck if he phoned Headquarters again. Morning light poured through the blinds, stirring him awake. He jumped out of bed, cursing the hours wasted sleeping and made a dash toward the bathroom. From the bathroom, he heard Olivia's voice, along with another, which raised the hairs on the back of his neck.

Anderson.

26

THEY sipped coffee over the remains of breakfast, plates littered with crumbs and the faint scent of bacon lingering in the air. Pharo had settled down beside Anderson, on the alert for a handout in case there were any going. Still in a temper from sleeping in, Jack manhandled a chair across the floor with a scrape and sat down just as Olivia jumped up, her expression rapidly changing from pleasure to dread.

"You look like you need a large dose of coffee," she said, too loudly, and hurried into the kitchen. She came back carrying a mug and a pot of coffee. Jack ignored her and stared straight at Anderson.

"The face that would sour milk." Anderson leaned back and arched his brow as he studied Jack. He took a casual sip of coffee, his gaze flickering between Olivia and Jack. "Anything the matter?"

Jack's eyes narrowed, searching Anderson's own for any knowledge about Max's disappearance and if he was concealing the truth for Olivia's sake. Then again, Anderson had probably already surmised that she was hiding something. Anderson's eyes went from questioning to resolved, and Jack's suspicion turned to hope that Anderson would likely think Jack's ongoing grudge against Olivia soured the mood.

Olivia poured his coffee, then touched his arm, and Jack turned an accusing gaze on her. She moved slightly so that Anderson couldn't see her face. "A good breakfast to start the day?" She tilted her head toward Anderson and mouthed a silent no. Jack ignored her.

"How'd you get here, and why?"

"I flew into Villeneuve Airport," Anderson replied coolly. "An errand for the boss. And to make sure she's behaving herself, following all the rules," he added. He held up his cup for a refill. Olivia obliged, smiling at him, but her hand was not steady, and coffee slopped over the rim. Anderson stared for a short second at Olivia, then nodded a thank you and took a sip, eyes switching to Jack. Olivia put the coffee pot on the table and slipped back into her chair, then immediately jumped up again. "Breakfast," she declared but made no move to leave. As if afraid to leave them both alone. Her eyes, the difference in colour apparent, stayed on Jack's.

Anderson laid his mug down and faced Olivia. "It doesn't take a Geiger counter to measure the sudden electricity in this room," he offered, his tone mild. "Anyone care to let me in on what's going on between you two?"

"Nothing. Now you've seen for yourself that Olivia is alive and well, I expect you'll want to leave so you can report to your boss." Jack gave him an evil smile. "But finish your coffee first."

Anderson's face remained impassive, but Jack sensed a shift in his posture, a tightening of muscles that signalled readiness. Olivia drew in a sharp breath. Pharo moved closer to Jack, sensing the undercurrents. He pawed at Jack's leg.

The three sat in taut silence until the phone's shrill ring shattered the tension. Pharo yodelled. Anderson's glance went between Jack and Olivia, his eyes calculating and expression pinched. Jack went to answer the phone.

"Mr. McGruber would like to speak to you," Apple said, his tone sharp.

"I'm all ears," Jack quipped.

"No need to be sarcastic, Jack. I'll put you through to his line."

"You sound just like a switchboard operator," Jack said, but all he heard were clicks in return.

"Yes, I find Mr. Macintosh more indispensable every day."

"Apologies, Mr. McGruber. I'm letting tension get the better of me."

"I understand." Phineas McGruber paused. "About the conversation we had yesterday. There may be some answers in the new industrial zone near the airport. A warehouse owned by a firm called Everything Kitchen. I'm afraid I cannot be of more help. Perhaps your . . . partners will go from there. Good morning, Detective Tuesday. We've never spoken."

"Thank . . ." Jack began, but the line went dead. Heart thumping, he pushed the plunger and dialled again. "Rory? Listen, can you find out if there is a warehouse in Nisku owned by an importer dealing in kitchen products? The name might be "Everything Kitchen." He listened, then said, "I'll be here. Seconds would be better, but the best you can do." He hung up and turned, only to find Anderson right behind him.

"Is Max still sleeping?" Anderson's voice was conversational, innocent. "Teens can sleep through any noise. Seems like a long time since I could."

"Right. I'll tell him you missed him and said hello," Jack improvised.

"You do that," Anderson said, flints of ice sparking in his eyes.

"Got any more of that coffee, Olivia?" Jack asked and picked up his mug, happy to see that his hand was steady, contrary to what was happening inside him. "Toast too, if there is any going." He returned to eyeing Anderson, this time considering a new idea.

Olivia silently slipped into the kitchen, her footsteps barely whispering against the floor as if she were trying not to disturb the fragile quiet. Unspoken resentments in the air wrapped around them like a thick fog.

The phone rang again, and at the first ring, Jack picked up the receiver, muttered his identity, and listened. He wrote an address, then disconnected. For a long moment, he inspected what he had written, then decided. Without glancing at Anderson or Olivia, he fingered Edina's number on the dial.

"I need you to do something for me," he said as soon as she answered.

He heard her indrawn breath. "Have you news?"

"Eddie, I have to know you're safe. I don't know if Max has talked or if Howard did. Maybe given your name. They will do anything to get what they want. I'm sending someone over to stay with you, and I want you to do whatever they suggest. Can you do that without asking me questions now?"

"Of course." No hesitation.

"So, two people and Pharo will be at your house. It's safer than here, I think. One person is Olivia, the other is a . . . friend, name of Anderson. I don't know how long they will be there, but Anderson will know what to do. They'll be there within the hour." He drew a deep breath. "Okay?"

"Be careful, Jack. You can explain later."

Jack turned to Anderson and Olivia. "I need your word that none of this goes further than this room."

"Yes!" Olivia immediately said, her tone eager. Anderson only glared at him. Jack's eyes didn't waver, and Anderson got the message. He had no choice; his first duty lay with Olivia, even as he navigated the delicate balance with her father while keeping himself insulated.

After a moment, Anderson huffed noisy air between his lips. "Lay it on me."

"Everyone associated with me, including Olivia, needs to be secure and vanish for a time. I hope to have this cleared up by the end of the day. You're the only one here that can keep them safe." He locked eyes with Anderson. "You don't want to know what they did to Howard Winslow." He paused, letting the weight of his words hang. "Just as important, you can't talk about this. If you need to explain your reason for being here, perhaps Olivia talked you into sightseeing or whatever. I don't care what. You know what I'm saying?" Jack quit before he lapsed into begging.

"But, my classes," Olivia put in. "I'm scheduled to prep for the lunch at Ernest's tomorrow. I can't miss it." She set her mouth in a determined line, then took in Jack's expression. "On second thought," she improvised. "Getting there from wherever is not a problem. I know how to protect myself." She nodded at Jack and Anderson as if that settled it.

Anderson looked like he wanted to curse, already regretting his presence. "I should have listened to you the first day and taken her back," he told Jack, his tone fierce.

Olivia stared at him as if he'd just slapped her. "I thought you were on my side," she whispered. "The opportunity . . . you wanted it too, and . . . to be together." She gulped, her hands cupped her mouth as if she was about to throw up. Jack caught a fleeting glimpse of anguish on Anderson's face before he turned away, a silent admission which told Jack that Anderson was using this moment to distance himself from her.

Compassion jabbed at his chest, making it feel tight. "That was then," he replied to Anderson's comment, cutting through the moment before it spiralled into something darker. "And this is now. Things change. She's part of this family, and I've decided she should stay as long as she wants." From the corner of his eye, he saw Olivia's despair morph into surprise, then gratitude.

She straightened and turned to Anderson, "You have to do what he asks. Dad will make me go back. You can't just leave. Not now."

Anderson let his shoulders sag, giving in, but Jack saw bitterness and acceptance of his lot. "Just this once. I'm in." Pharo padded over and took his hand in his mouth. Anderson closed his eyes like he wanted to snatch it away. Jack pasted a grin on his mouth, and Anderson frowned and glared at them all in turn. "Pretty low, sending in your dog."

Jack got down to business and talked. Anderson listened closely, nodding, and Jack was thankful he asked no questions or pleaded for alternate scenarios. Anderson glanced often at Olivia, assessing the information. "I know I've put you into a difficult situation," Jack said wryly, "but you asked for it in a manner of speaking. If you'd stayed in Winnipeg where you belong, you wouldn't be in this situation."

"I can handle it," Anderson shot back.

Just the same, Jack caught a flash of indecision, making Jack wonder if he was rethinking his strategy. What side was he really on? Whose loyalties? Had he turned?

A wave of sympathy washed over Jack. It must be awful to have his job, he thought, not for the first time.

JACK parked at headquarters and saw Wager's car pull in beside him. Without a word, they headed into the building and up to the squad room, where the rest had gathered. Jack knew Wager had been busy since his call—just as he expected.

"Okay, what have we got?" Simpson ordered as they all sat and faced him at the front.

Wager began to summarize, but the information was scant. "Anyone add to that?" He looked around the room.

"Um," Hank Vassar said, drawing all eyes to him. He consulted his notes. "Mirabelle's." He spoke directly to Jack, explaining. "All the shops and street businesses on that block where you dropped him off. I thought maybe someone may have seen Max."

"Yes, Hank," Wager prompted.

"I interviewed Mirabelle's kitchen staff." Vassar looked pleased with himself at being the centre of attention. "A sous chef said he passed someone who fit Max's description when he entered the bridge on the South side. So Max must have been at least as far as Saskatchewan Drive and 109th." He forestalled Wager's question. "He said Max was walking fast but didn't look like he was being pursued."

A police sergeant spoke up, "A lot of traffic merges from different areas around that spot. Easy to pick up and drop people off without notice. Other than the theatre, which is closed at that time of day, not much else. We drew a blank, searching for anyone who might have seen him on the south side of the river. So, I'd say that's where he was taken."

After a moment's quiet, Simpson spoke. "Okay, that's all for now.

Except for those directly involved, carry on with your duties. We need to outline and agree on a plan and get the right people." By that, Jack assumed the right people were Inspector Dave and his staff sergeant. "Until then, nobody makes a move. Understand?" Simpson continued.

Jack kept his expression neutral but his resolution firm. *To hell with the right people,* he wanted to shout. The plan first, then move was a better choice.

"Did you get any word from those two Intel?" Wager asked Simpson.

"To hell with them," replied Simpson, surprising Jack and raising eyebrows around the room at the sudden switch. "This is one of ours, our people," he went on, allying himself. "There's a category four storm moving in on the horizon, and time isn't on that boy's side."

Jack had no arguments against that statement.

27

"*CAN* we duplicate this notebook?" Jack asked, holding it up for Wager and Simpson to see. He quickly explained what Max's pages contained. "It has to look original, and I've marked the four pages that must not be copied."

"We have to let the RCMP Intel know," Simpson said.

"Respectfully, no," Jack stated. "Not until we know Max is safe. They'll confiscate it, tell us to do nothing, and it will be another week before they act. Max will either be dead or in East Germany by that time, which amounts to the same thing." He held the book out of reach, like a kid in the schoolyard. "We'll tell them afterward. We don't work for them."

Simpson's gaze shifted to Wager, silently seeking confirmation.

"Tuesday's right, sir." Wager chewed his moustache as if it pained him to admit it.

Simpson frowned and used his fingers to massage both temples. "So, tell me what you have in mind. And it'd better be good. I don't want to hear any swashbuckling hero plans."

Jack told him. Simpson sat back in Wager's chair and harrumphed. "Detective Tuesday, you make early retirement seem desirable. Someone should have warned me about you before I accepted this post."

"Since the wall went up, so has the Cold War, sir. With the amount of Soviet agents in Canada, we are bound to run into them." Jack said, hoping Simpson was already aware of that and Jack wouldn't have to give the same rant he'd already laid down to Wager.

"But why you?" And then why me, his silent plea seemed to add. "Do you lie in bed at night and make up these lavish prevention tactics?" He gazed across at Wager as if it were his fault.

Wager pointed to his hair. "Chief says sometimes we should let our people tilt at windmills." And shrugged one shoulder as if to say higher ranks sometimes had odd opinions.

"You realize you'll have to go in unarmed?"

Jack nodded. "They must believe I am following their orders and have no backup. Just delivering what they want."

Simpson shook his head and looked around the room as if wondering how he got there.

"It's simple, really, sir," Jack continued, showing more calm than he felt. "All depends on the timing, of course. Timing is crucial." He glanced at Wager, whose eyes never wavered from his. Did they look a trifle sad? "But we're no strangers to operations like this," he told Simpson, wanting his assurance.

Simpson's gaze steadied on him. "It's pretty short notice for the tactical team. They won't like it."

"Isn't that what a tactical team is for? Emergencies can't be scheduled." Jack paused, staring at his superior, then added, "Sir."

Simpson considered and puffed air out of his nose. "I think they will jump at it. Show off their training." His compressed lips said he'd be watching to see if they were up to snuff. "I want a statement, Tuesday, in your own handwriting, that you came up with this . . . scheme, and that you decided on your own to get in ahead of the team. If it all goes cock-up, you will not take this division down with you. Is that understood?"

"Yes, sir."

"On my desk in the next few minutes would be nice." Simpson rose. "With me, Wager," he ordered, stalking out of the room without waiting.

Wager picked up his notes and prepared to follow Simpson. Grinning at Jack, he said, "I'll let you know the order of battle."

Pausing for a moment, he reached out and shook Jack's hand.

Jack froze for a moment and pinched his brows together—the move felt so out of character for the burly sergeant. Wager held his gaze. "Be careful."

Only able to nod in reply, Jack watched Wager leave the room, then took the stairs two at a time to Administration to get the notebook duplicated.

28

JACK slowed down as he came to the address in Nisku that Rory had given him. The building was unremarkable, its dull blue paint emphasizing a white sign that read '*Everything Kitchen.*' A walkway spread across the entrance area continued around to the side of the building. The blind slats across three windows were drawn, and Jack imagined a showroom or front office space hidden behind them. The double glass main door sported a closed sign. Empty parking spaces in the unpaved area gave an air of desertion over the building, questioning the business as a going concern. It confirmed McGruber's instinct that the kitchen business was more of a convenient title than a busy enterprise.

Jack drove on, past signs promising new developments to come and a few already established. He passed a delivery truck alongside a tow truck, both drivers conversing over the delivery truck's open hood. Jack recognized one of them and accelerated, turning down a side road. He passed an electrical supply distributor where two men unloaded packages from the building to a lone van. They didn't seem in any hurry. Dropping their load, they lit cigarettes and leaned against the van's front end.

Jack continued until he spotted the industrial office building he was looking for, entered the parking lot and slid into a spot labelled *Visitors*. He peered through his side mirrors at the building, assuming Rory had chosen it because it was closed on Sundays.

A few minutes later, Rory parked beside him.

"My guys kept watch on it all morning," he told Jack after they shook hands. "They took turns so none passed by more than once—just enough to look like they had business in the area. They all reported the same thing: men, solo or in pairs, enter the building, but oddly, nobody brought cars. All of them were dropped off by someone else."

"A private club, maybe?" Jack asked, thinking of the closed blinds.

Roy snorted. "Sure. One that people don't want others to know they are members." He wiggled his fingers." Risqué things being done there, and all."

"How many?" Jack asked. "Would they be workers?"

Rory raised his eyebrows. "Not unless they hire executive-types wearing business suits. I counted about eight or nine, but more could have gone in before I got here. As far as we know, they haven't left." He paused, eyeing Jack with a raised brow. "Are you going in there?" When Jack said nothing, he added, "Want company?"

Jack shook his head. "It's all arranged. But you can keep your eyes open if you are so inclined. Just in case. But I'd advise you to use binoculars and stay a good distance away from the place. As well as any of your men still around."

"Speaking of binoculars." Rory motioned to the building. "There's a loading dock at the back—and a guard. So be careful."

"Of course. Thanks, Rory." He gripped Rory's hand. "Appreciate your help."

Fifteen minutes later, Jack crouched at the edge of the building, scanning the area for the guard. A dumpster blocked his view of the loading dock, so he took a step to the side for a better angle when he heard a cough and smelt cigarette smoke. He flattened against the building again, hoping for another sound so he could pinpoint the location. Hearing nothing, he picked up a small stone and tossed it at the side of the dumpster. A small flock of sparrows gathered along the top of the open dumpster rose up and flew off. As soon as the man stepped around the dumpster, Jack sprang forward, wrapping his forearm around his neck and squeezing tight behind his ear. The man crumpled, and Jack let him fall. He dragged him around the side of the building and made his way to the back metal door. The flock of birds resettled themselves along the dumpster and resumed their pecking along the rim. Jack carefully tried the handle. It turned, and he eased it open a crack, pausing to listen.

Nothing.

He experimented with another harder push. Too late, another mass fluttering of the birds behind signalled a warning. He felt a sharp pain in the back of his head. "Don't be shy, Detective Tuesday," said a familiar voice. Jack cursed himself for not checking the guard hadn't been alone with his cigarette. He flinched at a harder poke, urging him forward. "Keep going,"

Jack shifted to the side, bringing his left hand up to seize Alec's wrist, which held the pistol, and give it a sharp twist. Alec resisted, his palm smashing hard against Jack's wrist, breaking his hold. Before he had time to retaliate, another arm gripped him from behind, pulling him backward, a knee painfully digging into his back.

"Come quietly," a rough voice said, and whoever it was manhandled Jack forward, giving him a quick shove so that he stumbled through the door, striving to keep his balance.

Inside, Jack turned. Still pointing the pistol at him, Alec jerked the barrel up, showing Jack should raise his hands. He did. Out of the corner of his eye, he saw the back of the other man disappearing through the door again.

"I thought you'd be here yesterday," Alec sounded disappointed.

Jack said nothing, his eyes scanning for any sign of Max. Nothing but a dark expanse, broken only by the sliver of light coming through the open door. Next to him stood a long table containing a selection of plates, saucers and cups, and serving pieces—laid out like a showroom display, which, of course, it was.

Jack nodded toward the table. "All this to entice prospective buyers into thinking Everything Kitchen might be real? Or only for looks if an inquisitive customs inspector comes along?" His gaze shifted over the elegant setup, and he had to admit it looked impressive. Delicate bone china gleamed under the light, arranged in a way that screamed wealth, various modern patterns mingling with classic designs, offering options for any buyer. Farther along, a shining display of cookware in copper and steel caught his eye. There was fancy glassware nearby. Not your everyday stuff, and Jack smiled, thinking about McGruber.

A muffled sound and a scrape from beyond the table made his heart rate increase. "Where is he?" he said and lowered his arms.

"Keep them up," Alec jerked his pistol higher, and Jack obeyed.

The other man appeared again, this time carrying a paper bag and cans. Jack smelled onions and hamburgers.

"Good thing I got back in time," he told Alec. "But I'm sure you would have beaten him in the end." He sneered at Alec, his manner condescending. His hard eyes inspected Jack. "Is that him?"

"Meet Detective Tuesday, the father," Alec mimed introductions. "This is Hans."

Jack's eyes inventoried Hans, the same man he had seen at the entrance to the Chateau Lacombe with Hudek. Couldn't miss that butch, military haircut. Hans elbowed the door shut and laid the soda cans on the table. He wore jeans, which looked new and probably were. Which marked him an East European or, Jack guessed, East German. Muscle thickened his arms, his upper body stocky but solid. If he'd been shorter, he'd have looked square, but instead, he was more of a blocky rectangle. Beneath the bulky vest over his t-shirt, a noticeable bulge pressed against his left side—another pistol. He moved easily with assurance, which told Jack who the physical person was in the room, compared to Alec. This was the dangerous one and the man who had probably killed Winslow.

But who was the boss? His scalp prickled. Jack heard another muffled sound and a louder scrape. Alec smiled and, keeping his pistol on Jack, moved to the wall and switched on the lights. Jack's gaze remained fixed on the source of the noise. Max, bound and mouth taped, was rocking the chair back and forth. His eyes implored Jack, and his throat moved as he tried to make a sound. Jack's gut twisted, and he took an impulsive step toward him.

"Not yet." Alec waved the pistol at Jack again. "As you can see, the boy is unharmed. But he denies all knowledge of the questions we need answered."

"Names?" snarled Jack. "I told you he didn't bring any names with him. Not the kind you want, anyway."

Alec raised his eyebrows. "Now we are getting someplace. Tell me more about the names."

Jack lowered his arms again. They were aching. Alec shook his head and indicated with the pistol barrel that it was not acceptable. Jack sighed and spread them halfway to the side.

"Names of people you think helped him defect," he told Alec. "You weren't very subtle when you asked me the first time. But then, you people can't do subtle, just demand unrestrained obedience." Jack managed a sigh as if Alec wasn't very bright. "If you haven't accepted it yet, nobody but his mother helped him, and she's dead, so reprisals are out. She knew better than to trust anyone." Jack eyed Alec up and down. "That Stasi thrives on blackmail and people who accuse their neighbours. That's how you guys work."

Alec shrugged. "As long as it brings results. We have to eliminate traitors."

"Must be nice to walk in your shoes. Always looking over your shoulder. Never able to trust anyone." Jack saw his gibe hit home. "Being on alert twenty-four-seven must be tiring."

Max made a muffled sound again. "What's the point of keeping his mouth taped shut?" He pointed a finger at Hans, standing easily and looking relaxed, which Jack knew was false. "That hamburger for him?"

"Only if he tells us what we want to know," Hans rumbled, his English good, which told Jack that the big man was even more dangerous than he thought. He went over to Max, taking a knife out of his pocket. Max tensed, but Hans only cut the tape and pulled hard. Max let out a yelp and sucked at his lips.

"Sorry. It can't be helped," Hans said, his grin showing he wasn't sorry at all.

"Water," Max whispered, and Hans obliged. He pulled the tab on a can and tipped it over Max's mouth. Max tried to swallow, but most of it ran down his chin. He twisted his mouth away. "That's awful," he croaked.

"What? You don't like Canada Dry?" he laughed again.

Just drink it, son, Jack pleaded silently. He resisted the urge to tackle Alec while his attention was on Hans and Max. Hans was too close to Max for any success. Instead, he thought of sneaking a glance at this watch and, just in time, saw that Alec's brief break in attention was over.

Max was still watching him from the other side of the room, beyond the table. "You all right, son? Have they hurt you?" Max looked whole besides a red rash around his mouth where the tape had been. Jack backed up. "Don't move," Alec said.

"I don't intend to run," Jack said, still backing up, hands raised. "Not while you have my son." Alec raised the pistol, but Jack could see the uncertainty in how he followed, as if unsure of how to stop him

"I'm just going to see if he's okay. Alright?" He had made it to the end of the row of tables before he felt a forearm wrapped around his neck. "Never mind the boy," Hans told him. "We have more important things to talk about." He dragged Jack, who had no alternative but to stagger backward or choke. Smiling, Alec followed.

"Bring a chair over here," Hans indicated the row of chairs stacked against the far wall, and Alec hastened to obey.

Alec placed the chair beside him, and Jack delivered a kick at his knee while Hans yanked his hands behind him. Alec yelped loudly and swore. Hans produced a knife from nowhere, and the cold steel bit sharply into Jack's thigh. His breath hitched, and his yell came out more like a deep growl. The pain radiated up his leg and hips.

"What's all the noise out here?"

Alec and Hans immediately straightened up, almost jumping to attention. Hans kept his hand pressing down on the nerve in Jack's shoulder so that his resistance had about as much success as escaping a cement cast. Hans's violent grip confirmed he was responsible for Howard, and Jack let the knowledge sink in and fester in his gut.

Twisting his head, he saw Hudek frowning at them all. His eyes raked over Jack, then at Max, rapidly assessing the situation.

"You're sure he came alone?" he asked Alec. "Did you check?"

"Yes. I know the procedure," Alec said, his tone defensive with a tinge of resentment. He prodded Jack.

"I followed your instructions," Jack hurried to say. "No police. Now you can do your part. I'm here. Let us go. Don't think I haven't made plans. If anything happens to us, your names and what you do will be posted on every police bulletin board in the Province and across Canada. You won't get away."

Alec nodded. "When I cornered him, he was nervous, uncertain. It told me there was no backup nearby. His son was the bait, and all we had to do was wait."

"I warned you once, Detective, but you ignored it, and now, here you are." Hudek narrowed his eyes at Jack, who stared back and kept quiet.

"Yes, here I am," Jack said. "Right where you planned it."

"You might have avoided all this." Hudek's high tone lectured Jack. He pointed toward Max. "If you had listened to Alec when he pleaded with you." A flash of suspicion flared in his eyes. "What do a few names matter to you? You had your son, what you wanted. You should have been content. Now . . ." he let his reproach drift off, leaving a definite chill in the air as if there was nothing he could do about what was to happen here.

Jack's arms tingled. "Your deal was the names, and we'd go our separate ways."

"Of course," Hudek said. "And I keep my promises. It's all simple. Satisfy us that everything you give us is complete and accurate, and you are free to go."

He turned to Hans and moved him away, saying, "Keep it quiet," His lips curled into a cold smile. "We wouldn't want our comrades in front to lose their concentration.""

Jack snorted. "Preaching garbage and calling them comrades. Promising things you won't deliver," he said. His pant leg felt wet, and he glanced down to see blood soaking through. It only felt numb as he tightened his thigh muscle, hoping the wound wasn't deep or had nicked something vital. He felt blood dripping down his calf. He ignored it and continued, "Oh yeah, I remember now. It doesn't matter what promises you make. Just make everything sound possible and within reach. Preaching to the suckers."

Hudek's eyes raked over him. He muttered something in an undertone to Hans, then walked back toward the front showroom.

Hans glared and pushed his palm against Jack's mouth. He tightened his other hand into a fist and resumed what he started before being interrupted. Delivering a blow to Jack's head. He raised his knife to Jack's throat.

"Don't hurt my dad," Max's interrupted voice croaking. Jack turned his head, glad to hear something and cheered by the message.

Hans laughed and delivered a light punch, which made Jack's ears ring. He managed a head shake at Max, sending a message and wanting to hug him because, for the first time, he had heard the word Dad.

"You should listen to your partner," he told Hans. "The more you abuse my son, the more I will resist giving you what you want."

Alec forgot about his knee. After all, it wasn't a very hard kick. "Enough wasting time. You have the names?"

"I do," admitted Jack, putting on a sheepish expression. He dared a glance at Max and saw his puzzlement as if he wondered what all this was all about. Jack wordlessly told him not to say anything. "If you let my arms free, we can bargain."

"No bargains," interrupted Hans. As Jack knew he would, he ran his large hands over Jack until he found the notebook. Looking smug, he leafed through it and then handed it to Alec. "Check it over. See if it's complete."

Alec drew another chair from the stack and carried it to the table, far from Jack's leg and reach. Before he sat, he examined the notebook, cover, and pages inside. His brief prayer did nothing to mollify a tremor in Jack's stomach that he might notice the missing pages.

Finally, Alec closed the notebook and nodded at Hans. He limped over to Max and waved the book in his face accusingly. "You said there was nothing you brought. But here it is."

Max looked at Jack, then at Alec. "I didn't trust you. How did I know for sure whose side you are on? You could be part of him . . ." Max tilted his head at Jack, "his police organization. Besides, it's only my competition record. You already can get that information in the records filed in Germany."

"Then why not admit it? You lied for a reason."

"He's telling the truth," Jack interrupted. "I only found it by accident and have never seen it before, which proves he kept it secret. You people never learn that sometimes things are exactly like they seem."

"That's true," Max said eagerly. "And now, will you send me back to GDR?"

Both Alec and Hans stared at him and then laughed out loud. Jack sat straight, stunned. What was Max doing?

"Maybe we should," Hans said to Alec. "Let's see what his sports directors think about that when he turns up."

"Let alone our State Security," Alec added, which sent them into another round of self-appreciation for their humour.

"But that's what I want," Max insisted. Which stopped the two in their tracks of self-congratulation. Even Jack couldn't hide his surprise. Max's plea felt so genuine.

"You want to go back?"

"Yes, please." Max laughed. "I don't like it here. Everything is too loose. There are no rules, and that makes me feel like I am falling apart." He looked from one to the other and then finally straight at Jack.

Alec's eyes narrowed to slits. "A minute ago, you were worried your father was going to be hurt. Now you want to desert him?"

"Hurting him will create trouble," Max explained. "He is a policeman. Think if it happened to you at home where any threat or hurt calls out all his Stasi comrades. Same here. Do you want to invite all that trouble with everyone looking for you?"

"Why, Max?" Jack said, only half believing him. Absolutely opposite to all the things Max had said he liked about Canada. Was he only feeding him hoopla? Jack closed his gaping mouth.

"Yes, you are my father," Max rasped, his bitter words hitting Jack like darts. "But I only see it as an accident of birth. An illusion. GDR has nationhood; each of us has a piece of that. What the West sees as indoctrination, I see as structure." Max's eyes bored into Jack's. "I can go on, but you and those like you will never understand the will of our nation and people."

Those words were followed by silence so loud it burned into the air. Jack could feel Hans relax beside him.

"You did not know, did you? I was successful that you didn't suspect." Max smirked.

Alec looked both pleased and amused. Dumb from shock, Jack could only shake his head. He stared at Max, and a quiver of rage started in his belly.

Max nodded his head at the book in Alec's hand. "There is nothing in there that isn't already in the records at home. A list of competitions and my scores, that's all. Mutter thought he would be interested. I had no interest in him, so I forgot to show them."

"We shall soon see, won't we?" he said, but his smile was gentle.

Max nodded his head at the paper bag on the table. "What about that hamburger? Is it for me? I could use it, and you haven't given me food for twenty-four hours."

Alec jerked his head at Hans. "Untie him. Let him eat and drink. He can do nothing even if he wanted to."

Hans didn't look convinced. "It isn't what he said all day yesterday."

"Why didn't you ask outright?" Max yelled at him. He curled his lip. "You only knocked me around shouting out you wanted names." His bound arms tugged at the chair's back. "Besides, life in GDR taught me to hold something back until we all know where we are with each other." He added something in German that made Hans flush. His fists tightened, and Alec chuckled.

"It sounds logical, but I still have doubts," Alec said to Hans and turned to appraise Max. "Why did you avoid me when I met you at that lake? You could have told me then. Instead, you gave the impression you'd like to kill me."

Max shook his head as if he couldn't believe such a silly question. "I was trying to let you know the man who took me there was suspicious when you kept coming near me. He suspected you might be someone who goes after kids and was ready to confront you."

Alec mulled that over. "Let him go to the toilet," he finally ordered Hans, adding a long sentence in German. Jack saw Max's eyes widen in shock, then become neutral quickly as both men turned back toward him.

"Help me get home. Let's get this over with." He put his head down, but not before Jack saw his eyes close, wincing in pain. "But I will eat at that table first."

When they studiously avoided looking at him, Jack heard the death knell. If Max had decided to join the enemy, there was no chance of them letting him go. He knew too much, and it could only end in one way now. Hudek had probably given Winslow the same promise. Jack calculated how much time he had. Where was the team?

He watched while Hans went over to Max and heaved him out of the chair. Max swayed, and Hans snickered, watching him try to get his balance. Max finally got his feet working and unsteadily headed to the toilet, Hans following.

Alec opened the notebook again and wandered close to Jack's chair but remained out of reach.

"You gave us the tip on where to find Howard Winslow," Jack said softly.

Alec lifted his head from the notebook and stared at Jack. "What?" His eyes went to the door where Hans had taken Max, then back to Jack, pale face showing evident alarm.

Jack saw his guess had hit home. "Don't worry, I won't tell," he said. "I can see you don't agree with Han's brutality. Watching him torture Winslow must have been nerve-wracking." Alec's eyes squeezed shut as if to shut out the memory. Jack kept on. "He's insane, isn't he? Gets his kicks by killing?"

Alec opened his mouth but closed it again as Hans brought Max back from the toilet. Without permission and with every confidence, Max fetched the chair they had tied him to and carried it to the table and sat. He took a massive bite that only teen boys were capable of, his expression showing nothing but self-satisfaction. *As if nothing important was going on,* thought Jack, wanting nothing more than to get his hands on him. Max casually snatched a small plate from the stack before him, as if he hadn't a care in the world, and spread out his hamburger on it.

"Be careful with those dishes," Alec said. "They are exclusive, expensive, and special to Mr. Hudek. If damaged, you wouldn't want to be the object of his displeasure."

Max paid no attention. His concentration was on chewing, only reaching out to grab the ginger ale to pull at the flap. He ignored the rest of them.

Alec watched for a minute, then sighed and beckoned Hans over, showing him the inside of the notebook. He said something in German. Hans replied. Alec nodded and closed the book, placing it in his jacket pocket. Hans prodded him and spoke again in German. The tone did not sound to Jack like they were discussing Max's hamburger. Alec replied briefly, then they faced Max, and Hans spoke again in

German. To Max? It had been so long since his time in Germany, Jack struggled to catch even the simplest words, and gave up trying. Alec and Hans were staring as if waiting for a response from Max, who paid them no attention. Alec reached into his pocket and came out with a repressor, which he fitted to his pistol. Were they going to shoot Max? Jack opened his mouth to shout a warning, but they both turned and faced him. Jack let out a sigh of relief.

Hans dug into his back pocket and pulled out a woman's nylon stocking. Not taking his eyes off Jack, he wound the ends around each hand, then grinned as he snapped the stocking taut.

Jack's insides recoiled as if he were asked to swallow something slimy and still quivering. "What you intend to do will be a big mistake." He tried to keep his tone matter-of-fact and not show the horror he felt inside. "Pay attention to the boy's advice." Jack drew out the word *boy* as if it were a curse. "He is correct when he says you will never leave here if you kill me."

Inside, he prayed. *Okay, fellas, now would be a good time to do your thing. Another minute will be too late.* He shot Alec a quick glance, hoping common sense might hit him, but Alec only shrugged as though apologizing for something out of his control. Hans started toward Jack, but Jack caught a glimpse of movement behind Alec. Max stood, wiped his mouth with the back of his hand, then picked up the plate that had held his hamburger and massaged the edge, cleaning off the crumbs.

Desperately, Jack kicked out at Hans as he approached, but Hans quickly got behind him. Jack felt the stocking tighten around his neck. He tried to take a deep breath and couldn't. Twisting only helped pull the stocking tighter, and it felt like his face was going to burst. Lights danced behind his eyes. Daylight darkened, and he felt his bladder let go. He hardly felt the chair tilt, sending him crashing on his side to the floor. He thought he heard Max yell. Or was it Hans? The pressure on his neck suddenly ceased. He gasped, gurgling from the pain in his throat. His vision cleared to a foggy blur.

The last echoes of Max's yell mingled with Han's hysterical scream. The pressure on Jack's throat eased. Desperately sucking at the air, Jack turned his head to see Hans's fingers scrabbling at the steel pot lid, cutting into his eyes. Another roar from Max, a whizzing sound, and a bone china plate quickly found its mark on Han's bare arms, still clutching at the steel lid, causing his hands to jerk against his eyes. With an agonized cry, Hans fell to the floor, not resisting the barrage of plates hitting him. Jack could only marvel at the force of throws in rapid sequence and how they found their mark on Hans. Pieces of shattered bone china skidded across the floor or wedged themselves in his clothes.

Mewling like a wounded animal, Hans sprawled on the floor amongst broken plate shards, still clutching his eyes. Probably making the wounds worse, thought Jack, pleased at the idea.

Glad he was still alive, Jack fought against the rope, twisting his wrists to find a weakness in the knots. The pain in his throat stopped him from cheering Max's hits on target. A sound like a motorcycle exhaust from out back took his attention off Hans. *Please let it be the team,* Jack prayed. He searched for Alec and found him behind a chair, trying to get a line of sight on Max. Max danced around in a wild pattern, yelling *hey-hey,* his left arm holding plates against his ribcage while his right hand winged them without pause. Crouched and throwing, aiming low, he reminded Jack of a Japanese ninja-style exhibition he'd seen on R&R leave during Korea.

Alec ducked and fired blindly in Max's direction. Finally, face red with anger and desperation, he switched his target to Jack. Fire ripped at Jack's upper arm, then burning pain, knocking him back so that he rolled in the chair he was still tied to. His arm throbbed, and he felt wetness dripping down. Alec switched his posture and took aim again. Before he could fire, another stainless steel lid found its target at an oblique angle, then bounced away. Alec dropped his pistol and put both hands to his neck as if reassuring himself his head was still intact. Another throw, and a plate bounced off his head, adding pieces of china to the mess on the floor.

Hudek's high voice, loudly protesting from the front, interrupted. Thinking the man was coming to investigate the noise, Jack shouted a warning to Max that sent fire into his throat.

Instead, arms held high, Hudek and his group of partners paraded before armed men, prodding them along. Reinforcements burst through the back door, weapons sweeping in arcs around all areas of the warehouse. Jack never thought he'd be so glad to see Edmonton's own task force, Staff Sergeant Carter in front, and Wager and Chen at the end, following behind them all.

Max paid them no attention and ran over to Jack. "Dad, Dad." He pulled at the chair, trying to right it. "You're bleeding," he said, his voice tight, half sobbing, like he couldn't get his breath. His pale face was over Jack, his eyes darting frantically in different directions as if looking for new hazards.

"You called me Dad," was Jack's inane reply. All he wanted to do was take Max out of the atmosphere of violence. It was the next best thing until someone cut him loose, and he could hug him. The pain in his throat threatened to make him vomit. "Easy, son, you're safe now." Tears filled his eyes. He tried to nudge his body against Max's side, gasping against the pain in his shoulder. "You are a great actor. Damn it, you had me fooled."

A bulky form dressed for battle pushed Max out of the way and pulled the chair upright.

"About time," Jack croaked, complaining to cover that he wanted to cry from relief. Someone released his tied arms, and Jack tried to massage his wrists, but his arms seemed paralyzed. He managed instead to squeeze his upper arm in a tight grip to ease the pain. "You were all sitting out there just waiting for our guys to do the dirty work first. So you can swoop in at the end and claim all the glory."

"Stop talking, and save your throat." Inspector Dave said, his voice mild. He inspected Jack's arm, then his thigh, and beckoned the EMT people. "You're okay," he said to Jack, but he looked grim.

A paramedic bustled over, took a look at Jack and started searching in his case.

Chen got there next, Wager behind him. Both peered over the Inspector's shoulder. "You okay? We'll debrief later," Wager said, giving him a thumbs up.

Chen elbowed Dave out of the way. He looked Jack over and noted the wet patch on the crotch of his pants. Lips surrounded by a white circle pinched tightly together, his eyes swivelled to the red circle on Jack's neck, and he blinked hard. "I'm okay, Chen," Jack hissed against the pain in his throat. He laid his hand over Chen's and squeezed.

Chen nodded and swallowed. "Sure you are, pal."

Wager gave Chen a rough push, and they hurried off to help secure the prisoners, including Hudek, his nasal voice protesting while nobody listened. Staff Sergeant Carter shoved a piece of paper into his face. Hudek eyed it, and lip curling, he pulled back and stepped on a shard of china and lost his footing. Down on one knee, his horrified eyes took in the mess around him. A constable lifted him to his feet while Hudek peered around for the guilty party. His search swept past a dazed Alec, who avoided his eyes and hit on Jack.

"You will pay for this insult," he said, teeth set in a rictus line of fury. "I do not see Hans." His lips spread in what might have been a triumphant leer. "He got away, didn't he? I promise he will find you, for Hans does not forget. Everyone you love will pay."

"Look again," Jack said. "Hans is going nowhere but prison. He is not going anywhere. Not unless someone leads him." Hudek's gaze followed Jack's pointed direction. Two paramedics shifted their position, revealing a form with heavily bandaged eyes, now lying quietly, having been pumped full of morphine. Hudek ogled him, then dismissed the sight with a disgusted shake of his head. So much for loyalty, Jack thought. The man wasn't interested enough to ask about Han's injuries.

Hudek turned to the Staff Sergeant and declared, "I have diplomatic immunity. It is not too late for you to reconsider my arrest before it becomes a public embarrassment for your government."

"Sure you do," Carter said, then ignored him and shouted into his radio connected to HQ, probably calling for transportation. He signalled the two holding on to Hudek, and they pushed him, still objecting, toward the front, along with the rest of the group.

Jack caressed his throat, wincing. Dave looked over the shoulder of the medic and suggested water. "Can't you get him some water?"

"Negative," the medic shook his head. He asked Jack to open his mouth while he looked at his throat. He fastened a collar around Jack's neck.

"I'm curious," Dave said, "how did you know my men were here?"

"Those so-called electrical workers down the street," Jack whispered. "Looking as if they had nothing much to do. I knew they weren't ours, so they had to be yours." He smirked at Dave. "No union men would be mucking around on a Sunday. And that van probably has a bunch more listening devices inside. D.C. Simpson must have acted fast to get yours here."

Dave smiled. "Intel came in from our guy that Hudek had organized a group meeting. We planned to get them all at once. Then we heard from your deputy that you were going in all gung-ho. It screwed up our plans. We had to arrange a combined action sooner than planned." He paused, eyeing Jack. "Your Deputy Chief Simpson claims you trawl in choppy seas without permission and need to dock permanently. Beats me how you lasted this long."

"Chief Mackie understands me," Jack thought a moment more, visualizing the Chief's face. "Within reason."

"This one will be a stretch." Inspector Dave's tone was dry.

Jack shifted his weight and suppressed a groan. "No choice. What kind of father waits for someone else to save his son?" His throat was really burning now, so he shut up and put his good arm around Max, ignoring a sudden dizziness, and pointed to Dave. He tried to speak, but nothing came out.

Dave grinned and reached over to shake Max's hand, inspecting his face. His eyes immediately went to Jack's, questioning.

Jack blinked, confirming he was aware of Max's post-action condition. "He saved my life. You can't believe the act he played. He deserves a medal." The thought reverberated in his head. Max had saved his life, and the truth brought a lump to his throat. "And probably a few of your men, too. That guy," he whispered, pointing to Hans, attended to by a medic who wrapped a bandage around his eyes, "tortured and killed Howard Winslow. And probably enjoyed it. Hudek used him as his go-to guy for enforcement. Concentrate on Alec. He'll break quickly and tell you everything."

Dave looked at Max, his eyes speculating. "That's a lot of damage with a few pot lids and plates."

Max nodded shyly. "My mother taught me that if I was in danger, use whatever was at hand to save myself."

"Good advice," Dave said, but his eyes looked questioning.

"You should see him throw a Frisbee," Jack managed. "Like bullets."

"I was champion of my polytechnic competition," Max explained.

"Ahh," Dave said as if that explained it, but his eyes stayed on Max like he was considering a new idea.

Jack groped for Max in defence, then remembered the names. "Inspector, I've got four names for you. I'm bothered . . ." The floor shifted like sand, and his vision had black edges around the perimeter. The blackness closed in.

The last thing he heard was a frantic "Dad!"

29

JACK came to life in the ambulance, with Max bending over him, holding his hand and looking destitute.

"Hey, I'm okay," he whispered. His throat protested, and he contented himself with searching Max's face for signs of after-effects he knew would hit before the day was out. Even those trained, who coped with danger every day, suffered ill effects from encountering violence. What Max had experienced inside Everything Kitchen could haunt him, and he'd need counselling before it solidified like cement. He used his good hand to grip his son's and felt an appreciative return pressure.

Jack tried to sit up, and the EMC pushed back. He was already wrapping a pressure bandage around Jack's thigh. "Needs stitches," the EMT muttered, "but it could have been worse." Jack bent his upper body to get a better look. "Take it easy. You'll need surgery on the arm." He finished up on the leg and spun to examine the area around his throat, probing and pressing. Jack flinched.

"Any headaches?"

Jack shook his head, then wished he hadn't.

"How about numbness in your arms and hands?" Eyes searched Jack's expression, waiting for an answer. Jack paused, then shook his head again. "Any blood from your throat?" The EMT paused for a long moment, watching Jack. "I need you to tell me if you have the effects of strangulation. Don't ignore them."

"Just a burning throat," Jack said. "My whole body is just one big pain everywhere. But my thinking is okay."

"How about breathing? Any tightness or difficulty?" Again, Jack said no while the man watched him.

"You seem okay now, but if you notice anything I mentioned, tell the doctor immediately." He handed Jack something in a small paper container and turned his attention to Max while Jack downed whatever it was. Tasted like honey.

"Could you use your radio and ask the hospital to phone someone?" Jack croaked, reciting Edina's phone number. "Tell them to inform the person who answers that we're both okay."

"Can't it wait till you get to the ER?"

"No," Jack lied, tilting his head at Max, hoping the medic got the message. "Police business." The ambulance started off, using a sporadic whoop of its siren to ease its way between police vehicles and cops clogging the area around the front of the warehouse.

"YOU again?" The doctor slipped around the curtain in the ER, and Jack sighed, recognizing him. The same doctor who had treated his amnesia after his car accident, and again, had patched him up after a beating by wanna-be bikers—only months ago, though it felt like years. "Missed us, did you?" he said, examining Jack's arm.

"Not you," Jack whispered, his mind foggy and tongue thick. Had they given him painkillers? He couldn't remember. "But the food. Yup, the food is to be longed for. Ouch." Jack flinched as the doctor prodded his arm. "Where's my son? They brought him in with me." What was the doctor's name again? Had he even known it?

"Bullet's still in there," the doctor said, without replying. "We'll see about the damage. You're lucky it wasn't the shoulder. Would've caused a lot more trouble."

"My son?" Jack rasped.

"I'm going to him next." the doctor said, but Jack noticed the quick flash of concern in his eyes. "Was he involved in your . . . game?" He moved his inspection to Jack's throat, his fingers probing while he asked the same questions that Jack had answered inside the ambulance.

"Nobody's going home today, so you'll see him later. Someone will be in shortly for blood work."

"I've already lost enough," Jack slurred, but the doctor had already left. Jack heard him talking to the nurse about surgery.

A half-hour later, Jack and Max were upstairs, ensconced in a semi-private room, staring at each other from opposite beds. There was a constable by the door outside in the hall.

"Am I under arrest?" Max asked, looking resigned but uneasy too.

Jack hastened to assure him they were safe. "The constable is for our protection. There could be more people involved than those present today." Max seemed to relax, his face a normal colour.

"Why am I here? I am not injured."

"Just keeping us isolated is my guess," Jack said, matter of fact, not wanting to raise more anxiety. "I expect they have questions about what happened before the task force and the RCMP raid. We can testify that Hudek knew you and I were being held in the back, so he can't claim innocence. They want answers while it's all fresh in our memory. Thanks to you, the raid was a success."

"But if you had not come before the police, they would never have set me free, and I'd be already dead when the police entered," Max reasoned, as if they were discussing a movie plot. His lack of emotion worried Jack. The flat tone sent a shiver down Jack's spine. It was a sign that his son was burying his feelings, and if left unchecked, they would fester, only to emerge in ways that Jack didn't want to think about.

"When the doctor examined you," Jack probed. "What did he talk about?"

Max shrugged. "He asked if I had a headache and poked me all over with his fingers. And said you enjoy coming here because you like the food." Max fiddled with the bedsheet, not meeting Jack's eyes.

"That's all?" Jack pushed. "I always get asked questions about my feelings after a fight like that."

Max shrugged. "He wanted to know how I kept strong while they had me."

"What did you tell him?"

"Nothing, just stuff," Max said, his shoulders reaching his ears. "I saw him getting serious, then he said he would ask another doctor to come in and talk to me." Max pursed his mouth. "I know what he wants. For me to tell him all my secrets."

Jack managed a brief laugh, and then Max joined in. "I'm in for the same interrogation," Jack confessed. "But it's all for the good. We can't let Hudek win." *I'd like a turn at him myself,* Jack gritted his teeth, looking at Max's young face. He'd never rid himself of memories of severely wounding two humans—even if his actions were to preserve his own life. *And mine.* "Anyway, think of how popular you'll be at school when the news gets out. The girls too." Max flushed, but his eyes went blank as though considering the possibilities. Jack smiled.

An influx of people were attempting to bypass the constable at the door. Olivia moved in on him and gave him her pitiful expression. Jack's mouth aped the constable's likely *'poor little thing'* thought as they all trooped past him. Edina followed Olivia, then Anderson, whose scowl said he wanted to be anywhere else but here.

Olivia immediately went to Max's bedside and leaned close, hugging him. "I was so worried."

"Get off me!" Max squirmed, turning red with pleasure.

Edina kissed Jack, sat on the only chair, and took his hand. "Is it over?" Her eyes wandered to his arm, and she shivered. "Well, I've learned today what life with you is going to be like. But it had better not be something you get good at, Jack Tuesday."

Anderson leaned his bulk against the foot of the bed and smirked at him.

"You're not changing your mind, are you?" Jack said to her, only half joking.

"Of course not," Edina said. "Why would I give up days of worry, terror, and strange people coming into my house with excuses to protect me? Not to mention a weird dog who plays on your sympathies to get what he wants." Edina's blue eyes behind her glasses looked calculating for a moment. "Sort of like his master, come to think of it."

"Where have you put Pharo, by the way?"

"He's in the car, in the parking structure, so it isn't too hot. He wasn't going to be left behind."

"You got him in the car without fuss?" Jack's eyebrows lifted.

"Anderson held the door for him, and he jumped right in."

"Figures," Jack grumbled.

Anderson's lips twitched. He actually chuckled, then it vanished just as fast. "Tie up all the loose ends?" he asked, giving Edina an oblique glance. Jack recognized Anderson was still uncomfortable with the whole situation, and for a brief moment, he felt a pang of guilt about the predicament he'd dragged the man into with Luke. He shook it off, thinking about how Anderson had tricked Jack at the courthouse by hiding Luke's plan to move Olivia to Edmonton.

"Not quite," Jack admitted now. "Another day to get the ones behind the scenes. But we've got solid evidence."

"So you don't need me. I have to leave soon and fly back. My boss is antsy." Anderson twisted his fist in the palm of his other hand as if he were getting ready to pitch a ball. "I'm afraid he already is aware of . . . things."

Edina glanced around at Anderson, puzzled, then turned to Jack again. "Things? More things? It isn't over yet?" Her face clouded over with worry.

"Only to do with Olivia," Jack said. "Her father is overprotective. Anderson here has to convince him everything is normal."

Anderson's frown deepened, but he didn't speak.

"Olivia is a lovely girl." Edina leaned forward and whispered to Anderson, "Her maturity amazes me. You tell her father not to sell her short and that Jack is more than capable of protecting his daughter." She smiled warmly, leaning back a little. "After all, he knew Jack was a policeman when he asked if she could live with him and Max, so he can't complain now." She looked from Anderson to Jack. "Can he?"

"No," Jack said slowly, then conversely. "Yes. He knew."

Anderson's shoulders lifted as if the argument was moot. "I'll mention it. And now it's time I left." He glanced over at Max and Olivia. "He's okay?"

"Needs a bit of time and understanding," Jack said, getting a perceptive nod from Anderson.

"Will we all be seeing you again in Edmonton?" Jack pushed, wondering if there had been further discussion between Anderson and Olivia.

Anderson paused. "Probably not," he said, face blank.

"A hard decision, but best for everyone all around," Jack murmured, a sympathetic gesture to show he appreciated what it had cost Anderson to tell Olivia her affection was one-way.

Anderson glared at him. "Unless other business matters come up," he said, adding a spiteful addition to his earlier statement. Telling Jack that Anderson's personal affairs were out of bounds.

His comment spiked Jack's attention. "And do you? Have other business here?"

"My boss has his eye on a new business venture." Anderson's bad mood ramped up a notch. His hands became fists.

Jack's lips thinned considerably. "No way," he mouthed.

"Thank you for the protection today, Anderson," Edina interrupted. She had been listening quietly to their banal exchange, eyes measuring the resulting tension. Her lips tightened. Rising out of the chair, she took a few steps to Anderson. "Well, I hope we see you again." She leaned forward and kissed his cheek. "From me. And Pharo. We'll miss you." A hand on each of his elbows, she gave him a little shake. "Say goodbye to Olivia. She likes you." Edina gave him a wicked smile and winked.

Anderson's eyes narrowed to slits. He looked even crabbier, if possible. Another comment and he'd explode, Jack estimated.

A nurse and her tray entered the room. "Okay, everybody out. We're going into surgery."

"*We* are?" Jack grumbled. "Hope there's room on the table."

A young man in scrubs, a stethoscope around his neck, entered the room, caught a gander at Olivia and stared, his mouth opened and closed like a landed fish. Anderson scowled and crossed his arms, the tattoos on his biceps inflating.

"How long?" Edina asked the nurse.

"Waiting room down the hall, if you like. Check in later."

Wager appeared. Scarcely stopping, he flashed his badge to the constable and entered the room, He stood aside to let the others leave.

"I need a few with Detective Tuesday," he said to the nurse. Inspector Dave appeared, flashed his badge at the constable, and then halted, looking over Wager's shoulder.

"No can do, officer," the nurse said smartly. "We're on the clock here with the OR. So come back later."

"When he's all doped? He won't be any good to me," Wager protested.

"Only a minute, and we'll make it fast," Jack pleaded. He wanted to know the score and if Wager needed his input to lay charges.

"Tough bananas." The nurse turned Wager around and pushed him out the door, then flapped her hands at the inspector for good measure in case he had the same idea.

"The place is like a zoo," she muttered, then spotted Max staring at Jack with a worried face. You!" she ordered, pointing to him. "Get some sleep." Her face softened as she gently straightened the surrounding sheets. "He'll be back before you know it."

30

THE hospital released Max early on Tuesday morning but not before scheduling a series of follow-up appointments. Edina had suggested that Max stay with her the previous day, but Olivia pointed out that St. Albert was too far for him to travel back and forth to school. Max, ever stubborn, insisted he could take care of himself. But as Max packed to leave, Rory arrived to firmly settle the matter—he would stay with him and Tommy—the boys exchanged a high five, and Max went with a smile on his face.

Left alone in the room, Jack lay on the half-erect bed, thinking of ways to convince the doctor he was well enough to leave. He could do physiotherapy just as well at home as in the hospital.

Not an hour later, Wager and Inspector Dave arrived together, notebooks in hand.

"Am I glad to see you," Jack said.

"Which proves you are sicker than we thought." A small smile tugged at Wager's mustached mouth. Dave took the only chair, and Wager sighed, dragging another from beside the other bed.

"Just pull your rank and get me out of this place," Jack grumbled, his voice still raspy. He swallowed hard and resorted to whispering. "I'm full of antibiotics and god-knows-what-else. It makes me dopey. And coping with the food, I may end up in a lunatic asylum."

"Where you'll be right at home," Wager said. Inspector Dave snorted, and both men opened notebooks in tandem.

"Down to business," Wager continued. "Start at the beginning, right up to when we got there." He glowered at Jack and tugged his moustache. "Don't keep any secrets."

"I don't have secrets. I told you and D.C. Simpson everything when we planned the raid."

"You told the Inspector here that you had names. Just before you fainted." Wager allowed himself a slight grin. Jack felt his face flush. "After you unburden yourself, the Inspector and I may have more questions."

"That's why you came in together?" Jack huffed. "You don't trust me to give you both the same version?"

The guys didn't say a word; they just held their pens like they were ready to pounce.

So he recounted everything from the information he got from McGruber to Rory's confirmation of the address and what happened inside. He had made an easy capture by Alec look difficult so he could bargain Max's release for the notebook. What he hadn't bargained for was Hans.

"Finding the place was the simple part. As you know, Nisku Industrial Park is just starting development, and tenants aren't plentiful yet. I suppose that's why Hudek chose it—they could come and go with little notice, and it's close to the airport." Jack thought for a moment and said to Dave. "There has to be some cooperation with customs if the stated imports and records don't match. I suppose you're on to that already?"

"We are," Dave stated and shot Jack a look that said, 'Don't tell us how to run our business.' "And the matter of the names? The names which were so important to Hudek's crowd. It's puzzling why and how they had reasoned that Max had them."

"Remember that I told you Howard Winslow suspected Hudek was using the law firm's trust account for illegal business practices, cheating the tax department, for instance?" Jack glanced between their matching sardonic expressions. "He posed as a bellhop, hoping that if he found proof, he could quietly stop it before the firm got into serious trouble."

He paused, agreeing silently with the unspoken skepticism from the two men. "Winslow was a veteran of Air Force intelligence, so I guess it made some kind of crazy sense to him."

Jack took a rough breath and continued, "By ingratiating himself with Hudek and listening in on conversations, he found out that Hudek was a foreign agent, and the transactions were only a cover to receive money. They were funding something much darker: disinformation, propaganda, recruiting and setting up cells of foreign agents. To disrupt wherever they could."

His eyes dropped to his hands. "I told Winslow to get out, but he insisted he needed another day. He waited too long. Hans tortured and killed him." Jack swore under his breath and clenched his fists. I'm glad Hans will spend the rest of his life in prison. Blind."

"The names, Jack." Dave probed.

"Stop interrupting," Jack waved his hand and then massaged his throat. "It's important that you understand Howard's part in this. Aside from being a good person, he was trying to protect his firm— and Timothy Gordon's reputation. The firm will probably close when the Law Society finds out. They might even disbar the lot of them. The trust account is only to be used to hold a client's money while a contract is being processed. Like if you buy a house, the buyer doesn't get the title until he satisfies the lawyer that he's met the conditions and the title is free of encumbrances." Jack's gaze lit on his listeners, both stared back, glassy-eyed.

After a beat, Wager said what they were all thinking, "Winslow must have discovered there was someone in the firm who colluded with Hudek. Either under threat or for money, or whatever."

"Right," Jack said. "That's the key. The main reason why they killed him. He knew the name of that person."

"Yes, yes, but back to the four names you mentioned," prompted Inspector Dave. "What's all that about?"

Jack nodded and sighed. "Max's mother sat in on the meetings of Russian defence officials with their satellite countries. She was their expert on their nuclear programs. I suspect she was privy to classified material because Max said they never allowed her out of sight. No travel to anyplace outside of the GDR where she might disappear."

His gaze darkened as he remembered. "Ursula spent years planning Max's defection, slowly, quietly. Then, when she found out she had incurable cancer, she accelerated the plan." He paused, taking a long, measured breath. "Her life . . . It wasn't an easy one. She'd taken it on willingly to save her brother."

Wager and Dave kept silent, giving him a moment to think. Wager scratched a few lines in his notebook, not looking at Jack but his mouth pulling down the corners of his moustache.

"She compiled a notebook of his competition record, including all the names of his competitors. It was for me," Jack gulped back emotion, "so I could imagine his competition successes. Ursula had made him promise to never lose it and to give it to me. When they grabbed Max, I took a serious look at it. I knew she had to have left a message in it somewhere." He smiled at the two men, a pride for his past love swelling in him.

"And she did." Dave prompted.

Jack nodded. "I came across an English name, which seemed out of place, but then I figured it might be another birth from the allied occupation. Then I saw three more names, and they were connected to countries that weren't involved in swimming competitions."

"What countries?" Dave leaned forward.

"France, Italy, Netherlands, Canada."

"And the matching names?"

Jack told him and watched while Dave copied them down. "I can give you the actual pages from the notebook. I gave Hudek a copy of the notebook but excluded those pages." He saw Dave's eyes widen as he looked at the four names. "Do you recognize any?"

Dave nodded, face pale but for red blotches on his cheeks. "M. Harris. Probably stands for Malcolm." He swallowed. "He's Canadian, an official of NATO." The others stared at him, disbelieving.

"Good God," Wager exploded after a long silence. "They are Soviet spies. Inside NATO."

"No wonder Hudek wanted those names," Jack said. Max had been the carrier of that knowledge, innocent and unaware of the danger, but still marked for death because of those same names. An angry fire gripped him at the idea. Then, just as fast, he relented, remembering the high price Ursula had paid to get those names. She'd entrusted him to carry out her revenge, he told himself.

But a new worry wormed its way in. "How did Hudek know there was a list? And that Max had it? Who told him?" Jack said aloud. The three exchanged glances.

"Someone in East Germany knew." Dave looked at the names. "And let someone here know." His lips thinned. "Great. Just great."

FOUR days later, Jack appeared in front of Wager's desk.

"What are you doing here?" Wager looked up at him, then down at the report he was reading. "They let you out? Just don't try to convince me the doc cleared you for duty already."

"Six days in the hospital is long enough." Jack flexed his arm but gently. "No considerable tissue damage, no fragments. As long as I'm careful, and with physiotherapy, I'll be as good as new. My thigh is healing nicely, no infection. Sore as hell, though, if I climb stairs."

"You'll be on desk duty for at least six weeks or more." Wager snorted at Jack's expression.

"I'll have full use soon," Jack said, brushing off the comment. "The shrinks say I'll be fine. And my throat only hurts if I sing." He lied easily, then took a seat without an invitation. "I missed Howard Winslow's funeral while in the hospital. Did you go?"

"Chen and I went," Wager said and leaned back, his chair springs creaking ominously. "We saw nothing unusual. Only the family and the law firm's staff were there, including wives and husbands." Wager moustache quivered. "Kepler's wife sobbed openly, quite dramatically. But it didn't seem to smear her makeup. Kepler finally had to hold her up. You'd think she was Winslow's wife"—Wager turned thoughtful—"who stood up well."

Jack thought of Catherine Winslow. Edina's report was much the same as Wager's. Catherine, leaning on her son John's arm, had remained controlled and dry-eyed.

"But I think she was suffering underneath," Wager said, surprising Jack. He'd never openly shown sympathy for a victim before. Usually, he viewed them as a receptacle of hidden motives. Jack narrowed his eyes, wondering if Wager had become interested in her. "She's the type that hides her emotions in public," he told Wager.

Remembering his interview with her, Jack wasn't so sure she would suffer for long, but maybe he was being too harsh.

"Why are you really here, Jack? Go home, or I'll put you to work."

"I need you to come with me to Gordon, Winslow, and Kepler," he told Wager.

"No."

"You said it yourself, Wager. Somebody in that office is involved in Winslow's murder. I'm thinking Kepler's it."

Wager's eyes widened. He opened his mouth and closed it as the phone on his desk rang, and he gave Jack a dirty look instead. "What!" he barked into the mouthpiece. "No, nothing urgent. Get back in here. Fifteen minutes. I need you on the desk here while I go out."

"Vassar," he said to Jack, his expression benign, but his eyes were not. "Now, since you seem to have taken over my job, do I get to know why I'm going with you to see . . . whoever?"

"This morning, I made an appointment with Kepler." Jack looked at his watch. "For an hour from now. I told his secretary the purpose is to pick up Max's permanent papers."

Wager looked apprehensive. "And what? You need me to hold your hand?"

"You have to drive." Jack pointed to his arm, then his thigh.

"Is that all? Otherwise . . . nope, not going."

"Hudek," Jack said simply. "Kepler adores Lottie, his wife. I suspect Hudek threatened to harm her. And Hudek used Jassy's death to show Kepler what the consequences were if he didn't obey."

"And you know that, how?" Wager said.

"The staff said Kepler went berserk after Jassy's death. He was near collapse and had to be helped by Gordon." Jack nodded his head. "Jassy's murder may have been a warning to Kepler that his wife, Lottie, could end up the same way."

Wager didn't look impressed. "That's conjecture."

"We'll find out, won't we? That's why we have to both be there. Otherwise, Simpson won't believe me."

Wager's chair came forward, giving the springs a sigh of relief. "Oh boy, Simpson. I hope you aren't looking for a warrant. I found out that Gordon was the one who did the legal work on Simpson's house purchase when he moved here. They hit it off right away. Now, Simpson thinks Gordon epitomizes a lawyer's character."

"Great," Jack said, thinking, why me? "So that's why Gordon called upon him after my visit."

Wager bobbed his head, exaggerating Jack's logic.

"No need for a warrant yet," Jack said, taking control of the conversation. "This is just fact-finding. We'll be circumspect in questioning."

"Do you even know what that means?" Wager grumbled, but Jack could see the curiosity and a hint of expectation on his face. *Poor Wager, he misses his old position,* Jack thought. He seemed chained to his desk since taking over Hawke's job as Detective Sergeant.

THE door opened, and Kepler stepped into the reception area, briskly shaking hands with both men. He gave a quick glance around the area to make sure there were no clients to see two police officers, even those in suits and ties.

Inside his office, Kepler sat and opened Jack's file, leaving them to seat themselves.

"All complete," he said, his tone brusque, handing Jack a trio of papers. "Your son is now your son and a permanent resident of Canada. You can also have notarized copies if you wish, and you can place the originals in your safe deposit box." The last paper he handed Jack was the legal bill. "Our receptionist can handle that for you," he added, then folded his hands and sat back. "It's been a pleasure completing this work for you. Do you have any questions?" His glance went from Jack to Wager.

"Thank you. It seems pretty thorough." Jack said. He paused, then added, "I'm sorry to have missed Howard's funeral service. I just got out of the hospital."

Kepler's face paled. He examined each of his fingers, bending them as if they might be arthritic. "I heard the news about the arrest. Hudek phoned me, wanting me to attend him. I told him I don't do criminal cases." He left off examining his fingers and used them to rub his temples as if he had a headache. "Poor Howard."

"And yet, Mr. Hudek was your client," Wager remarked softly, his tone gentle but probing. Jack couldn't help but admire Wager's skill—he hadn't lost his touch. He kept his eyes trained on Kepler, noting how Wager's quiet understanding seemed to ease the man's anxiety, coaxing him to speak more freely.

Kepler let out a long breath. "I didn't know," he began, his voice faltering. "Well, that's not entirely true. I suspected . . . . strongly. I knew the transactions didn't follow the normal routines through our trust accounts. Fooled myself, I suppose. It was because they were foreign transactions." Kepler clicked his tongue against the roof of his mouth. "Stupid now. We'll have a lot of explaining to do to the Law Society when they audit our trust accounts."

"Were you forced to make these transactions against your will?" Wager continued.

"What?" Kepler dragged out the word. His surprise was genuine, Jack thought. "Good heavens, no. Not one of us suspected he wasn't on the up and up. Until Howard got suspicious, I guess." Kepler linked his hands again. "God, what a tragedy."

"Bad luck," Jack said, sympathetic, digging, looking for connections. "Starting with Jassy's death and going on from there."

Kepler shuddered. "A terrible business. Poor girl." He looked across them, eyes wandering to the far wall. He shuddered. "You know, my wife was supposed to be with her that day. Jassy had offered to introduce her to a dressmaker my wife had heard of. But she had a headache and cancelled it. God," Kepler's voice faltered, "When I heard, all I could think of was she would have died as well. It doesn't bear thinking."

Wager exchanged a glance with Jack, the unspoken message clear: Jack had lured him here under false pretenses.

Jack's mind raced. Something didn't add up. *If it did not compromise Kepler, then why was Hudek so confident he could get away with it?*

"Mr. Kepler . . . Bernie . . ." Jack smiled. "If we can get back to Hudek. Tell me, how did he come to be your client?"

Kepler frowned, then closed his eyes, thinking. "Last year, yes. At the Chamber of Commerce Christmas cocktail party. You know that type of celebration." He waved his hands vaguely. "A social gathering, but in reality a place to trade business cards, meet influential business heads who can be useful, future prospects, that sort of thing. Timothy dragged Hudek over and told him to talk to me. I wasn't sure whether he was serious or just fobbing him off on me so I could get rid of him. But I listened." Kepler shrugged. "Not sure how it ended. The usual thing," he added vaguely, "nothing direct, you know." Kepler paused, eyes looking inward, turning it over in his mind. "He showed up with an appointment right after the holidays." Kepler lifted his shoulders. "Maybe I did encourage him at the beginning. I can't remember."

Jack's spine tingled, and a chill ran up his arms. He shot Wager a warning glance and gave his hand a slight wiggle beside his knee, signalling for Wager to go along with him.

"Bernie," he said calmly, but his voice was firm. "I want you to listen to me now. This is important. Collect anything personal and go home. Leave a note in your handwriting that you are resigning as of yesterday and are no longer a partner in this firm. On the way out, give it to Sheila to hand to Mr. Gordon. Then I'd advise that you post the resignation notice in the Edmonton Journal for tomorrow's issue."

"I can't do that!" Kepler's eyes went wide in shock. "Are you mad? Everyone, including Gordon, will think it's because of Hudek. That I was colluding with him." Kepler stared at him as if, indeed, Jack was insane.

Jack held up his hand, palm out. "I also want you to keep quiet. Not a word to anyone. Just leave. If you care about your career and profession, you'll do as I tell you. In the next day or so, you'll see why."

Wager tensed beside Jack but kept still. Kepler stared at them both for a long moment.

Wager broke the silence. "You can expect an RCMP officer to visit you at home. He'll have answers and some questions for you." Despite Wager's sympathetic tone, Kepler's mouth settled in a thin, defiant line, then despairing, showing plainly the conclusions whirling around in his mind. He shook his head, denying it, followed by resignation, finally accepting his conclusion. His hands hovered over this desk, shaking. "What about the staff?"

"You can get in touch with them later. But it's imperative, for your safety, that you say nothing to anyone for the time being."

"Lottie?" he breathed out. "My wife?"

"Best not," Wager said gently. "You understand?"

"Yes." Kepler stood, shoulders slumped, and peered around his office with unseeing eyes.

Wager stayed silent all the way out of the building until they both got in the car, Jack in the passenger seat. "I get what you are thinking, but you can't possibly have proof. Simpson is going to go ape. This time, your days are numbered."

"All we need to do is ask the right question," Jack said as Wager put the key in the ignition. "Like Howard said, he looked at the file to find the source who recommended the client."

"The Chamber of Commerce?"

"Yes." While Wager reversed from the parking spot into traffic, Jack told him who he thought it was, the motive, and how he knew. "We need to get Inspector Dave back here and get an arrest warrant. They've been at it long enough to have the rest of the information needed to nail it."

"Your hidden insights again." Wager mattered, rolled his eyes and sighed. "I should be used to this by now. Off on a wing and a prayer."

"What else could we do? Try to keep Kepler out of the worst, that's all. Why'd he allow them to use him this way in the first place? Disbarment is the least they might do for misusing a trust account. At the worst, prison, if it's bad enough, and even treason could qualify."

"If he advertises his resignation before this mess becomes public, it looks like he's innocent of any collusion."

"It might give him a fighting chance," agreed Jack.

"Learning the hard way. No profession is immune, I guess."

31

PHARO greeted him as if he'd been gone for weeks. Jack showed his gratitude with a gentle pat using his good arm. Pharo wriggled in ecstasy, giving deep-throated gurgles of joy like only a Basenji could. Olivia took one glance at Jack, ordered him to sit on the couch, and said she'd bring him coffee. "I'll have a beer instead," he said.

"Along with antibiotics and inflammation medication that you call god knows what? No way."

Jack leaned back, realizing he was bone and brain tired. Added to that, his whole arm throbbed. Sensing his discomfort, Pharo laid his head on Jack's knee with ears alert and dark hazel eyes mournful. When Jack's eyes closed, he hunkered down, half lying on his foot. Feeling a new presence, Jack opened his eyes and saw Max bending over him.

"You okay, Dad?" his lanky frame towered above Jack, grey eyes bright with worry.

"Hey, when I see you here in front of me, calling me Dad, nothing else in this life could be better." Jack pointed to the space beside him. "Sit here where I can see you properly. I have a couple of questions."

Max stepped over Pharo and sat, his legs stretching out awkwardly in front of him.

"Are you growing?" Jack asked. "You seem taller."

Olivia came in and handed Max a glass of something orange and fizzy. "Probably," she said. "It's all my good food and vitamins." She saw Jack's hidden question. "Well, you told me to give him vitamins." At Jack's sheepish expression, she added, "You forgot, didn't you?"

She rolled her eyes at Pharo. "Men," she told him.

"You seem chipper," Jack told her. "I mean, after . . . well . . ."

"He didn't mean it," she said airily. "He'll be back."

"Who?" Max asked, looking bewildered while Jack squinted at her, squelching a sarcastic comment about dreaming. Olivia gave herself a secret smile and returned to the kitchen.

Jack turned to Max, pushing Olivia's fantasies out of his mind. "About your uncle . . ."

Max looked blank. "My Uncle? What uncle?"

"Your mother's brother?" Jack reminded him. "Were you a close family?"

Max grimaced. "Christof?"

"Was he a good uncle to you?"

Max's lips curled. "I didn't like him. He was too . . . what do you call it when people are nice to you, but you see they don't mean it?"

"Back Stabbers? Double dealers? But didn't he appreciate that your mother saved him from prison by going back to East Germany?"

Max shook his head. "I am sure the Stasi never had him at all. He would look for ways to be in their favour and trick her. He was always watching her, trying to trap her into something he could accuse her of. Mutter didn't have to tell me to be careful when Christof asked questions." Max guzzled his juice all at once and said, "The bugs used to crawl over my neck when I was near him."

"For real?" Jack sat up, interested. "Feeling like bugs were on your neck?"

Max flushed as if he had spoken out of turn. "You will believe it strange," he said, his tone defensive, "but when people lie to me, or like my uncle, is just a bad person, something walks across the back of my neck." He looked at Jack from the corner of his eye. "Like a warning. Is that possible?"

Jack grinned. "You're my son, alright. It happens to me, too, and I've learned to trust it."

"Okay." Max examined his empty glass.

Jack leaned back against the sofa, thinking. *Christof.* A misnomer if there ever was one. *A complete Stasi, suspicious of everyone, including his own sister.* He knew she didn't like East Germany and assumed she'd be a traitor. When Max ran, he'd imagine a way to get revenge. No big leap from there to imagine that Max would carry a gift along with him for the enemy. Names of GDR agents would be the easiest, even knowing it might not be true. Any accusation would do just to get even with Max for escaping.

Disgusted, Jack closed his eyes. He felt motion and opened his eyes only long enough to see Max gently take the cup from him before the coffee spilled.

After dinner, Max offered to take Pharo to the park, and Jack accepted readily, grateful to just relax. "Are you taking the Frisbee?" he asked, then mentally kicked himself at Max's expression. "On second thought," he added quickly, "just let him do his thing and run after chewing gum." But it was too late.

Max turned away, face still pale. "We will not play with the Frisbee."

"I mentioned it without thinking first," Jack apologized smoothly. "But let's not ignore the reason either, now I've said it. Doing the right thing always carries a price, Max. But together, we'll beat it, you and me. Right?"

Max jiggled the leash, and Pharo came running. "Yes, Dad, I know. The doctor told me I would remember such moments. He called them flashbacks. I might use the Frisbee sometime, but not today." At the word Frisbee, Pharo wagged his bushy tail. Max laughed and headed toward the door.

TWO days later, Inspector Dave and Wager came back from a session with D.C. Simpson. They had not invited Jack. Wager had presented his written report and an oral backup of Jack's official report. Poor Wager, he probably had to repeat the whole thing for Dave.

Now, Jack inspected their sober expressions and wondered what had happened. Wager beckoned him over and told him what was to happen next.

"Thank you. It's my case, and I deserve to be in at the end, But . . ." Jack's eyes zoned in on Dave. "There's one condition."

"Condition? You're imposing a condition?" Dave looked amused and over at Wager to intervene. Wager tucked his moustache into his bottom lip and looked at the ceiling.

"I know that in cases like this, you are the chief authority," Jack continued. "And I'm along only for polite recognition of city police cooperation. But I insist on taking the major role."

Dave said nothing; he just raised his eyebrows at the word insist and folded his arms. He shook his head. "Not done."

"I need this, Dave," Jack said. "My son could have died. I want the satisfaction of the arrest."

Dave studied Jack's face, considering. "Okay. Let's talk."

So, Jack and Dave now sat upstairs waiting in the reception room outside Timothy Gordon's spacious office. There was no sign of the nameplate of his secretary, Mrs. Roberts, anywhere near or on her desk. Jack glanced at his watch. One-thirty, right on time. Behind the closed door to the inner office, they heard Gordon in a one-sided conversation, which Jack assumed was the telephone. After a brief silence, Gordon appeared at his inner office door.

He waved them in, his manner unruffled and wearing a professional face. A grey, bespoke suit over a white shirt and dark blue tie with matching hankie peeking out of the breast pocket. When Jack and Dave stood up and came closer, Jack saw the crisp shirt had narrow faint blue lines the colour of the tie. *Nice*, thought Jack, smoothing his own jacket, knowing it didn't fit as well as Gordon's suit. Inspector Dave seemed indifferent. He headed into the office and stood until Gordon had closed the door. Without offering a handshake, Gordon sat, gesturing to the chairs on the other side of the desk.

"I assume you're here about the nasty business of Bernie and his transactions with that man, Hudek." Gordon's mouth took on a distasteful expression as if he'd swallowed a bug. "First Howard, now Bernie. I shoulder all the blame for not policing their cases more closely." He frowned. "But they are supposed to be lawyers if you can believe it now. Professionals." He stopped as if he had realized he was talking too much. He sat back. Jack decided Gordon wasn't as upset as his words implied. He looked satisfied, in control, almost distancing himself from the whole mess after a superficial acceptance of responsibility.

"But Howard Winslow was trying to stop it," Jack said. "Before it damaged the firm." *And you,* he wanted to add.

Gordon had the grace to flush as if understanding Jack's inference. "Yes, that's what I gather. Don't misunderstand me. I cannot and will not suggest he was involved, like Bernie. Only that he never considered confiding in me." He shook his head, face soured in regret.

"Mr. Kepler has resigned, I understand," Jack said. "And publicly. It implies he only realized Hudek was an agent of the GDR when we arrested him last Sunday."

Gordon's face turned sorrowful, like a person at a funeral service who can't believe the corpse is dead. "Imagine. A foreign agent. I read it in the paper, but I confess I discounted it as speculation, unproven." He took a deep breath, and his shoulders lowered while he let it out. He flapped his hands helplessly. "Which makes everything all the worse." He looked at them under lowered brows. "You know, I suspected her, then denied it. She has been with me for years, and I never supposed . . ."

"Her?" Jack interrupted. He didn't look at Dave.

"Mrs. Roberts. You must have noticed she is not at her desk. She's gone, taken off. No doubt as soon as the news hit about the arrest." Bewilderment on his face, Gordon looked at Jack, then Dave. "Isn't that why you are here?"

"Tell us what you know," Jack said with a sideways glance at Dave. "You are sure she is the leak in your firm? The one Winslow honed in on during his investigation?"

"Yes, absolutely," Gordon said, nodding emphatically. "Her actions over the last few weeks raised my own suspicions." His face flushed with anger. "But I resisted the idea. Mrs. Roberts has been with me from the start and, over the years, came to handle minor administrative aspects of the firm's affairs. She knew my mind and what my decisions would be and anticipated my directions. If Kepler had questions about Hudek, she handled them." Gordon's lips pressed together. "Foolish in hindsight. I also let my involvement in public affairs take over. Now, I admit it was wrong to let them take precedence over my duties here." He patted his hands on the desktop for emphasis. "But demands for my presence in charitable affairs have increased to where they all want a piece of my time." He glanced at them both, inviting consolation.

"Yes, I'm sure. Once involved in public activities, it's difficult to refuse when asked for more." Dave agreed and received a grateful smile from Gordon.

Not forgetting the same activities net new acquaintances resulting in new business for the firm, Jack thought.

"I trusted Helen . . . Mrs. Roberts," Gordon continued, in a firm address-to-the-jury voice. "She never gave me cause to regret it. Until now." He bowed his head and groaned. "To a certain extent, I must accept the blame. Howard . . ." Gordon wiped his palm across his eyes as if to blank out the sight of Howard's fate. "And manipulating our trust account? I will inform the Law Society, of course, and take full responsibility." He swore softly, and his face turned red with suffused anger.

"You don't know where she is?" persisted Jack. "Mr. Gordon, we can all save time here. You know the procedure. If you have solid proof of her involvement, we insist you hand it over."

Gordon's hands tightened into fists. "She scarpered off. To where is a puzzle? I wish I could help you there." Gordon shook his head in apology. "I can only testify that she directed that man Hudek to this office. She lied. I told Kepler he had my approval to use the trust account to transfer funds from their source to his bank account. All under falsified import and export documents." He frowned. "They must have looked real to pass scrutiny. Do you suppose he had agents inside Custom's too?" The idea widened his eyes in pain, and he put a palm to his forehead. "Good Lord. It only gets worse."

In his peripheral vision, Jack saw Dave's restless stir. Probably getting set to take over the questioning, He thought. Jack put forward his next question, leaving Dave no room to butt in.

"But can you show us proof, sir?" he persisted.

Gordon shook his head. "Nary a scrap. When I found she was gone, I searched her desk and file cabinets. I found a copy of a letter to Hudek, inviting him to consider us as his solicitors, signed by Mrs. Roberts for me. I never allowed it. But in a courtroom, they could challenge my statement." He spread his hands. "But I haven't done a thorough search yet. I'm sure there is something I've missed." His eyes flickered, and Jack caught it.

"So, what I'm hearing is that you did not know what was going on in your own law firm?" Jack's tone seemed mildly surprised. "Despite the fees swelling your profits and permitting a client to use the firm's trust account as his private bank. Surely you must have been aware that much of your revenue came from that client's trust account transactions?"

Gordon's face showed no emotion. *His courtroom face,* Jack mused. The advocate hiding his thoughts, even if they are critical to the case for or against. "Certainly, as the senior partner, I would know our firm's financial position. But my partners never abused my trust and always conducted business with due regard to the law. We all performed due diligence when taking on a new client." He pursed his mouth in regret. "I neither involved myself with Mr. Hudek nor knew him. You must find Mrs. Roberts."

After an interval, Jack looked at Dave, who nodded. "We already have," Jack told Gordon. "Mrs. Roberts surrendered herself at the Edmonton Police Headquarters this morning."

Gordon tensed, his eyes widened, then his hands spread out with his smile. "There we are then! I suppose she reasoned it was useless to run." He blinked several times as if the idea of Mrs. Roberts surrendering was illogical. "I should like to be there when you question her. You'll find I had nothing to do with Hudek besides knowing he was our client." His mouth turned down. "To our great misfortune. A huge understatement, considering all the new information now available."

Jack considered where they should proceed now. His arm throbbed. Still, his attention centred on Gordon, admiring the man's self-control. But then, any man who was an experienced litigator had the insight to insulate himself against accusations of malfeasance.

"We know how Mr. Hudek became a client in your law firm, Mr. Gordon. I also discovered where Mr. Winslow disappeared before his murder, and I questioned him. He told me where to look and what I'd find. The result is that I found out you brought Mr. Hudek into this firm as a client, Mr. Gordon, and assigned Bernie Kepler to him. Any doubts he had about using the trust account you smoothed over."

"What?" Timothy Gordon's eyebrows met his hairline. He barked a short laugh. "How . . . what?" He put out his hands, palms forward. "He lied, they are lying." His eyes narrowed. "Are you trying to make me fully responsible for this catastrophe?"

Dave cracked a smile when Gordon's practiced expression went from denial to insult. Jack sat back and let Dave do his part.

Inspector Dave reached into his breast pocket and brought out a folded sheet of notepaper. Deliberately taking his time, he unfolded it, and Jack saw that it was a typed list, a sort of timetable. He cracked a smile.

"We are not new at this game either, Mr. Gordon. This is a list of dates, places, and times that you and Mr. Hudek have met over the past months." Dave peered over the sheet at Gordon. "Your lawyer is free to receive a certified copy."

Jack saw shock and then calculation appear on Gordon's face before he shrugged as if the accusation were nothing. *He'd be some guy to watch in a courtroom,* Jack thought.

"I would be most happy to have that list, Inspector," Gordon said calmly. "I'm sure that a comparison with my appointment diary will prove yours to be counterfeit. Especially if I can supply witnesses." His expression became stern. "Even if I cannot account for every item, I'm sure there will be enough to cast doubt on your ridiculous charge."

"I failed to mention that all these meetings have corresponding photos taken by our agents. The camera automatically dates the time and place."

Inspector Dave leaned forward in his chair, relaxed, but Jack saw his thigh muscles coiled, ready to spring. "A foreigner by the name of Aleci Ionov has been under surveillance. He uses the name of Alois Hudek. He's a Soviet agent."

"Hudek is a soviet agent?" Gordon's mouth dropped open. "That's preposterous!"

"Cut the act, Mr. Gordon," Jack said, butting in, tired of Gordon, tired of sparring. "Mrs. Roberts located the documents you planted implicating her, and she was smart enough to take them when she cleared out." Jack let his open disgust show. "They prove you are also a soviet agent, and Ionov is your handler. Mrs. Roberts particularly hated your lack of appreciation for her years of loyalty."

Gordon lurched upright, then sat. Jack tensed, his eyes on Gordon's hands gripping the edge of the desk, ready for a movement toward his desk drawer. The hands relaxed. If Gordon had a weapon in there, he had decided it was too late.

"Timothy Gordon," Dave rose. "I am arresting you under the authority of the Royal Canadian Mounted Police for suspicion of espionage, a violation of Canada's national security laws." Dave laid a copy of the warrant before Gordon while reciting the formal line; authorities, cautions, and rights under the Canadian Bill of Rights, including the essential right to remain silent and retain and instruct counsel without delay. "Do you understand these rights?" Gordon probably knew them by heart, but he listened carefully, likely searching for a fault for which Gordon could accuse him later.

Gordon snorted and rose, his lips twisting in scorn. "Just another official government dupe," he snapped. "Debasing Canadians who have sacrificed their all for this country. They use them like cannon fodder, but when it's payback time, what do these poor fools get? Shoved off to the sidelines, and good riddance."

"You are the one who has betrayed these men and your country, Mr. Gordon." Jack's accusation was sharp.

"So what?" Gordon spit the words out. "Payback time. This country sent my son to Korea. He gave everything this country asked of him. Everything! And when he came back, shot to pieces, sick in spirit, what did you do for him? Nothing! Let him rot in his nightmares, fighting battles he couldn't win! Spirit broken, unable to function." Face red, Gordon swiped the back of his hand over his mouth, wiping off the spittle. "Veteran Affairs ignored him and doled out feeble attempts to help. In the end, they got him hooked on pills. Pills!" Gordon cried out, almost keening on his emotion. "They turned him into a zombie. He finally took his own life to end his misery." Tears rolled down his cheeks.

Throughout the rant, Jack sat frozen in his chair, trying to get his breath. Images of men he served with, Apple, his other comrades, the freezing mud and filth, beatings in the prison camp. The images loomed up in front of him, urging him to curl up underneath his chair for safety. He opened his mouth for oxygen. Dave's hand gripping his arm below his partially healed wound pried him back to the present. "Ahhgg," Jack sucked in a breath of pain. Dave gave the arm a reassuring pat, apologizing, his eyes still on Gordon.

"I'm sorry," Jack stood as if Dave's gesture had been a signal to stand. "A terrible loss. But what you have done will not bring your son back. Jassy and Howard," he continued, woozy and nauseous. "They had families. Howard started out because he wanted to protect you. And you had him killed." At the front of his mind, the faces of men who served with him in Korea gathered. "I served in Korea as well, Mr. Gordon. Many men experienced the same hell. But they all stand tall, proud of their service, in spite of their own difficulties or spirits." Jack took a deep breath, his eyes staring straight into Gordon's. "Given half a chance, your son would tell you the same thing. If you had listened."

"Go to hell," Gordon told them.

32

"LET'S set up a celebration," Jack stretched his legs in grateful comfort, Edina tucked inside his good arm. They were on the sofa in her living room after a satisfying steak dinner at the Keg. "Just enough people to fill my apartment. Wager, if he'll come, and Rory and Tommy. To thank him for his help and for looking after Max while I was in the hospital. Olivia will make something special. She'll like that."

"Will Gordon get off?" Edina asked him suddenly, her cheek nestled on his chest, head under his nose. She fitted against him perfectly, as though made in the beginning for the purpose. He pulled her closer. Her hair smelled like a spring morning. "Being well versed in the law, he will have considered all possibilities," she added.

"No, he won't get off. He as much as admitted it in front of the inspector and me. And they have photos and probably more on file. We've got Alec and Hans for Howard's and Jassy's murders. What other knowledge they have about Hudek's operation remains to be seen. We might only get the summary of his charges. The RCMP won't give away their methods or secrets." Jack gave a sigh of relief. "I'm just glad it's all over and Max is safe." He kissed her forehead. "And you."

"It's hard to imagine that a man like Gordon would have taken steps to harm anyone connected," Jack said, feeling Edina shiver at the thought. "He had no qualms about the murder of his own staff," Jack reminded her. "We don't know how many of Hudek's contacts are still in the wind, ready to act. I wasn't sure if he had your name, but a man with his courtroom experience never leaves things to chance. He knowingly twisted his moral values to suit his idea of revenge. Yes, Eddy, there was an obvious threat. Don't underestimate it."

Edina stayed silent, and Jack cursed himself. Had he emphasized the risk beyond her estimation of it? What if she started imagining danger where there wasn't any? Disturbed, Jack let the silence linger while he stared at the fireplace, appreciating how nice it would be to sit as they were, winter outside, fire inside. It wouldn't be long now. The trees were already bright yellow, and the nights were decidedly chilly. Maybe finally, it was the right time to invest in a house. For Max, Pharo, and he glanced at Edina—her. There'd be enough yard to have a garden, a patio with a table and chairs under a sun umbrella. He'd build the patio himself, a herringbone pattern of bricks.

"The man you all call Anderson," Edina's voice stabbed into his daydreams. "He is respectful and pleasant enough, but he belongs to a biker gang if I've ever seen one. And anyone with eyes will notice how he and Olivia dance around each other." She raised her head to face Jack. "I have a feeling there's more to those two than what's visible. Do you care to let me in on it?"

She turned her blue eyes up at him, questioning, really saying she didn't want to be taken for a fool. She wasn't joking.

"I suppose now is as good a time as any," Jack bit his lower lip. It had to be done. He straightened up, holding her at arms-length and eyeing her square on. "Olivia isn't my pretend niece," he said, diving in headfirst. "She's my brother's daughter. And Anderson is my brother's . . . employee."

"You have a brother," Edina said, looking at him, her lips pursed. "So. Why is that a secret?"

"We are . . . alienated . . . I guess that's the right word."

"Why, Jack?"

Jack hesitated, uncomfortable, and ran his fingernails up and down the back of his neck. "It's complicated, Edina. I've hidden it for so long that I hardly consider it myself anymore. Only the business with Harry brought Luke back into focus, and even that only briefly. Up to that time, he supposed I was dead. And I wanted it to stay that way."

"Harry." Edina examined him for a long moment. "Then, because of Harry, don't you think I deserve to know?" She touched his arm. "My brother and I were close, Jack. We discussed many things, including you." She smiled at his raised eyebrows. "I learned much about you before we even met. Yes," she nodded at his cynical expression, "otherwise, why do you think I agreed to hold his tapes for you? Harry's trust wasn't instinctive. He said your reputation as an honest policeman was solid, but he looked into your background and found information up to a certain point. Beyond then, it was as if you didn't exist."

"God," Jack said, questioning his own surprise. Harry McNaughton was an experienced crime journalist, and it was a mistake to assume he would only be curious about the cases he wrote about.

"When you asked me to trust Anderson," Edina went on, "and said he'd make sure I was safe, I wasn't exactly green enough to take your word at face value. As soon as he appeared and we talked, I strongly suspected he belonged to the people Harry wrote about."

"I should have guessed," Jack admitted sourly, unhappy about being so transparent. His stomach nerves fluttered. "Truth?" he started. "I am so afraid I'll lose you . . ." He pressed his lips together. ". . . but I realize a relationship is not real if there are secrets."

"And the longer you find excuses not to tell me, the worse you'll find my reaction," Edina promised. "Best to get it over with, and we'll go from there?"

"I feel like I'm going down for the third time," Jack agreed. He began by telling her of his father and how he blamed Jack for his wife's death in childbirth. "It didn't help that I wasn't into the business. On top of that, my resemblance to her fueled his resentment."

He told how their last altercation when he was seventeen, ended with Jack drawing his father's blood. Afraid of revenge, how he'd run and enlisted in the Army, his Korean war service, Ursula, and his return to Edmonton, where he joined the Police Service. He finished with Luke and Anderson's connection, only leaving out Anderson's role as an undercover RCMP.

"A crime boss?" she whispered, pulling back from him. He saw her mouth turn down in disgust. "Selling drugs? One of those people? The scum of the earth?"

"No, no, Eddy. My father . . . well, now Luke too, never deal in drugs. Their number one rule. Seriously, I can vouch for that. Anyone connected with drugs soon disappears." He squinted at her, making sure his assurance had convinced her.

"No drugs? You sure?"

"I promise. But," Jack snorted. "There's plenty of other unsavoury acts if you count in price fixing, union organization, protection rackets, bidding wars, murder. The Jackson gang's organization has its fingers in a lot of pies."

"So your name isn't Tuesday?"

"My baptismal name is Daniel Jackson. But I've been Jack Tuesday for longer than I was Jackson. So that's my name. Period."

Edina whistled softly through pursed lips while she digested the information.

"Sounds like the plot of a bad movie, doesn't it?" Jack sighed, wondering how much she could digest in one night.

"May as well admit it," she agreed and smiled up at him. "The day of the week, Tuesday, was first the Norse God Tyr. God of Justice and something," she offered. "It started as Tyr's day. A bit apropos," she frowned and shut her eyes as though her trivia were an attempt to blot out his confession. Jack shut up, glad it was all out, but deflated and half reconciled to the outcome. He wouldn't say more. Delving into the workings of a criminal organization would take all night. The loyalties, the enemies, the perimeters of territory. He'd already said enough.

"Besides you, my story for anyone else is"—he said, bringing the topic back to himself—"I grew up in an orphanage in Winnipeg and have no known parents or relatives. Definitely no connection with Luke Jackson or his criminal activities. Nor will there ever be." He averted his face away from hers. Had she already decided in the middle of his recitation that she wanted no association with him?

Suddenly weary, Jack gently disengaged himself from her and rose, making it easy for her. "It's late. I should let you get some rest and reflect on what I've told you. My only plea is that you don't make a quick decision and keep our conversation between us." He gave a short laugh, more of a cough. "And now another apology from me. I know you well enough not to take that for granted." He shot out an exasperated bark. "God, I sound like a used car salesman." Pulling her up on her feet, he let her go and stood apart. "Damn it, Eddy. I've never been as sure about anything as I am now. I love you, Eddy Chambers," he said to her face, then turned away, prepared to leave.

"Hey, hey, Jack Tuesday," she ordered, her hand on his arm. "Kindly shut up and let me get a word in, will you? Only Harry ever called me Eddy," she said as if it had just occurred to her. "I asked you to be honest, and you really came up with a doozy." She shook her head in disbelief. "You didn't impress me with your family tree, but considering you and your occupation, I can understand why you must keep it secret." She wrinkled her nose. "Living a lie can't be easy." She turned her eyes away from him, looking down at the front of his shirt as if counting the buttons. The message was unmistakable, and his throat tightened.

Was she working up to a rejection? Jack hoped he wouldn't cry. "But . . . ?" he prompted her.

She drew in a shaky breath. "I admit it, Jack. It bothers me. Shouldn't I have known at the beginning?"

"I've been living as Jack Tuesday for over twenty years, Eddy. I've only seen Luke once since then, and that was last spring. It's rare that I even think of my life back then."

"I know, Jack. Neither of us could foretell we would get serious.

But we are serious, aren't we?" Edina's jaw set in a hard line. "What if Luke wants revenge on you for interfering with his plans? Up to now, there has been only you. Honestly? I don't want to spend my life wondering if he might take his revenge out on you by targeting me."

Jack grabbed her hands and held them. "Is that all? My father had a strict rule that no harm would ever come to any wife or girl. It's inviolable." He released her hands and put his arms around her. "Policemen's wives put up with a lot of things, Eddy. But never fear harm from Luke." His smile was grim. "We—you don't have to decide now. Take all the time you need."

"Thank you for that," she continued, "but I don't need time. I've done nothing else but think since we met. Nor do you need to prove yourself to me, you fool. My heart and my head tell me what's right." His face turned rosy. "Yes, we've only been together a few weeks, but with all the action, it seems like months."

"Too intense?" Jack couldn't help but ask, probing into the danger zone.

"Sort of," she admitted. His fear increased. "But at least I found out that I'm still alive, and perhaps I don't want the simple life but a life worth living. Is being with you always like this?"

"No. Most days are boring. Otherwise, I'd look a lot older than I do now." A smidgeon of hope rose in his mind.

"Well, Jack Tuesday, I'm willing to give us a shot and see how we turn out. But no holding secrets back from me anymore, you hear?" She gave his arm a shake, which Jack felt in his wound. He winced. "Oops," she said. "I forgot."

"I don't care," Jack told her, pulling her close. "Some hurts feel good."

From the depths of his chest, she mumbled, "One last thing before you go. About Olivia. I sense a thing between her and Anderson, and he isn't happy about it. I suppose she and I will be in each other's company often. So tell me about them so I don't put my foot in it."

"She thinks she's in love with him," Jack said. "But Anderson has pretty well informed her there will be no relationship. Not only is she about eight years younger than him, Olivia will never condone the life of a crime boss, and Anderson knows it." Jack told her about Olivia's mother and her bargain with Luke. "Anderson is Luke's chief fixer. Knowing what he does about the organization, Luke will never let him go. Luke will see Anderson dead first. So Olivia and Anderson share the same prison."

Edina could only stare at him, her eyes round with shock.

"She convinced Luke to let her attend NAIT," Jack continued. "And Luke consented with the proviso that she lives with me." Jack pulled a face. "Luke's way of telling me he has power over me. I've been trying to oust her ever since she moved in."

"But why?" Edina gave him a gentle slap on the chest in reproach. "She's a lovely girl. Her head's in the right place. Beautiful too. A rare combination."

"How can I be sure he isn't demanding information about police work, and she giving it out of fear? Things I let slip in conversation?" At Edina's curled lips, he said, "She could also let slip who her father is. I'd be out on my a . . . er, butt if they found out what I'd been hiding all these years. I won't take a chance." His forehead creased in a frown.

"Any evidence so far?"

"No," he admitted, somewhat ruefully. "She's promised to follow my instructions. Her culinary arts program and her classmates take up almost all her time. She practices on us and is a superb cook. Max and Olivia already act like brother and sister. He likes her."

Thinking he might be the only one who didn't like her, he told himself he was neutral. "Well, power works two ways," Jack added out loud. "I can find out what he's up to as well. Make sure he hasn't any ideas about moving his operations to Edmonton."

"So, what are we going to do?"

"Nothing, so far," Jack said, liking that she included herself in any action. "Just admitting Olivia is part of our existence. I won't tell her to move out as long as Anderson stays away. Luke will bring her home and ruin her career plans. Until she's twenty-one, she's pretty well tied up. She's young, a life ahead of her. Time will heal, and forget a life with Anderson. I'll invite Chen to our celebration."

Edina raised an eyebrow. "The detective who was with you when you talked to Catherine?"

Jack nodded. "Chen's smitten. He tells Olivia stories of his grandmother's kitchen and makes her laugh."

"I'll be there if she ever needs to talk," Edina said. "Now go home. I think I've had enough shocks for one night. My brain is overloaded."

"You won't change your mind, will you?" he asked, only half in jest.

She leaned in to kiss him and yawned. "If you stay any longer, I might. Goodnight, Jack."

Driving home, he kept reminding himself Edina hadn't rejected him. Unaccountably, his thoughts turned to the day he ran from his father and joined the Army. On the bus leaving Winnipeg, not knowing his future, his spirit dulled with the full force of Luke's last edict; that Jack should forget his family and never return.

The realization hit him—the memory didn't raise bitterness this time, he no longer cared. As if telling Eddy erased old resentments. Cheered, he opened the car window and let the chill night air clear his head. The day seemed one long episode after another, and he slowed his speed on the St. Albert road into Edmonton if only to counter the hectic race of the day's events. It worked, and his mind settled into a familiar post-day calmness. He turned on the radio. Roberta Flack crooned, *'The First Time Ever I Saw Your Face.'*

Eddy was the person he wanted beside him for the rest of his life. Trite words, but he meant them. She had seen the worst of him and he'd witnessed her resoluteness when thrown into turmoil. *We're a good team,* he silently told Brodie, his first partner when he joined the Service. But then, Brodie had been his only family. Now, he had a whole new one.

In a city he called home.

THE radio station announcer began the late news as he drove down the last street before the apartment. Jack barely registered the reports. A huge art heist in Montreal, with over twelve rare paintings stolen, and locally, a small plane was missing, overdue in Vancouver from a Calgary takeoff. Jack cut off the announcer's voice as he pulled into his parking spot, happy to be home.

Pharo met him at the door, tap dancing and wanting a trip outside. Jack could hear laughter from Max's room and Tommy's voice too. Jack grabbed Pharo's leash.

"You up for a dinner party?" he asked Olivia, hunched over a pile of books at the table.

She put one finger on a place in her textbook and laid down her pencil.

"How many?"

"Oh. Well, Edina, me, you, Max, Tommy, Rory, and anyone else if you wish. Chen?"

That's seven. One more to make it even. He could ask Wager. "Anyone else you want? Nothing big, just something to show Rory appreciation for his help."

"Sure," she said, noncommittal. Jack kicked himself. One more, like Anderson? She'd be trying not to think of him. "I'll make it nice." She smiled at him, her eyes darkening, making the colour more even, and returned to her text. In his happiness, Jack dismissed a spurt of sympathy. She was young, a life ahead of her. Without Anderson. How old was he anyway?

Twenty-six, twenty-seven? She was eighteen. Better heartbreak now than later. The phone rang, and she jumped up, tearing past him to reach it first.

"I'll tell everyone," Jack said to nobody there. He rattled Pharo's leash and raced the dog to the door. A strangled sob stayed his hand on the doorknob. Olivia was staring at him, eyes wide in horror, face white. Her lips moved, but no sound emerged. Jack ran and caught her as her legs gave out underneath her. He laid her gently on the floor and took up the receiver, hearing Luke's voice still talking as if she was still on the other end.

". . . West of Calgary. It's gone missing over the mountains."

"What's gone missing?" Jack said in spite of himself.

"Oh. Hello, Danny." Luke's tone was almost snickering, but Jack could hear the agitation behind it.

He looked at Olivia sitting on the floor, looking up at him pleadingly with tears streaming from her face. "Anderson's plane," she whispered.

THE END

JACK TUESDAY: GAMBIT

If you enjoyed this book, *or even if you didn't,* please consider leaving a review on Amazon or Goodreads.

There is no better way to support an author.

Thanks!

Florence Nelson Smith, otherwise known as "Flee" was born in Medicine Hat and has been writing most of her life; novels, short stories, and poetry. She has an accounting designation and a degree in Economics from the University of Alberta. Besides writing, her hobbies include genealogical research and figure skating. After a career working in various cities in Alberta and British Columbia, she now resides in Red Deer, Alberta.

Follow F. Nelson Smith on Twitter @Fleesbooks

www.fnelsonsmith.com

ACKNOWLEDGEMENTS

Writing is a lonely business, but at the same time, no author writes alone. In the background are several people who provide encouragement, details, corrections, research and embellishments. Without all that, the story would not reach the final product seen on a store bookshelf.

I am grateful to my editor, Tessa Barron, who patiently convinces me of the writing when I plead for mercy at her cutting parts of my best prose. I also appreciate her artful book covers, which I truly believe are the best out there. I am so lucky to be the recipient of her talent.

Thank you also, Bear Hill Publishing, for your skills and all that you do in the background to prepare a book for publication. Thank you, also, K.E. Barron, for taking time out from writing her own excellent fantasy novels to edit my drafts. She, along with Brenda Roath and Nancy Nelson, has boosted my confidence that a story is worth plugging to the finish.

I hope you enjoy the second book, which follows Jack Tuesday as he marches along his road pitted with potholes and lessons of life.

More titles by

F. NELSON SMITH

NO STRAIGHT THING

"Ultimately heartwarming despite its macabre circumstances, No Straight Thing is an engrossing historical mystery."

— *Clarion, Foreword Reviews*

"With its vivid atmosphere and unforgettable characters, No Straight Thing is a treat for fans of suspenseful historical fiction."

— *BlueInk,* **Starred Review**

Available anywhere books are sold

JACK TUESDAY

Available anywhere books are sold